POISON CASE
NUMBER 10

and

MURDER CASE
NUMBER 33

from the files of the
Michael Joyce Agency

POISON CASE NUMBER 10

and

MURDER CASE NUMBER 33

*from the files of the
Michael Joyce Agency*

Louis Cornell

COACHWHIP PUBLICATIONS
Greenville, Ohio

Poison Case Number 10 / Murder Case Number 33,
  by Louis Cornell
© 2022 Coachwhip Publications edition

Poison Case Number 10 first published 1931
Murder Case Number 33 first published 1932
CoachwhipBooks.com

ISBN 1-61646-531-x
ISBN-13 978-1-61646-531-5

POISON CASE NUMBER 10

CHAPTER ONE
Friday—The Incredible Client

Inspector Michael Joyce settled his robust frame comfortably in his leather-upholstered desk chair, crossed his legs and threw a glance around the private office of his detective agency. He said:

"Kay, you're now going to write a letter that marks a milestone in the history of this outfit."

The red-haired girl with the shrewd gray eyes, whose status for some time had been much more that of an assistant than of a secretary, reached promptly for her notebook and pencil.

"All right, Inspector."

"Never mind about taking dictation. You can write a grand letter yourself without my slinging the words at you. Drop a line to Mr. Bischoff of the Standard Trust Company, and tell him that his terms are satisfactory. We'll guard his old bank for him, the main building and its four branches, as well as handle such confidential matters as may come up."

Kay flashed a curious look straight into her chief's quizzical eyes.

"What's there so remarkable about a letter like that?" she challenged. "We've already got the Murray Hill National, the Gansevoort Trust, and a slew of other banks."

Inspector Joyce shook with an infectious Irish chuckle.

"I thought I'd have you guessing. Well, I'll tell you. With this new contract, my business goes into the three hundred thousand dollars a year class. It's the mark I've been shooting at for years. Three hundred grand, clear net profit, will keep the lot of us out of the poorhouse—so now, Kay, I'm getting old, and ready to loaf."

"I can't quite see you doing that," the girl answered, a trifle uneasily. "It doesn't fit in with my notion of your temperament at all. Besides, the agency would go to pieces without you."

"Don't you believe it. The Joyce Detective Agency can run itself now. My son Tom can sit in this chair—with Mr. Symes to coach him a little, now and then."

"Young Mr. Joyce has a great deal of ability," said Kay, an absurd touch of sadness in her voice.

"But he isn't a born detective, eh?" The chief's blue eyes clouded. "You got that from me. I've raised hell with him often enough, God knows. But you must have heard me tell him also, that fifty detectives are made by discipline and experience for every one that's born smart. I think Tom is close to a finished job now."

"I didn't mean even to hint at a criticism of him," the girl protested, flushing unreasonably.

"And I'd not be suspecting you of the same," Inspector Joyce bantered. "The question before the house, Kay, me darling, is my right to loaf. I've earned it, by God! and I drilled the boys out there, and they'll work hard for any one I place in charge. They're an able and loyal bunch."

He threw his arms wide, and indicated beyond the glass partitions of his private office a scattering of men engaged in one of three simple-seeming occupations. They were either writing at desks, telephoning, or consulting records among the serried squads of steel filing cases. The suite

was not crowded, for the reason that most of the operatives were out covering assignments. An air of tenseness,
hurry and impending drama was nevertheless conveyed by
the stooped, busy forms. A newspaper office on the fringes
of the rush hour is much like that. The men worked with
their hats on. A girl employee had sat down in a corner
to bang off a report on the typewriter, without taking the
time to remove her coat.

Through the open windows could be glimpsed a drift
of clouds against a blue September sky, and a distant view
of the lumpy silhouette of the Statue of Liberty. The Joyce
Agency occupied the twenty-fourth floor of a building on
lower Broadway, overlooking the harbor.

"When I say loaf, I don't mean I'll go and sun myself
on a front porch in Florida," boomed Michael Joyce, not
waiting for an answer to his last remark. "But I'm sick of
routine. I want time for my hobbies."

"Your museum of deadly weapons?" said Kay. "I've
heard you tell that you found your best specimens, including the antiques, through working on queer cases. But
even I didn't know you had any other hobbies."

"Several of them—at the back of my head. Things I've
never had the leisure to follow up. Can't you figure the
temptation to become one of those guys that call themselves moneyed connoisseurs? I can do it with the best of
'em."

"Not you, Inspector. Never!"

"Why not?"

"You'd miss the thrills of the game down here. There's
not a day when something strange and exciting isn't
brought to you for a solution, because you're the greatest
private detective in America."

"Every single day? Three hundred and sixty-five real
hot cases each year? Kay, me darling, you're exaggerating."

"Either a new case, or a development in some old one."

"There hasn't been one today."

"There may be," she insisted stoutly.

"Aw, you're a romantic girl, though I will say I prefer you to most men as a side-kick when there's a job of roping some white-collar crook. Talk about the detective instinct. You've got it, Kay." The grizzled detective's voice was rich with blarney, a sure sign, if Inspector Joyce were speaking to one he was fond of, that he meant what he said. "There's no girl can kid me out of retiring. I'll put it up to the Sheriff here."

He turned to a desk behind his own, where, throughout his conversation with Katharine Carey, commonly known as Kay, a man had been working on a bulging dossier of brown cardboard concerning the activities of a notorious safe-cracker. This operative had apparently seen nothing and heard nothing that his chief was doing. He had labored with a peculiar self-effacement, a preternatural silence, which had prevented the very papers under his hands from rustling.

As Joyce turned, however, the man also swung around automatically, so that they met each other half way, and it was obvious that not a word which had been spoken had fallen on deaf ears. The assistant was small of stature, and both in the matter of features and clothing he was so drab and inconspicuous that a reporter would have found it difficult to find words to describe him. He was typical of nine out of every ten men who ride beside one in the subway, or dine at the next table in a restaurant. If, later on, some untoward circumstance makes it important to mention traits that would help to identify such a person, one is at a complete loss to do so.

But in addition to being typical of the herd, which gave him his protective coloration, so to speak, a quality invaluable to the Joyce Agency, G. Borden Symes had perfected a

technique of evasiveness which extended even to the motions of his body. Two minutes after you had observed him
in a certain spot, you were not sure that you had seen him
at all. That he should be nicknamed the Sheriff seemed
farcical, since that title is associated in the popular mind
with bluff and hearty men from the West. But Symes had
actually found his way into detective work through having
served a term as sheriff of an upstate county.

"What's your answer, Sheriff?" asked Joyce. "Of course
you heard what I was saying."

"You have earned a rest, if you want one, Inspector,"
murmured the Sheriff, in the most colorless tones imag-
inable.

"Aw, now, cut loose! Be a human being, for once, will
you? Miss Carey thinks it's not in me to retire. She as good
as claims I can't do it. You've known me long enough to
have an opinion as to whether that's true or not."

The lack-lustre eyes of the Sheriff brightened a little.

"I'd say that idleness would make you very unhappy,
Inspector. Don't you remember how you carried on when
you were laid up with a sprained ankle, just as the Saun-
ders kidnapping case was coming to a head? You ran the
whole business from your sick bed. And you were hobbling
through the dives of Red Hook on the trail of that Sicilian
bombing plot, a week before the doctor discharged you.
You're not the man to quit at fifty, Inspector."

Joyce reached for a cigar, and as he lighted it he straightened in his chair. "Nonsense," he retorted, a little curtly. "I see every job through to the finish, of course. But
I'm not a slave to this damned detective work. I've been
dreaming all my life of things that have precious little
to do with chasing murderers and the rest of it, and now
thank God I can pay for my fancies."

The Sheriff's body flowed from the waist upward, rather
than turned, back to its crouched position above the

dossier relating to safe-cracking. His long fingers rearranged a couple of sheets without producing a sound. About the corners of his lips there hovered the phantom of a smile.

"Get off that letter to Mr. Bischoff, there's a good girl, Kay," pursued the chief. "But before you sit down to the typewriter, will you find Tom and send him in to me?"

"Okay, Inspector."

As Kay Carey went through the doorway, an office boy passed her, advanced to Joyce's desk and stood stiffly.

"There's an old gentleman outside wants to see you, sir," the boy said.

"What's his business, kid?"

"He wouldn't say, sir—wouldn't give me no name neither."

"You ought to know better than to bother me with messages from cranks like that."

"He was very particular about seeing you, Mr. Joyce. And—he's a swell old gink—one of those rich guys in a tall hat."

"A handsome old 'gink' in a silk hat, eh?" chuckled Joyce whimsically. "He's probably lost his wife's favorite dog, and wants me to find it for him. Mr. Tom Joyce will take care of him in a few minutes. Savvy?"

"Yes, sir," the boy piped, and made a quick exit.

"Callers who won't send in their names are a nuisance, Sheriff," commented Joyce.

"Still—at a detective agency!" the Sheriff mumbled, deprecatingly. "Some of the best prospects act like nuts. I sort of hate to see you turn business away, Inspector."

"You have absolutely no temperament," groaned Joyce. "I should think I'd make it clear that I'm celebrating my liberty today. Prospects, from now on, are up to you and Tom."

A moment later, the office boy re-entered.

"The gentleman said I was to tell you, sir, that his father gave you your first job," he blurted out.

"My first job," Joyce repeated, his eyes lighting. "How come? Did he say any more than that?"

The boy looked embarrassed, and shifted from one foot to the other.

"He—he just mentioned that you'd want to see him, 'cause of his father giving you your—"

"I heard you the first time," interrupted Joyce. He frowned and tapped with his finger-tips on the plate glass that covered his desk. "All right, bring him in."

He stood up, a muscular and soldierly figure, to receive his visitor. The latter, as he entered, created an amazing impression of elegance rescued from some bandbox of the early years of the century. He was dressed in a cutaway coat, ascot tie, pin-striped trousers and spatted shoes. He held in one hand a silk hat, fawn-colored gloves, and a polished malacca cane. The salient feature of his face was a heavy white mustache that curved in impeccably barbered horns. But at the second glance one noted that he had weak brown eyes, and that the folds into which the flesh of his aristocratic face had relapsed were drained of blood until they had the unwholesome appearance of wax.

"To whom have I the honor of speaking?" asked Joyce curiously.

The old gentleman looked from Joyce to the stooped back of the seated Sheriff, and visibly hesitated.

"This is one of my most trusted assistants," Joyce gruffly explained.

"I understand, Inspector Joyce. I am Nicholas Van Zanten, of Van Zanten Manor."

"Where's that?"

"Van Zanten Manor? Why, Staten Island, of course!"

"Happy to meet you, Mr. Van Zanten. But—er—what's this about my having worked for your father?"

"Not precisely for him. In 1900 he was acting Treasurer of the United States, and it fell to him to cope with a conspiracy of counterfeiters. You were one of the young detectives on the case, and I remember his speaking highly of your talents."

"Well, I'll be darned!" exclaimed Joyce, reverting to the informal manner that was most natural to him. "I remember that case. I started with the Pinkertons in 1900. They were hot on the affair of the cross-bones yellow-backs, so called because a flaw in the design of the false tens and twenties which flooded the country looked under the magnifying glass like a set of cross-bones. That *was* my first case. But I was only a cub, and it's great to know Treasurer Van Zanten took notice of me."

"He did, indeed. And I have followed your career with warm interest as a result. I admired your work in the New York Police Department, where you rose in less than ten years to be an Inspector."

"The title has stuck to me ever since," chuckled Joyce.

"I used it myself just now. Need I say more to prove that I am a devotee of the chronicles of your fascinating profession?"

"You're a sure enough fan. But you didn't come here to discuss that, I take it. Are you worried about anything?"

Van Zanten seated himself slowly in the nearest chair, crossed his hands over the head of his cane and rested his chin lightly upon them. His watery eyes roved the office. A look of the most dreadful apprehension and grief flitted across his features. Yet when he answered the detective, he did so with a forced laugh.

"I admit to having been worried, Inspector. I thought I needed your help. But I am almost ashamed now of the impulse that drove me to you. I fear I am nothing but a nervous old man, and I'm minded to let this be just a social visit after all."

Joyce was familiar with the reticence complex, which crops up at the last moment when certain men face their chosen confessors. Physicians, lawyers, dentists and priests encounter it, no less frequently than private detectives. It operates to suppress tragedies rather than trifles. In the case of a courtly weakling like Nicholas Van Zanten, it moved Joyce to keen curiosity.

"Suit yourself, sir. I may not be at this desk tomorrow. But I am today—and you're here. It wouldn't do you any harm to get my advice." He snapped out the words, launching them like darts against the armor that masked the other's timidity.

Notwithstanding, Van Zanten continued to temporize.

"Have you a son, Inspector?" he asked.

"Why, yes. My boy Tom is twenty-five years old."

"Is he in this work with you?"

"He is."

Van Zanten sighed.

"You are a fortunate man. A brilliant career which you have built up for yourself, and a son to share it with you! I should like to meet your Tom."

"That's easy. He's standing outside the door. I'd sent my secretary to fetch him, just before you called."

Joyce signaled through the glass partition with his right hand, and Tom and Kay Carey entered. He presented them briefly to Van Zanten.

The old gentleman bowed with elaborate ceremony to the girl. One had the feeling that he restrained himself with difficulty from kissing the back of her hand. Then he turned and stared at Tom with cryptic intensity. Tears misted his eyes, and his lower lip trembled.

"A fine, upstanding young fellow," he said. "The double of my Jimmy. But you were wiser than I, Inspector. You married in time to have a grown son of this sort, before you were too old to be a companion and guide to him. I did not take a wife until I was nearly fifty."

Michael Joyce felt slightly irked by the display of sentiment. It struck an odd note in the precincts of a detective
agency, and it was a form of time wasting in which it did
not seem proper for an unheralded caller to indulge.

"You touch me in a soft spot there, Mr. Van Zanten,"
he muttered. "But I'm kind of anxious to get to the bottom of your business."

The other resumed his seat, threw back his head and
said with unexpected firmness:

"Yes, I have decided to tell you the story and obtain
your best judgment regarding it."

"Perhaps you would prefer to have Tom and Miss Carey
step outside?"

"It is not necessary. They are confidential employees, I
suppose, no less than the other man who is present."

"Right. Well, I'm listening to you."

"Inspector Joyce," said Van Zanten, his voice hard and
appallingly convincing. "I am afraid I am going to be murdered."

CHAPTER TWO
Friday—Can This Be Poison?

When Nicholas Van Zanten declared with the very accents of truth that he was afraid he was going to be murdered, the atmosphere in Joyce's private office abruptly changed. The social pleasantries were thrust aside, and the room grew charged with a psychic current as definite as electricity. Tom and Kay stiffened into attitudes of professional attention. The noiseless Symes turned his blank face toward the center of interest.

But it was Michael Joyce himself who underwent the most complete transformation. His good-humored, jesting Irish mannerisms fell away from him, and he became at once the keen analyst of mysteries. His blue eyes glittered like blades.

"What's your main reason for thinking yourself in danger, Mr. Van Zanten?" he asked.

"Within the past year, two members of my family have died in suspicious circumstances," the man answered starkly.

"Was there a police inquiry in either case?"

"Oh, no! Nothing like that."

"Then it's merely your own suspicions that have been aroused?"

"Perhaps. Others may be alarmed, but if so they have kept their fears hidden from me."

"Have you discussed the matter with any of your relatives or friends?"

"No."

"So much the better, if there's foul play to be investigated. Now tell me the story from the beginning."

"Willingly. I—"

"Just a minute," interrupted Joyce. "Say first why you think your death might follow the two that have already occurred." It was a favorite ruse of his to get a narrator started, and then to wrench the all-important conclusion from him before the threshing over of facts and fancies had possibly caused him to substitute some new-born theory.

"Because I am the next in line save one, Inspector," replied Van Zanten, flustered. "That is—that is, if a plot to destroy us all indeed exists."

"Hm! We'll come back to that when you've finished talking. Go ahead."

"But I don't know where to begin."

"No vagueness, please. Tell me about your family."

"Ours is one of the oldest names in New York." Van Zanten brightened. "We trace our ancestry to the early Dutch settlers. The founder of the line built a house on Maiden Lane, Manhattan. Since the Van Zantens moved to Staten Island, our home has been handed down from father to son for five generations."

"Are you wealthy?"

"Moderately so."

"Would you say the crimes you suspect are being committed for vengeance, or for money, or what?"

"There can be no question of vengeance. No one has any cause to hate us. But the million dollars or so that the estate is worth has a curse on it. It has inspired deeds of violence for the past hundred years."

"Are you tormenting yourself about supposed murders that have stretched over a century?"

"No. Dear me, no! What happened in the long ago was often terrible, but not mysterious. Two gallant men lost their lives in 1846, in duels for the hand of a Van Zanten heiress. My great-grandfather was a suicide."

Joyce shook with exasperation as the other came to a stop. Van Zanten's devious approach to the real issue and the necessity of coaching him were hard for a detective to bear.

"Please state, sir, who the persons were that died recently, and why the circumstances were suspicious," he said severely.

"A year ago, almost to the day, my brother George was seized with violent stomach cramps which came and went for three days. At the end, his tongue seemed paralyzed. Just before the final attack, he tried to gasp out some last message to us, but could not pronounce a word."

"Poison, eh?"

"I fear so."

"And the second case?"

"I attended yesterday afternoon the funeral of George's daughter and only child, my niece Mary. Her symptoms had been different, and even more alarming. We found her in bed in convulsions on Tuesday morning. She obtained a little relief toward nightfall, not sufficiently to tell a collected story, alas! An hour after dawn, she was dead."

"That might have been poison, too, though not the same kind of poison. Did both patients receive medical treatment before they succumbed?"

"Yes."

"What causes of death were certified?"

"George died of acute indigestion, the doctor said. Our little Mary of angina pectoris, culminating in the bursting of a blood vessel on the brain."

There was something infinitely pathetic about the tremulous tone in which Nicholas Van Zanten uttered the phrase, "our little Mary."

"Were autopsies held on the bodies?"

"No, Inspector."

"Great grief! Why not? It would have been the logical thing to demand, since you evidently didn't feel right about what happened."

"To tell you the truth, I suspected nothing wrong when George died. He had been a life-long sufferer from indigestion. He had had several attacks which resembled the fatal one."

"Then the man may actually have been taken off by indigestion?"

"I even consider that probable. I am not convinced that George was murdered."

"But you consider it strange that his young daughter should have followed him, I take it. Why didn't you have a post mortem in her case?"

"I suggested it," said Van Zanten. He hesitated. "But—but I was persuaded that that would be foolish. Some one in whom I have great confidence pooh-poohed the idea."

"The attending physician?" snapped Joyce.

"Oh, no! A—a valued employee and loyal friend, sir."

"Now we're getting somewhere. Who is this individual?"

"I refer to Mr. Alexander Fawcett, the manager of the Van Zanten estate."

"Is he a relative?"

"No."

"A salaried employee, then?"

"I provide him with an income, of course. He is an extremely competent man."

"Do you suspect him of having had a hand in the deaths of George and Mary Van Zanten?"

"Absolutely not. I was not being ironical when I called him loyal. He is closer to me than any other living person. I only fear that the warm humanity of his nature, his distaste for evil thoughts, misled him when he advised me not to have an autopsy performed on the body of my niece."

"I see." Joyce reflected for a moment. He perceived that he would be forced to probe for the continuity of Van Zanten's story, that every fact would have to be dug out of the man by a process of direct questioning.

"You have hinted," he went on, "that these deaths may have been brought about to affect the inheritance of your million dollar fortune. Also, that you may be a victim because you would be the next one in line for elimination. Is that right?"

"Yes, God help me! But I said the next save one."

"Who is that one?"

"My spinster sister, Constance," replied Van Zanten with a peculiar brusqueness.

"Your sister is the only immediate surviving member of the family, except your son?"

"Yes."

"And if you and Miss Constance die, the entire fortune will fall to your son?"

"Obviously. But do not imagine that I have thought of Jimmy as the plotter. That would be too grotesque."

"You perhaps believe that he is being made the beneficiary of crime, without his knowledge."

"That would be more likely, though I am loath to believe it."

"Is there any outsider whose own interests would be served by such a scheme?"

"Jimmy is engaged to a girl of whom I do not approve," said Van Zanten slowly, and dragging out the words with difficulty. "Her name is Celestine Curtis."

"Ah! Why do you disapprove of her?"

"She is not his social equal. She comes of a poor working family."

"Poor, eh!" growled Joyce, seizing on the significant word. "But what about her character, her personal qualities?"

"Just a pleasure-seeking, cigarette-smoking flapper," declared Van Zanten wrathfully. It was characteristic of him to use a term already outdated to pillory this daughter of the modern era.

"Did I understand you to say that young Mr. Van Zanten was about the same age as my Tom—twenty-five?"

"No, Inspector. The lads resemble each other. But Jimmy is a few weeks less than twenty-one years old."

"Not quite of age, then! He can't marry without your consent. Might that be a factor in the mystery?"

"Possibly." Van Zanten frowned and stroked his white mustaches. "It has a greater significance, however, than this—er—this silly betrothal. My son's minority, I mean. I should tell you that, as a precaution in view of my advancing years, I had appointed my late brother George to be Jimmy's legal guardian, should I pass away first."

"But it was Mr. George Van Zanten who died," commented Joyce drily.

"Precisely. Discovering nothing sinister in that fact at the time, I simply appointed another guardian."

"Who?"

"My manager, Mr. Fawcett."

"Did he suggest it?"

"Why no, Inspector. We are in the habit of talking over everything that comes up affecting the estate, Mr. Fawcett and I. At our first conference after George's funeral, it naturally occurred to me to pass on the responsibility of the guardianship to him."

"Supposing that murder has been done, do you now fear for Mr. Fawcett's life?"

"Hardly. George Van Zanten, in addition to being guardian, had a share in the fortune which passes to surviving members of the family. So had Mary. But the small legacy I have made Mr. Fawcett would go to his own heirs, if he died. Nothing would be gained by destroying him."

"Logical enough, if you hold to the idea that this is a plot against the Van Zanten million. Do you consider your son in danger?"

"He may be. Indeed I cannot guess how sorely we are to suffer. All is conjecture in my mind, Inspector."

"Has it taken the form of wondering whether the scheme might be to establish Miss Constance as the sole inheritor?"

"No, no—that would be insane. Constance is a religious woman, whose time is occupied with charities."

"Are you in sympathy with her charities?"

"I cannot say that I am, Inspector. In fact, they irritate me. She is passionately devoted to the work of a mission which seeks to convert the tranquil islanders of Bali from their Brahmin faith. She also maintains a home for stray dogs and gives tombstones for the dog cemetery connected therewith."

For the first time since Van Zanten had said he was menaced by death, Joyce's lips twitched in amusement; but his gravity returned swiftly.

"Outside of those you have named, what persons compose your household?" he asked.

"There is only Mrs. Fawcett."

"Anything remarkable about her?"

"She is a gentle, modest woman of about forty and performs her duties of housekeeper most unobtrusively. We are all fond of her."

"How many servants have you?"

"Five, including a butler, a gardener, a cook and two maids."

"Do you consider them trustworthy?"

"Decidedly. All of them have been with us for years."

Joyce fell silent and stared at the wall beyond Van Zanten's head. His hand reached automatically for a paper knife which was really a finely-wrought damascene dagger, and his thick yet sensitive fingers wandered over the surface of the weapon, searching out the convolutions of the carved handle, testing the edge of the blade, weighing the few ounces of the deadly trifle, and passing it from finger-tip to finger-tip, from palm to palm. It was a trick he had when he was thinking. His collecting of lethal instruments and his love of toying with them was the form which an odd impulse toward dilettantism had taken in the case of this ex-Pinkerton sleuth and police official.

But Nicholas Van Zanten fidgeted at the prolonged pause. "I feel sure, after talking to you, that there should be a confidential inquiry into the deaths," he said. "Will you undertake it?"

Joyce looked around. "No," he answered bluntly. "This is no job for me."

"Why, Inspector? Why?" the other wailed, in naive disappointment.

"Your course is very clear and simple. Have the two bodies exhumed and the contents of the viscera analyzed. Any investigator would demand that as your first move. If poison is not found, there's no mystery. If it is, the affair becomes a public scandal and the police step into it right away. What need have you for a private detective?"

"But if I choose to employ one, is that not my privilege? I want a secret inquiry, in advance of any possible post mortems upon George and Mary Van Zanten. I understand you were in the business of accepting such commissions."

The drab countenance of Sheriff Symes reflected, by a general drooping of the muscles rather than any expression about the mouth and eyes, its approval of the client's sentiments and its grief at the indefensible reluctance of Joyce. Kay Carey and Tom looked more patently worried.

"I am on the point of taking a vacation," declared the chief coldly. "But it goes without saying that if you are so good as to employ my organization for detective work of any kind, my assistants will take care of you."

"I want you, Inspector Joyce—you yourself," pleaded the old man unhappily.

"I'll not mince words with you, Mr. Van Zanten. The evidence isn't convincing enough to force me to clear the decks and go into action, at the expense of personal plans. Any death *may* turn out to have been a murder. But your facts don't spell murder."

"They don't?"

"No, except as a long chance. Two members of your family have died a year apart. Their symptoms were alarming, but not unique. A reputable physician has certified that they perished of natural causes. You're pretty sure that your brother had nothing but indigestion. You haven't made me believe that the girl was poisoned; do you believe it?"

A morbidly crafty expression, founded upon some deeply-rooted horror, took hold of the waxen flesh of Van Zanten's face and remained fixed there. He fumbled for his wallet and pulled from it an unmounted photograph of post card size, which he handed to Joyce.

"I was with Mary when she died," he said harshly. "I asked Mrs. Fawcett, who had been nursing her, to step out of the room for a minute. I fetched Mary's own camera from a cupboard and snapped this. Nobody saw me do it. An—an instinct told me to get a picture of our little girl before the undertakers went to work on her."

Joyce's lips tightened about the stub of his cigar, as he scrutinized the photograph. It had been taken with a strong Graflex lens, and could not have been clearer. He

saw the well-shaped head of a young woman against a white
pillow. It was impossible to judge whether the features had
been beautiful, so terribly were they distorted. The eyes
were wide open, and rolled to one side in their sockets.
The jaw had fallen, yet the lips were sucked against both
the upper and lower teeth, forming a ghastly rictus with a
leftward sag. Pinched nostrils and taut cheeks completed
the register of anguish. Lumps in the bed clothes indicated
that Mary's hands were clasped above her breast and her
knees drawn up to her stomach. The body was on its back.

Joyce looked from the picture to Van Zanten, and stared
wordlessly.

"The dead face says, 'Poison!'" the old man croaked.

The detective beckoned to Symes and Kay and Tom.
They advanced and examined the photograph over his
shoulder. Kay shuddered. But after a moment, all three
withdrew in well-trained silence.

"I have something else here," said Van Zanten, his voice
under better control. "Mary could not talk after her seizure, but she made signs that she wanted paper and pencil.
This is all she had the force to write."

The half-sheet of notepaper which Joyce accepted bore
an indefinitely labored scrawl, ending in strokes that were
barely legible:

"DANGER—YOU—I AM D—"

Joyce clipped together the picture and the note. "With
these in your possession, it was a hell of an idea to let any
one pooh-pooh you out of holding an autopsy," he said
grimly. "But why, at least, didn't you show them to me
right off?"

"I was ashamed of seeming melodramatic," replied Van
Zanten. "Sooner or later, I would have shown them to
you."

"You need a guardian yourself."

"Perhaps I do," the old man admitted humbly. "But Inspector, I implore you, take my case."

Joyce turned his shoulder on him and addressed his secretary.

"Kay, get a dossier started," he ordered. "Make as complete a report as possible on what you've heard this gentleman say. The full name is Nicholas Van Zanten, of Van Zanten Manor, Staten Island."

Efficient and swift, Kay turned to a filing cabinet and selected a stout manila folder. She lettered across the front of it the words:

POISON CASE NO. 10

CHAPTER THREE

Friday—The Wrong Man Is Stricken

Now that he had accepted Van Zanten as a client, Joyce treated him with courteous firmness. He knew that he would have to be tolerant of the man's devious approach to the crux of any question, but he proposed to control and anticipate him as much as possible. The case claimed from him an absolute professional loyalty. Van Zanten had become simply one of the human factors through which he expected to reach a solution.

"I'm at your service," he said. "A secret inquiry should, and shall, be made. What strikes you as being the best way to have me meet your family, without their knowing who I am?"

"I'd been thinking about that, Inspector. Suppose you come out with me as a house guest. I'll introduce you as a former business acquaintance."

"Not bad. Call me Charles P. Ryan, a construction engineer who's just returned from South America. This is Friday. I can stay over the week-end. If it's necessary for me to remain longer, we can fix up a story."

"That will be splendid. Can we start at once?"

"No, Mr. Van Zanten. I have some details to attend to in the office, and a bag to pack. Besides, it wouldn't look normal for me to show up with you in the middle of the afternoon."

"What then?" The other's face twitched nervously, as if he feared that Joyce was going to slip out of his hands.

"You return home now, and announce my coming. Have your car meet me, if you will, at the St. George ferry at six o'clock."

"Your wishes are my wishes, Inspector."

"Very good. And, by the way, in an affair of this kind a woman assistant would be invaluable to me. Allow me to bring Miss Carey."

At the mere mention of a person of the opposite sex, Van Zanten forgot his tragedy and became gallant. He turned toward Kay, smiling and bowing from the waist. "Delighted. The pleasure will be all mine," he said. "But how am I to explain the presence of so charming a stranger?"

"She can pass as my daughter," answered Joyce crisply. His manner brushed sentiment out of the way. "Please take care not to make any slips of the tongue in using our names. I'm to be Ryan—Charles P. She becomes Miss Dorothy Ryan."

"I shall be very careful, Inspector," replied Van Zanten meekly.

He and Joyce stood up at the same moment, and the detective left the office with him, to see him to the elevator. A businesslike air prevailed for a moment after their going. Not one of the three assistants so much as commented upon the grim photograph of the dead Mary; they had seen others almost as terrible. Symes had resumed his compilation of the chronicles of a safe-cracker. A sheet of paper in Kay's typewriter was already half-filled with notes concerning the events at Van Zanten Manor.

But Tom passed his fingers through his thick blond hair. He flushed, and his eyes looked troubled.

"I've bought a pair of seats to take you to the *Follies* tonight," he said sulkily to Kay.

She shook her head, without glancing up. "You heard the boss. He's adopted me over the week-end. I'm your sister, Tom. Isn't that nice?"

"Don't kid me, please. I never was more serious in my life. I—I don't want you to go out on this job."

The girl interrupted her typewriting then, and stared at him. "Why?"

"It's no work for a woman. It cheapens her, and it's often dangerous. Dad should know better than to drag you into it."

"Your dad is a great detective," Kay replied indignantly. "He loves his profession, and he's taught me to love it. What's good enough for him is good enough for me. Old-fashioned notions about woman's place in the world leave me cold."

The two talked without the least embarrassment in the presence of Sheriff Symes. They took it as a matter of course—and they were right—that among his friends he was all of the three monkeys of the Japanese toy rolled into one: he saw nothing, heard nothing and spoke nothing of what had not been intended for him. The man had a curious faculty for conveying this impression. It made him the ideal ferret type of sleuth. For strangers, to their sorrow, also imagined him to be uninquisitive and discreet.

"Maybe this is not a good time for me to tell you, Kay," said Tom Joyce, "that I could like you a whole lot better if you weren't so wrapped up in the private agency business."

"Isn't it sweet of you to like me at all!" she answered pertly. "Have you stopped to consider that I'd think more of *you* if you took a greater interest in detective work?"

Tom parted his lips to make a retort, but interrupted himself as his father strode into the office.

"Will you jump into a taxi and run up to the flat, Tom?" he asked with smooth authority. "I don't want to phone and trust this to servants. Pack my week-end bag. You know, the set-up, the one containing nothing that has initials on it. Stop by Kay's house and have her sister do the same stunt for her. You can be back here by five-thirty."

"Surest thing you know, Dad," the young fellow replied briskly, and hurried away.

"And I'm going to spend the time, Kay, refreshing my memory on poisons and toxic symptoms in the human body. If the telephone rings, you answer it and say I'm busy."

Joyce went to a bookshelf in the corner. He took down a bulky volume, over which he pored with intense concentration as he walked back and forth or rested one shoulder against the nearest support. It was one of his idiosyncrasies seldom to read seated. He made no notes. But occasionally he raised his head, a slight frown between the eyebrows, and gazed blankly at the wall while he mentally analyzed some knotty scientific point. His memory was prodigious.

At exactly five-fifteen, he restored the book to its shelf, sat at his desk and watched the door fretfully for Tom's reappearance. His son arrived within five minutes with the two bags, and Joyce's face lit up. He was far from being a fidgety man, except sometimes where Tom was concerned. He had taken to worrying that Tom might fail him in small matters.

"All right, Kay," he cried. "Let's get started."

The girl arose like a soldier coming to attention. She went to the women's cloak room, and was back with her hat and a light coat on, her nose powdered and her lips rouged, in less time than it takes the average girl to wash her hands. Joyce admired that quality in her. He grinned his approval, and nodded ever so slightly. She flushed with as much pride as if she had been awarded a medal of honor.

They descended to the street and caught a cab to South Ferry. It was at the height of the rush hour, when clerks of both sexes, laborers and honest burghers who have been in town shopping, swarm in their thousands aboard the municipal ferry boats. The movement toward the island borough of Richmond is one of the lesser streams of New York's commuting traffic, but between five and six-thirty each evening it makes a brave showing.

Joyce and Kay struggled with their bags into the main cabin of the *Dongan Hills,* the most recent addition to the harbor fleet. There was not a seat vacant. They found the decks almost equally crowded, and the men's section below was a horror of unwashed humanity in the mass and of billowing tobacco smoke. The broad, open aisle that ran from end to end of the boat was jammed with trucks and private cars, with their motors and lights off and their brakes on. One had the alarming feeling that if the unwieldly craft should give a sudden lurch, this tangle of vehicles would be catapulted into the water.

The engines of the ferryboat had begun to throb and she was nosing her waddling course out of the slip, when Joyce and Kay decided to remount the interior stairway. The latter was clear. Swinging doors shut it off from the passengers; it was a perfectly tranquil retreat.

Half way up, Joyce set down his bag and laughed. "This is against the rules of the Department of Plant and Structures," he said. "No one may ride on the stairway, as you'll notice by that sign. But cops and ferry bootblacks usually do. So why shouldn't we?"

"It's the only place where we can talk," remarked Kay.

"Precisely."

They sat side by side on the steps, like a couple of children. Kay was burning to ask a dozen questions about the case on which they were bound, but she was far too well disciplined to start the ball rolling. It was for her chief to speak, if and when he was ready. She hoped he would tell her what poison he thought had been administered to Mary Van Zanten. But he opened up along a different line.

"Kay, girl," he said, "who do you believe our old fashion-plate client suspects?"

"Celestine Curtis, his son's fiancée," she replied promptly.

"You're wrong. He certainly got all steamed up when he mentioned her. But what did he accuse her of? Of pleasure-seeking and cigarette-smoking. He called her a flapper. A gentleman of that school would never think of 'murderess' and 'flapper' in the same breath. He'd have promoted her to be a vampire, at the very least."

"Yet she may be guilty. A motive can be pinned on to her."

"If it *was* a murder, anybody may be guilty."

"Surely that unfinished message proved a murder."

"Not conclusively. 'Danger—you—I am d—' Blank! That's what it said. Mary may have intended simply to end with the word 'dying.'"

"She'd already written 'danger.' Could she have meant that she thought herself suffering from a contagious disease?"

"Pretty far-fetched. A dying person doesn't need a reason for going hysterical over the idea of danger. But I was asking you for your impression of Van Zanten's suspicions."

"Shut out Celestine Curtis, and I'm at a loss, Inspector. He evidently has complete faith in his manager, Fawcett, and he looks upon his sister as a harmless simpleton."

"Granted, Kay me darlin'. Where does your process of elimination bring you?"

Kay thought for a moment. "His son!" she gasped.

"Just so."

"But why—why?"

"Which 'why' do you mean? Why Van Zanten suspects his son? Or why I knew that that was what he had on his mind? We'll let the first drop, because it's too early to express an opinion."

"I guess I did mean the other thing."

"That's better. I want you to think straight, before you express yourself. You'll never be a detective until you do."

Kay hung her head.

"When the old man first came in, he was mighty sentimental about sons in general. He almost cried over Tom," Joyce went on. "You heard him envying me. Yet he was scared for his own life, and not for his son's. He's trying to kid himself that some one expects to benefit through this Jim becoming the sole inheritor. But his real fear is blacker still."

"Do you think there's much chance of his being right?"

"I think he's easily hoodwinked, and that's all."

"The man who got himself made the heir's guardian and then advised against a post mortem on Mary's body doesn't seem to me to be above suspicion."

"Fawcett? Not a bad theory, Kay. But it's too obvious. Until I meet these people and size them up, I refuse to commit my mind on any suspect."

They continued to discuss the mental quirks of Nicholas Van Zanten, but Joyce studiously avoided the question of poisons. If he had obtained hints from his tome on legal medicine and toxicology, he preferred for the time being to keep them to himself.

The twenty-minute voyage to St. George was made by the pair in a seclusion as complete as if they had been riding in an empty subway car. No sounds reached them except the pulsing of the engines and an occasional echo of the churning paddle-wheels. They missed the splendid pageantry of New York harbor on a long September afternoon. When they left the boat, however, on the heels of a crowd that dashed madly in the direction of waiting trains, busses and trolley cars, bright sunshine was still flooding the scene. Daylight saving had several weeks yet to run, and the actual solar time was five o'clock.

They went to the cluttered square outside the Ferry Building, which like all other public places on Staten Island gave the impression of a provincial city remote from New York. The square was nothing but a stone platform resting on pillars, between the railroad cuts on either side. A flock of shabby taxis waited there. The eye readily picked out the only car of any pretensions, a limousine of an ancient model. Joyce and Kay walked over to it.

"Is this Mr. Van Zanten's car?" the detective asked.

The driver turned quickly in his seat. He was a man with a broad, stupid face and gnarled hands. His uniform fitted him badly.

"Yes, sir," he answered. "You Mr. Ryan?"

Joyce nodded.

Instead of getting out, to open the door and help with the bags, the driver manipulated the catch from the inside. The visitors were left to settle themselves in their seats as best they might. The limousine glided forward.

Through the glass partition, Joyce studied the fellow's broad back for a moment. He lowered his voice and addressed Kay:

"Does this chauffeur say anything to you?"

"Mr. Van Zanten spoke of having five servants. He did not include a chauffeur. Driving the car is not this man's regular job."

"Good girl. But suppose he's from a garage."

"No. His coat wouldn't be lumped up between the shoulders, in that case, and he'd have better manners. It's not the butler, because they couldn't spare the butler so shortly before dinner. Besides, I noticed his hands. It's the gardener."

Kay's eyes twinkled as she spoke. This was an old game with Joyce, to test her on the A.B.C. of detective observation. It was a joy to her to show him how rapidly she improved. But she had not anticipated the warmth with which he suddenly covered both the hands in her lap with one of his great palms.

"Sure, I'd look far to find a daughter that could make me prouder," he said.

The possible double meaning in his words left Kay Carey speechless.

The car circled the Richmond Borough Hall and climbed a long, winding street leading to the top of the hill on which the homes of St. George clustered. A few tall apartment houses had recently been thrown up, here and there, amidst the weather-stained brick and frame dwellings of the older inhabitants. But the township was soon left behind. The limousine gathered speed and flew along a broad turnpike, pompously named Victory Boulevard, which ran down the center of the island. Pleasant suburban houses with lawns and shade trees now succeeded each other at short intervals. It was amazing to realize that this was an integral part of the City of New York.

Barely two miles beyond St. George, the car turned westward into a side road which curved in an easy grade over a low ridge of land and terminated at a gateway flanked by crumbling gray pillars. The iron gate was closed, and the chauffeur was forced to jump out twice, to open and to shut it. After that, the route lay along a private driveway, far from well kept, but bordered by trees of noble proportions. Cows and horses grazed in a walled field. A fine old house, of late Colonial architecture, was visible straight ahead.

"Van Zanten Manor," commented Joyce. "It's a regular estate. Several such have been held intact on Staten Island."

There was time only to observe that the lawn was as smooth as velvet, and that a fine rose garden adjoined the house on the left, when the limousine drew up in front of the porch.

Joyce and Kay got out briskly. But a watch had evidently been kept for them. The front door opened before they could start for it and a maid came hurrying to take their bags. Over her shoulder, they could see the neat figure of Nicholas Van Zanten, who was awaiting them just beyond the threshold.

The old man shook hands with them nervously. His waxen face bore the stamp of some new worry. He recalled the coaching he had received, however, and greeted them as if by rote.

"I am so happy that you could pay us this visit, Mr. Ryan," he said. "And here is your charming daughter, of course. How do you do, Miss Ryan."

"We're delighted to be with you," answered Joyce. He stared hard at Van Zanten, to encourage him to hint at what was really on his mind.

"But you'll have to put up with the company of old folks tonight—just my sister Constance and I. Unexpected difficulties have arisen."

"Yes?" questioned Joyce, impersonal and polite for the benefit of any servants who might be listening.

"My son did not know until I got home this afternoon that you would be coming. He had made an engagement which will keep him out until very late."

"But I can meet your son tomorrow. There is no hurry."

"Something else has happened. My manager and dear friend, Mr. Fawcett, is ill and confined to his room."

The detective felt a thrill of excitement run through him. But before he could ask a question concerning Fawcett's malady, a tall and cadaverous figure stalked out of the adjoining parlor, remarking in a voice that rasped:

"Our guests, I presume."

Her severe features, flat chest and untidy gray hair proclaimed the spinster, Constance Van Zanten.

Joyce shook hands with her. She demanded, without prelude:

"Do you like dogs?"

Repressing his impatience, he replied that he liked most dogs and was informed that the lady owned a number of unique canine pets which could not fail to arouse his admiration.

As soon as he could politely do so, he turned back to Van Zanten.

"You said Mr. Fawcett is ill. Is it anything serious?" he inquired.

"The doctor reserves judgment until he sees whether there is a recurrence of the attack."

"Oh, you have had a doctor for him! What were Mr. Fawcett's symptoms?"

"He was seized with a fit of vomiting at about five o'clock."

Joyce needed no physician to tell him that the majority of lethal poisons cause vomiting.

CHAPTER FOUR
Saturday—The Clue in the Tomb

The darkening mystery of Van Zanten Manor was not discussed at the cheerless first meal which Joyce and Kay shared with their hosts. Constance's tongue wagged in a persistent lecture on her philanthropic hobbies, and she continued to monopolize the talk after the diners had adjourned to the parlor.

Dogs were her chief preoccupation that evening, but the welfare of the islanders of Bali came next. Some missionary society had convinced her that their peculiarly narrow view of the seven deadly virtues should be made to prevail in that far tropical paradise. She gave the better part of her income to bring the dubious result to pass, and she enjoyed harping on it.

Van Zanten broke away at about eleven o'clock and saw Joyce to his room. The old man was eager to sit up for further talk, but Joyce cut him short with a single request.

"Please go and see how Fawcett is doing," he said. "Give me an exact report on his condition, and after that we'll go to bed. You're tired, and so am I."

In due course, Van Zanten returned, his face beaming.

"Mr. Fawcett is much better," he stated. "His stomach was sensitive for several hours after he vomited. But the medicine Dr. Henkle left with him had a soothing effect.

He is now free of pain, and his strength is fast coming back."

"That's fine. Is Henkle the same doctor who attended your late brother and niece?"

"Yes, Inspector. He is our family physician. But about Fawcett—the doctor's first opinion that it was just a touch of ptomaine poisoning seems justified, eh?"

Joyce smiled cryptically. "The patient is out of danger, at any rate. Let's get some sleep. Good night, Mr. Van Zanten."

"Good night, Inspector, and rest well. Breakfast will be served at eight."

In defiance of the accepted conventions of sleuthing, Joyce did not start to prowl through the house the moment his host was out of sight. He did not even lie awake and apply his master mind to an analysis of the strange circumstances surrounding the deaths of two members of the Van Zanten family, as well as the present illness of Fawcett. Most casually, he undressed, got into bed and slept with the soundness natural to a perfectly healthy man.

He opened his eyes at half-past seven, because he had mentally set that hour for arising. Like all experienced detectives, soldiers and travelers, he had trained himself to need no alarm clock. He bathed, shaved and dressed swiftly, and entered the breakfast room downstairs precisely at eight.

The only person ahead of him was a young man whose clean-cut features and blond complexion were not unlike those of his son Tom. But this youth had cheeks that tended to be hollow, a tight-lipped mouth and precociously weary eyes. He was evidently more serious for his years than Tom Joyce. He advanced courteously to meet the visitor, and held out his hand.

"Mr. Ryan, I presume," he said. "My father has told me a lot about you. I am James Van Zanten."

Joyce made small talk, while he appraised the other keenly. "He tries hard to be a forceful character," he thought, "but there's an inferiority complex gnawing at him. The result of some one obsession, perhaps. He's not always sure of himself."

"By the way, have you heard how Mr. Fawcett is this morning?" the detective asked, at the first convenient pause in the conversation.

"He's quite all right," the lad answered, his eyes suddenly growing hard. "In fact, he's up and at his gardening already."

"His gardening?"

"Sure. The garden is his special hobby. That's why we have such grand flowers."

Jimmy waved his hand in the direction of the French windows, and for the first time Joyce glanced outdoors. He saw a perfect riot of the hardier blooms that do not vanish with summer. Chrysanthemums of many shades were especially noticeable. Close to the house, a dozen varieties of roses were still blossoming. A man with a pair of shears was hovering about a bed of fading hollyhocks in the near distance. Farther down, another man crouched on his haunches, plying a trowel.

"An honest to God garden," commented Joyce. "It's a sight for sore eyes."

At that moment, the elder Van Zanten and Kay Carey entered the breakfast room together.

"Good morning, Mr. Ryan. 'Morning, Jimmy," the old man cried in the cheeriest tones that Joyce had heard from his lips. "I found this young lady in need of a guide around the old house, and here we are. What a lovely day it is! And the scent of those roses is mighty sweet."

He introduced his son to Kay, naming her meticulously as Miss Dorothy Ryan, and they all sat down to breakfast.

Constance Van Zanten, it was explained, was not in the habit of arising so early.

They chatted across the table about matters of no importance. Joyce refrained from saying anything that might have led the Van Zantens to mention recent tragic events. He preferred to study the peculiar gravity of Jimmy's demeanor throughout a talk of a nature gay rather than grave. Had the boy been harder hit by his cousin Mary's death than the family realized? Joyce wondered. Or was he suffering from remorse? Why, too, was he unable to suppress a certain note of frigidity whenever the name of Alexander Fawcett was mentioned?

Of lesser interest to the detective, but still important, were the personalities of the maid who served at table and of the housekeeper, Mrs. Fawcett, who dropped in for a few minutes. Joyce found the two women utterly colorless, as he had found the butler at dinner the night before. All were of the stolid servant type, including Sarah Fawcett. The latter lacked the social presence expected of the wife of a man who had risen to be manager of a great estate. She stammered, and she wore her hair in an incredibly old-fashioned "bun" at the back of her head.

"You must let me show you and Miss Ryan about the grounds," Joyce heard Van Zanten saying. "There is much to see. The early morning is the best time, before the sun gets too warm."

"We'll enjoy that immensely," the detective answered.

Kay, who had been devoting herself to Jimmy, addressed the lad with a touch of coquetry: "It rained a bit last night. You can help me over the puddles, if there are any."

But Jimmy looked at her moodily. "I'm awfully sorry, Miss Ryan. I have to leave right away, to attend a lecture in Stapleton."

The oddity of this assertion did not escape Inspector Joyce. "A lecture on a Saturday morning. That's real devo-

tion to the cause of self improvement," he remarked in an
off-hand manner.

"Jimmy is taking a preparatory course before he enters
Johns Hopkins," said old Van Zanten.

"Johns Hopkins! Is he going to be a doctor?"

"Why, yes. He has always had a passion for medicine."

"You bet I have," said Jimmy.

The statement interested Joyce profoundly, though he
did not reveal that fact by so much as the flicker of an
eyelash. He felt irritated anew at the secretiveness, or the
lack of clear thinking, which marked his venerable client's
methods. Why on earth had Van Zanten not told him that
Jimmy was a medical student?

At nine o'clock, the group arose from the breakfast
table. Jimmy went to the garage, and presently reappeared
in a small roadster. He sketched a vague salute with his
left hand, and drove toward the gate at breakneck speed.
It was evident that his nerves were in shreds.

The others stepped hatless into the autumn fairyland of
the garden. It had been years since Joyce had seen a private
tract to compare with it, and the mild, sweet weather that
morning made it the more delicious. Flowers of almost
every description were cultivated there, to deck the chang-
ing seasons with color. Many of the annuals had ceased to
blossom, and their leaves were withering. But their places
had been taken by the sturdy chrysanthemums and asters,
and an exotic note was struck by giant tiger lilies from
Japan. Decorative shrubs abounded, plants grown for the
sake of their vivid leaves, as well as borders of boxwood
that had been clipped into a variety of formal shapes.

The garden stretched for a full acre behind the house.
Starting with the rose-beds that adjoined the wing, it
curved also toward the southwest and ended at a greenhouse some thirty feet long. The whole tract was meticulously tended, the earth spaded and freshly manured. It

seemed as though it would tax the capacities of four men, much less of the two who were working there.

As he approached the men, who had drawn closer together, Joyce observed them covertly. The crouching one with the trowel proved to be, as he had expected, the chauffeur of the evening before. The other was a loosely-built, stoutish man in his later fifties. He wore his hair a trifle long in the back, which gave him the appearance of a politician of the William Jennings Bryan school. Seen face to face, his salient features were his smooth, plump cheeks which showed no traces of the years, and a pair of remarkably bright hazel eyes. Even when the rest of his countenance was in repose, his eyes appeared to be beaming.

"Mr. Ryan and Miss Ryan," said Van Zanten pompously, "I want you to know my manager, Mr. Alexander Fawcett."

Fawcett transferred a huge pair of shears to his left hand, and extended his right. He turned his face to the sunlight as he did this, and his complexion was revealed as being abnormally pasty, with a bluish tinge about the nostrils. Nevertheless, his eyes laughed.

"I'm happy to meet you," said Joyce. "But your courage in getting to work so early has me worried for your sake. I hear you were very ill yesterday."

"Not *very* ill—oh, no!" answered Fawcett, drawling his words. "My stomach was upset. The doc called it ptomaine, but I think a little roach powder or something like that must have fallen into my soup. It didn't feel like ordinary food poisoning."

"I hope the ill effects have all worn off," remarked Van Zanten solicitously.

"Sure, sure. Thanks for your interest. I feel fine. I'm a hard man to kill."

"This garden is the best medicine for you, no doubt. The family tells me you're responsible for it. It's a marvelous garden," Joyce threw in.

Fawcett's eyes positively danced. "Isn't it!" he cried, with childish vanity. "I give it every spare minute of my time, and Mr. Van Zanten can tell you I don't neglect the business of the estate either."

"The abundance of flowers is only half of it," declared Joyce, for want of something better to say. He was by no means a connoisseur of horticulture. "I'm just as much impressed by the wonderfully neat appearance of the beds."

"Constant care does it—care and love of the plants." Fawcett automatically clipped off a dead leaf with his shears. He stepped back and studied the appearance of the bank of asters he was tending, then snipped twice again.

"Pruning is important," he went on. "And you've got to fight the confounded weeds, too. Weeds! I hate 'em." He stooped and tore up an offending straggler by the roots.

As Van Zanten, Kay and himself strolled on to the far end of the garden, Joyce mused that Alexander Fawcett, whatever else he might be, was a character.

The rolling meadows of the estate, with tall isolated trees here and there, gave the feeling of the deer-park of an English country seat. Unfortunately, there were no deer, but Van Zanten proudly led the way to the quaint walled field which the detective had noted on his way in.

"A corner is reserved for horses," he explained. "See, a paddock has been fenced off for them at one end. I may ride in an automobile for convenience sake, but I keep a few horses all the same to remind me of the good old days."

Joyce glanced at the pathetically aging steeds. He was more interested in the small, but first-class, herd of Hereford cattle that grazed in the main section of the field.

The handsome blooded beasts with their red bodies and
white faces were good enough to be the pride of any
gentleman farmer.

"Huh! Swell cows!" the detective grunted. "Who takes
care of them?"

"They are one of Mr. Fawcett's fads. He thinks it good
business for the estate to exhibit them at shows, where
they usually win prizes."

"Fawcett can't possibly look after them himself. The
flowers keep him and the gardener hopping. There must
be a herdsman."

"That's right. A man who lives outside the gates reports
for duty at certain hours. I had forgotten."

"Does he ever come up to the house?"

"Seldom. Only on pay days, as a rule."

"I see. You realize, Mr. Van Zanten, that I've got to
have the low-down on every single person who's been in
contact recently with the members of your family."

These words seemed to remind Van Zanten that, for the
first time that morning, he was free to address Joyce in the
latter's actual role of a private detective.

"What do you make of things here, Inspector?" he asked,
his voice rising sharply. "Was Mr. Fawcett poisoned? You
heard what he said about roach powder, and—and his being hard to kill. He has suspicions. It is fantastic. I can't
for the life of me see what the criminal would gain by
murdering Mr. Fawcett."

"Nor I," answered Joyce noncommittally. He threw up
his hand. "Don't excite yourself. I'll discuss the whole
business with you when I'm ready, but not before."

Van Zanten's face fell. Looking suddenly and pathetically older, he turned from the cow pasture and went with
his mincing footsteps down a path that did not have the
appearance of leading anywhere in particular. He pointed
out ancient trees, which he said had been standing when

his ancestors bought the property a hundred years before. He called attention to the fact that between the trunks of two elms one caught a glimpse of a silver ribbon which was the far waters of the Kill Van Kull.

Joyce felt a trifle bored. But shortly after they had left the greenhouse in Fawcett's garden behind them, the pathway dipped abruptly, the manor and its environs were wholly lost to view and a fresh landscape unrolled itself. The most prominent object now was the pointed roof of a small chapel, some fifty yards distant.

"What's that?" the detective inquired, his interest quickened.

"The entrance to our family vault," Van Zanten replied.

"I thought so. A private burial place, eh?"

"Yes. Many generations of the Van Zantens lie ."

"Are the bodies of your brother and niece there?" Joyce interrupted.

"Of course."

"Let's take a close look at it."

They advanced along a graveled walk, and presently were peering through the iron grill-work of the chantry. The chamber on the ground level was about fifteen feet long by eight wide, big enough for a coffin to be easily turned around in it and to furnish standing room for a dozen persons. In the east wall there was a mullioned window, below which hung a plain black cross. A narrow shelf obviously had been intended to do service as an altar. A trestle stood ready to be converted into a catafalque. The floor of the chapel otherwise was bare.

"I guess it was the custom long ago to hold the last rites here, instead of in the house," remarked Joyce.

"Only when the person had died of a contagious disease. Small pox and cholera used to be terrible scourges, and the dead were isolated as quickly as possible," explained Van Zanten listlessly.

"Hm! That flight of steps straight in front of us leads to the vault, of course. Is it one big chamber down there?"

"Yes, with ledges around the walls, upon which the caskets rest."

Joyce's eyelids narrowed, and his blue eyes glinted as they made a slow survey of the chapel. He raised his left hand and tugged at his chin.

"The funeral of your brother George took place here a year ago, did it?" he demanded.

"Yes, Inspector."

"And that of Mary Van Zanten two weeks ago?"

"Why yes, yes." The eyes of the old man clouded with facile tears.

"Has the chantry gate been opened since Mary's burial?"

"Certainly not."

"How many sets of keys are there to this chapel and vault?"

"Just one set. A key to the chantry and a key to the door of the vault." Van Zanten's face twitched nervously.

"In whose possession are they?"

"In mine. I keep them in a wall safe in my bedroom. But why do you ask? What—what do you think has happened?" vociferated the old man, his voice soaring to a tormented treble.

Joyce thrust his hand between the bars of the chantry grill, and pointed. "Look at those footprints," he said. "They can't be more than six hours old. It rained last night, and they are still wet."

Blatantly visible, now that attention had been called to them, the tracks of a muddy pair of boots described a zigzag, both going and coming, from the door to the head of the vault stairway.

CHAPTER FIVE
Saturday—Why Joyce Did Not Quit

The knowledge that some secret prowler had been fumbling among the coffins of his ancestors at the dead of night seemed to have a more demoralizing effect upon Van Zanten than anything which had occurred hitherto. The man's already waxen cheeks paled to a sick gray. He clutched at the bars in front of him, and it was necessary for Joyce to fling an arm around him to save him from sagging to his knees. His mouth fell open grotesquely, beneath the curling white mustache.

"What object can the ghoul have had?" he mumbled, when he could control his breath.

"Should I know, just by looking at the footprints!" Joyce answered on a note of sarcasm. "I must ask you to get a grip on yourself, Mr. Van Zanten. This business calls for horse-sense and steady nerves."

Kay thought that she had never known her chief to be so openly contemptuous of a client. She wondered why this should be. Clients, after all, were traditionally held to enjoy the privilege of indulging in hysteria.

"I want to help you," said Van Zanten meekly. "But what can I do?"

"Nothing much, except keep your eyes open. Funny stuff may be pulled when I'm not looking. Watch out for it. And be sure not to act as if you'd seen a ghost down here."

"I shall try, Inspector."

"Then let's go back to the house. Slip me the keys to this place the first chance you get, and I'll find a way to check up on the dirty work unnoticed."

The three retraced their steps silently. When they reached the garden, they saw Fawcett's assistant working at a distance among the roses. The man's back was turned toward them.

"What's the gardener's name?" asked Joyce.

"Andrew Burns."

"Have you had him long?"

"About five years."

"Suppose you take us through the kitchen. I want to see the cook, as well as your second maid—the one who didn't serve at breakfast."

This is the time to find all the servants together," agreed Van Zanten. "Cook will be serving them their second meal of the day, before she prepares our luncheon. They're at work so early in the morning, it is our custom to let them eat ahead of us."

As befitted good detectives, Joyce and Kay tagged at the heels of their host through the rear quarters of the mansion, showing interest in the ancient bake-ovens and the copper pots and pans, but apparently caring little about the persons who worked there.

The second maid, Pearl Brown, was of a kind with her fellow, Sally Jenkins, and the butler whose ponderous name was Bucklestrope. But the cook earned covert attention for more reasons than one. In a poison case, a cook was patently a factor to be taken into consideration. This cook happened to be a creature who would have aroused curiosity under any conditions. Joyce had expected her to be a family retainer of American stock, or perhaps a motherly German. She was a Negress so black that her skin appeared to have been dusted with soot, her lips a dark purple and her eyeballs yellow. Her lean old frame and quick, nervous movements suggested the life of the jungle. She was the antithesis of the kindly Negro mammy type one associates with American households. The gaudy bandanna handkerchief with which her head was bound completed, somehow, the impression that she was no stranger to the rites of Voodoo.

"Where are you from?" Joyce asked her bluntly.

The woman gave him a blank stare, and Van Zanten replied for her, an odd, fussy note of challenge in his voice:

"Aunt Ellen is a Jamaican—a native of the British West Indies, you know. She has been with us for a quarter of a century, no less."

"I see," commented Joyce with a pretense of indifference. But as soon as they were out of earshot of the kitchen, he said:

"That cook's a queer-looking specimen. Do you really feel all right about having her around?"

"I trust her more completely than any other servant in this house," answered the old man earnestly. "Why, Inspector, she's a simple-hearted savage, and she's devoted to us. She ran away from a sailing vessel that dropped anchor off Staten Island twenty-five years ago. She came here begging food, and we gave her a job. In all that time, she's never once crossed the harbor to New York City."

"What was she doing on the ship in the first place? They don't have female cooks at sea."

"She claims to have been selling fruit to the sailors in a Jamaican roadstead. A sudden storm forced the vessel away from land, and she was brought up here."

"Huh! It's quite a story. Mr. Van Zanten, I've now met everybody I need to meet, except two persons: your family physician and your son's fiancée."

"Dr. Henkle will undoubtedly be here this morning. He'll drop in to learn how Mr. Fawcett is feeling after last night. He may be here already."

"That's good. And the young lady—Curtis is the name, isn't it?"

"Celestine Curtis is foisted upon us every Saturday without fail," snapped Van Zanten venomously. "Jimmy meets her in Stapleton when his lecture is over, and brings her here for lunch. You'd think she'd know her company displeases me, but this younger generation has no sensitiveness."

Joyce concealed a grin behind his hand. "If she weren't coming today, you'd have to invite her," he said drily.

They went on to the parlor, and as Van Zanten had promised, they discovered there the very logical presence of Dr. Alphonse Henkle. The latter was dressed in a morning coat of correct style but shoddy material. He was just drawing on his gloves. His bag stood on a chair. The moment he heard footsteps, he turned, threw his head back and smiled theatrically. One perceived then that he wore a pointed gray beard which matted on his cheeks, and that the black ribbon attached to his eyeglasses was unreasonably wide.

"Good morning, Mr. Van Zanten," he cried heartily. "You look prime. But the patient—*tse, tse!* What a man! Out in the garden working since six o'clock, he tells me, and not a sign of the ptomaine that laid him low. Nature is the best physician, after all, Mr. Van Zanten. I've done my duty and given our friend a prescription, but I fear he'll toss it under one of his rosebushes. Ha, ha!"

"This doctor is the biggest ass I've seen around here," thought Joyce.

Nevertheless, he exerted himself to be pleasant, and in his role of a construction engineer lately returned from South America he answered the series of banal questions

hurled at him the moment they had been introduced. He
asked none in return. And when Henkle had gone strut-
ting to his decrepit sedan, the detective merely inquired
of his host:

"Where does the doc practice?"

"In St. George," answered Van Zanten.

Joyce whistled softly between his teeth. "Well, it's getting on for midday," he remarked. "I suppose we'll be having lunch soon, and I can take a slant at Miss Curtis."

"Quite so, Inspector. She and Jimmy will be here any
minute now."

"Does she play bridge?"

"Bridge!" repeated Van Zanten indignantly. "Of course,
the little fool plays bridge. They all do nowadays."

"Are you and Mr. Fawcett able to play it?"

"We know the rules. But it's a stupid game, not to be
compared with old-fashioned whist."

"Never mind. I want you to start a bridge party after
lunch."

"I find that an extraordinary suggestion when I have so
much to worry me."

"You'll please do what I say," replied Joyce imperturbably. "Suggest a rubber for the entertainment of my girl,
and they won't be able to refuse. I need to get Mr. Fawcett
tied up for an hour or so. Your son, too. Be sure that those
two play, whoever else does not."

Van Zanten nodded slowly. "I see what you have in
mind. You wish to visit the vault unobserved."

"That among other things. Suppose we run upstairs
now and get the keys."

As they started away, Joyce caught Kay's glance and
almost imperceptibly puckered up the skin at the corner
of his right eye. It was a secret signal between them when
he thought he was beginning to see to the bottom of a
mystery. Her heart throbbed with excitement. She had no

inkling of what clues he might have discovered. To her, the puzzle was as obscure as ever.

Luncheon brought together the entire household of Van Zanten Manor, with the dynamic addition of Celestine Curtis. The clear gray eyes, the virile blond hair and the wholesome sun-tanned complexion of this plebeian girl declared her to be a devotee of life itself rather than of a mere cult of modernity. She might smoke cigarettes avidly, but she had the free, light carriage of a dancer and the strong shoulders of a swimmer. Her blunted features were so vital that it seemed of small importance that they were not conventionally beautiful. Her talk was a jet of eager self-expression which Van Zanten would inevitably find lacking in social poise, but which did not justify him in calling her a fool.

To Michael Joyce, ex-policeman and the descendant of sturdy Irish immigrants, Celestine seemed attractive beyond the average. He commented to himself that the slightly anaemic young heir of the Van Zantens was showing good sense in planning to marry a woman whose blood would rejuvenate their strain. The snobbish rudeness of the spinster Constance, whenever the young girl opened her mouth, stirred the detective's bile and made him doubly a partisan of Celestine. Constance Van Zanten! A walking ruin of womanhood, loveless and eccentric, who had stalked in to luncheon with two French poodles on leashes, and who fed the beasts with dainties from her plate. If that was the sort of thing that ladies could get away with, Joyce knew that he preferred the commonest of healthy clay.

"You haven't told me a tenth of what I want to know about South America," Celestine was crying when they arose from table. "Golly, I'd like to travel in those countries! Give me half a chance and I'd make the trip on a small schooner and take my turn with the rest of the crew."

"You'll be making it one of these days in your own yacht, maybe," laughed Joyce. "Then you can boss the crew, which will be more fun."

Nicholas Van Zanten, precise and conscientious, interrupted with the speech he had rehearsed on the subject of bridge.

"Our charming guest, Miss Ryan, is—ah—fond of cards," he said. "It seems to me that a rubber or two would help pass the afternoon most pleasantly."

Celestine clapped her hands. "Great. We've got a bridge player in our midst. I'm certainly glad I came today."

The withering Constance snorted and took her departure swiftly, dragging her poodles on their leashes when their corpulent bodies balked at the stairs.

"Count me in," said Jimmy quietly. "I suppose you'll take the fourth hand, Mr. Ryan."

Joyce shook his head. "Thanks, but I don't play the game."

Alexander Fawcett's beaming eyes were turned upon Van Zanten with a raising of the brows. "Why, Nicholas, are you figuring on letting them draft one of us?" he asked, in mock dismay.

The detective thought it worthy of note that, for the first time in his hearing, the estate manager had called Van Zanten by his Christian name. He had not believed the pair to be quite so intimate.

The old man fussed and preened, stroking his mustaches to cover his embarrassment. He made a self-conscious plotter. "Just so, Alec, just so!" he said. "We've got to help the young folks out. It had better be you. I am really—ah—so infernally slow at cards."

"All right. I can spare an hour from the garden," answered Fawcett promptly. He smiled genially at everybody and wagged his head, as much as to say that their punishment would be on their own heads for asking him to be a partner at bridge.

The maid Pearl went to fetch the collapsible tables. Joyce stretched his arms and then lighted a cigar. "I'll go and read for a while, if you don't mind," he said.

"By all means, sir. I propose to watch these experts and get some pointers on the game," remarked Van Zanten.

Joyce sauntered over to the library, which was in the opposite wing of the house. He made a swift survey of the books. Except for a few modern novels on a center table, they were all old editions, sets of Washington Irving and Hawthorne, Dickens and Sir Walter Scott. The glass doors of the cases had been kept meticulously clean on the outside, but apparently had not been opened for weeks. The strip of shelf in front of each row of books was covered with a thin film of dust. If the family did any reading, it was not from the collection in their ancestral library. There were no reference books; he checked that point carefully.

Within ten minutes, the detective slipped quietly upstairs. He located Constance's room by the yapping of her dogs and the muffled sound of her harsh voice chiding them. The doors of other bedrooms stood open negligently, as if their occupants had nothing to hide. Joyce glanced through the one nearest to him. It was plainly the room of Jimmy Van Zanten. Boyish possessions were scattered about: fishing tackle, tennis rackets and balls, a kodak. Piled on a little table were some half dozen text books for the study of elementary medicine.

A little farther down the corridor, the detective came upon the room of Alexander Fawcett. He entered it cautiously, because he was not sure of the whereabouts of Mrs. Fawcett. But he was quite unhindered. The upper floor remained tranquil and silent. In the brief moments that he could spare, he scrutinized only one feature of the estate manager's belongings: the books. There were two shelves of them, and every volume dealt, as might have

been expected, with some phase of the science of horticulture. Tomes on the perennials, and particularly roses,
jostled treatises on the annuals best suited to northern
climes. There were several books on general botany, as
well as a few on the composition of soils and manures.
Chemistry from the medical viewpoint seemed to play no
part in Fawcett's pursuit of knowledge.

Joyce returned to the ground floor. He took his hat
from the rack in the hall, and left the house unobtrusively
yet with no excess of secrecy. The voices of the bridge
players could be heard in the parlor. He thought it probable that his departure had not been noticed.

Avoiding the garden and striking straight across the
fields, Joyce walked at a leisurely pace until he was out of
sight of the house. He then made for the burial vault of
the Van Zantens. Drawing the keys from his pocket as he
approached it, he was about to insert the larger one in the
lock of the chantry. But he held his hand and stood for a
long time staring between the iron bars of the door. His
eyes gleamed, though otherwise his face was impassive. He
had made an observation that interested him vastly.

The muddy footprints he had seen there some three
hours before had vanished utterly. The floor of the chapel
had been wiped clean with a mop.

Finally, the detective stooped and scraped the soles
of his shoes with a knife. He stamped on the gravel of
the pathway until the soles were dry and would leave no
tracks. Then he turned the key in the lock, swung the gate
open and entered the chapel. He descended the flight of
steps, fumbled with the much more complicated lock on
the door leading to the vault itself and in time forced it to
yield. He was now in the presence of the dead.

Accustomed as he was to visiting even more gruesome
places, such as the morgue or the dissecting rooms of hos-
pitals, the dismal atmosphere of the Van Zanten vault

chilled his blood. It was an oblong crypt fully thirty feet
long, and it was faintly lighted by a single airshaft protected by a grating above his head. Three ledges ran all the
way around the chamber. The middle ledge was filled with
caskets lying end to end, and the one nearest the ground
had but a few vacant places. A number of ancient coffins
were stacked on the floor in a far corner. The top ledge
was reserved for the pathetically small boxes of infants.

Joyce produced a pocket electric torch and went over
the vault slowly. He first examined the floor and discovered, as he had expected, that it had recently been mopped
here and there. The cleaning process had not been as thorough as in the chapel, but all footprints had been erased.

The detective turned his light upon each coffin. He
paused longest in front of a brand-new oaken casket on the
middle ledge. Here, without doubt, lay the body of Mary
Van Zanten. He could find no indications that it had been
tampered with. Adjoining it was the slightly time-stained
box that held her father. Joyce stooped and examined the
name-plates on the lids, to make sure that he was right.

Then he swung about brusquely and left the sad charnel house, locking the doors behind him. He walked back
to the mansion without concealment of his course. As
he passed through the garden, he again saw the gardener
Burns at work among the rose bushes. The hulking fellow
saluted him, and he returned the greeting.

Joyce re-entered through a back door which stood ajar,
and found his way to the parlor. Kay Carey was sitting
there alone, reading a magazine. The bridge table with
cards scattered all over it still occupied the center of the
room.

"Well, what happened to the game?" he asked curtly.

She jumped up, smiling and shaking her head. "It was
no go, Inspector. Mr. Fawcett played so badly that Jimmy
and Celestine got mad. They all got to scrapping, and

old Mr. Van Zanten went upstairs in a huff. Mr. Fawcett quit, too, to attend to his prize cattle. The kids have gone driving in the roadster. They asked me, of course, but I pretended I had a headache."

"It doesn't matter. I've made up my mind about the situation here—and we're going home."

"Home!" repeated Kay, astounded. "You're dropping the case?"

"Yes and no. I'm willing to be consulted, but I can't waste my time snooping in this family circle. If there *is* a case, there's only one way to open it up. The police must be called in and the bodies exhumed. I told Van Zanten that already, and I'm going to tell him again."

The girl's quick mind leaped to a conclusion. "You found out something at the vault?"

"I found that the footprints we saw in the morning had been carefully wiped away," said Joyce grimly.

"But surely that's a very strange and suspicious circumstance. Why did somebody sneak in there, in the first place? And why is he covering up his tracks?"

"Suppose Van Zanten himself did the sneaking, because his nerves are all shot and he thinks ghouls have designs on the bodies. He claims to have the only set of keys. Listen, Kay, that old fellow is as dippy as hell. He sees a crime behind every sickness, including indigestion. The rest of this crowd, except Celestine, are the usual collection of morons and parasites you find on these country estates run to seed. There may be a poisoner among them, but I'll have to be shown."

"Remember the photograph of Mary Van Zanten and her last message," pleaded Kay.

"Ye-es—that photograph," said Joyce slowly. "It had me hopped up for a while. But is it evidence? Not on your life. The only evidence would be toxic substances in the dead girl's viscera, as revealed by a post mortem. If I stay here, I'll have to demand such an autopsy at once. The moment I do that, the investigation is no longer secret. I might as well quit gum-shoeing now."

"You think there's nothing in the idea of our advance work saving Mr. Van Zanten?" asked Kay respectfully.

"The surest way to save him would be to make his suspicions public. Exhume Mary's body and scare off the poisoner—if any. I'm going right upstairs to tell him so."

Joyce strode out of the parlor, crossed the hall and started to mount the stairs. His foot was barely on the third step when a shrill and dreadful scream broke the Saturday afternoon silence of the old house. A pause during which the echoes still seemed to resound, and then a crescendo of shrieks and the sound of running footsteps. The maid Sally Jenkins appeared at the head of the stairway.

"What the devil is the matter with you?" roared Joyce.

Sally reeled against the balustrade and clutched at her throat. "Poor old Mr. Van Zanten—" she gasped. "Oh, God! He's been murdered."

"Murdered! Where is he?"

"In his own room, sir."

Joyce rushed by her and flung himself into Van Zanten's bedchamber.

The body of the old aristocrat who had prophesied this denouement just twenty-four hours before was slouched in a big armchair between the bed and the window. His head was thrown back, with mouth and eyes wide open, and his chest was arched forward as though he had suffered a violent convulsion. His arms were hanging on either side of the chair.

The detective knew at a glance that Nicholas Van Zanten indubitably was dead.

CHAPTER SIX
Saturday—A Flitting in the Dark

Joyce was far too experienced an investigator of crime to touch the corpse of Van Zanten before the arrival of the examiners specified by law in such cases. He briefly studied the old man's contorted face, and made a few mental notes. Then he commenced a rapid survey of the room, in a quest for clues that might hint at how the grisly result had been brought about.

On the window sill, within arm's length of Van Zanten's chair, there stood a carafe half filled with water and a glass which had recently been emptied. Fingerprints on the outer surface of the glass and the modicum of water inside pointed to the fact that the victim had drunk from it. This was the most obvious medium for the poison which probably had caused his death, whether he had been murdered or was a suicide. Because his keen eyes seldom missed a detail, Joyce noticed that there was a flaw about the size of a grain of wheat close to the upper rim of the tumbler.

He refused to be satisfied with the water as possible evidence, and looked, without avail, for subtler indications of foul play. While he was thus engaged, the tall and bony Van Zanten spinster Constance appeared in the doorway. She was deathly pale and leaned on the jamb for support. Since her bedroom was located only a few steps down the corridor, Joyce knew that she could have arrived more promptly. It was unthinkable that she had failed to hear the screams of the maid. Horror—or some other motive—had caused her to hang back from the scene.

"My brother!" she said in her harsh voice, which tended to stammer rather than to gasp. "Wh-what has happened to him?"

Joyce waved his hand at the body in the chair. "You can see for yourself. He's been dead for at least a quarter of an hour."

"Dead! *You* can't be sure. We must call Dr. Henkle."

"Call him, if you like. But at the same time phone the police. This is murder, or suicide."

The dread words moved her to irrational anger. "No, no, no!" she shrieked. "Such a thing couldn't be—not in our home. You're a madman."

"Thanks," said Joyce drily. "All the same, I insist on the police being notified."

"What right have you to give orders? I'll get Dr. Henkle over here."

Joyce was tempted to tell her who he was, but thought better of it. With Van Zanten gone, their verbal contract was canceled, and his only legal standing in connection with the death was that of a private citizen who had knowledge of suspicious circumstances. Before getting high-handed, he would wait to see what could be done with Fawcett and Jimmy.

And at that moment, footsteps were heard upon the stairs. Constance stood aside. Fawcett, his wife Sarah and Kay entered the room. The estate manager's head was cocked at a queer angle, which caused his longish hair to droop toward one shoulder, and which brought his slight double chin into relief. His eyes gleamed, but had lost their kindly merriment.

"I came in from the paddock just now, to find the women yelling murder downstairs. What's going on here?" he demanded.

Joyce stared narrowly at him, and again pointed at the corpse. "Dead!" he said.

"Oh, my! My poor friend Nicholas. Oh, my, my!" Fawcett repeated the inadequate words over and over again. He wrung his hands, then used them to cover his face. Tears oozed out between his fingers. "How could he be struck down this way? It doesn't seem possible."

The detective made no answer. He preferred to let Constance Van Zanten speak.

"Dr. Henkle must be summoned, Fawcett," the acrid spinster snapped, with a curious new note of authority in her voice. "This Mr. Ryan, however, this house guest of ours, says that the police ought to be called in, too."

The manager lowered his hands and looked at Joyce, frowning. "Why do you consider that necessary, sir?"

"Mr. Van Zanten told me yesterday that his brother and niece had both died suddenly in this house. Now he passes away, in a chair—like that!" Joyce was measuring every word. "Don't you think yourself that the cops should look into it?"

Fawcett moved his head slowly up and down. "There's a lot in what you say. All these sudden deaths—and my own illness last night. It may be a poison plot."

"Poison!" exclaimed Constance, her teeth suddenly chattering. "Stuff and nonsense."

"Well, an autopsy will tell the tale." Fawcett was galvanized into activity. He turned to his wife. "Sarah, please phone at once to Dr. Henkle."

The drab woman who looked like a servant scurried to obey him. For the past several minutes, she had been gazing with expressionless eyes at Van Zanten's body.

"It is only due Henkle to call him, as family physician," Fawcett went on to explain. "Let him pronounce Nicholas dead, and I shall then be in favor of asking the police to investigate."

"You are within your legal rights there," said Joyce. "But I warn you not to allow any unnecessary tampering with the corpse, or with the objects in this room. The suspicion is likely to be that it's murder."

"You seem to know a great deal about the law," sneered Constance.

"I do, Madam," replied Joyce curtly.

"There isn't going to be an autopsy," she cried. "I won't allow it. I won't have my brother butchered with knives."

"If the law requires it, we must submit," said Fawcett soothingly.

But the spinster was not soothed. "I won't have the police here at all, unless Dr. Henkle says Nicholas was poisoned," she shouted. "You're trying to take a lot upon yourself, Fawcett. I am the head of this family now."

The manager shook his head. "Pardon me if I contradict," he said coldly, but politely. You are only one of the executors of the will. Young Mr. James is the heir."

"He is a minor, Fawcett you fool."

"True. But I am his guardian for the next four weeks, until he comes of age."

"That is a lie."

"Pardon me again. Mr. Van Zanten signed the papers appointing me nearly a year ago."

Joyce, who knew this to be a fact, was interested chiefly to learn that Constance had not known it. She appeared on second thoughts to regard it as a likely action on her late brother's part. For, without demanding proofs, she threw a venomous look at Fawcett, strode back to her own room and slammed the door.

"Imagine losing one's temper in the presence of the dead! A woman who's so anxious to convert the heathen of Bali should set a better example than that," said Fawcett patiently.

He walked over and stood between the armchair and the window, staring down at the corpse. It was undoubtedly the best position from which to study that part of Van Zanten's face which was exposed, because the old man had died with his eyes turned toward the window. But Joyce watched Fawcett narrowly. He would have preferred not to have the light cut off by the interposition of the manager's bulky frame.

A grief-stricken expression crept over Fawcett's features, and in a few minutes it was evident that he could no longer endure the ordeal of this close inspection. He turned away.

"No man ever had a better friend than I had in Nicholas Van Zanten," he said, his voice shaking. "He took me when I was a failure at forty—gave me this job on his estate that put me back on my feet—made it possible for me to pursue my hobby of gardening. God, God! I can't bear to think of him dead in this terrible, sinister fashion."

The outburst of sentiment gave Joyce a more favorable opinion of Fawcett, who until then had struck him as having too many of the characteristics of the charlatan to be above suspicion. His present sorrow and his candor in admitting that he had been a nobody before he met Van Zanten threw new light upon his standing in the household. He was a protégé who had found it no trick to be more able than his patron, but who had never fooled himself. Joyce saw it now. This Fawcett had a hard job ahead of him, to control the eccentric Constance and the moody youngster Jimmy. He had every reason to regret the death of the man through whom it had been fairly easy for him to exercise control.

He decided that Fawcett, after all, was the best person to work with, in solving the poison mystery. And almost immediately the latter gave him additional proof of his shrewdness.

"Would you mind asking your daughter to step outside?" the manager asked gently. "I don't think that either you or I should stir from this room until the doctor comes. But I do want to say something to you privately."

Joyce glanced up at Kay, and nodded. "It's all right, girl," he said. "Will you please shut the door behind you, as you go out?"

The moment they were alone, Fawcett remarked:

"You see, it's this way. I know who you are, of course. I recognized your face from pictures I had seen in magazines."

"Yes?" countered Joyce, faintly startled. "What do you think of my being here?"

"This morning I thought it was absurd—a fresh proof of nerves on the part of my dear old friend Nicholas. Now I realize that he was amply justified in engaging a detective. His instinct warned him that his life was in danger."

"Instinct's a mild word for it," said Joyce. "The cases of George and Mary Van Zanten had put him on his guard."

Fawcett shrugged. "I confess that, at the time they occurred, neither of those deaths impressed me as being abnormal. I would no doubt feel the same way about today's dreadful event, if it had been the only tragedy of its kind to take place in this house. I am not given to suspecting crimes. But three in a row! It is too strange a coincidence, and should be probed."

"Do you want me to help, or will the police satisfy you?" asked Joyce bluntly.

"Please stay on the case." Fawcett dropped his hand on the detective's shoulder. "I shall support you in any step you wish to take. From what I've heard of the police, they're nothing but bunglers."

They talked for about fifteen minutes longer, when into the room there erupted the histrionic and verbose apparition of Dr. Alphonse Henkle. His bearded face was set in a mask of dismay, which only partly succeeded in conveying an authentic emotion. His eyeglasses dangled wildly on their broad ribbon, and in some fantastic fashion he made his coat tails whirl about his legs.

"Nicholas has had a seizure, they tell me. It's incredible!" he cried. "I simply won't believe he is dead. I saw him this morning, and he was in marvelous health—marvelous health, I say. He must have suffered a slight embolism."

Joyce fairly shook with rage at the antics of this burlesque physician. "Quit jawing before you've even looked at the body," he snapped.

Henkle threw him a startled glance, and calmed down in jerks.

"And be careful that you don't destroy any evidence that might interest the police," added Joyce grimly.

The doctor thereupon went about his examination in quite a competent manner. He applied the usual tests with the stethoscope, and then scrutinized the bloodshot eyeballs and slightly swollen tongue.

"Mr. Van Zanten has passed away. I judge that he died about an hour ago, and would ascribe the cause to heart failure," he said. He was unable to resist the temptation to introduce an artificial quaver into his voice at the finish.

"Heart failure is just another name for death itself," remarked Joyce coldly. "Would you sign a certificate that this man died of heart disease?"

"Why—why no!"

"Or indigestion, or a clot on the brain, or any of your medical rubber-stamps?"

Henkle looked thoroughly alarmed. "I am being ridi-
culed," he announced, with a striving for dignity that at
any other time would have been comical. "The symptoms
in this case prohibit my making a definite diagnosis without an autopsy."

"That's all I want to know from you. It goes to the
Homicide Bureau now."

"You charge murder?" shrieked Henkle. "Impossible!
Absurd!"

"I charge nothing—as yet." Joyce looked at Fawcett,
who swung his top-heavy cranium in a slow, up-and-down
movement.

"I'm afraid we've got to have the police in," the estate
manager said, addressing Henkle. "This is going to be hard
on Miss Constance, but we can't spare her."

Joyce thought it odd that only Constance should be
credited with finding the police irksome.

With a certain aplomb, the doctor agreed: "Well and
good. But why do we let this man dictate to us?"

"He is Inspector Michael Joyce," drawled Fawcett, his
hazel eyes glowing, as if he took pleasure in paying tribute to a distinguished character. "The name of Ryan was
assumed. He is the most famous private detective in the
country, and Nicholas employed him because he feared he
was going to be murdered."

The "Oh!" with which Henkle greeted this statement
was that of a genuinely thunderstruck and intimidated
person.

"Suppose you notify the police, Inspector," Fawcett
went on. "You know the ropes better than I."

"Sure."

There was an extension telephone in the room. Joyce
promptly lifted the receiver from the hook, and put
through a call to the Bureau of Criminal Information at
New York City Headquarters. Archibald Kane, the Deputy

Inspector in charge, was a personal friend. In a few crisp sentences, he gave Kane the facts about the death of the owner of Van Zanten Manor, and added:

"I suspect poison. Send your best analyst over to the Staten Island Morgue for the post mortem, will you? Make it a special assignment. Thanks. You're a pal."

Then, though Centre Street would pass on the news automatically, he also telephoned to 78 Richmond Terrace, in St. George, Police Headquarters for the Borough of Richmond. This hastened by a few minutes the dispatching of detectives from the Borough Homicide Squad, as well as an Assistant Medical Examiner, two police photographers and a stenographer. He knew that the Inspector commanding the detective division for Staten Island, the captain of the precinct and a representative of the District Attorney's office would not fail to come, too.

Then there remained nothing to do but to wait for the invasion of the house by the massed representatives of the Law. They came in half an hour and swarmed into Van Zanten's bedroom, where both Joyce and Fawcett still stood stubbornly on guard. The local Inspector looked curiously at the private detective whose name had become a legend since his resignation from the Police Department, but he refrained from saying anything. The most important persons for the moment were the photographers, who immediately set up their cameras and took pictures of the corpse from various angles, as well as views of the room to show the arrangement of every object in it.

The Assistant Medical Examiner then got to work. His procedure seemed to be cursory, but it was merely swift. Following some elementary tests and a shrewd, keen appraisal of the condition of the body, he stood up.

"The cause of death cannot be determined without a post mortem," he said. "This cadaver must be rushed to the autopsy room of the morgue."

The words were his own, but the spirit of urgency behind them had been inspired by Deputy Archibald Kane,
of Centre Street, Manhattan.

A stretcher was brought in, and Van Zanten's contorted
form was placed upon it. At the morgue, before the knife
of the surgeon touched it, a most elaborate record would
be made of finger-prints, the condition of the teeth, the
foreign matter lodged under the finger-nails, abnormal
stains on the flesh and a score of other details which might
serve as clues of foul play.

As soon as the body had been carried down to the ambulance, the detectives and the man from the District
Attorney's office started to interrogate every member of the
household. Questions and answers were recorded at length,
and it took considerable time. At about five o'clock, while
the last of the servants were being examined, Jimmy Van
Zanten walked in alone. He had left Celestine at her home
in Stapleton, and he had no sooner reached the gates of
the estate than he had encountered the first evidences of
tragedy. A uniformed policeman had been stationed there,
to hold back all persons who were not residents. Beyond
the gates, he had met the gardener, Andy Burns, who had
told him his father was dead.

His young face drawn and as white as chalk, his eyes
dull, Jimmy entered the parlor where the inquiry was being held. He uttered no exclamation of horror or surprise,
though clearly he was suffering mental torture. In view
of his proved absence since the bridge game, only a few
questions concerning the recent state of his father's health
were asked him. He made his replies listlessly, but with
clarity. That Joyce had lost the name of Ryan and was
functioning as a detective, he seemed to take as a matter
of course.

The moment they were through with him, Jimmy went
to his bedroom and locked himself in. Constance Van

Zanten had done the same thing. As last limbs of a decaying family tree, they were a neurotic pair.

Because the evidence did not as yet justify even a presumption of murder, no arrests were made, nor was any person held as a material witness. A policeman, however, was placed on guard in the death room, as is customary when the circumstances point to homicide. The borough officials and detectives then took their departure.

Unmitigated gloom settled upon the house. Joyce and Kay dined with the Fawcetts, and by a tacit agreement the talk was confined to the manager's homilies on flowers, with an occasional excursion into the general field of criminology. Joyce could not blame Fawcett for shying away from the Van Zanten case until the result of the autopsy was announced. But he learned with a certain amusement that the fellow's discernment in recognizing him as a detective had not extended to Kay. Fawcett believed Kay to be his daughter, and not an operative. So far, so good. It was an advantage to have at least one secret agent upon the premises.

They all went to bed early.

But in the morning, an enormous sensation broke, and the Van Zanten mystery became further complicated. Constance had disappeared. She had apparently taken a small valise and some toilet articles, which were missing from her room. There was no written word or other message to indicate where she had gone, or why.

CHAPTER SEVEN
Sunday—Sinister Lore

The way in which Constance had decamped from the Manor, as well as the route she had followed, offered no difficulties as a detective problem. She had gone down to the side door in the east wing of the house, had let herself out and walked to the gateway of the estate. This had been some time during the night. Presumably, she had continued afoot until she reached Victory Boulevard, where she would have been able to catch a bus or a taxicab.

With Fawcett at his heels, Joyce had searched for clues to indicate the method of her departure, and he had found them quickly. From the sill of the east door, her tracks were deeply imprinted in muddy soil, running in a fairly straight line until they reached the drive some fifteen yards distant and were lost in the gravel there. It was impossible to mistake her footprints. She wore a large shoe for a woman, with heels of medium length. Joyce brought one of her old shoes, and fitted it into the traces; they corresponded perfectly.

Her motive in making this flight in darkness down a lonely road was much harder to explain. Fawcett shrugged his shoulders when Joyce asked him for his opinion.

"She is a very eccentric woman, Inspector, as you must have noticed," the manager said.

"Eccentric enough to skip at a moment when it makes her look as if she has something to hide?"

"Well, she has done it. That answers your question."

"Perhaps. Has she ever run away from home like this before?"

"N-no. But the death of her brother—coming on top of two other deaths in the family—might have destroyed her last vestiges of common sense."

Jimmy's contribution was scarcely more helpful. The pale-faced boy folded his arms and included both Joyce and Fawcett in a stare that tried to be truculent.

"So Aunt Connie's gone!" he said. "What are you going to do—set the police to looking for her as a fugitive from justice?"

"Don't be silly, Jimmy," answered Fawcett mildly. "No one has any right, as yet, to mention murder, or talk about fugitives."

"If you know of any places where she's likely to have gone, you might telephone them," suggested Joyce.

"All right. There's her missionary society, and one or two old maid friends she has in New York."

But a little while later the lad reported that Constance had not been seen at any of her favored haunts. Joyce noted the addresses.

A preliminary report of the findings of the post mortem on Van Zanten's body might be expected around noon. If the evidence were positive in character, it might even be conclusive. But until it came, there was nothing to do but mark time. Joyce called Kay, led her to the parlor and sat down for the first private discussion of the case they had had since their chat on the ferryboat. She had been looking forward to this.

"Kay," he asked, "what do you know about poisons, any way?"

"Not a great deal, Inspector," she replied. "Just what a secretary who's ambitious to be a real assistant would pick up in a detective agency."

Joyce smiled. "That could be a lot. We've had some curious poison cases, though none to compare with this one since you've been working for me."

"You believe that Mr. Van Zanten was poisoned, then?"

"Who wouldn't, on the dope so far? But let's dig into the subject in a general way. Poisoning has been popular since the beginning of history, for bumping off an enemy or simply getting rid of a person whose life is blocking your plans. The last-named is the commoner reason in our times. The automatic makes killings that grow out of hate and rage so darned easy, your modern feudist doesn't take the time to bother with poison. Not very often. Poisoning is a coldblooded proposition. It's always premeditated. The criminal tells himself that the cause of death will not be found out—and half the time he's right."

"Really?" murmured Kay. "I thought our present methods of chemical analysis of the contents of the viscera were almost infallible."

"They sure are. But suppose it never gets as far as a medico-legal examination. Suppose some doctor who's a boob, or a crook, gives a certificate of death by natural causes. That's what the poisoner counts upon. You probably think this Doc Henkle you've seen around here is a unique specimen. I wish I could believe it. Guys like him have made it possible for many a poisoner to go unpunished."

"What are the substances generally used?" asked Kay inquisitively.

"I was coming to that. There's arsenic and bichloride of mercury, strychnine and cyanide of potassium—all of them common, easily-obtained poisons that have figured

in criminal cases without end. I'd say that arsenic is the
stuff that has found most favor with murderers, because
it's tasteless and sure to cause death if given in sufficient
quantities. The knowledge of it is as old as civilization.
The basic element is orpiment, found as a pure mineral
in certain places. What we call white arsenic is one of the
oxides that is extracted from orpiment."

"I see you read that big book in the office to good
advantage," the girl said, with affectionate raillery.

Joyce smiled. "It brushed up my memory on certain
points, but really I'm quite a sharp on poisons. Now, as to
arsenic; it's used for all sorts of legitimate purposes. Doctors prescribe it in tonics and for the treatment of skin
diseases. Every drug store carries it. It's the main thing
in most fly-papers, and in sprays employed to kill insects
and even weeds. So you see it's not much of a trick to get
hold of it.

"What your poisoner of the dumbhead sort overlooks
is that arsenic lodges in the system and can be detected
months and years after the death of the victim. Absolute
tests for the finding of arsenic have been worked out. The
same is true of antimony, mercury, cyanide of potassium
and all the other mineral poisons."

"But the vegetable toxicants?" demanded Kay.

"Not quite the same story. Many of them evaporate
rather fast, and an early autopsy is necessary to turn up
direct proof. Yet they're apt to cause certain changes in
the tissues which an expert analyst can't miss. Take strychnine, which is an alkaloid derived from nux vomica, the
seed of an Oriental tree; and also from the St. Ignatius
bean and some other plants. Strychnine causes the most
terrible convulsions, and at death the arms and legs become as stiff as wood. This rigidity has been found in the
bodies of victims that had been buried for six months and
longer. It's an extreme example, but you can take it from

me the vegetable poisons can be trusted to leave a sign of some kind."

"All of them?"

"Well, not *all*. Aconitine is an exception. That is the most powerful of the alkaloids obtained from the plant called wolfsbane in Europe, and aconite here. But aconitine is a mighty rare poison. It has cropped up in only one or two murders in the police records of the last hundred years."

"You said that strychnine wasn't hard to get. Why?"

"Because it's a standard medicine. In small doses, it's used as a heart stimulant and for the treatment of nerve trouble. There again, you have a weapon that can be had at any drug store."

"I should think it would be hard to get the necessary prescription from a doctor," said Kay. "At least, for a quantity large enough to be used for murder!"

Joyce grinned out of one side of his mouth. "Prescriptions!" he sneered. "They can always be bought, by crooks—from crooks. And there are other ways. Strychnine is often sold on the q.t. by druggists, who take a chance on the story that the buyer wants it to kill rats or stray dogs. In almost every strychnine murder that has been brought to book, the accused has hollered to Heaven that he had the stuff around to fight vermin. It makes swell rat-poison, and that's a fact. The victim got some of it into his food by mistake, of course, if you were to believe the argument for the defense."

Kay made no comment, and after staring at the ceiling for a moment, Joyce went on:

"Some other darned interesting, but uncommon, poisons are hemlock, antiarin and curare. Hemlock was the stuff they handed Socrates. It was distilled from a bush resembling fennel, and it produced a merciful, slow paralysis which ended by hitting the heart. Antiarin is taken from the sap of the upas tree. If you've read the ancient travel books, you'll remember that the bozos who first toured the Orient were told that it meant death to sit in the shade of the upas. The real lowdown was that the juice, when placed upon the tips of arrows, destroyed an enemy within half an hour after he was wounded. Curare comes from the bark of a South American shrub, and is what the Orinoco Indians use to doctor their darts."

"In naming those, you haven't begun to exhaust the subject, have you?" suggested Kay.

"You said it. There are snake poisons, as well as venoms extracted from the glands of frogs and the bodies of many kinds of insects. Exhibits for a chemist's chamber of horrors, all right. But for practical purposes, we aren't likely to have to go beyond arsenic, or some of the other standard concoctions I told you about."

Kay took her cue promptly. She knew how Inspector Joyces mind worked. His dropping of so broad a hint meant that she was at liberty to question him.

"What poisons do you think may have caused the deaths here?" she asked.

"Between you and me, and assuming there's been murder done, George Van Zanten a year ago seems like an arsenic case. He had recurrent stomach cramps for three days, culminating in a violent seizure which finished him off. That's a typical result for a real strong dose of arsenic. The symptoms might pass as those of indigestion. Absorbed in smaller quantities, the powder has been known not to kill for several weeks."

"But the paralysis of the tongue which our client mentioned?"

"Queer! And it certainly throws doubt on the arsenic theory. The man being old, however, there may have been a normal tendency toward paralysis, which fastened on the tongue when he was dying."

"Are there any other poisons which produce similar symptoms?" inquired Kay.

"None of the usual ones. C. P.—that's cyanide of potassium—works like lightning. It scarcely has time to reach the stomach before the victim drops dead. That's why so many suicides go for it. Bichloride of mercury, on the other hand, tears the organs to pieces slowly, especially the kidneys. The sufferer is gnawed by horrible pains until he finally goes into a coma."

"And strychnine?"

"Lord, no! The convulsions I just told you that strychnine causes are ten times more severe than the stomach cramps of arsenic. The patient twists around like the damned in Hell. There is frequent vomiting, with periods of stupor in between. Death can follow in less than twenty-four hours."

"Then Mary Van Zanten was very possibly murdered with strychnine?"

"Good girl. I hoped you'd draw your own conclusions. It seems crazy, of course, that any physician could diagnose it as a death by natural disease. Yet it has been done. In the John Parsons Cook case in England, in 1855, several doctors declared that the man had died of angina pectoris. He had been poisoned with strychnine, and a guy named Palmer was finally hanged for the crime. If you claim that medical knowledge has advanced since 1855, you're right. But science is no help if the wrong person is using it. Doc Henkle may be more of a dummox than the English medicos of seventy years ago."

"You're taking the stand that he's likely to have been a dupe in this whole business?"

"So far—yes. The plot appears too deep for Henkle to have originated it. It's working too smoothly for that comic even to be the main agent. No one would trust him to keep a secret. I'm including him among my possible suspects, however."

Joyce lighted a fresh cigar, and puffed away for a moment in silence.

"You may wonder why I now have poison theories about George and Mary Van Zanten," he continued, "when I'd started on the tack that exhuming the bodies was the only thing to tell the tale?"

"No, I don't wonder. You had nothing to go upon. The circumstances surrounding the death of Nicholas Van Zanten have occurred since then."

"Smart kid. But that's not all. I hadn't seen Doc Henkle in action. The first two bodies had been buried on certificates signed by a supposedly intelligent physician. He might have been a crook, but how could I picture him as a sap who'd find it hard to recognize the nose on his own face? The proper caper was to take a look at what he had buried, and then form theories.

"But when I heard him shout, 'Heart failure!' over a man who had obviously been poisoned, I just naturally figured out the real meaning of the symptoms he had called 'acute indigestion' and 'angina pectoris' in the earlier cases."

"It's great to listen to you thinking aloud like this," said Kay. "I sort of flatter myself I'm the only person you'd do that with."

"You're right, Kay. I'm close-mouthed until I've reached a solution. But I want to train you to use your bean the way I use mine. You've got it in you to become the finest woman detective in the business."

The girl flushed, gratified beyond words. She touched the back of his hand with her finger-tips, then drew them away swiftly. Joyce smiled, and with a bearish gesture stroked the curls that were flying loose above her ear.

After a prolonged pause, she asked:

"Do you have an idea what it was they fed to the old man yesterday?"

Joyce shook his head. "Let's leave that until we get the report on the post mortem."

"Then perhaps you can tell me why the family vault was visited by the prowler, who later erased his footprints?"

"Ask me a hard one. That visit was probably for the purpose of tampering with the viscera of George and Mary Van Zanten."

Kay shuddered, in a sudden access of feminine horror at the picture his words evoked.

They had exchanged a few more desultory comments on the mysterious affair when the telephone in the hallway rang. The maid Sally Jenkins answered it, and presently called Joyce to the phone. Kay heard him say: "Hello! . . . Yes, yes . . . Read it to me, will you?" and then there was a long pause while the detective listened. He said: "Thanks very much, Doc. I'll get in touch with you later!" Walking back into the parlor, with a face set as hard as stone, he stared at Kay and announced:

"That was Doctor Allison Swift, the best autopsy surgeon in the Police Department. He was assigned to the Van Zanten case by my friend, Deputy Inspector Kane."

"Well—what did he find?" inquired Kay tensely.

"Absolutely nothing. The stomach, intestines and organs of Nicholas Van Zanten have revealed no proof that he died of poison."

CHAPTER EIGHT
Sunday—The Clutching Hands

Late that afternoon, Inspector Joyce held a conference with Alexander Fawcett and Jimmy Van Zanten. They consented to it, it seemed, with a shade of reluctance; for they had heard the preliminary report from the Morgue without understanding what effect that would have upon the case. Jimmy expressed the naive opinion that nothing further should be said about his father's death until the body had been sent back to them for burial.

But Joyce had insisted, and the three men met in the library behind locked doors. Kay had been excluded, because the fiction still obtained that she was only the detective's daughter.

"I have here a copy of the police surgeon's memorandum," said Joyce, drawing from his pocket an envelope which had been delivered to him by special messenger an hour before. "Let me give you the gist of it:

"Dr. Swift found that the only signs of disease in Mr. Van Zanten's system was a slight hardening of the arteries, due to age, and an enlarged heart. This condition would have lowered the old gentleman's resistance to shock of any kind, physical or mental. The stomach, et cetera, contained no substances of a deadly nature that could be recognized. Yet the stomach was in a bad state—red and irritated. The doc's exact words are that 'death may have resulted from some unknown poison which has acted upon the nerves and other centers.'"

"Which means precisely what?" asked Jimmy Van Zanten. "There can be no verdict of death by poisoning, can there, unless the poison is located and named?"

"Correct. But they're going ahead with a chemical analysis of the organs, as well as the contents of the viscera."

"Is that usual, when there is so little reason for presuming a murder?"

"Not unless the police have suspicions of their own, or unless there's a demand from some quarter. I demanded it, charging foul play."

"You surprise me. The ordinary post mortem calms my fears. My father appears to have been a heart case, after all. But I guess you feel obliged to live up to the commission he gave you."

"I do."

"And this—ah—this chemical analysis, is it sure fire?"

"Yes, so far as the great majority of poisons are concerned. But I'll say this: Mr. Van Zanten was knocked over, as if by something he'd just swallowed. In that case, the stuff should still have been in his stomach, unchanged. It didn't have time to be soaked up by the organs. If Dr. Swift couldn't find it in the stomach, it's unlikely that the analysis will turn up a positive sample."

Joyce refrained from saying that he had arranged with Swift that Stas's process should be applied. This infernally cunning method devised by a Teutonic chemist consists of reducing the physical parts examined to their component elements, extracting the alkaloidal deposits and isolating that which is abnormal in a human body. The alkaloid thus arrived at may be so mixed as to defy chemical identification. Yet when tried upon a sacrificial guinea pig, it may produce the known symptoms inseparable from some rare poison. It is then considered proven that the original subject died of the same cause that killed the guinea pig.

Fawcett bobbed his head slowly. He fastened on the reminder that his late employer, if poisoned, had probably absorbed the lethal substance a short while before his death.

"I noticed that the police took away the carafe of water and the glass from Nicholas' room. I suppose they tested them. Do you know the result?" he asked.

"Yes. The water in both receptacles was pure. No clue there."

"Well, then—" Jimmy hesitated. "What is the object of this conference? What do you want to do now?"

"Can't you think of something that it's our plain duty to do?"

"Why no, Inspector."

"I want the bodies of George and Mary Van Zanten exhumed, and autopsies held on them."

Jimmy leaped up, his peaked face working convulsively. "No, no!" he cried. "I can't stand any more messing with corpses. Uncle George and Mary weren't poisoned."

"How do you know? Your father thought they were," said Joyce coldly, and as the lad replied only with sobs, he queried the estate manager with the raising of one eyebrow and the lifting of his chin.

Fawcett sketched a large negative gesture with his right hand. "I can't agree with you, Inspector," he returned mildly.

"Unless those police chemists you talk about decide that Nicholas died of unnatural causes, I'd not feel justified. How long do you suppose they'll take?"

"At least a week."

"We'll forget George and Mary for that time."

Joyce got to his feet. "As you say. But if you won't be guided by me, I'll pull out of this case."

"Please don't." Fawcett had risen, too, and he dropped his broad, calloused palm of an amateur gardener upon the detective's shoulder, while his eyes glowed earnestly. "I'm thinking of this grief-stricken boy and the poor, foolish lady who's gone into hiding. I can't wound their sensibilities by disturbing the last sleep of their dead, with so little cause! Really, until the police make a final report on Nicholas, it would be unseemly. But I want you to stand by us, as long as the faintest suspicion exists that Nicholas was murdered."

Joyce thought to himself: "Well, I'll be damned! This Fawcett is a mushy tear-jerker. If *he* did the killing, his acting is good enough to land him in the movies." He was on the point of replying, when Jimmy cut in:

"I'm opposed to having a private detective mixed up in this. The Police Department is as much as we can stand."

Fawcett turned on the boy in ponderous distress. "I'll thank you not to antagonize the Inspector, Jimmy," he said. "Remember I'm your guardian for a month longer. I am the one to say whether he stays in this house."

There was something odd in the way Jimmy quailed before the benign and refulgent eyes of his mentor, and Joyce reached a quick decision.

"I'll stay, all right," he announced, "but only on the condition that you engage me in writing."

"In writing?" repeated Fawcett, astonished.

"Yes. Just make it clear that I'm authorized to take any steps I see fit to learn whether poisons have been fed to members of this family. You needn't worry about the bodies in the vault. A Board of Health permit, applied for by you, would be necessary before an autopsy could be held on either of them."

He had thought that Fawcett might refuse, but the manager sat down immediately at the nearest desk, drew out a letterhead stamped with the Van Zanten crest, and wrote:

"Michael Joyce, private detective, is hereby authorized to investigate, at his discretion, the alleged poisoning of residents of Van Zanten Manor, Staten Island, New York.
    "Alexander Fawcett,
    "Legal Guardian of James Van Zanten."

"First rate," remarked Joyce, after he had glanced at the document. "Now, have the young gentleman countersign it, if you don't mind."

Fawcett silently raised his eyes to Jimmy, and the latter responded like a physical automaton. Nevertheless, rage and a sort of obscure hatred contorted his face, as he scrawled his name, below the one already on the sheet. He walked from the room, without uttering a word of apology, or stating where he could be found.

"I'll be going back to my flowers now," sighed Fawcett. "There's still quite a spell of daylight left."

"Yeah," said Joyce, with seeming indifference.

He left the library shortly after Fawcett had departed, looked up Kay and drew her to a secluded corner of the parlor.

"I want you to hop over to New York as fast as you can make it. You'll go to the office first. I'll phone to have Tom and the Sheriff wait for you, but I don't want to give them orders over the phone. The orders mustn't be overheard by anybody here."

"Right, Inspector," the girl answered, and stood by like a soldier for further instructions.

"You see, it's this way. I've got Fawcett to appoint me in writing, and we're going to rip this case wide open."

"If Fawcett did that willingly, he can't be guilty," Kay said.

"Maybe not. He acts as if he's innocent. I'm kinda for him, but perhaps it's just that he's smart. Now listen. You'll tell my son to check up on all sales of poisons in the Borough of Richmond during the past year. He can put two or three operatives on the job, and after they're through with the Staten Island drug stores and doctors' prescriptions, let 'em canvass the nearby Jersey towns. The city-wide reports at 505 Pearl Street—Department of Health—should be looked at for a possible clue. The likeliest poisons are arsenic and strychnine, and the idea is to learn whether they were bought by a person from this house. Tom's bright enough to look after that end of it."

"He certainly is," said Kay.

Joyce smiled. "As to the Sheriff, I want him in St. George. He's to snoop for information about the personal lives of the Van Zantens, Fawcett and his wife, Celestine Curtis and Doc Henkle. I want the neighborhood gossip, and most of all some dope on where Fawcett came from before he landed the job here."

"You don't think you should ask Fawcett the direct question?"

"Better not to. It might make him suspicious, and I want the dirt, if any. Of course, I'll draw him out as much as I can, and also see what I can get on the servants. But I'm planning to stick close to this house. Let Symes do the gum-shoe work round about the whole section. He'll find a way to report to me as a phony gas inspector, or something; he knows that game."

"Okay. I'll tell him."

"And now for your own assignment. You're to try to find Constance Van Zanten in New York City and trail her, until further orders." Joyce handed Kay the list of addresses of the spinster's haunts, which he had obtained from Jimmy the day before. "I hate to lose your help here. But none of the boys at the office have seen the woman, and you have. Maybe it won't be for long."

"I'll do my darndest."

"I know you will. As you go upstairs to pack your bag, stop in the old girl's room and take one of the pictures of herself. If you fail to locate her easily, we'll have the office work from the photo. Now hurry; there's a good kid."

While Kay was getting ready, Joyce put through a call to the city, and in guarded terms instructed his assistants to await a messenger. Then he sauntered out to the garden, where he found Fawcett troweling the roots of a bed of magnificent dahlias.

"I've decided to send my daughter home," he said, without preliminaries. "Would you be so kind as to have her driven to the ferry right away?"

The estate manager got to his feet, brushing red soil from the knees of his trousers. "Surely, surely," he answered. "I don't blame you for sending her from this house of gloom."

Fawcett waved his hand rather theatrically at his man of all work, Andrew Burns, who was raking manure among the rose bushes a few yards distant. "Climb into your uniform, Andy, and take Miss Joyce to St. George. Use the limousine."

As the hulking fellow approached, distinctly sullen at the idea of doing emergency duty, it struck Joyce for the first time that his broad, clodhopper's face reminded him vaguely of some one. Perhaps he had seen him in other circumstances. Perhaps Burns was a man with a police record, who had been involved in one of his thousands of cases.

But the next minute he acquitted the gardener of being a crook, or at all events a crook who had passed through his hands. Upon this point, Joyce's memory was photographic and almost fabulous. He never forgot the face of a criminal, though often the name and other data had slipped him, and the precise identification would have to be made by searching through his records. He now concluded that Burns must have crossed his path in some quite trivial manner, such as riding on the same train, or working at some menial task on which the detective had cast an eye.

He watched Andy's slouching figure until it disappeared in the garage, and then kept small talk going with Fawcett. The safe departure of Kay assumed an exaggerated importance in his eyes, he did not know why. It was not long delayed. She was ready as soon as the car was, and waved her handkerchief like a good little daughter until a curve in the driveway carried her out of sight.

"Fond of her, aren't you?" remarked Fawcett.

"I'll say so—very fond."

The estate manager rubbed his chin. "By the way, I didn't want to bring this up before Jimmy—he's so morbid—but the keys of the burial vault are missing from the late Mr. Van Zanten's safe. Did he give them to you, Inspector?"

Joyce looked at the other steadily. "He did. He had me visit the place yesterday."

"And did you discover anything strange?"

"No." He had made up his mind on a hunch not to mention the ambiguous and vanishing footprints, or to tell Fawcett that he feared a duplicate set of the keys existed. Not yet, at all events.

"My, my! The vault had a horrid fascination for Nicholas. He used to slip down there himself, when he thought nobody was looking."

Joyce had uttered the same idea to Kay, as a suspicion. From Fawcett, it sounded like an attempt to hide behind a dead man who could not contradict him. But in the next breath he said, with a naivete that Joyce found it difficult to believe was bluff:

"I think you should give the keys back to me."

"Why?"

"Because they have become one of my responsibilities. If you need them at any time, I'd be glad to lend them to you."

Joyce handed the keys over, without a word. He had taken the precaution that morning of impression of them in wax scraped from an old candlestick.

"Guess I'll look the garden over," he said. "Don't interrupt your work to show me anything. I'll just blow around."

"That's the best way to enjoy flowers," beamed Fawcett, and promptly resumed his tending of the dahlias, turning his back as he troweled.

There was something queer about the landscape design of the garden, Joyce noticed. It was terraced more abruptly than the contour of the land required, to form a central lozenge, of which the long points were depressed and the middle domed. Even an amateur surveyor could tell that there was room there for a subterranean chamber. Joyce played with the idea, because Fawcett's devotion to the garden prodded at his brain. "If he's the guilty one, I bet he hides his poisons out here. He'd maybe buy them long before he intended to put them to use, and he wouldn't risk keeping them in the house. A guy like him would have a cache right in his own territory," he told himself. Yet the notion of an underground retreat was far-fetched, he admitted. The mound had probably been built up with rocks.

He drifted here and there, looking for a concealed entrance to a grotto and finding none. The tool shed interested him briefly. It was an earth-stained lean-to, which gave no evidences of being used as laboratory. Then he gave himself up to the enjoyment of an autumn riot of vivid blooms, and the intoxication of perfumes among which the honeyed sweetness of jasmines predominated.

Having strayed to the extreme northern end of the garden, Joyce was behind the mansion, and he had lost sight of Fawcett. An outhouse which he had observed before, though with no great attention, impinged upon his

consciousness because of a muttering that penetrated the
clapboard walls. Two or more persons were in there, wag-
ing a heated argument.

The A.B.C. of detective work called for an investigation, and Joyce stole forward. He could soon make out the
voices more distinctly, but the words were lost and he only
gained the impression that one of them had an extremely
odd timbre. Circling the hut—for that was all it was—he
found a single window, and peered in. To his amazement,
he saw Jimmy Van Zanten shaking his fist in the face of
the old Jamaican Negro cook, known as Aunt Ellen. The
bandanna handkerchief on her head was awry, and her
hands clasped in front of her in a gesture of pleading. She
was saying: "No, Marse Jimmy! No, Marse Jimmy!" over
and over again. Joyce could tell that much by lip-reading.

He was about to rap on the window to attract their
attention, when the boy seized Aunt Ellen by the throat,
pushed her against the wall and shook her fiercely, as if
trying to choke her to death.

CHAPTER NINE
Sunday—Jimmy Accuses

Joyce had no intention of allowing the weird old Negro woman to be killed by Jimmy Van Zanten. Besides, the motive behind this attack might throw valuable light upon the case, and he wanted Aunt Ellen's testimony. He leaped around to the door of the cabin, smashed the flimsy lock with a blow of his shoulder, and dragged Jimmy away from his victim.

"What the devil!" he said. "Are you crazy, mistreating her in this way?"

The lad was as white as chalk, and trembling all over. "You have no right to interfere," he gasped. "She's our servant."

"But not your slave—I don't think. Her being a Negro doesn't give you power of life and death over her. What's it all about?"

Jimmy morosely declined to answer. He made a move to leave, but Joyce threw up his hand. "You'll stick right here for a moment," the detective ordered, with unmistakable authority.

He turned his attention to Aunt Ellen. A packing case turned end up now served her as a chair. She was staring ahead of her, a perfectly blank expression in her black eyes. Her sooty skin and purplish lips had been tinged with gray during the struggle, but were now resuming their natural barbaric colors.

"Why was he quarreling with you, Aunty?" Joyce asked politely.

The Negress simply shook her head.

"Oh, come now! You can't be uppish with me. I represent the law here. I'm a detective. Did you know that?"

"I knowed it, sah," she replied in an excessively odd British West Indian accent, "but I ain't a-goin' to talk."

Joyce glanced slowly from the cook to her young master. It was difficult to tell which of them was the more surly, and despite the scene of violence he had broken up, they were most obviously in cahoots against him. He was about to make a new attempt to bully Jimmy into giving him some enlightenment, when the interior arrangements of the outhouse stimulated his curiosity in a new direction.

The place was a single room, with a bed in one corner and a small cooking stove in another. An ancient rocking chair stood beside a table in the middle of the floor. A couple of grocery boxes, on one of which Aunt Ellen was sitting, and a larger packing case fixed up as a dressing table, constituted the only other furniture. There was, however, an unpainted board shelf above the bed, and this was crowded with a collection of jelly jars and candy boxes, from which protruded such incongruous objects as the stems of clay pipes, dried herbs and bits of colored ribbon. On the little center table lay a Bible, and tacked to the wall was a picture of the late Queen Victoria of England, cut from a newspaper.

"I take it that Aunt Ellen lives here?" remarked Joyce, looking at Jimmy.

"If that seems important to you, there's no reason why you shouldn't know the truth," the boy replied sarcastically. "She does live here. She never liked to sleep in the house. This used to be a chicken coop, which my father fixed over for her years ago."

"Really! A chicken coop. And does she make it her home winter and summer?"

"Yes. She's all right, except in zero weather, when she takes refuge in the big kitchen and sleeps beside the stove like a dog."

Jimmy spat out his words viciously. The intonation he gave to the phrase, "like a dog," was not kind, seeing that he had attacked Aunt Ellen with his hands and she was refusing to bear witness against him.

Joyce dropped his manner of a good-natured mediator. "I've got to have a private talk with you," he said sternly to Jimmy. "Please step out on the lawn."

"Forget it. I don't have the time. I'm going driving in my car."

Until that moment, the youngster could not have been blamed for thinking that he had to deal simply with a private detective who knew his business, but whose sense of professional etiquette never allowed him to lose his temper. Crooks and insubordinate policemen without number could have told him that if one insisted on scrapping with Inspector Joyce, one caught a Tartar.

The blue eyes suddenly hardened, and the pleasant Irish mouth became as grim as a shark's mask. "You'll do as I say, Mr. Van Zanten. On the lawn, within ten feet of this shack," he ordered icily.

Jimmy wilted, and went out.

"I want you to stay here until I come back," Joyce said to the old Negress. But as she glowered at him blankly, he decided to take no chances with her. He had himself broken the lock to get in. So he pulled the door shut, and dragged in front of it a block for chopping firewood which he found outside.

The heir of the Van Zantens was standing under an apple tree, at the point where the garden stopped and the lawn began. Joyce walked up to him.

"Get this straight. I'm investigating three deaths that look like murder. You've got to co-operate."

"What right have you—"

"You signed a paper employing me," Joyce interrupted. "But that's not really important. It only protects me from a technical charge of trespassing on this estate. Why, you damned pup, I've the right of any citizen to collect evidence that may result in bringing a murderer to justice."

"Go ahead, then. Mr. Fawcett wants you here, and I've agreed to it. But you can't do anything to make me suffer if I leave you to your own devices."

"No? Has it struck you that your father died more than twenty-four hours ago, and there hasn't been a single newspaper reporter come to get the low-down on the story? Funny, isn't it? The tabloids just eat up a poison mystery, especially when the victim is a rich man. Well, I'll tell you why the news hounds haven't been around. I blocked 'em. I used to be an Inspector in the Police Department, and I've got enough pull to have kept the death of Nicholas Van Zanten off the blotter, so far. One word from me, and the bars will be down."

"The newspapers will have to find out some time," muttered Jimmy, his peaked face going a shade whiter.

"Sure. But if we can fix the guilt before they start blatting, you'll be saved a lot of grief. You don't want them to prejudge the case, do you, and write you all up as if you were monkeys in the zoo?"

"I'll lock myself away from the reporters."

"Like hell you will! If you don't talk to me now, you won't get the chance. I'll have you placed under arrest as a material witness, and you'll be facing the reporters from behind the bars of the County jail."

The force of Joyce's personality and the manner in which he bit off his words had the effect of a third degree upon the boy. His will broke. A hard, dry sob shook him, and tears came into his eyes.

"What do you want to ask me?" he gasped.

"Did you murder your father?"

"Oh, God—no!"

"Do you know how he was killed?"

"I do not."

"Have you suspected foul play?"

"Yes."

"In the cases of your uncle and cousin, also?"

"Yes."

"Poison?"

"Yes."

"Then why have you done nothing to bring these events to the notice of the police?"

"Mr. Fawcett and Dr. Henkle said Uncle George and Mary died natural deaths. Dad believed them, so why shouldn't I? I—I guess I believe them still. When Dad was hit yesterday, I found the house full of detectives, including yourself. I hated to admit the idea of murder, so I just left it to you."

"You're a medical student, aren't you?"

"Yes."

"Well, let me tell you, Mr. Van Zanten, you show signs of making one of the world's worst doctors. You'll bring disgrace on the medical profession, you will, if you don't make a better use of the scientific knowledge that's pounded in to you. You must have picked up a lot of dope on poisons—more than the layman knows, any way—and yet you've allowed these deaths in your family to occur without investigation. You ought to be ashamed of yourself."

Jimmy's shoulders drooped, and suddenly Joyce struck at him from a new angle.

"Why were you choking that old Negro woman?"

"I—I don't like her, Inspector."

"That's a fine reason to give me. Not trying to say you wanted to kill her, are you?"

"Of course not."

"Why don't you like her? Out with it."

"It's a long story. She came here as a sort of tramp, and Dad took a fancy to her, as he may have told you. I was always scared of her as a kid. I don't take to savages—don't like any of the wild exotic stuff that goes into adventure stories, and that most boys think romantic. Aunt Ellen isn't an American darky. She's from some tropical island, and her ways give me the shivers."

Joyce shook his head. "That's not good enough. You grew up with this woman around, and you must have got accustomed to her. No one jumps at a person's throat—but, oh hell! Quit stalling. Give me the real reason."

"She practices voodoo," muttered Jimmy.

"She does, eh? On exactly what do you base that statement?"

"As far back as I can remember, she has tried to make us drink herb teas which she brews with God knows what. Ghastly stuff! She doesn't call it medicine, but claims it has magic properties. Dad sometimes fell for the idea, to please her. I've heard him kidding her about how much better he felt after one of her potions, but there were times when I was darned sure that the muck made him ill."

Joyce pricked up his ears. "This is kinda interesting," he said. "Go right on. Spill all that comes back to you about Aunt Ellen and her teas."

"She isn't given so much to prescribing them for sickness, though I've known her to do that, too. She considers them good for old age, or to restore happiness, or to put one in the right frame of mind to succeed in an undertaking.

Things like that. She mumbles charms over the cup before she hands it to the person to drink."

"And what about the other side of the story? What about curses? Does she ever fix up a brew intended to bring trouble upon an enemy?"

"She's said more than once that it's possible to do that, but that such is the devil's work and she's opposed to it. I think she's an old hypocrite. Still, I've never had proof that she harmed any one."

"Hm! Have you drunk her teas yourself?"

"When I was a child—yes."

"What effect did they have on you?"

"None that I could notice. They tasted filthy, that's all."

"Has everybody else in this house drunk them, one time or another?"

"Everybody except Mr. Fawcett. He'd laugh when they were offered to him, and tease Aunt Ellen, and blame Dad for encouraging her superstition."

"Do you know her methods—what herbs she puts into the pot, and so forth?"

"I do not. She's everlastingly at it in that chicken coop of hers, but I've shut my eyes to it. Until today, when I got to thinking of her mumbo-jumbo on top of my other troubles, and I went out and raised the deuce with her."

With a pretense of complete skepticism, Joyce stifled a yawn. "Of course, I'm taking this with a grain of salt," he said. "It comes too pat. Murder and sudden death, and a witch doctor to finish the picture. Hot stuff!"

"You don't believe she brews voodoo teas?" demanded Jimmy indignantly.

"Can't say that I do—not a hundred percent, anyway. It seems to me your father wouldn't have talked poisons in my office without mentioning this funny-business. Fawcett, too, would have sprung it, for his own protection."

"Fawcett thinks Aunt Ellen is a joke—" began Jimmy. He interrupted himself, and started back toward the hut. "Please come this way, Inspector. I bet I'll be able to prove it to you."

Joyce hesitated, but decided to follow the lad.

"She was preparing to make some of the stuff when I butted in on her half an hour ago," Jimmy whispered, as they approached the window stealthily. "That's what got me so sore."

Peeping through the same dusty glass that had first revealed Aunt Ellen being choked by her young master, Joyce got glimpses of a bizarre spectacle.

A kettle was boiling on the stove, and giving off clouds of steam. Ranged on the floor were three small, uncovered pans. The ancient West Indian sat on her haunches in front of the stove, and with the greatest care selected dried leaves and twigs from a miscellaneous bunch clutched in her left hand. She dropped an herb in one pan and then in another, observing no sequence, but apparently concocting three different recipes with the ingredients she lit upon. Her lips worked continuously, and it was clear that she was either praying or uttering an incantation. Once she reached suddenly for the Bible on her center table, kissed it and replaced it before she went ahead with her dubious task.

Joyce glanced at his companion, and raised his eyebrows. "Why the Bible?"

"Oh, she's very religious! High Church of England, if you please!" the other answered under his breath. "But I've been told that that never stopped a savage from practicing voodoo."

"You're right enough."

Aunt Ellen had now exhausted her handful of parched vegetation, except for a few stalks which she stowed away in a bottle that had contained raspberry jam. She rose to her feet, took the kettle from the stove and poured a little hot water into each of the pans. The vapors that floated up from them appeared to be extraordinarily thick.

The Negress then fell upon her knees. She clasped her hands, and stooped until her body was hanging over the receptacles containing her brew. Her position was such that the watchers could see only her back, and the steam curled on either side of her bent head.

Joyce drew back from the window, and faced Jimmy Van Zanten.

"Queer goings-on, all right!" he said. "Now get the rest of it off your chest."

"I don't know what you mean, Inspector. There's nothing more to tell."

"Just a natural born liar, aren't you? You must have a bad conscience, and a low opinion of my smartness into the bargain." Joyce seized him by the collar and shook him. "Come across pronto! Come clean!"

"What do you think I'm hiding?" the boy panted.

"Your motive for attacking Aunt Ellen. You say her voodooism got your goat on general principles. Bunk! What has she done that has a bearing on this case?"

Jimmy hung his head. "I—I wanted to get a confession from her before I talked," he stammered. "But the fact is, she—she gave Dad one of her teas to drink yesterday morning."

"And he swallowed it?"

"Yes."

"Why?"

"She claimed it would calm his nerves."

"Does any one in the house except yourself know that he drank this stuff?"

"I don't think so. I happened to be standing by. It was just before breakfast."

"A few minutes ago, Mr. Van Zanten, I asked you whether you had any information as to how your father met his death. You swore you had not. You wouldn't so much as share a suspicion with me. You lied and lied, until I broke you down. It comes a bit late, but now's your chance to get it all said."

"I accuse that Jamaican witch of poisoning Dad," Jimmy screamed. "She probably killed Mary and Uncle George, too, and she'll murder everybody here if we don't put her in prison."

CHAPTER TEN
Sunday—A Lesson in Black Magic

As soon as he had forced Jimmy Van Zanten to put into words his accusation that Aunt Ellen was the poisoner, Joyce relaxed the pressure he had brought to bear upon the boy. He seemed almost to lose interest in him. Carelessly, the detective tapped him on the shoulder and said, as though he were giving advice rather than issuing an order:

"You can go to your room. It will be dinner time in a little while. I don't think you should be off the estate more than you can help until this investigation is over."

"I'd intended to drive to Stapleton and bring back my fiancée, Miss Curtis, to dinner," Jimmy replied.

"Oh, all right! I'll be glad to have another talk with the young lady. She struck me as being a sensible girl."

"Are you going to question Aunt Ellen now?"

"Yes. And don't get ahead of me in letting Fawcett, or anybody, know that you and I discussed her."

"You can trust me not to, Inspector," Jimmy assured him, suddenly tractable.

Joyce watched his retreating figure until it disappeared into the house. Then he stepped back to the door of the Negress' hut, shoved aside the chopping block with which he had barricaded the door and entered without knocking. He found Aunt Ellen sitting bolt upright on the same packing case where she had been when he left her. His

swiftly roving eyes noted immediately that the three pans
which held her brew had been hidden from sight. The kettle was still on the stove, but simmering faintly because it
was over to one side. Joyce assumed that the woman had
heard some of Jimmy's final outcry at the window, and
that she had prepared against his own prompt return.

He stood looking at her for a minute or two, without
speaking. His voice when it came was gentle and coaxing.

"I'm not trying to harm you at all," he said. "I'm your
friend. If you'll answer a few questions I want to ask, we'll
get along nicely."

Her irises were so black they could not be distinguished
from her pupils; they were like round pebbles framed by
her yellowed eyeballs. Into these strange orbs there now
seemed to come a flicker of light, but her lips remained
stubbornly closed.

"Mr. Jimmy treated you very badly just now," he pursued. "I didn't approve of that."

The old body stiffened. "Marse Jimmy can do what
he like to dis-hyah nigger. He's de son of my own Marse
Nicholas, God rest him!"

"I know how you feel, Aunty," said Joyce, pleased to
have found a way to pierce her shell. "But the young
gentleman *was* a little rough. I don't think he understands
you."

The Negress shook her head ambiguously.

"In fact, I'm sure he doesn't," Joyce continued. "He was
giving me his ideas about you, and he had a lot of things
quite wrong. Wouldn't you like me to tell you at least one
of them, to show what I mean?"

Her curiosity was betrayed by a quivering of her eyelids
and twitching of her hands. She condescended to nod.

"Well, he called you a voodoo woman. I know that you
aren't one of those, Aunt Ellen. Voodoo is what they do in
the forests of Haiti, and the Haitians got it from some of

the wickedest tribes in Africa. Slaves brought it over long, long ago. It's the worship of the devil, and the priests think nothing of sacrificing human beings and drinking their blood. That's voodoo."

"Mr. Detective, you know what you's talking about," she cried in an astonishingly clear voice. "I swear to God I have no dealings with voodoo."

"Of course not. That's what I said myself. But it's no secret to me what you do go in for."

Joyce had assumed that since she was not a native of Haiti, it was highly unlikely for her to be a practitioner of true voodooism, which is confined in the western world to the French-speaking black republic and to certain sophisticated circles in Harlem, New York's Negro quarter. The cult of the serpent—both the Petro and the Legba rites—excite horror among the natives of the other West Indian islands. The last-named have only a vague idea of what it is all about, but they have heard of the slaying of "the goat without horns," as the human sacrifice is called, and they associate it with Haiti, a land with a bad reputation in such matters.

Furthermore, it was equally easy for Joyce to guess at the milder form of African sorcery which a woman from Jamaica was likely to practice.

"You think you know all my secrets, white man?" Aunt Ellen asked, with a faint grimace that passed for a smile. "Let's hear how you call 'em."

"You do a little obeah," Joyce told her. "The church people would blame you for that. Your minister would be very angry, if he found out. He'd make you confess before the congregation and pray to God for forgiveness. But you can't see what harm there is in going back to the wisdom of your fathers. Religion is one thing for buckras, and it's another for black folk. They have their mysteries that they keep to themselves, so you have yours. Suppose you cook

some leaves and say the right charms over them; yes, and
fix up a good-luck or a bad-luck sign with chicken feathers, bones and red string! Why, it's just obeah, isn't it?"

The woman had been listening to him with a growing
amazement. Her jaw dropped, but her eyes became as alert
as those of some wild creature. "Where you learn about
such things?" she demanded. "Who tell you we call white
folk 'buckras' where I come from? Who teach you to talk
obeah? Marse Nicholas neber knowed dat, nor Marse Jimmy neither."

"I've traveled more than anybody in this house, Aunty.
Sure I've been in your country—in Jamaica. I lived up
in the Santa Cruz Mountains for a long time, and I rode
horseback all the way from there to Spanish Town." Joyce
glanced about the room, as he spoke. His eyes fell upon a
large knife-like implement, the broad blade of which was
about eighteen inches long and widest at the tip. He lifted
it from the floor.

"This is a machete, though you Jamaicans also call it a
cutlass," he went on. "It's used to chop grass and bushes,
to dig in the ground and almost everything that needs to
be done on a plantation. I'll bet there's no other tool you
fancy as much for cutting the things you need for obeah."

The Negress wagged her head, and replied with a certain friendly awe: "You suttenly is a learned gentleman,
sah!"

Now that he had obtained her confidence, Joyce proceeded more boldly. "I guess you won't mind telling me for
what reason you've been making teas and putting charms
on members of this family?"

"Dere's good obeah, and dere's bad obeah," answered
Aunt Ellen obliquely.

"I know it," said Joyce, and diplomatically left it to her
to state her own claims.

"I love de Van Zantens, Mr. Detective, and I only try see how I can help dem. I use good obeah."

"Did you do anything to Mr. George, who died a year ago?"

"After him fall sick, I give him a powerful draught. But I no can save him."

"And Miss Mary?"

"She die too quick. I no have time to make medicine for her."

"What about your old master yesterday?"

"I give him a draught to keep him safe, but him go jus' de same."

"Then your obeah has not been working?"

"No, sah."

"Why is that?"

"Since twelve months, dere is a curse on dis family."

"Whose fault is it? Who put the curse on?"

Aunt Ellen shrugged her shoulders in exaggerated fashion. "It's de Debbil's work. But I no like dat doctor who laugh loud all de time and stroke his beard. Why he no save my white folks?"

"Dr. Henkle may not have been able to do anything to save them," Joyce said noncommittally. "What do you think of Mr. Fawcett?"

"He make mock of me, but I no can say he is a bad man," she replied, with an air of scornful indifference.

So far, Jimmy Van Zanten's version of the old woman's relations with the members of the household had been upheld, save for his damning charge that she was the author of premeditated murder. Joyce took a fresh tack.

"What plants do you put into your teas, Aunty?"

She moved her body restlessly. "I jus' knows dem when I sees dem. No can find all I want. Bush here is different from Jamaica."

"Well, let me look at some samples."

She hesitated, but took down several of her jelly jars from the shelf and handed them to him. He made a selection of all the varieties of leaves and twigs he could find, and stuffed them into his pocket. Aunt Ellen began to mutter incoherently.

"Which of these went into the tea you brewed for the old gentleman yesterday?"

She indicated two or three specimens, and he made a mental note of them.

"What you do?" she inquired. "You tell the law on me?"

"I am the law," he said gravely, and choosing simple phrases in order to impress her. "I'll never punish you for your obeah. But your master is dead. I've got to test your plants, to be sure they are not poisonous."

She looked relieved. "No poison. Good medicine."

"Glad to hear it. The next thing is to show me those three mixtures you were cooking a little while before I came in. I saw them through the window, but you've got them hidden now."

The old woman bestowed a perfectly inscrutable stare upon him, which softened in a moment into one of her rare smiles. Without making any comment in words, she got up and fetched the pans from the narrow space between the stove and the wall, and ranged them on the floor at his feet. Joyce stooped to examine the liquid, which was no longer steaming.

Dusk was falling outdoors. It was getting quite dark in the hut. Aunt Ellen busied herself with the trimming and lighting of an old-fashioned kerosene lamp, which she placed on the center table. Then she returned to her seat upon the packing case that had once held groceries.

The detective smelled the concoctions one after the other, dipped a finger in each, and touched it to his tongue. He could make nothing of either the odor or the taste.

"Who are these for, Aunty?" he asked.

"Marse Jimmy."

"All of them?"

"Yes, sah."

"But they are different, aren't they?"

"Oh yes, sah!"

"What way do you think he should take them?"

"One is for now, so's him no fall sick. Nex' one for supposin' his belly hurt him. Las' would save him, if he's a-gwine to die," declared the aged sybil.

"And do you figure you could get him to swallow any of them?"

"Mebbe so—mebbe no!"

Joyce scratched his head. "Well, promise me you won't try to put them into his food or drink, without his knowing it."

Aunt Ellen made the sign of the cross, and he was reminded of the bizarre fact that she professed the creed of the extreme ritualistic branch of the Church of England. Many of the colored people in the British West Indian colonies are of that persuasion. "I swear it," she announced solemnly.

"Would you say that Marse Jimmy is in danger of falling ill soon?"

"Yes, sah."

"Why?"

"I tol' you already. Dere is a curse on dis family, an all de children of God dat live in de house of de Van Zantens."

Without asking her permission, Joyce got up and fumbled among the objects on the shelf where she kept her bottles and candy boxes. She watched him with an intense concentration of her coal-black eyes, and he could hear the quickened breathing of the half-savage creature. Yet she raised no objection to his free and easy behavior.

He lifted the lids of the various boxes and saw a jumble of trivial objects: the feathers of birds, especially the soft neck feathers of chickens; round pebbles from the beach, the tiny bones of bats and mice, and a large selection of colored threads and twine. This he knew to be the paraphernalia of obeah. Absurd and harmless stuff, he felt sure, and he did not take the trouble to examine it closely. The potions that Aunt Ellen mixed were really all that mattered in this business.

He ended by selecting three empty phials from one of the boxes. He rinsed them carefully in a pail of water which was standing on the floor, and filled each of them from a different pan of the recently manufactured brew. They fitted into his waistcoat pockets, and as he stowed them there for future chemical analysis, he looked at Aunt Ellen and smiled. The woman's natural intelligence told her that he was appropriating them for the same reason that he had taken samples of her dried herbs, and no exchange of words was necessary. He left her in possession of the main supply, and this fact built up a confidence on her part which the detective could feel as though it had come to him on a wave of telepathy.

The atmosphere in the little cabin, lighted by one archaic oil lamp, became subtly weirder as the dusk deepened out of doors. Joyce had the sensation of being in the lair of a witch doctor, far away from New York in the depths of some tropical forest.

"You've said twice that there's a curse on this family, Aunty," he remarked. "Three deaths do make things seem pretty bad. But I don't want you to talk about curses to anybody but me. It scares folks, and it's kinda crazy any way."

"It's crazy?" she queried in a surprisingly loud voice. "No, sah! Dead and bury is not all. I knows what I's seen."

"You've seen something you haven't told me?" Joyce asked curiously.

She nodded, and suddenly became reticent once more. "De curse! De curse!" she repeated morosely to no matter what question he put to her for the next few minutes.

"I'm not denying it," he at last admitted craftily. "I was just asking you not to frighten people who are not as wise as you and I, Aunty. We know there's magic in this world. Now, what did you see?"

She leaned forward and scrutinized his face in the dim light.

"Miss Constance leave dis house las' night a-walkin' on her hands," she said with stark abruptness.

"What?" he exclaimed, thunderstruck.

"A-walkin' on her hands—yes, sah! My blood turn to water when I see dat. It is a bewitchment."

"You must tell me more about it," said Joyce softly. "How can you be sure that you weren't fooling yourself?"

The old woman touched her eyeballs with the fingers of both hands. "True, I's a little blind. No can see far. But it was moonlight las' night. I's a-roamin' on de grass when I see Miss Constance come out of de side do' with her feet in the air. Can't make no mistake about dat."

"How did you know it was Miss Constance, Aunty?"

"Well, I no could have took my oath befo' God dat it was her, until dis morning when I hear she leave de house in de middle of de night. Dere ain't nobody else dat has gone away from here."

"That's right—nobody else," agreed Joyce.

"She walk clump-clump, mighty hard, until she reach de carriage drive. I run to my bed an' hide myself from such works of de Debbil."

As she talked, Inspector Joyce's mind had been swiftly analyzing her amazing statements. Of course, Constance Van Zanten had not left the Manor walking on her hands. That idea was preposterous. The aging spinster would have been incapable of gymnastics of the kind, nor would she have had any reason for indulging in them. But some one else might have had a powerful motive for making it seem that she had departed normally, for creating the footprints which had convinced Joyce himself when he had examined them that morning. The person in question must be a man; a woman would have been able to put on Constance's shoes, and do it simply. The man had resorted to placing his hands in the shoes and covering the distance to the graveled drive in the manner Aunt Ellen had described.

The sinister implication of this theory was only too obvious. Constance Van Zanten had not gone away. Yet she had disappeared. She, too, had been murdered, and her body must be hidden somewhere on the premises.

CHAPTER ELEVEN
Sunday—Tell-Tale Faces

When Joyce returned to the house after his unexpectedly long interview with Aunt Ellen, he found Jimmy, Celestine Curtis and the Fawcetts just completing a haphazard meal. Since he had been monopolizing the time of the Negro Cook, the solemn and conventional butler, Bucklestrope, had made the best of it and put some dishes together. He now proceeded to serve cornbeef hash and half-cold vegetables to Joyce, with a slightly injured air.

The members of the household and Celestine drank their coffee and excused themselves. The detective's mood of the moment caused him to be well satisfied that they should do so. He wanted time to think. Before allowing his mind to probe, however, into the intricacies of the evidence, he issued a curt order to Bucklestrope.

"Phone Dr. Henkle," he said. "Ask him to be here by ten o'clock. Use the extension in the kitchen, so that no one overhears you."

Thereafter, Joyce ate slowly, lingering over his dessert and coffee, while he mused about the extraordinary complications of the Van Zanten poison case.

He first appraised the mental condition of old Nicholas Van Zanten, when the latter had come to his office two days before. The man had been genuinely terrified. Why?

Because he had feared for his life, and events had subsequently proved in ghastly fashion that his suspicions had not been chimerical. He had seen his niece Mary die in agony, and had been shrewd enough to assume that a rapid poison had been administered to her. This had caused him to think back to the death of his brother George and to imagine that he, also, had been murdered.

Nicholas apparently had not known what poisons were employed, nor how they had been taken into the systems of the victims. Yet he had failed even to hint at the peculiar circumstance that an old Negress was in the habit of mixing barbarous and totally unscientific potions for himself and his family. He had evidently not believed Aunt Ellen capable of doing harm, intentionally or otherwise. Joyce was not prepared to acquit her so easily, not at any rate until he had had her nostrums analyzed.

Again, the deceased head of the house had been vague about the motive for the killings and had been doubtful whom to suspect as the master plotter. He had tried, unconvincingly, to make a case against Celestine, as an upstart who wished to marry into the family and get her hands quickly upon the million-dollar inheritance. Actually, he had seemed secretly to dread that his son Jimmy was guilty. Yet he had failed to mention that Jimmy was a medical student, with a presumptive knowledge of poisons. There was simply nothing that Van Zanten had done or said which would help in solving the mystery. The only testimony he would now be able to give would be the silent testimony of his post mortem. And the same, Joyce firmly believed, was true of the vanished Constance.

Searching for a definite theory, Joyce told himself that there were three main points at issue. First: what was the object of the series of murders? Second: to whom did the finger of suspicion now point? Third: what lethal means were employed, and how?

It was increasingly clear that the object must be the destruction of Van Zantens. All the Van Zantens who had been living in the Manor a year ago? That was not so sure. There was only one of them left now—Jimmy—and the plot might well have reached its climax. Joyce had been given to understand that, except for a small legacy to Fawcett, Jimmy was the sole heir. Who then would benefit by Jimmy's death? No one in this immediate circle, for Celestine could enjoy his money by becoming his wife. There must exist, all the same, an heir at law who would get the fortune in case Jimmy perished before he had time to marry. Joyce decided that he would insist on seeing Nicholas' will, and also learn the identity of the next of kin. It was by no means impossible that the holocaust was being engineered, through an agent or agents, to benefit some person whose name had not as yet been mentioned. In that case, an attempt would be made upon Jimmy's life—and made quickly.

Going on the assumption, however, that the plot was confined to residents of this house and their close associates, who was most likely to be guilty? Jimmy Van Zanten himself? Joyce admitted that on the known facts it looked black for the boy. The latter's surly resentment of an investigation did not inspire confidence. His having charged Aunt Ellen with being the poisoner meant very little. His real reason for the visit to the chicken coop might have been to bully the Negress, because she knew too much about what he had done. Her loyalty in not accusing him, despite the bad treatment she had received, was typical of a family retainer with her primitive background.

Still Joyce found it hard to believe that the youthful Jimmy had been the perpetrator of cunning and ruthless murder. He behaved much more like a person who knew what was going on, and did not have the moral courage to denounce it.

If four human beings had been done to death, therefore, to put Jimmy in possession of a million dollars, who was doing it? And what could be the scheme for personal gain? As Joyce saw it, the actual killer might be planning, in that event, to blackmail Jimmy with the threat that a tip to the police would go a long way towards incriminating him, and the resulting autopsies on the dead would be disastrous.

Fawcett or Dr. Henkle might have been foxy enough to think up something like that. Fawcett was probably the cleverer man, but Henkle was a physician. Henkle would know exactly what could be accomplished, and how on a show-down to make his original certificates of the cause of death seem like mere errors of judgment.

To be sure, any one of the servants might be guilty. Poisoning was a lamentably facile act, if the poisoner chanced to be an individual who had no conscience. But it took a certain amount of vigor to turn the results to account afterwards. The butler and the two maids were hardly the type. The gardener, Andy Burns, appeared to be too much of a moron to plot anything subtle. The dour Mrs. Fawcett probably was guided solely by what her husband instructed her to do.

Yes, it simmered down to Jimmy Van Zanten on his own hook, Fawcett or Henkle for purposes of blackmail, or old Aunt Ellen running wild with her infernal obeah.

Joyce arose from the dining table at about half-past nine. He was thinking now of Kay Carey, and wishing he had not sent her on that wild goose chase to the city. She could have been useful to him here. Mighty useful in roping the suspects, and helping him to solve the third and most important of the problems he had posed. What poisons had been used, and how—and when? He could form all the theories he pleased about crimes and motives, but if he failed to prove the means and the circumstances, there would be no conviction for murder.

He had no line on where Kay was apt to be at the present moment. But he first called up her home, and as he had feared he did not get any information. The girl was on the trail of the undiscoverable Constance, and like a good operative she would forget family ties until the chase was either ended or abandoned. However, she would keep in touch with the office. It was a bit late for any of the important assistants to be at the office, but Joyce took a chance, and while he was waiting for his phone connection an idea occurred to him that made him grin at one side of his mouth.

The phone was answered by a very intelligent detective named Dennis Sullivan.

"Hey there, Dinny!" the chief said. "Can you tell me where Miss Carey is?"

"Trying to locate Constance Van Zanten, Inspector."

"Yes, I know. But when did you last hear from her?"

"She phoned from the Bali Missionary Society half an hour ago, and said the woman had not been seen there."

"Good. She'll sure call again. Stick around for it. Now get this. . . ." Joyce quit speaking the English language, and substituted for it a strange collection of syllables which but slightly suggested any known tongue. He lowered his voice and constructed his phrases slowly. An eavesdropper would have recognized only the occasional use of the name, "Kay." The jargon was an invention of Joyce for communicating with his men in emergencies.

Sullivan, at the other end of the wire, answered: "Okay, Inspector! I get you."

He had no sooner hung up than Joyce heard the front door open, and the bombastic voice of Dr. Alphonse Henkle reached all the rooms on the lower floor in a volley of greetings and optimistic remarks, which swelled almost to the proportions of an uproar.

The detective walked quickly to the parlor, where he found the young people and Fawcett exchanging trivialities with the doctor. He nodded brusquely.

"How are you, Mr. Joyce?" cried Henkle. "But I need not ask. You look in the pink of condition—Oh, very well indeed! Now—er—what can I do for you? I understand from the worthy Bucklestrope that it was you who requested my presence here."

Fawcett pursed his lips, and an expression of anger flashed across Jimmy's face. Neither of them liked to hear that a step had been taken without their knowledge. Joyce could have cuffed Henkle for springing his line about the butler so tactlessly. But it really didn't matter. He was getting a group together for a purpose, which he was willing to bet they would find it impossible to penetrate.

"That's right, Doctor. I've some questions I want to ask you in the presence of these folks," he said coolly.

Henkle looked uncomfortable, but replied: "I shall be glad to give any information that may help in this sad case. That is to say, so long as—er—I am not asked to violate my professional ethics."

"You needn't worry. This is going to be painless. I want your angle on the fact that the old black cook here has been dosing the family for years with mysterious herb teas. And, mind you, she's a voodooist." Joyce purposely avoided the term "obeah," since it involved a shade of meaning unfamiliar to most Americans.

"Are you sure? Why, this is preposterous!" exclaimed Henkle theatrically.

Fawcett wagged his large head, and smiled. "So you are on to Aunt Ellen's childish superstitions! Is that what you were talking about to her this afternoon? I'd have mentioned her herb remedies myself, if I'd thought them important."

Ignoring the estate manager for the moment, Joyce concentrated on Henkle: "Are you trying to tell me you did not know that the woman prepared such draughts?"

"I said nothing of the kind. Of course, I knew it. But it never occurred to me that she might be practicing voodooism."

"Whether she did or didn't may not cut any ice. Voodoo is only a name. What I'm chiefly after is this: what did you think of your friends actually swallowing the stuff?"

"I disapproved, sir. Any doctor would."

"Did you try to prevent it?"

"I gave my advice to that effect. But—er—that is about all one can do with wealthy patients. They have the habit of behaving as they please."

"Did you ever look into the nature of the mixtures—ever analyze them?"

"N-no."

"Then all I can say is, you're a poor excuse for a family physician. The cook may be a dangerous faker, and you should have checked that up."

Henkle looked extremely crestfallen. Joyce swung around to Fawcett:

"What about you? Did you ever test 'em?"

"A few times," the manager replied tranquilly. "I poured out some of the horrid stuff my poor old friend Nicholas was going to drink, and tried it on a dog. On another occasion, I poured it down the throat of a chicken. Neither of them came to any harm."

"Well, that was one way of doing it. Better than nothing, I'll say!" Joyce extracted a wisp of dried herb at random from his pocket and showed it to the doctor.

"What plant would you say that was?" he demanded.

"I—I really don't know," answered Henkle, after he had stared at it somewhat helplessly. "I am not a botanist."

"And you, Mr. Fawcett? Can you give a name to it? It's one of Aunt Ellen's favorite samples."

Fawcett took the sample, and used his thick gardener's fingers to straighten out the withered leaves with extraordinary delicacy.

"Why, it's common dandelion," he announced. "I guess old women in all parts of the world make dandelion tea."

Joyce smiled, and put the herb back into his pocket. This line of questioning was killing time beautifully, but wasn't leading anywhere in particular. He took a surreptitious glance at the clock.

"I now want you to call Mrs. Fawcett and the servants in here," he said.

"All of them, Inspector?" inquired the manager, his countenance expressing a vague amusement.

"All except Aunt Ellen. Let's see; there's Andy Burns, your assistant, and the butler, and the two maids Pearl and Sally. Be good enough to round 'em up."

Fawcett went in search of his wife, and presently the drab woman returned with him, and followed by the four astonished domestics. They stood in a row by the door and gazed at the detective with various degrees of alarm at this sudden inquisition.

Joyce patiently asked them, one by one, whether they had ever taken potions prepared by the ancient Negress, either as remedies or good-luck stimulants. He figured that Aunt Ellen's practices were no secret in this house, and that it would do more good than harm to create the impression that his suspicions were becoming centered upon her. If some one else were guilty, it might make that person careless in covering up his tracks.

The replies were diverting, and a commentary on the unreasoned contradictions of human nature. All the witnesses except Andy Burns admitted that, more or less, they had been patients of the obeah woman. The coarse-featured gardener simply made a gesture of contempt, and grunted:

"Such truck don't fool me."

Surprisingly, Sarah Fawcett was galvanized out of her customary reticence and expressed an earnest faith in the virtues of the nostrums.

"Doctors don't know it all," she said. "The old-fashioned healers, whether they be white or black, have done a lot of good in this world and saved many a mortal from the grave. I've often been helped by Aunt Ellen. Her teas seemed to cheer me up, and they cured my palpitation of the heart five years ago."

Dr. Henkle shook his head, and made absurd gestures with his hands. But it was at Fawcett's face that Joyce glanced, following this declaration. The estate manager continued to smile. Known to be a scoffer at obeah, he nevertheless seemed utterly tolerant of his wife's fancies.

Pearl and Sally declared with a certain embarrassment that they had allowed themselves to be talked into trying drinks, which Aunt Ellen had promised would bring them rich husbands. No bad effects had resulted, but they were still unwed.

The case of Bucklestrope, the portentous butler, was a shade more humorous. His body quivered unhappily when it became his turn to answer. No one could fail to see that the forced confession was doing grievous things to his dignity. He held up two fingers.

"Twice since I have served in this home, Inspector Joyce twice in sixteen years—I listened to that ignorant Jamaican cook and imbibed her nasty doses."

"Well, why did you do it?"

"She said they would cure me of the blues."

"And did they?"

"I experienced no symptoms, pleasant or otherwise, sir," replied Bucklestrope dolefully.

Now that he had heard from all of them, Joyce was forced to acknowledge that the evidence was not in itself conclusive. These people had received non-poisonous drinks at Aunt Ellen's hands, but that fact did not by any means prove that she lacked the knowledge to mix a lethal draught when the circumstances appeared, in her warped brain, to demand one.

The detective abruptly addressed himself to Jimmy's fiancée, Celestine Curtis. The girl had been leaning against the mantel-piece, smoking cigarettes in her free, modern way and listening with intense interest to the rapid-fire dialogue. It was evident that she had never before seen and heard a crime-hunter at work, and the mere fact of being present gave her a thrill.

"You're the only person I haven't asked about this," Joyce said. "Did you ever experiment with the magic tea, Miss Curtis?"

She brought her head around with a quick, graceful motion that shook her virile blond hair into her eyes. "Golly, no, Inspector Joyce! I keep in training, and I wouldn't take a chance on crazy mixtures."

"Well, you've heard of Aunt Ellen's doings, haven't you?"

"Sure. They made Jimmy mad, but I thought they were funny. I'm a newcomer around here, anyway."

At that moment, the telephone in the hall rang. It was what Joyce had been waiting for, providing the call was for him. As Bucklestrope moved out to answer it, the detective went right on talking to Celestine. He spun out a long speech, without real significance, about the superstitions of West Indian Negroes. All he wanted was to hold the girl in conversation, so that in a moment it would seem natural to make a certain request of her.

Bucklestrope returned to the doorway and announced: "It's a call from your office, Mr. Joyce."

"Oh, is it? I wonder whether you'd mind taking the message for me, Miss Curtis. I'll come to the phone, if there's anything important. But I'd rather dodge a long routine report."

"You bet, Inspector," cried Celestine, and dashed with her smooth athlete's gait into the hallway.

She was heard to pick up the receiver and say: "Hello! The Inspector wants you to give me the message." A brief pause followed. Then Celestine gasped, exclaimed: "What? What? Are you sure?" jiggled the hook as if she had lost the connection, and finally hung up. She came back into the room, her eyes snapping.

"Your man just slung a few words at me and got off the wire. It's a short message, but it's a darned important one to us, Inspector."

"Well, go ahead and repeat it," said Joyce casually. "I don't object to any one present knowing, since you happened to get it first."

"Your daughter has found Miss Constance Van Zanten in the city. She's going to bring her back here, the first thing tomorrow morning."

As this preposterous and totally untrue piece of news was launched, Joyce's eyes swept the circle of faces with a lightning-fast glance. He had arranged with his assistant, Sullivan, to telephone the canard the moment Kay actually communicated with the office and received her instructions to come out in the morning, alone. The fact that she would arrive without the missing spinster could be then explained to the household, on the grounds that she had blundered into making a false identification.

But the hoax had its purpose for this evening. It was one of the oldest tricks in the science of detecting crime. Joyce felt reasonably sure that Constance had been murdered; but only the guilty person shared that knowledge, and he might well be startled into betraying himself when he heard the sensationally false assertion that the victim was alive.

Joyce had chosen Celestine to answer the telephone, because he suspected her least. He had preferred not to announce the message himself, since the murderer might be on the watch for a detective's subterfuges. But every one would believe that the girl was repeating exactly what had been told to her.

There was a general and inevitable start of surprise, and the sound of breaths being taken harshly. Dr. Henkle clapped his hand to his forehead and cried, "Thank God!" with a theatricalism that neither absolved nor condemned him. Then all the servants and Mrs. Fawcett expressed their pleasure, convincingly enough, at hearing that Miss Constance was coming home.

Fawcett bobbed his head up and down in his favorite gesture, and his eyes beamed. "The dear lady has caused us a lot of worry, but we can't wonder at her nerves going back on her," he said. "I'm glad she's been found."

Jimmy, who had not uttered a word at that session, parted his lips to say something, but checked the impulse visibly. His complexion always chalky, seemed unusually white. He dropped a meerschaum pipe he had been smoking, and it smashed to splinters on the floor.

"Jimmy Van Zanten," Joyce told himself grimly, "looks as guilty as hell."

CHAPTER TWELVE
Monday—A Verdict from Headquarters

So busy had Joyce been since he first heard the tale of the person who had walked upside down from Van Zanten Manor at the dead of night, there had been no time to search for the clues that instantly suggested themselves to his mind. Of prime importance was the body of Constance, which almost certainly had been disposed of within the house or in the grounds nearby. The crafty murderer had doubtless hidden it well, but a detective who could not count on locating it would not be worth his salt. Contributory evidence, such as the shoes into which the miscreant had forced his hands, and which should carry finger-prints, also would be of great value in building up the case.

When he was finished with the group in the parlor, therefore—after he had observed the effects of the false message about the return of Constance—Joyce went upstairs to scrutinize the vanished spinster's room from a new viewpoint.

On his way, he looked in at the bedroom where Nicholas Van Zanten had died. A uniformed policeman, horribly bored, was seated there with his arms folded. Nobody had paid the least attention to him, except to bring him his meals, for more than twenty-four hours. Because of the remoteness of the Manor, he had not even been relieved at the proper time, and had dozed as well as he could in an armchair.

It is a wise rule of the Police Department to station a sentry at any spot where a death which may have been homicide has occurred. The object is to prevent possibly important evidence from being tampered with. The duty is one that the average patrolman dreads, on account of its monotony. Only after the detectives on the case are satisfied that they have noted all the clues is the guard removed.

Joyce said: "Tim Cavanagh, isn't it? How are ya, Tim?"

The oldish policeman sprang to attention. He was not obliged to do this for a civilian, but such was the legendary fame Inspector Joyce left behind him in the Department, that the veterans still thought of him as their superior officer.

"I'm fine and dandy, Inspector," Cavanagh answered untruthfully. He was so tired, he could have fallen asleep on his feet.

"You were here the whole of last night, and real wide awake, I guess, for the first lap of this punk assignment," continued Joyce shrewdly. "I'm wondering whether you heard any funny business in a room across the hall, from twelve o'clock on."

Cavanagh ruminated. "There was footsteps some time between four and five. Nothing much. A door opened kinda soft, and a couple of people walked towards the back stairs."

"You're sure it was two persons?"

"I wouldn't swear to it. But it was more than one. These folks haven't been put under surveillance, and it wasn't up to me to snoop. So I stuck right here."

"Correct. You didn't hear voices, or anything like that?"

"N-no! But I tell you what. Some pet dogs in a room started to yap—you know, squeaky little barks, the way them silly beasts do. They were choked off quick. I figured they'd been shoved into another room, but one of them let outa short howl first, as if it had been kicked."

"Great, Officer, great!" exclaimed Joyce. "That's more dope than I expected to pick up from you."

As he turned away and headed for Constance's room, he considered that two or three highly important points had been established. There had been no struggle in connection with the killing of the woman. He had already anticipated that angle. Since poison was the favored weapon in this house, the supper which she had taken alone probably had been doctored. The person, or persons, who had come for her had come merely to remove a corpse. Joyce felt that Cavanagh's impression that two had walked down the hall was not necessarily accurate; a single individual struggling along with an inert body would sound like a couple of men. Still, there might have been a confederate. The deed, in view of the presence of a policeman in an adjoining room, had been daring, say what one pleased!

The matter of the dogs struck him as being especially interesting. That morning, he had noticed two of the spinster's obnoxious poodles running free in her room. Neither of them had showed signs of having been kicked. But there might have been a third one, which had later been knocked on the head to conceal its injuries, or removed to the kennels behind the kitchen. He must look the beasts over. All the poodles were in the kennels now. He had seen Fawcett during the afternoon throw the two abandoned ones in there.

That it had been possible to kick a dog in Constance's room was additional proof, Joyce thought, that the woman was dead or unconscious at the time. Otherwise, she would have squawked to Heaven at seeing her beloved pet hurt.

He proceeded to examine the ground with all but super-human thoroughness. Constance's bed had been

made up by the maid, which was a pity, for it might have
furnished valuable hints. The nap of the carpet studied
through a magnifying glass gave proof of having been
trampled by hobnailed boots to which sandy soil had been
clinging. The tracks had been partially erased, by means
of a brush having been passed over them. For the rest,
there was nothing to indicate who the intruder had been.
The valise which had been taken away to give color to her
supposed flight had been packed with a sure hand, which
had been careful not to touch any toilet articles save those
that were to go into it.

The shoes employed for the making of the false tracks
were nowhere to be found. This did not surprise Joyce,
because any murderer with the cunning that this one had
displayed would probably hide the shoes as effectively as
he had had to conceal the valise and the clothes Constance
was presumed to have worn.

It became, then, a question of searching for the body
itself. That was a fairly hopeless task at night, in the great
rambling house, with its outbuildings, its garden and the
broad fields where a grave might so easily have been dug in
advance. Nevertheless, Joyce prowled from attic to cellar,
looking into closets and poking behind heaps of rubbish.
He gave it up at about one o'clock, and went wearily to
bed.

He had expected the morning to produce a crescendo
of drama, but the initial drift of developments surprised
him. He thought the case had passed beyond the stage of
quarrels with Jimmy Van Zanten and debates with Fawcett
as to the propriety of his detective methods.

After breakfast, which he had eaten alone, he had deliberately given everybody the slip and had spent an hour
or two exploring the basement of the house more completely than had been possible in the darkness. The easy
assumption that the corpse had been buried in the coal

pile, or under a cellar floor, could not be allowed to rest in abeyance. He had satisfied himself that the solution did not lie in that direction.

Upon his return to the main floor, Jimmy and Fawcett promptly cornered him. The boy's manner was marked by a quivering aggressiveness, a hard-eyed obstinacy, which suggested that he had somehow assumed temporary leadership over the estate manager.

"Inspector Joyce, I rescind the authority given you in writing yesterday," announced Jimmy, with extreme formality. "I wish you to retire from this case, and to leave the Manor at your convenience. You will, of course, send us a bill for services rendered, and it will be paid."

The detective boiled. Three times since old Nicholas Van Zanten had originally sought him out, he had tried to side-step the whole affair. Now he'd be damned if he'd let himself be kicked out of it! He had made too much progress toward piecing together the scattered fragments of a truly amazing puzzle. The dossier of this "Poison Case No. 10" was destined to go into his files endorsed "Solved," or he'd know the reason why.

"Fired, eh?" he answered with savage sarcasm. "A contract's a contract, you young shrimp. You were only asked to countersign, anyway, to witness your guardian's signature. You can't bounce me."

He turned toward Fawcett. But the latter was frowning, nibbling at his lower lip, and unaccountably no longer beaming at the world through his bright hazel eyes.

"I'm afraid I'll have to uphold Jimmy in this and cancel the paper I gave you on my own account, Inspector," he declared solemnly.

As quickly as his anger had flared up, Joyce switched to a Machiavellian craft. "Well, put it in writing, too," he said carelessly. "You seem a sensible man, Fawcett, so I hope you know just what you're doing.

"We have come to the conclusion that it's undignified to have any but the regular police here," stated Fawcett, brightening.

"Undignified!" repeated Joyce, genuinely amused. "How come?"

"I think I'd better let Jimmy reply to that."

It did not escape Joyce that this guardian, who had made firm decisions on other occasions, was now oddly deferential to the boy.

"Sure, I'll tell you what's in my mind," agreed Jimmy truculently. "That girl you've been calling your daughter is a detective working under you. When I heard last night that she was bringing Aunt Connie back, I got on to it right away. I phoned your office after you'd gone upstairs, and asked for 'Kay,' as if she'd been a friend of mine. They told me 'Miss Carey' wasn't there. I thought it damned offensive that you'd fool us on a detail of that sort."

Joyce wondered whether the other really did not understand the nature of the previous night's subterfuge, or whether he was doing some creditable acting. Aloud, he said:

"So it's your opinion that I shouldn't use undercover agents when I'm investigating what looks like a series of the foulest murders ever committed?"

Jimmy winced. "I object to being surrounded by spies when I don't have to be. The Police Department detectives can go as far as they please, and I'll know who I'm dealing with."

"Is that all?" asked Joyce. He commented to himself that by dropping a few words at Centre Street about the taking off of Constance, he could become as big a factor in the case as he chose to demand.

"No, it's not all. You've been walking around suspecting me of murdering my father. You've let me see that you do."

"How so, young feller?"

"The way you talked to me yesterday afternoon, when you butted in on my argument with the cook. I was a fool to stand for it."

"The Inspector is not to be blamed for having tried to get at the truth," interrupted Fawcett, his sugared tones conveying a spirit of large toleration. "But he *has* been free with his suspicions. I'm sure he has suspected me, also."

Joyce was about to say something, but Fawcett turned to him before he could speak. "Yes, you have, Inspector. I haven't resented it, because it was so—so inevitable. Here I was, the manager of this property, and my employers dying one after the other. Yet I had nothing to gain by their deaths."

"I'm doing the resenting," declared Jimmy. "The matter is settled. Joyce goes. Then we'll fetch the body of my father home, and give it decent burial no later than tomorrow."

The idea of overruling the officials at the morgue was a bit pathetic, but Joyce refrained from saying so. He merely asked:

"Got any other plans?"

"Bet your life I have. I'm going to have that black witch doctress arrested today, charged with murdering Dad and trying to wipe out my whole family."

This was awkward, Joyce reflected. It would gum up his plans for a logical solution if Aunt Ellen were accused now. Under pressure, she would make damaging admissions about herself. The newspapers would call her a voodooist, and she might easily be railroaded to the electric chair without the real truth ever becoming known. But there was no way to halt her arrest, if Jimmy carried out his threat of asking for it promptly. Joyce's anger began to rise again. He thrust his clenched fists into his trousers pockets and strode over to the nearest window to get a breath of fresh air.

He found himself looking down the driveway to the gate. A taxi was speeding toward the house. He wondered whom it was bringing. Kay, perhaps? Or a man from the District Attorney's office? An official from Headquarters would have been likely to come in a P.D. car.

A few minutes later, a young man got out and ran up the steps. Joyce saw that it was his son Tom. Pretty quick action, he thought, for Tom to be here already. He must have something significant to report. The detective waited impassively until he was shown in, and then introduced him to Fawcett and Jimmy.

"These are the chief interested parties, Tom," he remarked. The harmless words constituted a code, and meant that reserve instead of frankness was desirable in their presence. With no preliminary explanation, therefore, Tom took two letters from his pocket and handed them to his father.

Joyce's face registered no emotions as he read first one letter and then the other. The curious eyes of his unwilling hosts were fastened upon him, but he ignored them until he had finished both missives. Finally, he looked up.

"I have here a confidential memo from Dr. Allison Swift, the police surgeon who did the first autopsy on Van Zanten," he announced. "You'll remember he said yesterday that death might have been caused by 'some unknown poison.' Well, Doc Swift is one of the finest analysts in the business, as well as a surgeon. He's worked twelve solid hours on the contents of the stomach and intestines, and it isn't guesswork any longer. He now knows why the old gentleman died."

Despite his recent bold front, Jimmy began to tremble. He wet his lips with his tongue, and said nothing. Fawcett spoke up, with a touch of irritation:

"Aren't you being melodramatic, Inspector? Why don't you let us have the verdict?"

"Nicholas Van Zanten was poisoned, according to Dr. Swift's findings. And I want to add that there isn't the slightest reason for believing that he committed suicide."

"What was the poison?"

"Aconitine. Swift's explanation is very technical, but I'll give you the gist of it." Joyce selected phrases from the memorandum, in preference to offering a simplified version. He glanced frequently from the page to the distressed countenances of Fawcett and Jimmy. Both of them, he observed, seemed horror-stricken at what they heard, but only Jimmy was frightened.

"Pure aconitine is the most violent poison known. One-fiftieth of a grain can be fatal, but the average amount needed to kill a man is one-tenth of a grain. A solution containing one-thousandth of a grain produces tingling and then a numbness on the tip of the tongue, and if rubbed into the skin in the strength of one-hundredth of a grain there will be loss of feeling, lasting for some time.

"If aconitine has been swallowed, the immediate cause of death is asphyxiation, because the throat has swelled and the tongue become paralyzed. But if the physician has not seen the victim die, he will note no typical symptoms except a dilation of the pupils. This last is common to many drugs.

"Swift goes on to say that there is not a single chemical test that is characteristic of aconitine. In his analysis, the alkalies, carbazotic acid, chloride of gold, iodide of potassium and bromine in hydrobromic acid—some tongue-twisters those—all yielded precipitates which might or might not have contained a solution of aconitine.

"The doc, however, took one of the precipitates and injected it into a cat with the hypodermic needle. The cat got weak, staggered around, breathed hard, became partly paralyzed and choked to death in fifteen minutes. That was a death he'd witnessed. It was a death by aconitine, and

the aconitine had been drawn from Nicholas Van Zanten's
body. I guess you realize what that proves."

"It proves so little that I'm surprised at you for getting
excited about it, Inspector," said Fawcett calmly. "No jury
is going to be convinced by such a round-about argument,
unless it can be shown that the poison you mention had
been brought into this house, and by whom."

"It could have been fed to him by Aunt Ellen," cried
Jimmy shrilly.

"Nonsense," countered Fawcett. "Where would that
ignorant old woman get hold of such a rare chemical preparation as aconitine?"

"If the police advance this theory of poisoning, let
them furnish the evidence," Jimmy shouted hysterically.
"Anyway, it's not Inspector Joyce's worry. He's out."

"Just a minute. I'd like to read you the second letter my
son brought me," Joyce challenged.

They stared at him. Both were on the verge of inso-
lence, the one bored and the other exasperated.

"It's from Police Commissioner Edmund D. Gilhooley,
and it's quite a short letter. It says: 'Michael Joyce, of
209-½ Broadway, New York, N. Y., is hereby appointed a
special deputy in full charge of investigating the alleged
homicide, or homicides, at Van Zanten Manor, Borough of
Richmond, City of New York.'"

CHAPTER THIRTEEN
Monday—Secrets of Van Zanten Manor

The two communications he had just read, and more particularly his appointment as a deputy by Commissioner Gilhooley, had been astonishing to Joyce himself. The contents of Dr. Allison Swift's report was in line with his own deductions; but he had not expected to receive it so soon, nor was it probable that it should have been forwarded to him through Tom. The letter from Gilhooley was a complete surprise. The idea of asking for police powers had occurred to Joyce when Jimmy Van Zanten had told him he was fired. But that the Commissioner should already have volunteered to grant them seemed almost too good to be true.

He spoke sternly to the abashed pair, who so recently had been treating him like a hired man.

"I notify you that you are under police surveillance from now on," he said. "If you don't know what that means, get an earful. You're as good as arrested as material witnesses. I can have you picked up and jugged any time I want to give the order. If you set foot outside these premises without permission, you'll become fugitives from justice."

"Are we to understand that you've been made a police official?" asked Fawcett gravely.

"Exactly. Until the Commissioner revokes the order, I am the deputy representing himself on this case. Mrs.

Fawcett and the servants are under surveillance, too. Please tell 'em so, though I'll be sending a cop around with the same message before the morning's over."

Fawcett and Jimmy started to leave, dazed. Joyce halted the latter with a final question:

"Who's your nearest relative—the next of kin, aside from your Aunt Constance?"

"What has that got to do with—?" began Jimmy indignantly.

"No back talk," snapped Joyce. "I'm questioning *you.*"

"There are no other members of the family left in this country. My nearest relative is a third cousin in Leeuwarden, Holland, named Cornelius Van Zanten."

"Good. That's all I want to know."

The pair walked out. Joyce turned to his son.

"Well, Tom, things are moving fast. Those letters you brought help a lot. Suppose you give me a report on what's been stirring at your end."

"As soon as Kay reached the office yesterday afternoon with your instructions, I went right to work checking up the sales of poisons, Dad. I was at it most of the night. I telephoned to every drug store in Staten Island. Then I came over here and had personal interviews with the druggists in St. George, Tompkinsville, Stapleton and Port Richmond. I kept after them until the last pharmacy closed at three o'clock this morning."

"What did you learn, son?"

"The records were in good order, and not one of the drug stores had sold poisons, on prescription or otherwise, to anybody living in this house."

Joyce's face fell. But he commented: "If we'd lined up the evidence that way, it would have been too easy. The murderer is a cunning divil, and he likely bought his stuff in the city, or in another State."

"I've set operatives to work all over, including Jersey and Connecticut."

"That's fine. Now, give me the dope on Doc Swift's analysis and the letter from the Commissioner. How did you get 'em?"

"After I was through with the Staten Island druggists this morning, I figured that Swift would have been working all night to give you prompt service. I took a chance and phoned him at his private laboratory, at Headquarters. He told me I could come at eight o'clock to get the report. So I was Johnny-on-the-spot."

"Smart work, Tom. But I'm still puzzled about Gilhooley."

Tom looked at the floor, shifted his feet and flushed slightly. He had the appearance of a college boy, about to make a confession in class which may excite the professor's wrath. "It happened through Dr. Swift and a line of talk I gave him. Kay had told me some of the difficulties you were up against out here. So I put it strong to the doctor, and asked him whether he didn't think the Commissioner would appoint you a deputy if he knew all the facts. I'd have liked to ask Gilhooley himself, but I feared I couldn't reach him. And I was sure Swift was a real friend of yours. You may bawl me out for taking so much upon myself, but it worked. Swift went with me to the Commissioner's office at nine sharp, and in ten minutes the letter was written."

For a moment, Joyce was almost insane with anger. This was just like Tom. Plenty of energy, but no professional viewpoint, no sense of discipline. The result obtained chanced to be of considerable advantage, and the broad streak of realism in his nature prevented him from being as severe with his son for a success as he would have been for a failure. He struggled silently with himself, and became calmer before he spoke:

"Joseph and Mary! A subordinate spreading the news about an unfinished case, and playing for favors without me even knowing it! It's lucky Gilhooley knows me inside out."

"What I did worked, Dad," Tom repeated.

"That's a politician's slant, or a newspaper man's. By God, Tom, you're maybe in the wrong calling, after all."

"Detectives often are forced to act on their own initiative," the other argued. "They're tricky, too. They have to be."

"Against the enemy, the crook—yes, son. But I'm not talking about that. I'm kicking because you schemed over my head with men who expect me to ask frankly for what I want. It's like a desk sergeant plotting to get the captain of his precinct promoted. It's not military." Joyce laughed, his good-humor restored. "Well, let's forget it. I'm darned glad to be appointed a special deputy on this case, and that's no lie."

"Three men from the Richmond homicide squad are to report here, subject to your orders," Tom said sensibly getting down to business without further apologies. "And the newspapers will have got wise to Gilhooley's action. I don't think you can hold off the reporters much longer."

"Hold 'em off! Just watch me. I think I hear cars driving up to the house now."

The two of them went to the front door, and watched a couple of Fords discharging passengers. The city dicks got out first, and approached Joyce, saluting. He motioned them into the house. Then a squad of news writers charged towards him, and were met by a stubbornly outthrust palm.

"It's no use, boys. I have nothing to say," declared Joyce.

They fired a volley of questions at him all the same.

"They'll tell you everything that can be told at Borough Headquarters, St. George, boys."

"Is it true that you're going to arrest Jimmy Van Zanten?" the representative of a morning tabloid demanded,

exactly as if Joyce had not spoken. But this young man had
never seen the former Inspector of the New York Police
Department in action.

Joyce took a single step forward, and the tense crouch
into which his body went was as formidable as that of a
lion about to spring. "Get out of here—and stay out!"
he roared. "If I catch any of you snooping around the
grounds, I'll have you jailed. I'm not answering questions,
d'ye hear?—not till I pass the word for you to come back.
That's final!"

The discomfited sensation hounds of the press took
their departure silently. But as a desperate gesture of
devotion to duty, a tab photographer raised his camera
and snapped a picture of the special deputy. Joyce grinned
faintly, and let him get away with it.

Inside the house, he spoke to the men from the homicide squad: "I'll have assignments for you soon. Meanwhile, keep an eye on the people living here, including
the servants. See that nobody leaves. You can get in touch
with the patrolman on guard upstairs, and if you can pick
up any clues in the room where Nicholas Van Zanten died,
why so much the better."

Alone with Tom, he gave the youngster a swift recapit-
ulation of the developments in the case since Kay had left
for town the preceding afternoon. He stressed mainly the
virtual certainty that Constance, supposed to be in hiding, was the latest victim of a wholesale murder plot, and
the bearing that Aunt Ellen's lurid story had upon this.

"You see, Tom, the authorities know of only one death,"
he explained, "the death of the old man, which happened
in such a way that it got on to the police blotter. Until I
tell 'em, they won't be searching for the woman. And unless I ask it, the notion of exhuming the bodies of George
and Mary Van Zanten, as possible poison victims, isn't
likely to hit them.

"Now, these flatfeet they've sent me—I'm not going to turn 'em loose on any hunt for Constance. I'll let 'em mark time, because I think we can solve the puzzle ourselves. I'm working up a plan, which maybe we can put across tonight. You can be of help. I want you here by eight o'clock, but put in the rest of the day checking up the Staten Island druggists you haven't yet visited."

"No matter how many persons we prove have been poisoned, we can't go into court unless we show where the poisons came from. That's certain," said Tom, without originality.

"Yeah."

"But something else strikes me. If two have been killed since you were brought out here, the murderer is the kind who'll stop at nothing. I'd say you were in danger of being poisoned yourself, Dad."

"Now you're talking. I'd thought of that, and I'm watching my step. But there isn't a whole lot I can do to protect myself, when I'm forced to eat the food they give me. Detective work is like war, Tom. You've got to take chances."

"Of course, the point I'm most curious about is, who do you think's guilty?"

Joyce sketched the characters of the chief figures in the mystery, as well as the arguments for and against their importance as suspects. He concluded with the statement:

"That young Jimmy, Fawcett and Dr. Henkle are the likeliest, in the order named, but nothing much to choose among them. The Negress is a strong possibility, too."

"Without having met him, I'd pick the doctor."

"Why?"

"He seems phony. He signed the first two death certificates on flimsy grounds. As a physician, he could write his own prescriptions for poisons, or buy them by mail from a wholesale chemical firm."

"When you reach my age, you won't do such honor to simple circumstantial evidence. It has fooled many a detective. I was talking wild in going as far as I did in naming names. Hell, anybody may be guilty! It's always so with murder, up to the moment when you nick your man. In this case, I'd be willing to bet money on the innocence of only one person—the girl Celestine Curtis. She's not the type, if I know anything about poisoners."

Tom nodded his head sagely, and prepared to leave. Joyce took from his pockets a strange diversity of objects, comprising the samples of dried herbs he had obtained from Aunt Ellen, the phials filled with her brews and a small tissue paper package with a rubber band around it.

"There's a good chemical laboratory in Stapleton," he said. "Look it up. Have these leaves and the contents of the bottles analyzed for poisons. In the package you'll find paraffin molds of two keys. Get the keys made on a rush job, and be sure to bring them with you tonight."

After his son had gone, Joyce fell to wondering why Kay hadn't arrived yet. He'd have liked to talk the new stuff over with her. He found himself more and more relying upon Kay for a certain psychic lift, which helped him to clear up knotty problems in his own mind.

But there was plenty for him to right then. He walked through the garden, where Fawcett and Andy Burns were working with a sulky concentration to mark their resentment of the fact that they were under police surveillance. Joyce did not speak to them, but unceremoniously looked the ground over for an entrance to a subterranean chamber, or any recent disturbance of the soil on a large scale. As had been the case the afternoon before, he was unable to discover anything out of the way.

He then went over to the dog kennels and examined the two poodles, the three spaniels and the single old black

Pomeranian which had formed Constance Van Zanten's menagerie. None of the beasts showed injuries resulting from a kick, but that did not prove a whole lot. Catching sight of the maid Sally, Joyce called her over.

"How many dogs does Miss Constance have?" he asked.

"Seven, sir."

"How many poodles?"

"Three."

"There are only two here."

"I guess she took the third one with her, sir."

"I see," remarked Joyce, keeping his opinion to himself. Perhaps the third poodle had been killed and its body done away with, at the same time that its mistress had met her end. But why?

The sound of a car's wheels crunching the gravel of the driveway took him back to the front of the house. He found Kay just about to ring the doorbell, and he chuckled with pleasure at the sight of her.

"Good morning, Inspector. Here I am emptyhanded," she greeted him.

"How did you lose the prisoner that Dinny Sullivan phoned me last night you were bringing in handcuffs?" he demanded, with mock severity.

"Sure, she gave me the slip and jumped, handcuffs and all, from the Staten Island ferryboat coming over. It's drowned she was," answered Kay, who often talked Irish to her boss when they were kidding.

Joyce laughed, and shoved her lightly away from him with one of his great fists. But there were serious matters to be discussed, and his tone sobered as he went on:

"I'm sorry I sent you off on a wild-goose chase, all the same. Things have been breaking here. I guess old Constance was murdered, too."

"Really, Inspector?"

"Yes, and—"

He did not complete the sentence, for at that moment there materialized, apparently from nowhere, the colorless figure of the Sheriff, G. Borden Symes. He was dressed in a gray tweed suit, which although of fairly good material resulted, somehow, in making him look a very unimportant person at whom nobody would glance twice. He wore a cap of the same color, which subtly placed him in a low rank of the social order. He appeared to be a minor salesman, or perhaps a worthy mechanic out of a job. His face was expressionless, yet not cryptic. He looked just plain ordinary. Under his arm, he carried an unwrapped box of cigars.

His unobtrusive arrival was incomprehensible, but it was typical of Symes. Joyce did not trouble to ask him whether he had sneaked through the shrubbery, or how he had come.

"I have a report for you, Inspector. Lucky I found you here, instead of having to give the servants a story," the Sheriff murmured.

"You don't need to gum-shoe any longer to see me, Mr. Symes. Commissioner Gilhooley has appointed me a special deputy in charge of this case."

"Oh!" he replied, as if an event of the kind were quite common.

"Well, let's go indoors and hear what you have to tell."

Joyce led the other two to the parlor and closed the door behind him. Symes placed his box of cigars carefully on a table.

"What's the idea of the smokes?" the chief asked.

"I bought them in town last night before coming over to the Island. They're five-centers. A good cover, in talking to storekeepers. I pretended I was taking orders for cigars, and every so often I'd give one away."

Joyce smiled. "Did you get any real dirt on the Van Zantens?"

"So-so."

"Spill it."

"The tradespeople in St. George and Stapleton—grocers, butchers, laundrymen, icemen and so forth—think that the whole family is sort of crazy," declared the Sheriff, who was quite capable of making a long and clear speech when the occasion called for it. "They are stingy with their money, and they've never encouraged the neighbors to be friends. The old man Nicholas and his late brother George hated the sister Constance; they'd burst out quarreling with her sometimes in the Ferry Building, when they were all on the way to New York. If she had been the first to die, every one would have believed she'd been murdered. Around St. George they say, too, that these Van Zantens were nuts to have a half-wild Negress as a cook for twenty-five years. They say the old woman has been known to walk up and down the lawn the entire night, singing."

"That isn't very hot. Your only important point is that Nicholas and George made a public scandal of their grudge against the sister," observed Joyce, whose mind played for a moment with the notion that Constance had killed for vengeance, and then had engineered her own disappearance cleverly.

"Well, I may dig up more later. I was out for dope on the Fawcetts, Dr. Henkle and Miss Curtis, too."

"What did you learn about them?"

"The Fawcetts are well liked. It appears that Van Zanten met them when he was traveling through Texas more than twenty years ago and brought them North with him. Their original home town was Hillsboro, near Dallas."

"Swell. We'll set the machinery to work, to get a report on them from my Dallas agents."

"Dr. Henkle is a flop in his profession," continued the Sheriff imperturbably. "The Van Zantens are his best patients, and they've been given to hanging him up—slow pay. Five years ago, he invested a thousand dollars in stocks on George Van Zanten's advice, and lost it."

"The hell you say!" exclaimed Joyce. He glanced at Kay and shook his head. "That's motive enough for a man like Henkle to turn murderer. It's queer what things come out in the wash!"

"But my information about Miss Curtis is a lot more interesting," pursued Symes.

"How so?"

"The Van Zantens have been good and sore about her engagement to the son, Jimmy."

"I know that."

"Yes, but you haven't heard their real reasons. The Curtises are dirt poor. They're up to their eyes in debt, and if Celestine doesn't make this marriage soon and raise some money, they'll be evicted from their home. That's forgivable, Inspector. It's something else again, though, that the family has had criminals in it for generations on the father's side. Celestine's own father died in the electric chair in 1910, for killing a man whose house he was trying to rob."

Joyce tensed. Less than an hour before, he had told Tom that he would bet money on the innocence of the wholesome-seeming girl. Now he was far from sure.

"In St. George and Stapleton they think that Celestine Curtis has been murdering off the older Van Zantens, so as to make sure of getting Jimmy," proclaimed the low and undramatic voice of Sheriff Symes.

CHAPTER FOURTEEN
Monday—Ghoulish Business

At ten o'clock that Monday night, the fourth day of his service on the Van Zanten poison case, Inspector Joyce summoned the members of his staff and the three detectives assigned to him from the Homicide Squad, to receive orders. They met in the parlor behind closed doors. He addressed himself first—and briefly—to the city dicks.

"Hennesey, Heinholtz, Boyle," he said, "I'm going to follow up a hot lead. My own men will be all I'll need, but I've got special work for you. Until we come back, I want you to stand close guard over the persons living in this house. I prefer not to place any of them under arrest just yet. They've got to be prevented, though, from snooping after me to see what I'm doing. Hennesey, you'll watch the chicken coop in the yard, where the old Negro woman sleeps. Heinholtz can take the general servants' quarters, and Boyle the corridor upstairs where young Mr. Van Zanten and Fawcett have their bedrooms. If a single one of 'em tries to go out of doors, warn him back to bed without an explanation. In case of an argument, take the necessary measures. Savvy?"

"Yes, Inspector," replied the well-trained detectives in chorus.

"Okay! Hop to it. But Hennesey, before you go to your post, dig me up some screw drivers of assorted sizes, a small crowbar and a lantern. You should be able to find them in the tool room in the basement. Bring them to me here."

The men went out, their impassive faces a mask for their secret curiosity.

Joyce turned to his son, the Sheriff and Kay. "You had those keys made all right, didn't you, Tom?"

"You bet, Dad." The young fellow handed over a couple of old-fashioned keys, each about four inches long, which the Inspector slipped into his trousers pocket.

"You'll be wondering what dirty work I've got for you," remarked Joyce.

"I know," said Kay in a low voice. The blood receded from her face and left her pale.

"I guess you do, girl. But I'll not be asking you to take part in it. Tom and Mr. Symes were not with us when we visited the Van Zanten vault." He cleared his throat, and glanced at the men. "The bodies of the uncle and the niece—you remember—were laid away in a private vault on this estate. I feel pretty sure now that they were both poisoned, and I'm going to take a look at them."

Neither of his assistants flinched. They simply nodded. Propositions like this were in the line of business.

"Of course, such a move is extra-legal," he continued. "I ought by rights to get a permit from the Board of Health, and since Fawcett as guardian and executor of the will is still a free man, he should be asked to sign the request. You can figure how long all the red tape would hold us up. I want some live evidence quick. If we flop on finding it, I'll keep mum about what we've done and demand a real post mortem later on."

"I did something like that myself once, when I was Sheriff of Algonquin County," observed Symes. "I had two of my deputies exhume the corpse of a motion picture actor who had been buried in a Potter's Field. Nasty work, but it brought about a conviction for murder."

"Yeah. On a big-time investigation, one can't always keep strictly within the law."

Kay had bent her head over a table, and was tracing patterns with her finger-tip on its surface. "I want to go along with you," she announced.

"What?" Joyce started. "I'll say not. You don't know what it means to open coffins, Kay girl."

"If I'm to learn to be a good detective, I can't balk at anything," she argued. "You could trust me to see this through, Inspector, without disgracing you."

"Better not. Some other time," he answered a bit sharply.

She hesitated, then said: "You'll need a lookout, and you haven't arranged for one. Why not let me stay just outside the vault?"

"Well, by all the saints, you're a persistent little divil! Hanged if I don't love you for it. We'll call it a bargain, Kay. You can come as the lookout, and it's a good idea at that."

Tom's lips were set in a thin line of disapproval, but he did not venture to criticize at a moment when they were about to start on a ticklish job.

A silence fell, while they waited for the return of Hennesey with the tools. Kay broke it, by commenting:

"I can't reconcile myself to Celestine Curtis as a suspect. No matter how bad her ancestry was, she's no criminal moron. How can we say a healthy, athletic girl like her is not chiefly a product of the mother's side of the family?"

"We don't say it," retorted Joyce, "but we've got to be shown. I'm not altogether sold on the heredity stuff in accounting for crime. Lombroso and some other big guys have believed in it, and it's not to be laughed off. That Celestine needs money so badly makes it look twice as black for her. I'll admit, though, that this whole angle on the case is a big shock."

"I'm astonished that Nicholas Van Zanten didn't tell you that her father had died in the chair."

"It's damned funny. Maybe the fact didn't cut any ice with him, any more than it does with Jimmy who's set on marrying her. All the old man could think about was her social errors and her cigarette smoking. Morbid eccentrics, that's what the Van Zantens are. You can't figure them. I'm going to worry hereafter only about cold evidence that can be proved."

They exchanged a few additional remarks on the subject of Celestine, and then Hennesey came with the screw drivers, the crowbar and the lantern. He now looked faintly disgusted at being consigned to the role of sentry over a Negress in a chicken coop, while exciting doings were evidently under way.

Joyce led his small procession through the garden, which was redolent with the perfumes of roses, jasmines and honeysuckle. An almost full moon was shining. The lighter hued flowers, especially the massed banks of white chrysanthemums, made a ghostly showing. But the minds of none of them were set upon the charm of blossoms seen by moonlight. It was impossible to forget that they were bound upon the ghoulish business of breaking into a tomb.

They came at last to the path that led across the fields and over the low ridge separating them from the family mausoleum. Joyce had made the journey twice before, and Kay once. The others followed glumly in their wake, unable to tell whether they would have to trudge a hundred yards or a mile.

When the pointed Gothic roof of the chapel loomed up, it at once imparted a dismal air to the night landscape. Isolated though it was—a lone tomb in a meadow—the

funereal, churchyard impression was inescapable, because
of the grilled door of the chantry and the cross above it.

The group paused on the very threshold, and for a moment nothing was either said or done. Finally, Joyce took
out the keys he had had made, and tried them one after the
other in the huge lock. They made a grating and rattling
noise, and he fumbled with them considerably until he
lost his temper and swore. Then he took the lantern from
Tom, and turned its light upon his operations.

"Great grief!" he exclaimed. "The lock has been changed.
Today probably. The screws are brand new."

Everybody uttered deep sighs, as if to relieve the tension.

"This is tough," Joyce went on. "We don't have the
equipment to bore through an iron gate."

The Sheriff pushed silently forward. He produced from
his breast pocket a neat little "jimmy," with which he
prodded for several minutes at the lock. Then he shook
his head.

"I can't do a thing with it from this side. It's a queer
old-time lock," he muttered.

"We're stumped," growled Joyce.

"Oh, no, Inspector! I'm not so sure. From the far side,
I think I could pick it. The lock is not enclosed in the
usual metal case."

"But how the devil are you to get to the far side?"

"I'm a thin man, and my joints are like rubber. These
bars now—I believe I could squeeze between them. You'll
notice the grill work only extends down the middle of the
gate. The two bars on either side aren't so close together."

"If you can manage that, Sheriff, I'll pin a medal on
you," said Joyce dubiously.

The self-effacing detective immediately got busy with a
demonstration that would have done credit to an acrobat.

He went feet first between the bars easily enough, until his hips became stuck. By dint of squirming and straining, he twisted the middle section of his body through, only to have his chest and shoulders present a seemingly insuperable difficulty. But the Sheriff's breast-bone must have been unusually elastic. After taking some punishment, it yielded audibly to the pressure. A final backward jerk, and the man had thrown himself on to the stone floor of the chapel.

He lay there until he had recovered his breath. Then, quite calmly, he rose to his knees, fished an odd, curved wire from a special pocket inside his waistcoat, and picked the lock with an expertness which proved that detectives and crooks may have almost identical talents.

The gate swung open. Joyce, Tom and Kay entered the chapel, pronouncing words of low-toned praise for the Sheriff. The latter ran down the steps to the solid iron door of the vault itself, and examined the lock there.

"This one is different," he said. "I can pick it directly through the key hole."

As he set to work, Joyce waved a forefinger at Kay.

"You're the lookout," he reminded her. "You mustn't stay in here."

The girl stepped outside and walked down the path for about ten yards. Her slender and alert figure could be seen taking its post in the moonlight, without a trace of nervousness. Joyce sighed.

The Sheriff had a delicate job, which he performed wordlessly and with an incredible absence of mechanical sound, while the father and son looked on. The mortuary chapel seemed to grow more eerie and depressing, the longer the men stayed there. But its atmosphere of gloom was innocuous compared with the effect when Symes swung back the vault door, and up from the gaping cavern there flowed a stream of the musty air which is inseparable from charnel houses.

Joyce and Tom moved forward, Tom carrying the lantern, while the Sheriff straightened and flattened his body against the wall to let them pass. They were well inside the vault, when Joyce noticed that Symes had not followed them. He had remounted the steps most silently, and was standing in the doorway of the chapel with his arms folded.

"Hey, there—Sheriff!" Joyce called softly. He got no reply, and because shouting appeared to be inappropriate, somehow, he hurried back alone and tapped his assistant on the shoulder. "Hey, there! We've got to get busy."

The little man stared at him, and hissed with an extraordinary intensity:

"S'help me God, Inspector, I can't bust into caskets! You'll have to excuse me."

"What's this?" gasped Joyce, astounded. "You helped us with the doors."

"That's different. It's the rotten corpses I can't face. I'd be sick at the stomach."

"But you said you were at the opening of a grave up-State."

"Not I. I meant that I sent two of my deputies to do it. The principle of the thing's all right. But the last scene is just too much for me, that's all."

"Well, I'll be damned!" muttered Joyce. "I suppose you think it's a picnic for me!" He knew that it was useless to command or argue against a panic of this sort. The crisis had revealed a hidden weakness in the man. Symes, who thought nothing of risking his life against living gangsters, could go so far and no farther in coping with the dead. He turned sharply on his heel, and rejoined Tom.

"We'll have to do this alone," he said curtly. "The Sheriff's sick—he hasn't been well for the past two days."

They proceeded down the right-hand side of the vault, to the spot where the coffins of George and Mary Van

Zanten lay end to end on the middle ledge. Joyce hesitated
between the two, then selected the casket of the young
girl. It was a little below the level of his chest, and as
easy to work upon as though it had been on a trestle in a
parlor.

"Hold the lantern so that the light falls downward,
Tom, and hold it steadily," he ordered.

Selecting a medium-sized screw driver, he inserted it
and twirled with a steady motion of his wrist. The screw
turned readily, but that was normal in view of the fact that
the coffin had been underground for less than three weeks.
Raising the entire number of screws, however, was a tedi-
ous task and occupied him for nearly fifteen minutes.

"We can lift the lid off now," he muttered. He stepped
back, took a handkerchief from his pocket and tied it
around his face, so that it covered his nose and mouth. He
signed to Tom to do the same thing.

When they were both ready, Tom put the lantern on
the floor at a safe distance. He moved to the foot of the
box, while his father took the head. They hoisted the lid
without much effort and disposed of it against the wall.
Then Tom stood by, the lantern again in his hand, and
Joyce bent over to take his first look at the mortal frame
of Mary Van Zanten.

The detective noted instantly that the body had been
tampered with. The mysterious visitor who had left footprints in the tomb three days before had, as Joyce had
anticipated, been bent on nullifying in advance any post
mortem analysis of the viscera. The visible scars of the
mutilation, however, were slight and had been covered
carefully over with clothing. The dead girl's appearance was
not in the least repellent. Her features had been molded
by an expert undertaker; the contortion which had shown
on the death-bed photograph of her, made by Nicholas

Van Zanten, had been erased. She looked peaceful, even beautiful, in the flickering lantern light.

Under these conditions, it seemed impossible for Joyce to determine whether Mary had died of poison. The tampering with the corpse implied as much, but it was not absolute evidence. A scientific autopsy might still prove a great deal. He was on the point of ending his scrutiny when it occurred to him to touch the arms and legs. The result caused him to emit a brusque cry of satisfaction.

The muscles of all four limbs felt literally as rigid as wood under his finger-tips. They were taut and twisted at many points into knots, which had subsequently hardened. Barring the possibility that a rare form of paralysis had been the cause, the symptom was acceptable evidence that the girl had been killed by strychnine poisoning. The crafty murderer who had thought to eradicate the proof of his guilt had overlooked this physical after-effect of the essence of nux vomica.

Joyce did not take the time to explain his conclusions to Tom. "Let's cover her up," he said. "This corpse is going to be a mighty damning witness against somebody."

They set the lid in place, and screwed it down as tightly as it had been before. Then they passed on to the coffin where George Van Zanten lay.

After a full year in the tomb, the remains of the old man had disintegrated to a point which made it hopeless for a lay observer to form any opinion of the cause death. Joyce's object in looking at it was simply to discover whether it, also, had been mutilated. He satisfied himself that such had been the case, and then closed the casket with all speed.

The ghastly job finished, he stood away and tore the handkerchief from his face. Tom lost no time in imitating him.

"Wow, I'm glad that's over!" he exclaimed. "And I've got to hand it to *you,* Tom. You went through with it like a soldier. It was your first chore of the kind, and must have been hard sledding."

The young fellow made a few incoherent sounds which were meant to be thanks for the compliment. He was easily embarrassed by praise.

"We'll give this hole the once over before we go," went on Joyce. "The guy who changed the locks may have dropped something we oughtn't to miss."

They made the circuit of the vault slowly, Tom swinging the lantern, and Joyce turning his pocket torch into the dark crevices. No objects of a suspicious nature were discovered. As they passed the heap of very old coffins, standing one upon the other at the far end, Joyce's eye caught a glint of raw copper on one of them. It did not strike him as significant, and he walked on.

The pair reached the foot of the flight of steps leading up to the chapel. They could see the back of the Sheriff, who still stood in the outer doorway, his shoulder against the jamb and his arms crossed upon his chest. At that moment, a sudden and stupefying diversion occurred.

A revolver shot rang out, and Symes started backwards as if he had been hit.

CHAPTER FIFTEEN
Monday—The Last Corpse Speaks

In lightning-fast reaction to the mysterious revolver shot, Joyce and Tom rushed up the steps. They shouted to the Sheriff, to ask whether he was hurt. He answered that he thought not, and already he had his gun in his hand and was slinking close to the wall, advancing cautiously to defend the doorway from assault. But Joyce was not so much worried about him. He was thinking of Kay, who had no weapon and was ten yards off in the open, alone. He cursed himself for having allowed her to act as a look-out unarmed, but with the residents of Van Zanten Manor under guard, a murderous interference was the last thing he had contemplated seriously.

Without pausing, he dashed out of the chapel, and was met by a second shot which went wild. He dropped behind a bush, and looked about him for Kay. She could be distinguished clearly in the moonlight, on her hands and knees, crawling in his direction. He called to her to be careful. But the attacker was not interested in Kay. The third shot came straight at the bush which sheltered Joyce, and clipped twigs from the top of it.

This time, Joyce had noted the flash of the revolver, a little to the left of the tomb. He aimed his own automatic carefully, and returned to fire with a burst of bullets. Tom and the Sheriff followed his example from the doorway.

This silenced the trouble maker for a while. In a few seconds, Kay had reached Joyce's side.

"Are you all right, me darlin'?" he whispered.

"Perfectly all right. I haven't seen any one, or heard a thing until the shooting started."

"Well, lie low. You'd better get back of me."

They waited tensely. Then from a new direction, three shots were discharged in quick succession, but with so inaccurate an aim that there was no telling what the target had been. The flashes had been masked, probably by a shrub, and Joyce was unable to retort intelligently. He fired several times, however, on general principles. The aftermath was a complete and protracted quietude.

"I could swear, from the report, that that gun is an old-style six-shooter," he remarked at last. "The bird may have had only one round of shells. If so, the party's over."

He decided a little later that there was a good chance of his surmise being correct.

"We'll crawl back to the chapel," he muttered. "I'll go first, but keep close to me."

They covered the short distance without mishap, and were soon standing beside Tom and the Sheriff. The latter closed the grilled gate as a precaution, with one of his customary soundless movements.

"This is a damned funny to-do," declared Joyce, rubbing his chin. "The way the attack was made was crazy. No regular thug would pull a thing like that. Half a dozen shots, and he's gone. But who can he be? If we don't find that one of the people who live here sneaked past the dicks, I'll be surprised."

"I think it's useless to try and hunt him down now," Tom argued.

"Sure it is. He's got all the woods around here to hide in," the Inspector answered. "We'll wait ten or fifteen minutes, and then return to the house. Of course, he may start shooting again when we leave cover, but I don't expect it."

The jangling of their nerves calmed gradually. Kay changed the subject by asking what the results of the investigation in the vault had been.

"I'm satisfied that Mary Van Zanten was poisoned with strychnine," Joyce told her briefly.

His mind went back to the events in the subterranean chamber, and for some reason that glint of copper that he had seen on one of the old coffins prodded at his memory. Caskets were sometimes made of copper, or trimmed with it, he mused. The handles and screws often were of that metal. But it was peculiar that an ancient box should have a spot on it that reflected the lantern light. Copper quickly became tarnished and coated with verdigris. He felt that it would be an act of carelessness on his part to leave without checking up this small detail.

"There's something I forgot to do down below," he announced crisply. "Lend a hand, Tom. The Sheriff will stay right here with Kay."

Father and son retraced their steps. They passed between the dismal files of Van Zantens, laid end to end with pitiful economy of space. It reminded Joyce of the crypts of churches he had seen in Rome, where bishops and archbishops had been stacked through the centuries in serried ranks.

He advanced directly to the pile of old coffins, and played the light of his pocket torch over them. Tom, at his elbow, held the lantern high. For several minutes, Joyce was unable to locate the scar of raw copper. Then he found it suddenly, immediately under his hand. It was the result of a gouge between the lid and the main section of a casket that lay breast-high and lengthwise. No other box was on top of it.

Joyce's heart leaped. He examined the screws narrowly and found that every one of them had recently been
worked upon. Oil had been used to lubricate the rusted
thread.

"By God, Tom!" he exclaimed. "This coffin has been
opened—and not by us."

"What do you suppose the reason could have been? It's
at least a century old."

"Damned if I know!" Joyce looked for the nameplate,
rubbed it fairly clean with his handkerchief and read:

Theodore Doremus Van Zanten
Born May 19, 1750
Died July 22, 1822

The detective gnawed his lip. There was no obvious
answer to the mystery of why anybody should tamper with
the resting place of this long-dead ancestor.

"We'll have to take a look ourselves," he ruled. "Can't
tell what clue we might be passing up, if we failed to do
that."

Tom handed him a screw driver, and he struggled for
many minutes with the antiquated fastenings. In spite of
the fact that they had lately been drawn, a few of them
stuck fast. A hammer had probably been used to beat the
heads flush with the lid, and the metal had spread.

"Well, here's where we find a use for the crowbar," Joyce
growled. "It's a lucky thing we brought it."

He inserted the tip of the implement at the very spot
where he had first seen the copper flashing red, and he
and Tom bore down with their combined weight upon the
iron bar. A harsh groaning and creaking vibrated along the
length of the rusted box. Then the lid gave way abruptly
and flew up. They took hold of it, jerked the last screw

out of its hole and transferred the cover to the floor. Tom raised the lantern.

A sight that absolutely staggered them—a discovery that they had not dreamed of making—was spread before their eyes in the dim glow cast by the guttering wick.

Theodore Doremus Van Zanten was nothing but a bare skeleton, to which clung a little dust of the past. The bones lay at the bottom of the casket. On top of them, and filling the space with not much margin to spare, were the stark remains of his descendant, the spinster Constance.

Her face was congested with blood, and her wide-open eyes had a dreadful fixed look, with the pupils even more dilated than those of old Nicholas had been. A faint odor of oil of bitter almonds floated up from her. Crammed between her left arm and the side of the coffin was the body of a poodle, undoubtedly the same beast which had been killed to stop its yelping in her bedroom.

CHAPTER SIXTEEN
Monday—Bullets Wild

A gruesome, but logical, process of thought had led the murderer of Constance Van Zanten to hide mistress and pet dog together in a spot where nobody would conceive of looking for them. Joyce was forced to admit that the device was diabolical in its cleverness. "What an idea," he reflected, with a kind of admiration, "to inter the newly dead in one of the oldest coffins in a vault!"

But it was odd how criminals nearly always committed some minor blunder which gave them away. It would have been easy to stuff the gouge under the lid with putty and then smear the latter with a little moistened dust to conceal all traces of tampering. Yet that had not been done, and the trivial clue of the glinting copper had been sufficient to guide the detective and his son to a sensational climax.

He glanced from the corpse to Tom and back again several times, without speaking. Then he said inadequately: "There she is, boy! There she is! I always knew she'd been murdered."

"This is some triumph for you, Dad," his son answered.

"I haven't beaten the case yet. I don't know who did it. But I'm sure this woman is another poison victim."

"How can you tell that?"

"Have you noticed the smell of bitter almonds?"

"Sure. I've been wondering what caused it."

"It's characteristic of prussic acid. You can't eliminate that odor. It comes up on the moisture that runs from the mouth. I see other symptoms that confirm it—the fixed eyes, for instance. Prussic acid is one of the deadliest, and one of the fastest-working, of poisons. But it isn't used much by killers, because any doctor knows the signs. Even Henkle couldn't have made a mistake here."

"I guess that's why the body was stowed away in such a hurry."

"Right you are, Tom. Risking a post mortem on Nicholas Van Zanten was one thing. This is quite another kettle of fish."

"What do we do next?"

"Help me close the coffin. Then you're going to see plenty."

They put the lid back in position, but did not trouble to screw it down.

"The body is going to be on its way to the autopsy room of the Morgue as fast as cops can come to fetch it," Joyce explained. "There isn't a hell of a lot of danger of it's being snatched in the meanwhile."

They ran up the steps to rejoin Kay and the Sheriff. Briefly, Joyce gave an account of what he had found. He was as restive as a hunting dog on the trail of game, and declined to enter into any details.

"Tell you more later. Get started back to the house," he said impatiently. "I think we'll learn something there."

Strung out in a line, and with revolvers held ready in the hands of the men, the party moved away from the chapel. A fresh attack from the person who had already fired six shots at them appeared to be a vital peril. But as they walked farther and farther across the fields, it became clear that nothing of the sort would occur. The enemy had decamped.

They arrived at the garden, and Joyce looked first for the detective Hennesey, who had been set to watch Aunt Ellen's cabin. The man was standing rigidly, a few feet away from the door.

"Everything all right here?" he was asked.

"Yes, Inspector."

"Did you hear any shooting?"

"I did sir. But ye'd ordered me to stay put, and I stayed."

"Correct."

Inside the house, Joyce mounted to the second floor and questioned Boyle.

"Are the Fawcetts and young Van Zanten in their rooms?"

"They are, Inspector. Divil a chance would they have to get by me. Fawcett tried to come out a half hour ago— to get some water, he said—but I chased him back. The young feller is in bed. You can hear him breathing through the door."

There remained Heinholtz, whose assignment had been to guard the servants. The latter slept in an attic on the top floor, which was reached by a service stairway. Joyce hunted for the detective on the three landings of the stairway. He called his name, but got no answer. He figured then that Heinholtz might have thought it best to wait outside the service door, which opened into the backyard. Coming from inside the house, Joyce pushed open that door and stumbled over the body of a man lying prone on the sill.

It was Heinholtz, felled by a blow on the head and groaning faintly. He had evidently been unconscious for so long a time that his injuries must be serious, and might cost him his life.

"Take care of him," Joyce ordered the Sheriff, and turned to rush back up the stairs to the top of the house.

He banged in quick succession on the doors of the four servants. The maids were probably unimportant in this,

but he compelled them to show themselves. They were
followed by the butler, Bucklestrope, blinking owlishly
and greatly upset in the matter of dignity. He answered
the questions that were thrown at him, but seemed more
concerned with hunting for a bathrobe to mitigate partly
the fact that he was wearing an old-fashioned nightgown
several inches too short for him. No, he had not been outside the house since eight o'clock, he protested dolefully.
It was impossible to doubt that Bucklestrope was telling
the truth.

Unable to get a response from the room of Andrew
Burns, the gardener, Joyce's eyes glittered wolfishly. He
found it probable that Burns had been the man who had
slugged Heinholtz, and then had gone down to the chapel
to discharge a mad fusillade. Yet when he lost patience and
flung the door open, there was Burns on his back in bed,
with his eyes closed and breathing heavily.

Joyce seized the gardener and shook him. The man
snorted. He shifted his head on the pillow, but did not
wake up. And though the detective tightened the clutch of
strong fingers on his shoulders, all the effect it had upon
Andy was to cause him to moan and to click his teeth, as
if in a nightmare.

Finally, in response to a cuff on the jaw, the gardener
sat up, rubbing his eyes.

"You damned faker!" roared Joyce. "Don't tell me you
haven't felt me shaking you. I made enough racket at the
door before that to rouse the dead."

"Huh—wha'—wha's that?" grunted Burns, in a voice
that was convincingly that of a half-aroused sleeper.

"I want to know what you've been doing. Where were
you in the last two hours?"

"Ben in bed all th' time," Burns mumbled.

"You're a blasted liar!" Joyce looked around frankly for
boots wet with dew, and for clothes that might have been

torn by thorns. The revolver, as a matter of course, would have been thrown away in the woods, or hidden. He failed to note any such indications of guilt. But he slammed his open palm on the bureau and shouted:

"I represent the law, and God help you if you try to fool me! You heard me come into this room, and you bluffed at being asleep. Explain that, Burns."

Behind him, Joyce heard a timorous footstep. He turned and saw Bucklestrope, enveloped now in a bathrobe of Tartan plaid.

"Really, sir, Mr. Burns is an unusually sound sleeper," the butler said. "In the many years I've known him, it has astonished me, sir. Knocking at his door, and even bawling in his ear, has almost no effect upon Mr. Burns when he is getting his first slumber of the night."

"Yeah!" answered Joyce sarcastically. Yet he was forced to admit to himself that many outdoor workers—farm-hands and gardeners, for instance—had the peculiarity which Bucklestrope claimed for Andy. He changed his tactics, and asked the butler:

"Are you willing to swear that Burns has not left the house this evening?"

"I couldn't swear it, sir. But I will say this: I wasn't resting very easy myself, and I think I would have heard him go out. There seemed to be no commotion in his room, except his snoring now and then."

Joyce felt almost convinced by this reasonable testimony. After all, the detective Heinholtz had been knocked over in the backyard. An interloper skulking around the grounds might have run into him and decided to put him out of the way, before proceeding to the vault for the shooting party. The crime had not necessarily been perpetrated by one of the servants.

Then his eye was caught by a detail, which it was amazing he had not observed before. In Andy's thick and

tousled hair, above the ear and toward the back of his
head, a small twig was sticking. It was not a piece of any
garden plant, but a twig from a coarse shrub, with one
leaf still adhering to it. Furthermore, the leaf had not yet
begun to wilt in the heat of the bedroom.

The implication was clear. Andy Burns had been roam-
ing abroad, had been crouching behind bushes as the man
with the six-shooter, down by the tomb, had done. On
returning to bed, he had been in such a hurry that it had
not occurred to him to comb his hair.

Joyce smiled cryptically, went to the head of the service stairway and called to his son Tom, who was assisting
the Sheriff to give first aid to Heinholtz. He knew that
Tom had in his pocket the only pair of handcuffs they had
brought from New York.

When the young fellow arrived, Joyce returned with
him to the bedroom and at once announced:

"Andrew Burns, I arrest you for assault with firearms,
with intent to kill. It is my duty to warn you that anything
you say now may be used against you."

"You're crazy, you big stiff!" Andy blustered.

Joyce shook his head. "Clap the handcuffs on him,
Tom," was all he said. His hand was in his pocket, touching the butt of his automatic. He was ready, in case the
gardener tried to pull a fast one. But Andy's courage had
already oozed away, and he held out his wrists for the
irons.

CHAPTER SEVENTEEN
Tuesday—The Doctor on the Grill

In making his first arrest on the case, Joyce was under no delusion that he had placed in custody the undoubted, or even the probable, poisoner of four members of the Van Zanten family. He had charged Andrew Burns with trying to shoot up the party that had visited the vault, and he believed him to be guilty of that. The action implied that he was a confederate of the chief criminal, or that at least he had an injudicious mania for protecting the latter. Brains enough to plot and carry through the entire tragedy, the gardener did not seem to have. Yet in a murder case, as Joyce had often told his assistants, anything was possible.

He preferred to have Burns behind the bars, because he was a crudely dangerous fellow who had furnished a specific and separate cause for his arrest. It was by no means the Inspector's intention to jail Fawcett and Jimmy Van Zanten on general charges. He preferred to leave them free to make some misstep which might enable him to pin crime upon the right person. And the same thing applied to Dr. Henkle and Celestine Curtis.

Immediately after Burns had been placed in handcuffs, Joyce had telephoned to Number 78 Richmond Terrace, St. George, the Borough Headquarters of the metropolitan police, and had given arbitrary instructions. His role as Commissioner Gilhooley's special deputy entitled him to do so. A medical examiner and men from the Homicide Squad, with an ambulance, were to come to the Manor at once. They were to remove the body of Constance from the vault to the Morgue for an autopsy, and the investigation of her death was to be handled upon the presumption of murder. The remains of George and Mary also were to be transferred for post mortems. If red tape classified their cases as exhumations, then red tape was to be cut and the act regularized afterwards.

Joyce had mentioned his arrest of Burns. He had asked that two uniformed policemen be sent to take the man to the county jail. He had sat up to see that all his instructions were carried out, and had got to bed at half-past four in the morning.

Nevertheless, he was up at nine, dressed and ready for action. He got together his own folks and gave them their orders for the day:

"Tom you'll buzz around Staten Island, keeping after the druggists and seeing whether you can find out if any of our suspects bought poisons, personally or through a dummy. You'll perhaps have time to visit Perth Amboy and Elizabeth, too, in Jersey. Mr. Symes, I want you to run over to the office in New York. Collect any answers which may have come to our wires of yesterday to Texas, concerning Fawcett. If our agent in Dallas has been slow, get him on the long-distance phone. Shoot some telegrams to likely people down there, police chief, newspaper editors and so forth. Do your best to bring me some dope by six o'clock."

The male assistants left promptly on their errands, and Joyce turned to Kay.

"You and I, me darlin'," he said, his voice unconsciously softening, "are going to pay a visit to a doctor, but he'll not be treating us for sickness—not if I know it!"

"Henkle?" she queried, her eyes laughing back into his, jesting with him over trivial quips, as she did often to relieve the tension of detective problems. "The best use to make of a prescription written by that guy would be to light a cigarette with it."

"Sure. Henkle. He mayn't be guilty at all, at all. But I think it's a good idea to size him up in his own office."

"It strikes me that way, Inspector."

"The reason for taking you along is not to have you vamp him. I guess I'll have you wait in his outer office. But I don't like to leave you alone in this house."

"There are city detectives here, and a policeman. I'd be safe. I might even dig up some evidence," argued Kay, becoming jealous of her standing as an amateur operative.

"Maybe. But I tell you, Kay, this house is as dangerous as if it were in a war zone, or as if the plague had hit it. There have been two poisonings since we came, and—God knows!—the next attempt may be to slip something to you."

"More likely to yourself, Inspector," she answered, her face sobering.

"I can take care of myself, but you—aw, what's the use of jawing? I want your company on this ride, Kay darlin', and that's reason enough."

She smiled affectionately at him, and went to get her coat and hat. Then, since Burns, the emergency chauffeur of the establishment, was in prison, Joyce invaded the garage, brought the limousine around to the front door and picked up his companion. They speeded down the driveway. It was the first time Joyce had left the Van Zanten estate since his arrival the preceding Friday, and this was now Tuesday.

They followed the Victory Boulevard until they reached the heights on which St. George is built, then glided around a sharply dipping curve and turned into the side street where Dr. Alphonse Henkle had his office. It was an individual frame house to which they came, a shabby structure which needed to be reshingled. The forlorn garden on one side of it did little to improve its appearance. The modest sign which announced the physician's name and profession was sadly in need of polishing.

"The Sheriff said he didn't have many patients," Joyce commented. "It sure looks that way."

They got out of the car and rang the doorbell. Henkle himself admitted them, and though it was virtually certain that he had observed through a window the arrival of the large limousine, he started backwards affectedly.

"Why, Inspector, what a pleasant surprise! Delighted to see you!" he exclaimed.

"Same here!" Joyce answered drily. "I want for us to have a private talk."

"By all means. Come right in. Your charming companion is as welcome as you are."

They went into a stuffy parlor. A pair of folding doors stood slightly open, and revealed a white table such as doctors use for making thorough physical examinations. Joyce pointed at it.

"You and I will go in there. Miss Carey—that's her real name, by the way—understands that she's to wait for me. Let's get down to business as quickly as possible," he said significantly.

"Oh certainly, certainly! Whatever you desire." Henkle was beginning to turn a little pale.

The two men passed through the folding doors, which Joyce took the initiative in closing behind them. They moved over to the desk. The doctor sank into his accustomed seat, while the chair reserved for patients on the opposite side of the desk fell to Joyce. The latter studied his man for several minutes in silence. The eyes, he noticed, were shifty and quite unable to meet a prolonged scrutiny.

"Dr. Henkle, I'm going to be very blunt with you," he declared at last. "You're a central figure in one of the most hideous murder cases of this century. You're smart enough to realize that much, I guess."

"Murder!" the physician mumbled, patently terrified. "My dear friend Nicholas seems to have died of poisoning, but I don't believe you have proved he was the victim of a crime."

"We'll pass him up, for the moment. I'm going to tell you some things you don't know. Constance Van Zanten is dead, too. I've found her body—I won't say where—and as sure as God she was killed with a dose of prussic acid. She's in the autopsy room of the morgue right now. Furthermore, George and Mary are out of their coffins, and with her. They were discovered to have been mutilated, to destroy evidence of the cause of death. But the medical analysts of the Police Department aren't blocked that easily. Poison, with a capital P, in every instance. That's the verdict I'm expecting."

Henkle covered his face with his hands.

"Take your hands down, you silly actor," cried Joyce savagely.

The other jerked them away, and said in a distracted manner: "As family physician, I'll—I'll be summoned to coroners' inquests. And if there are murder trials—on the stand—as a witness. Horrible, horrible!"

"Tougher than that, Doc! You signed death certificates in the first two cases which were either phony or proved you didn't know your business. You attended Fawcett last Friday for what you diagnosed as ptomaine poisoning, but which may have been the effects of an attempt on his life. You were supposed to be watching over the health

of Nicholas and Constance Van Zanten. It's all going to
sound pretty bad to the District Attorney."

Henkle suddenly became calm. "I have harmed none of
those people. I am not a murderer," he pronounced, in a
flat, dreary tone.

"And I don't have any reason to accuse you—not yet,
Dr. Henkle. Perhaps I'll never have. From now on, you're
to be considered a material witness, and I'll have to slap a
cop on your tail. Police surveillance; savvy? But if you're
innocent, that needn't worry you. I'm here today to give
you a chance to help me."

"Help you? How can I do that?"

"Just by being frank. Just by telling me all you know
about these deaths."

"Inspector Joyce, I swear to you that I am hiding noth-
ing. If there was foul play in the taking off of any of the
Van Zantens, I did not suspect it at the time," averred
Henkle solemnly.

"Well, let's put it on a broad basis. I say they were
poisoned. Accept that for Gospel truth, and some ideas
are bound to come into your head. How? Why? Where-
fore? You've known the family for years. What's the dirt
on them? Who might have had an object in bumping the
ones that have gone? Who's clever enough to have covered
up the traces so far?"

Henkle's reaction to the detective's volley of questions
was startling, but typical of the man in its prompt concentration upon the personal element. His body slumped
across the desk, and every muscle in his face relaxed in a
pitiful abandonment of the mask it wore. His pompous
professionalism was gone in a moment. His flaccid cheeks
and dull eyes looked as if never again could they assume
the histrionic joviality which had been his stock in trade
with creditors and patients.

"When you talk about covering up traces, you mean me, of course," he said heavily. "You're wrong, Inspector. I'm not clever. I'm the biggest fool who ever tried to practice medicine. I'm a bluff and a faker."

"No kidding?" sneered Joyce.

"It's only too true. I barely scraped through college. The sort of examiners we have today would not have given me my license. I have never had the least aptitude for making diagnoses. I can only keep the simplest remedies in my head. My prescriptions are jokes, I tell you, calomel, quinine, iodine, and—if I can't think of anything better—bicarbonate of soda. But I write them out with contractions the layman doesn't understand, and a big X thrown in here and there. Ask the druggists in this town. They've taken to poking fun at me whenever I call at their shops." His voice began to rise shrilly, in a passion of self-condemnation. "I confess that when George and Mary Van Zanten died, I didn't know what to make of their cases. Their symptoms seemed abnormal. Yet murder— brrr!—murder was farthest from my thoughts."

"Why didn't you call in another physician for a consultation?" asked Joyce severely.

"Because of my weakness of character. I'm not only a bluff, Inspector—I'm weak. I've never been able to talk down any one who's set up his will against mine. That goes even when the other person is almost as spineless as myself. I—I run away from a really strong will, Inspector. All my life I've trembled before people who have authority, or whom I depend on for a living, or anything of that order. Alphonse Henkle is just a puppet of hypocrisy and pretense and walking lies. These whiskers, for instance—" he clutched his beard viciously—"they're for the purpose of helping me to hide the truth about myself. Some men wear whiskers because they like them. I hate a beard. But if you ever saw my clean-shaven face with its receding chin and loose lips, you'd know why I cover it with hair."

Joyce let him rave on. The confession had taken a turn which hinted how a modicum of truth might be extracted from the doctor. He waited for a pause in the flow of hysterical words, and asked:

"Who bluffed you out of handling the illness and death of George Van Zanten in the right way?"

"Nicholas. He wanted to believe his brother had succumbed to indigestion, and I fell in line. Superficially, the diagnosis was justified."

"What about Mary?"

"We were all frightened by her terrible condition, and Nicholas even suggested a post mortem. But Fawcett talked him out of that. So I called it angina pectoris, which indeed it resembled. I did not have the backbone to sustain an argument."

"I understand you to say that Nicholas bossed you in all matters, little or big?"

"Yes."

"But that Fawcett had the drop on him?"

"Not altogether. Mr. Van Zanten had great confidence in Fawcett, and was apt to take his advice. But the manager of the estate is a shrewd fellow. He always remembered he was an employee, and did not try to force points that Nicholas disliked."

"Would you claim that Fawcett had a private motive for blocking the post mortem on Mary's body?"

"Far from it, Inspector. It seemed clear to me that he advanced the argument chiefly because he saw that Nicholas would be glad to find an excuse for avoiding the harrowing details of an autopsy."

"Hm! You figure him as playing the same game you did. Anything to please Mr. Van Zanten, eh?"

"Mr. Van Zanten was a very rich man," replied Henkle simply. "But I submitted to him out of weakness, while Fawcett catered whenever he didn't consider the question important."

"The son Jimmy is in this picture, too," commented Joyce. "Who had the most influence over him, his father or Fawcett?"

"Neither of them—and both," proclaimed the doctor portentously. "Jimmy is easily led, yet on the surface he resists all authority. A typical case of thyroid hysteria. He should be taken to a gland specialist, and probably have an operation."

"You're a fine one to talk about thyroid symptoms," said Joyce curiously. "You've acknowledged you're no good as a physician. The modern theories about glands are pretty deep stuff."

Henkle waved his arm, to indicate the books that lined two walls of the office. "I had to have some hobby to save me from dying of boredom. All the works that have any bearing on glands are on those shelves. I've collected them and read them all in the past fifteen years."

"Ever sit in on a consultation with specialists?"

"No, Inspector."

"Ever witness a gland operation?"

"No."

Joyce shrugged his shoulders. It was queer the eccentric characters one ran up against in criminal investigations, he thought. Yet Henkle, with his book knowledge about glands, might have a slant on Jimmy at least as sound as his own—so far. He returned abruptly to the subject of Mary Van Zanten:

"Is Fawcett such a fool that he didn't suspect foul play in the girl's death?"

"Fawcett doesn't know anything about diseases. He isn't to be blamed for assuming that Mary had died of natural causes, no matter how awful she looked at the last. He likely thought that the more quickly she was buried and forgotten, the better it would be for Nicholas."

"You're making this case seem damn jumbled to me. The old man came to my office and talked poison, and blamed himself for listening to Fawcett and allowing the funeral to be hurried through. Now you try to say that he actually wanted things handled that way."

"At the time of the funeral, that was exactly what he wanted, Inspector. Later, to be sure, he may have lost his nerve."

"What do you mean by losing his nerve?"

"He certainly did not have the intention of calling in a detective. He told me so. Yet he ended by going to you."

"I still don't follow you."

"It is my painful duty to suggest that Nicholas Van Zanten was half demented. If deliberate poisonings have been committed in that house, he was the only person who could have been guilty."

"Now I know that *you* are crazy. Nicholas was poisoned himself—with aconitine, in case you haven't heard. His sister died after he did. Yet you accuse him. It's a bughouse notion."

"Inspector Joyce," said Henkle with prodigious solemnity, "our late friend was the dupe of the Negro cook, the evil voodooist, about whom you questioned us all that evening. Suppose some of her potions were harmless. Others may have contained deadly vegetable poisons. Mr. Van Zanten was as eager as she was to have people drink them. He was perhaps a destroyer, without realizing what he was doing. He fell a victim to his own folly. I expect Jimmy to be the next to go. I have read that some of the voodoo poisons work fast, and others slowly. If mysterious deaths occur in this neighborhood for weeks and months to come, it will not surprise me."

"What do you figure Aunt Ellen's motive to be?" asked Joyce contemptuously.

"Just heathen mania, and cussedness. Voodoo is a kind of religion, a worship of the Devil. It isn't necessary to seek farther for a motive."

The detective did not take the trouble to explain the difference between voodoo and the Jamaican obeah practiced by the cook. He remarked: "She was mixing a draft for Jimmy when I interfered and took samples of her herbs. They're in a Stapleton laboratory for analysis. We'll phone right now, and get the result."

He reached for the telephone, and in a few minutes was talking to the chief chemist of the laboratory. Upon restoring the receiver to its hook, he announced:

"The dried leaves and stalks are absolutely harmless. They're mostly dandelion, wild thyme, fennel and grasses of one kind and another. The stuff in the bottles is made from them, in different combinations. Non-poisonous, the laboratory guy says, and even of some medicinal value as a mild stomach tonic."

Henkle threw up his hands. He was about to reply when the telephone rang for an incoming call, and he seized the instrument feverishly. The faint metallic buzzing of a voice could be heard in the room, but only he distinguished the words.

"Dreadful! Dreadful!" he cried, in answer. "Tell Fawcett I'll come over at once."

Joyce leaned swiftly across the desk, and intercepted the receiver before he could hang up.

"What was all that about?" he snapped.

"Another tragedy. Jimmy Van Zanten has been taken seriously ill."

"Yeah?" Joyce gave him a piercing look, then turned to the phone:

"Inspector Joyce speaking . . . Oh yes, Miss Curtis! . . . You'll have to call in another physician. Dr. Henkle is under close police surveillance, and not permitted to leave his house."

CHAPTER EIGHTEEN
Tuesday—The Evidence Piles Up

As soon as Joyce had fulfilled his threat and summoned, by telephone, a detective to keep a close watch over the doings of Dr. Alphonse Henkle, he rejoined Kay in the front parlor. His keen deductive mind had been at work on the new and startling developments in the case, and he felt ready to make a positive pronouncement. He said nothing, however, until they were seated in the car. Dispassionately, then, he told the girl that Jimmy had been stricken.

"It's a safe bet that he's been poisoned, too. With a real doctor on the job, we'll soon know, of course."

"And if he has been, Jimmy's name goes off the list of suspects?"

"Sure—unless the boy's trying to commit suicide, which isn't likely."

"That leaves it a toss-up between Fawcett and Henkle, doesn't it, Inspector?"

"You're forgetting Celestine Curtis. She's with Jimmy now. She phoned for Henkle to come and attend him, which doesn't say a lot for her good sense. Guilty or not guilty, she should have tried to keep this boob away from all future sick beds." Joyce paused, and ran his stubby fingers through his hair.

"Henkle was out to convince me that the old man Nicholas was the poisoner. Tie that! Says he dosed everybody with Aunt Ellen's mixtures, one of which killed him. Other potions, working more slowly, account for Constance's end—and now the illness of Jimmy, I guess he wants us to believe!"

"It's sheer bunk, don't you think?"

"It's improbable. To put it any stronger than that would prove us to be bad detectives. The weeds I took from Aunt Ellen were innocuous, but she may have used other kinds."

"Strychnine, aconitine and prussic acid are chemical preparations," Kay argued. "The symptoms indicate that they did the work. How would such poisons have come into Aunt Ellen's possession?"

"Suppose she stole them and put them into her draughts at the last minute! Well, if we can prove that against her, or any one else, it will be evidence. That's what we need— evidence! So far, we've been working only with theories. In a case of this kind, there's three main things: the body— the *corpus delicti*—without which there can be no charge of murder; the cause of death; and the dope that pins the crime upon the right person. We've got the first two, but without the third and last every son-of-a-gun in the whole mess will go free."

"Apart from Tom's inquiry in the drug stores, what do you think might be turned up, Inspector?"

"The reports from Texas may give us a new line on Fawcett. Constance's shoes—the pair some bird clamped on his hands, to fake her trail from the house—they'd be evidence, if they carry finger-prints. Only circumstantial evidence pointing to her murder, but pretty strong, taken in connection with the rest." He hesitated. "Then I'm wondering whether there mayn't be a secret laboratory at the Manor, a place where poisons are mixed."

"Why should that be necessary—the laboratory, I mean—when staple manufactured products were employed?"

"I'm not very clear about it yet, Kay darlin'. But the hint of a tie-up with Aunt Ellen's obeah drinks has set the idea to buzzing in my head. Henkle's talk about quick and slow poisons may have a meaning, too. Strychnine can be diluted and fed to a victim in small doses. It's just as deadly that way, though the symptoms are different."

"I see," answered Kay thoughtfully.

"We'll maybe do something with that later. The doc's verdict on Jimmy's illness is the big point today."

They had been driving slowly out of St. George, while Joyce talked over his shoulder to the girl. Now, as they reached Victory Boulevard, he bent over the wheel, put on speed and dashed back to the Van Zanten estate as though to make up for lost time.

Standing in the hallway, with his physician's bag and his hat in his hand, was a stranger, whom the detective Hennesey at once introduced as Dr. Arthur Wagenhalls, of Stapleton.

"I held him for ye, Inspector," he said. "I knew you'd be wanting to question him about the sick boy."

"Quite right, Hennesey." Joyce swung around to the doctor. "Well?"

"The patient's condition is alarming, but so far not critical," stated Wagenhalls formally. "It appears that be was suddenly overcome by giddiness and loss of muscular power. When I arrived, his skin was cold and his pulse feeble. The most peculiar symptom is a numbness and tingling in the mouth and throat, which makes it difficult for him to speak."

"What's wrong with him?"

"I am unable to make a diagnosis at the present stage. I shall pay my next visit at four o'clock, but if he changes radically for the worse in the meantime, you will of course summon me by telephone."

"God damn it, Doc, you're talking to the law, and not to a relative!" said Joyce bluntly. "I want your best opinion, even if you have to change it afterwards. Do you think the young man has been poisoned?"

"I perceive what you have in mind. I—I naturally have heard rumors about recent events in this house. Upon my word as a professional man, sir, I assure you that I do not recognize this as a case of poisoning. There has been no vomiting, which is the usual indication of the presence of toxicants in the stomach. I may be able to tell you more about it this evening."

"Fair enough. Does he need a trained nurse?"

"Certainly. I have taken the liberty of sending for a trustworthy woman on my call list. A Miss Curtis, his fiancée, is with him now."

Joyce dismissed the pedantic medico with a nod, and went upstairs. He knocked lightly at Jimmy's door. A strangled voice asked him to come in, and he found Celestine Curtis weeping by the bedside. The spectacle of the strong-minded girl in tears was so novel that Joyce stared, without questioning her. Her grief appeared to be perfectly genuine.

He then gave the recumbent figure of the boy a long scrutiny. Jimmy was breathing softly with his eyes closed and his limbs unstirring. He looked more like a paralytic than a poison victim. And suddenly Joyce noticed a slight swelling in his neck, to the left of the Adam's apple. It was the thyroid gland brought into abnormal relief by the way the head was held.

Perhaps Henkle was right, he mused. Perhaps Jimmy did need a thyroid operation. Chronic nerves, leading to hysteria and ending in this state of semi-coma, might well be the result of gland trouble.

He walked out again, dropped down the corridor a few doors and entered Fawcett's room. The estate manager was sitting by the window, with his hands folded upon his stomach. He wore a patient and slightly woebegone air. When he saw Joyce, he arose politely and greeted him without a trace of animosity. He hastened to set a comfortable chair in place for the detective.

"Sad about Jimmy," he remarked, his voice shaking and his bright hazel eyes dimmed.

"I'll say it is. Looks like a clean sweep of the Van Zanten family," answered Joyce, ironically naïve.

"And you are proving it's murder? I hear you found Constance dead, and that you've sent all the bodies to the Morgue for autopsies. A wise move. When I opposed it, I didn't know about Constance."

Joyce reflected that if this man were the culprit, he was also a cool and courageous bluffer.

"But in arresting Andy Burns, I think you made a mistake, Inspector," Fawcett went on. "That poor oaf is no poisoner."

"I haven't charged him with murder."

"No?" Fawcett shot a swift glance at Joyce. "I wonder how soon you'll be arresting me. The prospect does not frighten me, because I know I am innocent. But being a half-prisoner in the house is very irksome. I hate to neglect my garden."

"Sorry I have to hold you. The more help you give me, the sooner I may be able to set you free. I'm here to ask you to show me Nicholas Van Zanten's will."

"Really, until it is probated—"

"That makes no difference," Joyce interrupted sharply. "I'm claiming a police right in a murder investigation. The District Attorney can demand it, too, for the information of the Grand Jury."

"Just as you say," replied Fawcett, with the utmost calmness. "The will is unimportant to me. You will find its terms to be precisely what Mr. Van Zanten told you they were."

He reached into his trousers pocket and handed Joyce a bunch of keys. "The safe is in the library downstairs," he added gently.

The detective felt momentarily baffled by this willingness to give him the run of the safe. Then he reflected that if Fawcett had anything to hide, he would be crafty enough to put it in some other place. He could not resist tapping two new and shiny keys on the ring, however.

"These are to the vault, I suppose."

"Yes, Inspector. I changed the lock early Monday morning, because there seemed to have been some tampering with it. You needed only to ask me for the keys, and you could have had them. You would have been spared the trouble of picking the lock."

Joyce left without further comment. He spent a fruitless hour upon the contents of the Van Zanten safe. The will, which was dated within the past year, left the estate jointly to Constance and Jimmy, with the proviso that the survivor should inherit the whole. A legacy of twenty thousand dollars to Alexander Fawcett was relatively too small to encourage the suspicion that the estate manager, with his job assured for life, would commit murder to gain immediate possession of it. Nor did the other private papers throw the least light upon the series of crimes.

The Inspector then devoted several more hours to a hunt for the shoes he regarded as a vital link in the chain he was weaving. The rational, human assumption would have been that so damning a pair of objects as Constance's mystery shoes had been promptly destroyed. But Joyce knew from experience that malefactors are strangely reluctant to do away with concrete evidence. They prefer to conceal it, in the vague hope that its meaning can be falsified in an emergency and turned to their own account.

He failed utterly in his quest. It was the third time he had made the search vainly. This was not so good. The day had contributed only one important development, Jimmy's illness. A negative point, so far. "The case is hanging fire," he thought, "and I'd be a goof to kid myself that it isn't."

But at three-thirty in the afternoon, things began to hum. A special police messenger arrived from Borough Headquarters in St. George, with a preliminary report on the autopsies. Both Mary Van Zanten and her father were found to have been victims of strychnine, though the last-named had taken the poison into his system in small quantities spread over a week or more. Mary had died of a single powerful dose. Constance unquestionably had been the victim of prussic acid. A postscript to the report stated that the cause of Nicholas Van Zanten's death had been officially recorded as aconitine, the lethal alkaloid obtained from the root of the plant known as wolfsbane.

Joyce had barely finished reading it through when Dr. Arthur Wagenhalls came to pay his second visit to Jimmy. The physician was allowed to make his examination and on his return downstairs was asked for an opinion, which he expressed cautiously:

"I am still puzzled by the inertia of the patient. It is not characteristic of any common malady. A blood test is advisable. As soon as I know the results of such a test, I should be able to diagnose. Possibly by tomorrow."

Joyce smiled grimly, and showed Wagenhalls the report from the morgue on the four preceding Van Zantens who had been stricken in that house. "It's confidential, of course," he explained. "But I'm wondering whether it mayn't help you to understand what has happened to the lad."

An amazed look came into the doctor's eyes. His pursed lips relaxed, and his cloak of professional formality fell away from him.

"Damnation, Inspector!" he muttered. "Aconitine, strychnine and prussic acid—the three deadliest vegetable poisons known! Especially aconitine! Why, that's so rare that it's almost unheard of, except in a prescription. I did have an inkling that my patient might have taken a modicum amount of aconitine into his system, but it seemed fantastic."

"Then his symptoms do point to aconitine?"

"Broadly—yes."

"Can you save him?"

"It is very doubtful. That poison is fatal in a quantity of one-fifteenth of a grain. The boy could scarcely have been given less. If it had been as much as one-seventh of a grain, he would have died in half an hour."

"I know, I know! Well, do your best for him."

"Naturally. It will be essential that no one but the trained nurse prepares his nourishment and medicines."

"Is the nurse here yet?"

"Yes. She came while you were out of the house, she tells me. But that fiancée is with the patient, too."

"We'll fix that," Joyce promised him.

They went to the sick room, and the ultimatum was curtly served upon Celestine. She must stay away from Jimmy, until he was pronounced to be out of danger.

The girl had stopped crying, but her eyes were swollen and her face as pale as it could become through its coating of sun-tan. She stood up, to fight back:

"I won't leave Jimmy. You can't bar me from this room."

"'Can't' is the wrong word to use to me, young lady," Joyce answered. "You've no claims that I've got to respect, and if need be I'll have you jailed."

"I do have claims." She hesitated, then drew from the bosom of her dress a folded paper, which she handed to the Inspector. "I am Jimmy's wife."

Astounded, he read a marriage contract dated the day before. "How early in the morning did you pull this off?" he demanded. "I put Jimmy under police surveillance at about eleven o'clock."

"We were married in St. George at nine, before the bureau opened to the public. Jimmy had enough pull to arrange that."

"But the license? A minor has to give five days' notice in this State."

"We applied a month ago, but Jimmy's father opposed it. Yesterday morning, Mr. Fawcett, as guardian, gave Jimmy his written approval, and the license was issued to us all right."

"So old Mr. Van Zanten's death was important to your wedding plans, was it?" Joyce drawled meaningfully. "We'll talk about that some time. Your husband may be dying, and it's doctor's orders that only the nurse can be with him until further notice. So, mosey along. You're under police surveillance yourself, by the way. Have one of the maids fix you up a guest room here. You can't go home tonight."

He shooed Celestine into the corridor, and went to look for Kay. The latter was waiting for him in the parlor—and not alone. Sheriff Symes had made a quick round trip to New York.

"Reports from Texas on Fawcett, Chief," the Sheriff said, and handed him two telegrams.

The first message was from a detective agency in Dallas. It stated briefly that Alexander Fawcett had been known in the city and in the suburb of Hillsboro, until twenty-two years previously, when the man had gone North. He had been a jack-of-all trades, and considered a shiftless fellow. Subsequent to his departure, a woman named Ann Scott had asked the police to locate him, so that she might sue for the support of an illegitimate child. Nothing had come of this, and the woman had died.

The still shorter second wire bore the name of the Chief
of Police of Dallas, and ran as follows:

ALEXANDER FAWCETT NEVER ARREST-
ED HERE STOP SUIT OF LATE ANN
SCOTT FOR MAINTENANCE OF SIX-
YEAR-OLD SON OUTLAWED BY LAPSE
OF TIME STOP FAWCETT SAID TO HAVE
SEDUCED SCOTT WOMAN WHILE BOTH
WERE WORKING IN LOCAL CIRCUS
STOP FAIR REPUTATION OTHERWISE

A slow smile flickered across Joyce's face, as he half
closed his eyes and considered the new angles on Fawcett.
It was interesting about his having worked in a circus,
Joyce thought. In a small outfit, he would have had to
be some sort of tumbler or acrobat, to get by. With such
training behind him, he would not have found it difficult
to walk in a reversed position, with his hands thrust into
a woman's shoes. Significant, also, that Fawcett had been
a young man of low principles, capable of deserting a mistress and child.

"I did some long-distance telephoning, as you told me
to," the discreet voice of the Sheriff broke in upon his
reflections. "I thought we ought to find out whether that
son was alive. Nobody knows. He disappeared from Dallas
when he was eighteen—or ten years ago. His name was
Angus."

"Angus, eh? Angus Scott. It's a real Scotch name." Joyce
was looking very pleased with himself. He winked at the
Sheriff.

"Yes, Chief. And I learned something else about Fawcett himself. The longest time he ever held a job down was
between 1902 and 1905, when he worked as a gardener at

the Beeston-Bailey Botanical Research Park, near Amarillo, Texas."

"The hell you say!" Joyce slammed his open palm upon a table, and emitted a wolfish chuckle. "I've got a grand idea, but you'll have to do some fast jumping around for me, Sheriff."

"Work never scared me. That's what I'm here for."

"Then go to Stapleton or St. George, and be back pronto with two white rabbits. I don't care about the breed, or what they cost. But they've got to be white, and I want rabbits that haven't been fed for several hours."

CHAPTER NINETEEN
Tuesday—What the Garden Told

At eleven o'clock that night, the condition of Jimmy Van Zanten was unchanged and a static gloom enveloped the house. An observer from the outside world would have said that dynamic events were not destined to occur there within the next few hours. The atmosphere was one of complete lethargy and exhaustion. Even the city detectives assigned to the duty of awaiting orders, which failed to materialize, seemed stupefied by their inaction.

Tom had returned earlier in the evening, shaking his head over his failure to learn that Staten Island or New Jersey druggists had sold poisons to residents of the Manor. But Joyce had slapped him on the shoulder and told him not to worry any further about the matter. If information should be telephoned in as a result of his efforts, well and good. If not, the following day would be time enough to decide whether the old line of inquiry was worth pursuing. More than that, Joyce would not say. His assistants had a hunch that—despite the deceptive calm of the house—they would witness some excitement before the morning.

They were not surprised, therefore, to be summoned to the hallway on the ground floor at eleven o'clock. The waning moon had risen, but its beams were intercepted by the tall trees to the east, and the light outdoors was dim.

Joyce plainly held this to be an important point. From
time to time, he glanced impatiently through a window,
and when at last the moon thrust itself above the tops of
the trees, he grunted with satisfaction.

"We're now going to pay a visit to the garden," he said.
"Sheriff, are you ready with those rabbits?"

Shortly after dark, Symes had slipped into the house
in the most unobtrusive fashion. He had been carrying
a small wicker basket, which he had concealed behind a
desk in the library. Not even Joyce had seen him do it,
for it was the Sheriff's habit to perform all errands with
a ghostlike evasiveness. He had reported his own physical
presence, however, and the Chief had remarked that it was
a pity he had not been able to get back while there was
still daylight. That had been all. The next best thing had
been to wait for the light of the moon to make use of the
creatures he had brought.

The little man vanished and reappeared with his basket, and the party went into the garden, by way of the back
door. Joyce led them to the middle of Fawcett's beloved tract.
There he halted, and instructed Symes to set the rabbits
free. They hopped here and there clumsily, and then settled
down to the business of looking for something to eat.

"I wanted white ones so that we could see them easily," the Inspector explained. "Domestic rabbits are stupid beasts. They'll nibble at almost any plant, if they're
hungry. That may result in giving us some mighty telling
evidence."

"Do I get you right?" Kay asked, her voice soaring.
"You think they will find poisonous plants in this garden?"

"Yes."

"The ingredients of obeah draughts?"

"You're hot on the scent. But Aunt Ellen furnishes
nothing but the lead. When I found out that she'd been
boiling herbs, it should have struck me right away that

others could do the same thing. Dr. Wagenhalls made the remark this afternoon that all the Van Zantens had been killed with vegetable poisons. Finally, the Sheriff told me that Fawcett had worked at the Beeston-Bailey Botanical Research Park in Texas, and the connection clicked. That Beeston-Bailey outfit specializes on noxious plants—to use them in science, of course. An employee would learn a lot about poisons."

"Everything could have been grown here?" Kay questioned blankly, as if thunderstruck.

"Yes. And vegetable toxicants can be extracted in an amateur's laboratory. They're not like the mineral poisons—arsenic and so forth—which are unobtainable except from a chemist."

"Then Fawcett is the guilty person."

"He or Andy Burns. I figure Fawcett as being at least a confederate, but he *may* have been working with Doc Henkle. Don't forget that."

"It would be too wonderful if this theory is correct."

"We'll soon know for sure," said Joyce briskly. "Tom and the Sheriff—you watch the rabbits. Drive them away from ordinary flowers, but take samples of anything else they eat."

He produced his pocket torch, and sent the beam traveling in a slow arc across the nearer beds. When it reached a cluster of handsome flowers on a low shrub, he paused.

"There you are, Kay. That plant is wolfsbane—*aconitum napellus* the Latin name is. You'll notice that the blossoms are hooded, which is why it's sometimes called monkshood. By daylight, the petals are a clear blue, with two spurs under each hood. It's cultivated by gardeners, who don't dream that the deadly poison aconite can be extracted from the roots. By the way, the roots are shaped something like horse radish. They've been eaten by mistake often enough, I've read in books."

He pulled up one of the plants and thrust it, root and all, into his pocket.

"Now this," he continued, pausing in front of a bush some three feet high, with spiny leaves and bell-shaped purple flowers, "this is deadly nightshade. Belladonna and atropine are obtained from it. Observe how cleverly it's been grown, with morning glory trailing over it. The blossoms of both are of much the same color."

"What about the nuts from which strychnine is made?" Kay demanded.

"We'll probably find them in the greenhouse over there. They grow on two rather hefty tropical shrubs, the nux vomica and the St. Ignatius' bean, so called. The seed of either fruit fairly reeks with strychnine. But let's look for some more of the little fellows.

"Here's jimson weed, which is another kind of nightshade, and quite useful to a poisoner. Yes, and water hemlock or cicuta, if you please, on the edge of this irrigation canal. The same sort of draught that killed Socrates could be brewed from this hemlock. And I see a few stray plants of the Oriental poppy, which secretes opium. God, Kay, our man Fawcett and his assistant are a damn clever pair! They cultivate a show garden, and among the roses and irises and hydrangeas they scatter the most dangerous growths—like weeds!

"That's what these poison plants are—the weeds of the garden. It's impossible to have a garden without a few weeds in it, but Fawcett has been careful to provide that every one of the seemingly chance sprouts is an evil servant of his own. A visitor would never guess at their real character. Even I looked at the wolfsbane a dozen times, and only thought that it was a pretty flower."

It was the first time that Kay had ever heard her chief make so long a speech. But Joyce behaved like a man

inspired by his extraordinary discovery. The words poured
from his mouth in a steady stream, and on a low, resonant
note.

"The next stopping place is the greenhouse," he said.
"It's no doubt piped so that in the winter it can be oper-
ated as a real hothouse for tropical plants."

They found the door unlocked and entered the long
thirty-foot, glass-enclosed shed. Almost the first object
Joyce noticed was a small tree, growing in a wooden tub
which stood in the center of the building, with its topmost
branches touching the domed roof.

"That's nux vomica, all right," he commented.

The tree bore round fruit, about the size of a stunted orange. Joyce plucked one of them, and cut it open
with his jacknife. It contained many disc-shaped seeds. He
threw the fruit back into the tub.

"We could likely turn up a slew of rare tropical flowers, bushes and weeds that would be useful in committing
murder. A guy capable of importing nux vomica from the
East Indies, where it grows wild, and cultivating it for
years until it bears fruit, *must* be a bug on the subject.
I'll bet he grows poison plants for the pleasure of it, and
is proud of having a big collection. But we don't have the
time to search for any more."

"I'm still wondering about the prussic acid with which
Constance was killed. Could that have been made here,
too?"

"Nothing simpler. Cherry stones and bitter almonds
contain that poison in an almost pure state. I remember
seeing quite a grove of cherry trees on the edge of the
lawn. It's a funny thing but the acid has the almond smell
no matter what kind of fruit pit it's made from."

They returned to the main flower beds, where they saw
Tom and the Sheriff engaged in the faintly ludicrous task

of trailing the rabbits on their hands and knees. The two
men shouted that, so far, they had not caught the beasts
eating any leaves of a suspicious nature.

"I'm still of the opinion that a laboratory might be
hidden underground, right here in this garden," remarked
Joyce. "Some kind of lab would have been needed in preparing the poisons. They couldn't have been boiled in a
pot in the open. They had to be purified."

"Why underground?" countered Kay. "I've been thinking about that myself, and it struck me that maybe—" She
stopped, as if ashamed of some farfetched notion.

"Go ahead! Spill it. Any idea's worth looking into,
when you're trying to solve a crime mystery. You ought to
know that, me darlin'."

"Well, I thought of the cowshed down in that meadow
where the prize Hereford cattle are. Old Mr. Van Zanten said
the cattle were one of Fawcett's fads. Why wouldn't he have
cooked his poisons some place like that, way off the map."

"Suffering cats! That should have come into my thick
head. It's a hot idea, Kay, and we'll go straight down and
give the cowshed a once-over."

Joyce called to his assistants not to lose sight of the
rabbits, and he and Kay started across the fields. As they
left the garden, they had a momentary impression that
some one was following them, dodging from bush to bush
and hiding behind trees. But the moon just then was veiled
by drifting clouds, and they concluded that the shadows
had deceived them.

It took them fifteen minutes to reach the shed, and at
a glance they saw that any possible laboratory would be
located in the hay loft above it. The ground level was
given over to stalls for the animals, and there were no
adjoining structures.

They climbed to the loft, and explored for some time
without results. The place appeared to be filled only with

fodder. But as Joyce prodded at the bales of hay in a corner, one of the bales tumbled to the floor, and a wooden
partition was revealed. The latter had been built diagonal-
ly to isolate the corner, and the hay obviously stacked in
such a manner as to hide it from view.

Joyce pulled down the bales that were still in place.
He uncovered a narrow doorway, secured by a padlock.
But the planks were flimsy, and a few stiff drives with his
shoulder broke through them. The triangular space beyond contained a stove, resting on a sheet of tin, and with
a pipe to carry off the smoke. Pots and pans of various
sizes stood on shelves. The utensils were spotlessly clean,
and there were no bottles or other receptacles containing
the product of the work done on the premises.

Two objects, nevertheless, promptly caught Joyce's eye
and caused him to growl delightedly. These were a pair
of women's shoes with mud still clinging to the heels and
the edges of the soles, and an ordinary drinking glass. The
latter was marked by a flaw about the size of a grain of
wheat, close to its upper rim. The bottom of the glass was
stained by a whitish sediment.

"Constance's shoes!" gasped Kay.

"I hope so. But the glass maybe is going to prove every
bit as valuable. The last stuff it had in it was not plain
water—not by a long shot."

Joyce tied his own and Kay's handkerchiefs loosely
about his prizes and carried them in a gingerly manner on
the palms of his hands, in order not to erase any finger-
prints which might have been left upon them. The re-
maining contents of the secret room, he considered to be
merely circumstantial evidence.

Kay took up the pocket electric torch which he had
been manipulating, and led the way. They descended the
ladder which brought them to the gate of the cowshed.

Down there, a new development lurked to startle them. A human figure unquestionably was slinking in the lee of the shed.

"Who the hell's there?" shouted Joyce angrily.

Dumb silence was his only answer for a moment. Then out into the pale moonlight hobbled the bent form of Aunt Ellen, the Jamaican cook. She came straight up to the Inspector, and said in a surprisingly clear voice:

"Marse Jimmy's dying."

"What do you mean—dying?" he retorted. "How can you know?"

"Nebber min' how I know. I say he die now—*pam-pam*—unless you fix it so Aunt Ellen can save him."

"How would you set about that?"

She drew a bottle from the folds of her dress, and held it up. "Good medicine. My medicine, Mr. Policeman. Obeah is all dat can keep de las of de Van Zantens from his grave."

"I think you're crazy, old lady. He's got a doctor and a nurse attending him. They'd not allow you to dose him."

"You mus' allow me," the Negress persisted. "You been in my country. You know we black folk can cheat de Debbil. De white doctor is one big fool."

"Have you seen your Marse Jimmy?"

"Yes, sah. De nurse let me look 'pon him."

"Perhaps you're not talking such nonsense, after all."

"My young Massa's face is red, his skin is cold and his throat closing," Aunt Ellen cried, in a queer singsong. "In one hour he dead, if you no give me chance to save him."

"Damned if she doesn't describe the final symptoms of aconitine poisoning!" Joyce muttered to Kay.

He addressed the West Indian sybil:

"We'll all go now and pay him a visit. I'll say Yes or No to you then."

CHAPTER TWENTY
Tuesday—Rabbits and Obeah

Upon reaching the garden, Joyce found Tom and the Sheriff standing disconsolately over the forms of two very sick-looking rabbits. The beasts were flattened out in a curious manner on their stomachs, their heads extended and their legs spread wide. It needed no veterinary surgeon to proclaim that they were at the point of death from poisoning.

"They wouldn't eat the nightshade," elucidated Symes, who as a former country dweller was himself a fair authority on plants. "It's too bitter, I guess. But when they came to the wolfsbane here, they nibbled at the leaves, didn't seem to like 'em, and then began to gnaw the stalks and the roots that were exposed. They toppled over in a few minutes."

"Great!" said Joyce. "We'll get an analyst's report on what killed them. It sounds foolish, but a couple of rabbits that died this way under our eyes will impress a grand jury three times as much as the straight facts about the plants being grown here."

"I know, Chief. Building up an indictment is a science, like everything else."

"Don't touch the rabbits until they pass out. Watch 'em and let me know exactly how long it takes in each case."

"That's easy."

"Then preserve the bodies carefully. Kay and I are going with Aunt Ellen to see Jimmy Van Zanten."

"With the rabbits and all, you're planning to convict on circumstantial evidence, aren't you, Inspector?" Kay asked, as they hastened toward the house. "Don't you hope for a confession?"

"I may be able to force one."

"From whom?"

"That would depend upon a lot of things. For instance, the finger-prints in the shoes—if any—and the glass. I don't need to tell you that it's up to me to prepare a case as if no such help could be expected."

So far, it would be a weak case, because we haven't established a powerful motive. Why should any of the three chief suspects turn wholesale poisoner? They don't stand to profit by it."

"You're right, girl. There may be a revenge motive, but if so we've uncovered only picayune things—like the thousand dollars Henkle lost on the stock market. That forces us back to the criminal mania theory, and Fawcett doesn't strike me as being a nut. Andy Burns might be one, though. He's ignorant and brutish enough to be a thrill killer. This mystery is a long ways from being solved."

They had been talking in low tones, to prevent Aunt Ellen from overhearing them. Now, as they came to the back door of the house, they waited silently for the old Negress to catch up. All three went in together, and mounted the stairs to Jimmy's bedroom.

Celestine Curtis was leaning against the wall just outside the door, her face buried in her folded arms. She looked up sharply as the others approached, and her grief-stricken expression changed to one of anger.

"I've been allowed in to see him just twice since dinner, and then only for a minute. That cook has no claims above mine. If she goes in again, I shall."

"Miss Celestine, I'll be asking you to have a little patience with us," answered Joyce gently, his voice warmed by an extreme courtesy the like of which he had not shown to any one else during the course of the investigation. "Aunt Ellen knows something about this kind of illness. I want her opinion. In a while, I'll tell the nurse to let you visit with Jimmy."

It was fairly evident to Kay that he had mentally removed the name of Celestine from his list of suspects.

The young wife stood back, astonished and grateful, and Joyce, Kay and the Negress entered the sick room.

Jimmy was seen to be lying rigidly, his face presenting a far more dreadful appearance than it had in the afternoon. It was congested with blood. The mouth was half open, and the breathing was labored.

Joyce threw an interrogative glance at the nurse, who was hovering over the boy's pillow and wiping his forehead now and then with a piece of cotton lint. She came to the detective on tip-toe.

"I've phoned for Dr. Wagenhalls, of course," she whispered.

"When will he be here?"

"He was out on a call. They'll give him the message when he returns."

"That means that he mightn't arrive for an hour or more."

"I'm afraid so."

"The patient is dying," Joyce said.

The nurse shrugged her shoulders, unwilling to commit herself to a medical opinion.

"Don't stall with me. I'm a police official. How long has this boy got to live?"

The struggle that her professional ethics cost the nurse was almost humorous, as reflected on her drab countenance. She had been taught not to usurp the prerogatives of her physician in stating what was the matter with patients, or what was going to happen to them. Finally, she compromised by murmuring:

"You can judge for yourself. If I were a doctor, I'd be inclined to give him about fifteen minutes."

Joyce clenched his teeth. His own layman's judgment confirmed the nurse's estimate, and both were significantly in line with the prophecy uttered by Aunt Ellen. A quarter of an hour was a small margin of time in which to save a dying person. And, to look at it another way, any desperate remedy was better than none at this moment. He turned on his heel, and rejoined Celestine in the corridor.

"Your husband is at his last gasp," he said bluntly. "Aunt Ellen claims she can pull him through with an herb cure. I won't decide. You must. Do you want that tried?"

The last vestiges of color receded from the girl's cheeks. Her eyes widened. But her inherent strength of character was proved by the way she kept her head erect and squared her shoulders slowly.

"I've known he was going all evening. Is there no—no hope that the doctor can do anything?" she stammered.

"The doctor can't possibly get here in time."

"In that case, Inspector," she cried, her voice hardening with almost masculine resolution, "in that case, we'll see what obeah can accomplish."

Joyce patted her on the arm and led her into the bedroom. The moment they had crossed the threshold, he wagged a forefinger at Aunt Ellen.

"All right, Aunty. We're going to take a chance on you."

"Thank the Lord! The Lord's name be praised!" the old woman chanted, with her bizarre commingling of Christian piety and witchcraft. "He's letting me save my young Massa."

She uncorked her bottle, and muttering incomprehensible words in an African dialect, she advanced to the bedside.

The nurse started up in horror, saying: "This can't be allowed. The doctor—"

"Never you mind. I take the responsibility," Joyce interrupted. He thrust the nurse aside with a certain roughness, since her rigid loyalty to duty as she understood it led her to battle fussily like a hen with flapping wings.

Aunt Ellen put her arm under Jimmy's head. She poured a few drops of her medicine between his parted teeth. It trickled into his throat, and unable to swallow it at first he coughed and panted. She gave him another does, which went down more easily. At short intervals, for five minutes, she continued the treatment until four-fifths of the contents of the bottle had been administered. She then fell to mumbling her cabalistic runes.

Joyce signed to her to give him the almost empty bottle. She obeyed willingly, and he dropped it into his pocket. The nurse stood by with a scandalized air. Nobody paid any attention to her, and the leaden minutes ticked themselves away.

Celestine was the first to notice a change for the better in Jimmy's condition. "He's not so flushed," she whispered excitedly.

Aunt Ellen nodded. "Quick, quick now, young Massa get well," she broke her crooning and gibbering to announce.

Thereafter, the sick boy's improvement progressed with a rapidity that seemed little short of miracle-working. The weird anomaly of a flushed face, but cold skin, corrected itself by a return to normal of the circulation of the blood. The limbs relaxed, and the mouth closed. The constriction of the throat obviously was lessened. The breathing became easy.

After she had taken Jimmy's temperature three times within half an hour, the trained nurse was forced to admit that the crisis had been successfully passed. The patient was no longer in immediate peril of death, she declared with conservatism. The other persons in that room knew intuitively that his life had been saved.

Joyce looked at Kay. "The obeah was nothing but an antidote," he commented. "We'll likely never know now what poison Jimmy swallowed. Aconitine, I think. But if Aunt Ellen knows an antidote for aconitine, she's certainly a whiz."

Dr. Arthur Wagenhalls came, and went away again. He exhibited marked scepticism when told about the draught. Simples or no simples, the patient's constitution had been sufficiently strong to re-establish its balance, he averted pedantically.

At four o'clock, Jimmy opened his eyes. He was weak, but fully conscious.

"Celestine," he mouthed, exerting a great effort. "Celestine, darling."

His wife knelt by his pillow, and Joyce moved closer without compunction. He had been waiting up for this, waiting to hear what Jimmy would have to say when he came out of his coma. It might have an important bearing on the quadruple murder-plot, which had so nearly included a fifth victim.

"I—I've been ill," Jimmy gasped. "Very ill . . . bad dreams . . . pain . . . so much pain!"

"Yes, dear. You've had a bad time of it. But you're getting better now," Celestine answered softly.

The boy frowned. "Poisoned!" he said more clearly. "I felt poisoned . . . like the others."

It was difficult for his young wife to find an answer to that. He closed his eyes, and appeared to be falling asleep. "My will," he grumbled. "Show will . . . show it to Joyce."

A long silence followed. The detective tapped Celestine on the shoulder, and signed to her to come with him to the other end of the room. "What's this about a will?" he asked.

"Jimmy signed one immediately after we were married. He had it in his pocket, already typewritten. A lawyer and a clerk in the license bureau witnessed it."

"Do you know its provisions?"

"No, Inspector. He didn't offer to show it to me, and naturally I wouldn't press him."

"Where is the will now?"

"Right here in the room. He told me that Mr. Fawcett advised him not to put it in the safe downstairs."

"That's interesting. Will you get it out for me?"

Celestine's level, candid gaze met his for a moment or two in silence. "I'll do it," she agreed. "Jimmy's mind may have been wandering, but even so he said you were to see the will."

She stepped over to a bureau and brought out a small tin box, the key of which was in the lock. The last testament of the last of the Van Zantens lay on top of a package of love letters from the former Celestine Curtis. The document started in the usual formal way, with a request to the executor to pay all legal debts out of the first funds available for that purpose. The second clause bequeathed to the testator's wife no more than the one-third share in the estate which the Surrogate's Court would have assigned to her in any event. But the final provision contained a shock. It read:

> "I give, devise and bequeath to my guardian, Alexander Fawcett, *all the rest and residue of my property of every description, of which I may die possessed. I make this bequest as a token of love and affection, and to mark my gratitude for the wisdom with which my said guardian*

*has managed the estate inherited from my fa-
ther. As sole executor of this will, I name and
appoint* Alexander Fawcett, *imposing on him
the sacred duty of carrying out my desires in the
bequests above mentioned.*"

Joyce pondered his discovery briefly, his face like a
mask. Then he handed the will to Celestine, pointing to
the important clause as he did so.

"Why do you suppose Jimmy would leave two-thirds to
Fawcett and only one-third to you?"

"Mr. Fawcett has a great influence over him. I've always known that. Jimmy resented the bossing, yet he'd
let himself be talked down every time." She hesitated. "I
got the impression that morning we were married that the
will was bound up somehow with Mr. Fawcett's giving his
consent to our wedding. When he signed it, he mentioned
in a sulky sort of way that his guardian had said it wasn't
the right thing for anybody to drift along without making
a will."

"Yeah? Well, you've helped me a whole lot, Mrs. Van
Zanten." Joyce recovered the document and stowed it in
his breast pocket. "Stick close to your Jimmy now. He'll be
needing you when he wakes up."

He passed into the corridor and spoke to the detective
Hennesey, who was doing a turn on guard.

"Hennesey, me lad," he said, "round up your sidekick
Boyle and take that guy Fawcett down to the police station. Do it now. Book him for murder."

"Sure, Inspector, sure!" replied Hennesey, snapping
into complete wakefulness.

"I'm going to get a wink of sleep," concluded Joyce,
"but tell 'em at St. George Headquarters that I'll be along
myself at about ten in the morning."

CHAPTER TWENTY-ONE
Wednesday—Joyce Clinches the Case

Accompanied by his son Tom, the Sheriff and Kay Carey, Joyce appeared at Number 78 Richmond Terrace a few minutes before the hour he had set. He went first to the detective bureau, where he obtained the help of technical experts in establishing some simple points. He desired to know if the shoes and the drinking glass found in the laboratory above the cowshed bore finger-prints, and what the nature of the stain inside the glass might be. The bodies of the rabbits he sent out for analysis, but the result was of no immediate interest; it would be offered as supporting evidence for the indictment and subsequent trial of the person he believed guilty.

When he had the reports he had asked for, he took the shoes and the glass to a large, bare room on the second floor of the precinct jail. He placed the objects on a table behind a screen, and presently had added to them certain pieces of evidence which had been removed days before from the bed chamber in which Nicholas Van Zanten had died.

Then he sent a policeman to fetch Fawcett.

While awaiting the arrival of the prisoner, he issued brief instructions to his assistants:

"Kay, you will act as a stenographer and take down everything that's said here. Tom, if I should look at you

and close my left hand, you'll immediately go for Andy
Burns, lead him through this room in handcuffs and push
him kind of roughly into that special cell beyond the
barred door you see to the right. Go in with him, and stay
until I join you. Mr. Symes, you'll just hang around until
I call upon you for help."

He had barely finished talking when the policeman
returned with the estate manager. Fawcett was pasty-faced,
his smooth cheeks sagged like pouches, and his hair and
clothing were somewhat disheveled. His few hours in prison had done much to shake his complacency. But his hazel
eyes were still curiously bright and optimistic. His status
being merely that of a person held under suspicion, he was
not shackled and the privilege of smoking had not been
taken away from him. He was chewing upon the butt of a
cigar.

Joyce signaled to the uniformed officer to stand back
against the wall. He did not ask Fawcett to sit down, but
measured him with a cold appraising glance.

"What do you know about the murdering by poison of
four members of the Van Zanten family?" he asked finally.

"Nothing, Inspector. If I'd been able to answer that
question, I'd have volunteered the information long ago."

Joyce shrugged. "I thought I'd give you a last chance
to help the ends of justice. But you don't have to commit
yourself. Your lawyer, when you get one, will likely advise
against it."

"That means that you regard me as the murderer. How
you misjudge me!"

"I'm only looking for the truth. We'll pass up the four
deaths I mentioned. We'll not go into the illness of young
James Van Zanten, who was poisoned, too, as sure as hell,
but who's luckily recovering. We'll stick to a few side
issues, and take it from me, you've got to answer my questions about those."

Fawcett shifted nervously, bit on his cigar end and then spat it out. He reached for a fresh smoke, but withdrew his fumbling hand from his waistcoat pocket, as if he had changed his mind. "Well?"

"You are the manager of the Van Zanten estate. But your special hobby has always been the flower garden. Is that right, Fawcett?"

"Yes."

"How does it happen that the garden is filled with the most deadly poisonous plants? Some of them bear pretty flowers, and some of them look like weeds."

"Name them, if you please," countered Fawcett calmly.

"Wolfsbane, hemlock, the opium poppy and deadly nightshade to remind you of only a few."

"The first is an accepted garden blossom. If you have found the others, they are there by accident. Many weeds are poisonous."

"I suppose the nux vomica tree in the greenhouse is also an accident."

"Oh, no! I cultivated it as a curiosity."

"The fact that strychnine can be made from its seeds didn't interest you?"

"The idea never entered my head."

"Where did you get the cutting in the first place?"

"I bought it from a nursery that specializes in tropical shrubs."

"From the Beeston-Bailey Botanical Research Park near Amarillo, Texas, I guess."

Fawcett started. "Funny you should have heard of the place," he managed to say, with the greatest aplomb. "It has all others in its field beat hollow."

"But it's not exactly a commercial nursery. Funny you should have worked there for close on three years and taken a shine to nux vomica trees and such like."

Thunderstruck at this turning of a page from his past, the other was unable to muster a reply. He stared, and his eyes grew dull.

"It looks sort of ugly for you, Fawcett," Joyce went on. "And yet you've got me all wrong. I'm not trying to railroad you to the electric chair. Why should I? I haven't proved a thing against *you*. Your testimony is going to be important, and I'm out to get it. It was your garden, when everything's said and done, and if somebody else used the plants in it for murder, the law will hold you partly to blame. The questions I'm asking are mild compared with what the District Attorney is sure to fire at you on the witness stand. But if you're honest with him and with me, you may be able to get off easy."

This speech, which had been phrased in deliberately obscure terms, stirred Fawcett to new hopefulness.

"You're going to accuse another man?" he queried.

"Sure, if I can get a confession out of him by means of the third degree."

"Third degree?" repeated Fawcett, horrified.

"It's about to start." Joyce looked at Tom, and closed his left hand. "But there's no reason why you and I shouldn't keep on talking until I'm ready to get busy on the guy."

"Who is it? Who is it?" The estate manager's voice broke in a falsetto.

"Can't you guess?"

"God, no!"

"There was one other person who had access to the poison plants right along. And I do have something on that bird. He tried to shoot me. He's a natural criminal."

"You mean Burns?" screamed Fawcett. "You mustn't harm him, Inspector Joyce. He's not guilty."

"Seems to me you're worrying a lot about that gardener. What are you scared he'll confess? What has he got on you?"

"It's nothing like that. But I can't bear to think of an innocent man being tortured."

"Soft-hearted, aren't you?"

Joyce turned his head, as the door behind him opened and Tom entered with Andy Burns. The bucolic lout was manacled. He whimpered, as the young detective drove him across the room with cuffs and jolts of the knee.

Suddenly, Fawcett threw himself upon Joyce. He did not use his fists to strike, but flung his arms around the Inspector's torso and struggled to hold him, panting the while: "No, no! For Christ's sake! Don't hurt Andy!"

Taken by surprise, Joyce only was able to counter with a few short-arm punches at Fawcett's middle before the uniformed policeman descended on the prisoner and dragged him away by the collar. Fawcett became meek in a moment. He allowed himself to be gripped above each elbow, and stood blinking foolishly. His coat had been wrenched open, and because of the way he was being held from behind his paunch stuck out prominently.

"I—I promise not to lose my head again, Inspector," he stammered.

Joyce had a vague impression that while they had been wrestling, one of Fawcett's hands had passed swiftly across the front of his vest. But for the instant, he saw no significance in the occurrence—if indeed it had taken place. He looked coldly at the estate manager, and remarked:

"The officer will see to it that you don't repeat that monkey business."

Then he signed to the Sheriff to follow him into the cell to which Tom had taken Andy Burns. It was a narrow room with a few chairs and a table in it. At the far end was a second door.

"Chuck him in there. He'll be safe. There's no exit," Joyce whispered to his son.

When Burns had been disposed of in the second and more remote cell, the Inspector glanced from one of his assistants to the other and smiled grimly.

"You know what this set-up means. Cut loose. Make it sound convincing. Make Fawcett think we're beating the hide off of Andy."

Tom and the Sheriff each seized a chair and banged with it against the wall and upon the table. They purposely collided with the door. At intervals, the Sheriff uttered shrill and blood-curdling yelps, or groaned dismally. The Chief cut in every once in a while with a throaty bellow: "Come clean! You can't bluff me! Confess, you swine!"

Among them, they created a terrific racket. But over and above the noise, they were soon aware of the anguished shrieking of Alexander Fawcett:

"Don't, don't, don't! I'll talk! I'll tell all!

Joyce nodded to Tom and the Sheriff, and they ceased their play-acting. It was precisely then that he chanced to notice a cigar sticking half-way out of his waistcoat pocket. He had had one of his own there, but he saw at a glance that this cigar was thicker and darker-colored than the brand he favored. He took it between finger and thumb and looked at it. Superficially, it was not widely different from his cigar; just a panetela without a band. An eye less trained than that of a detective might have failed to observe that it was not the same. But Joyce knew. He held it up to the light. The closed end of the cigar, which the smoker would clip or bite off, and put in his mouth, was faintly marked for about an inch as if it had been soaked in water and then allowed to dry.

"By God, Fawcett switched cigars on me just now!" he exclaimed under his breath. "The damned sleight-of-hand artist! The circus faker! This one is poisoned, or I'll eat my hat."

He replaced the panetela and emerged into the outer room. He looked surreptitiously at the prisoner's vest

pocket and saw his own lighter-tinted cigar there. "Smooth
work!" he thought. "The bastard had it doped out to make
a poison victim of me this morning, before I'd gotten very
far with him." But he ignored the matter temporarily.

"Well, Fawcett," he challenged harshly. "What are you
ready to tell?"

"I am guilty, Inspector Joyce."

"You poisoned the four Van Zantens?"

"Yes."

"Spill the details."

"I see no reason to do that. I confess. That should be
enough for you."

"Don't be a blasted fool," shouted Joyce furiously. "You
may be doing this to save Burns for the time being. You
may crawl on your confession later, figuring that I can't
prove anything. I want the whole story or nothing."

"I have said as much as I intend to say. I am the guilty
man."

"And I'm going to put the screws on Burns again." Joyce
half swung around, but did not take his eyes from Fawcett's face. He saw the latter turn an even sicklier green-
ish white than it had been before, if that were possible.
Abruptly, the detective modified his tactics.

"I'll give you a sample of how much I know about you
already, Fawcett. I'll tell you just why it means such a hell
of a lot to you to protect Burns," he sneered, and paused.
"Andrew Burns is the former Angus Scott, your own illegitimate son, the child of the woman you deserted in Texas
when you came north to work for Nicholas Van Zanten."

In making this assertion, Joyce was shooting at a venture. He had deduced the possibility of the relationship,
but he was not sure. The effect upon Fawcett was crushing. His head sank upon his chest, and when he raised
it in a moment the optimistic glow in his hazel eyes was
tarnished forever.

"That is the truth," he said dully. "The boy came to me five years ago, and I found that I loved him. I wanted to make some reparation for the way I had treated his mother."

"So you turned murderer, to make millionaires of yourself—and him. Yes, I've seen the will you induced young Jimmy Van Zanten to sign. Pretty crude, by the way, poisoning that boy after the investigation of the other deaths had started."

"You think so? I'd been feeding him aconitine in infinitesimal doses for five days, since the morning of the day his father died. I thought nobody could ever find out. But what's the use?—I've talked enough."

"Don't kid yourself that I'm through with you. I'll show you another point or two I've got lined up, and then we'll dig deep for motives."

Joyce went behind the screen, and brought out Constance's shoes. "Take a look at these," he said. "You used them to make the false tracks from the house the night the woman was supposed to have run away. You and I know that you poisoned her with prussic acid and hid her body in an old coffin in the vault."

"You can't prove a thing by the shoes," replied Fawcett wearily.

"Perhaps not. I'll admit there are no finger-prints on them. You remembered to wear rubber gloves for that little stunt of walking on your hands."

The murderer's lips twisted in an ironic grimace.

"But there's a heap more to this exhibit." Joyce produced the drinking glass with the flaw like a grain of wheat close to its rim. "That afternoon when Nicholas Van Zanten lay dead, you came into the room and shed crocodile's tears over him. I saw you get between the body and the window sill where there was a glass standing. You substituted a clean glass for the other one, and that's why the police chemists had to report that they found no poison at the bottom. I didn't suspect it at the time. But I'd noticed the flaw in the first glass, and I remembered when I came upon it in your laboratory over the cowshed. Stupid of you to have kept it, Fawcett. It contained traces of aconitine, and your finger-prints are all over it. To cap the evidence"—Joyce lifted a second glass—"this one, the one that reached the police, doesn't have a sign of a flaw."

Fawcett's mouth sagged in a repulsive sneer of shame at his own carelessness. "You might have convicted me on that alone," he muttered. "To think I could have slipped up on such a little point!"

"Murderers usually do, somewhere in the plot. Now, are you going to tell the rest?"

"Anything you like, if you'll only order this cop to let go of my arms. I feel sick. I'd like to sit in a chair."

"Okay." Joyce pushed a chair forward, and glanced at the officer. "You can stand close by and see that he doesn't start anything."

"It would be a great favor, also, if you would permit me to smoke," the self-admitted monster pleaded.

Joyce's eyes narrowed. "He can have that cigar of mine, and welcome," he thought. "I wonder whether he figures it will put the idea of smoking into my head?" He could have laughed right out when Fawcett added:

"Why don't you join me? Tobacco calms the nerves."

But he held himself to replying curtly: "I may in a minute."

A look of grotesque and almost candid disappointment passed over Fawcett's face. He lit his cigar from a match thrust under his nose by the policeman, and puffed upon it avidly, drawing the acrid smoke into his lungs and chewing nervously at the butt. In a second or two, he began to talk:

"I'll tell you first about the poisonings. Strychnine was good enough for George Van Zanten and his daughter,

because I banked on clean death certificates from that
jackass Dr. Henkle, and I didn't fear an inquiry. But when
Nicholas got to worrying, I had to think up something
more subtle. I used aconitine on him and Jimmy, believing that even a thorough autopsy wouldn't turn that up. It
wouldn't either, if you hadn't been snooping around with
your infernal expert knowledge. In Constance's case, I had
to get rid of her in a hurry, because she really did intend
to run away from the house. I fell back on prussic acid,
which advertises itself almost as definitely as a pistol shot.
But you know how I schemed to dispose of the corpse.
Only an uncanny pest like you would have found it."

"Did you have any confederates?" asked Joyce.

"No. I swear it. I used to drop the poisons in food, or
in drinking water, at the last minute. The night I killed
Constance, I stopped Bucklestrope on his way up with the
tray, asked him a question that made him look over his
shoulder and put the acid in the old dame's milk. I never
confided in a soul."

"But Burns knew enough to want to kill us. He—"

"He was sore because you suspected me, because you
set a dick to guard me. Poor Andy! He's too simple-mind-
ed to be useful in a plot like mine. It was I—alone—who
tampered with the corpses in the vault, by the way."

Fawcett had started to speak very rapidly. His words
tumbled over each other. He fidgeted in his chair, and
sucked furiously at his cigar.

"You asked something about my motives," he almost
babbled. "I'll give you the truth. I—I always wanted to
be a millionaire—a millionaire and a country gentleman.
Not just a salaried employee. You understand? Plenty
of ambition, but not much ability. . . . Married badly,
and that held me back, too. Married a dumb servant woman . . . Sarah—good soul, but narrow-minded. She never
forgave me for having that affair—and the child—down

in Dallas, Texas. She'd not have tolerated Andy, but didn't know who he was while he worked for me. I—I intended to poison her at the finish." He came to a stuttering halt.

"Go on," urged Joyce. "Get it all off your chest."

"There isn't much more. Just that I wanted to be a country gentleman—the big garden—Hereford cattle—my own estate. I'd have educated Andy—trained him to be a real son and heir."

Fawcett's voice seemed to snap in his throat, and he laughed harshly.

"This—cigar—has—fixed—me—all right!" he enunciated with immense difficulty, fell over sideways and slipped from his chair to the floor.

Joyce had known from the first word of the final speech what was wrong. But it had been too late to prevent the climax. He covered the distance between himself and Fawcett in a single bound, and instead of testing the prisoner's heart he plunged his fingers into his upper left-hand waistcoat pocket. He brought out a broken cigar, his own panetela which Fawcett had taken from him when the sleight-of-hand exchange had been made.

Then he plucked the still lighted smoke from Fawcett's mouth. He understood perfectly what had happened. The dying poisoner had had two prepared cigars, one with which he hoped to kill Joyce and one for suicide. Failing to trick his victim and sensing he had failed, he had nevertheless been cunning enough to compass his own destruction. He had allowed the harmless panetela to show above the edge of his pocket, and when given permission to smoke he had crushed it down with the same movement that had enabled him to fish out the concealed deadly weed.

While the uniformed policeman went to fetch a doctor, Joyce turned to Kay.

"It's things like that which prevent a guy from getting too conceited," he said. "We had a perfect case, until I slipped up by allowing Fawcett to smoke after he'd wrestled with me. He has cheated the chair."

In view of the fact that the murderer could not be brought to trial, the poisonings at Van Zanten Manor never became widely known to the public. The conviction of Andrew Burns for the comparatively unsensational crime of discharging firearms with intent to kill attracted little notice. The gardener is still serving out a seven-year term at Sing Sing.

But "Poison Case No. 10" remains one of his star affairs in the mind of Inspector Michael Joyce. He sometimes discusses it with his friends and confidants. To complete the record, he identified the poison with which Fawcett had soaked the ends of the two cigars. It was the drug known to science as physostigmine, a product of the Calabar bean. On the West African coast, it is held in high honor for use at trials by ordeal, particularly the trials of witches and congenital liars.

A Calabar bean plant was found growing in the greenhouse of Fawcett's garden. Its longer tendrils were supported by a branch of the equally lethal nux vomica tree.

MURDER CASE
NUMBER 33

Dedicated to the memory of
George S. Dougherty
a great detective
and a good scout

MURDER CASE

NO. 33

by LOUIS CORNELL

AUTHOR of "POISON CASE NO. 10"

DUNNE

CHAPTER ONE
Death Stalks the Red Man

Idle days in the Michael Joyce Detective Agency on lower Broadway were rare, but on a certain soft April morning it appeared that never in the history of the agency had there been so little stirring. The balmy wind that sighed through the open windows overlooking New York harbor was laden with spring fever. "A sure-fire day," as Kay Carey called it, a day which just because it had begun so peacefully was certain to furnish some new and sensational case. As Inspector Joyce's confidential assistant rather than his secretary, Kay enjoyed the privilege of making such poetical remarks. She had a talent for correct hunches.

Michael Joyce, robust and youthful at fifty, a former Inspector in the City Police Force to whom the title had clung, lolled at his desk, his shrewd Irish lips clamped upon the butt of one of his everlasting cigars. His eyes rested affectionately on the nape of Kay Carey's neck as she bent over her typewriter, a few ruddy tendrils of fine hair fluttered by the April breeze.

"She's a great one," he told himself. "Efficient as hell, whether she's slinging words on paper or helping me rope some white-collar crook. A real woman, too. The man she decides to marry will be a lucky guy."

The last thought inevitably caused his glance to wander to the two other persons who shared his private office. He narrowed his eyelids as he looked at his son, Tom. It was no secret that Tom was in love with Kay.

"Yeah, Tom!" Joyce said under his breath dispassionately. "That would be one way of getting her into the family." But he wished that in addition to being an athletic, clean-cut young American, Tom showed more aptitude for the detective business. There had been moments, disturbing to his own vanity, when he had feared he should have launched his son in some other calling.

The fourth individual present, however, was by all manner of means a perfect sleuth of his type. G. Borden Symes, known as the Sheriff, combined an ingenious and observant brain with an exterior drabness that was little short of miraculous. No one ever picked him out of a crowd, so completely did he belong to the gray majority. He made no sounds in sidling through the world, or so it appeared. He was the ideal agency shadow.

Joyce's half-amused contemplation of the Sheriff crouched above a heap of typewritten memoranda and boring silently into them, was interrupted by the jangling of the telephone. He picked up the receiver, and was asked to stand by for a long-distance call.

"Okay!" he said curtly. Long-distance calls were no novelty in that office.

Half a minute later, his assistants heard him reply: "Hello! Joyce speaking." At intervals, he added: "Yes. . . . I get you. . . . Yes. . . . Yes. . . . Fair enough. . . . Good-bye!"

He pushed the instrument aside, rubbed stubby fingers along his outthrust chin, and then tapped on the glass top of his desk.

"Here's a hot sketch for you," he remarked, addressing the room at large. "Dan McCall, a big cattleman from Oklahoma, was just on the wire, talking from Washington. Said a pal of his was in New York, and would phone me during the morning. He wants me to listen to the bozo's story and do what I can for him. Yet he—Dan—refused to tell me a thing in advance."

Kay and Tom looked around briskly. The upper part of the Sheriff's body oozed from among the typewritten notes, and revolved noiselessly until the pale eyes were looking down the pinched nose at Joyce. It was Symes who spoke first.

"I take it that you know this ranchman, Inspector."

"I know who he is."

"He's never been a client of the Agency," commented Kay.

"Good girl. Trust you to remember all the customers' names. Fact is, I never was on any case connected with Dan McCall. But I read the newspapers."

Tom's face remained blank. The Sheriff pursed his lips, implying that he recalled something, but wished to marshal his points before he committed himself. But Kay Carey's eyes snapped, and she burst out spontaneously:

"McCall—from Oklahoma—and visiting Washington. He's been making a stab at learning who murdered several rich Osage Indians near the oil town of Tulsa, or maybe Pawhuska. Probably, he's now trying to interest the Bureau of Indian Affairs."

"Right, to the last word, Kay me darlin'."

The girl's cheeks flushed with pleasure. "But that about lets me out. I'm not familiar with the details of the affair."

"That's not surprising. There's been very little about it in the Eastern papers. Not yet. But I figure that, sooner or later, it's going to break as a national case. Hand me the folder marked 'Osage' from my special file, please."

Kay extracted the correct folder with lightning-fast precision, and Joyce pawed over the contents. He chose a clipping from a Kansas City newspaper, and refreshed his memory from it.

"A full-blooded redskin named Harry Roan was shot between the eyes, at close range. His body was found at the wheel of a parked car, on a country road," pronounced Sheriff Symes in colorless tones.

"Right," said Joyce. "The killing of Roan, however, was the third murder. It occurred last December. Two had taken place before that, and there have been three since—all of 'em blood connections of a single Osage family."

"Was the motive robbery?"

"It isn't clear. Some valuables have been lifted. In the Roan case, a $25,000 insurance policy seemed to have a meaning of its own. For the rest, it looked like vendetta stuff, or the bumping off of more and more people so as to keep their mouths shut about the first of the murders."

"And we're to believe they were really rich Injuns?" said Tom irrelevantly.

"Rich! They were millionaires—every one of them."

"Then, I can't understand why it hasn't caused more talk, Dad."

"A dead Indian isn't such a whale of a sensation, even if he *is* wealthy. We whites butchered too many of them in the early days, I guess, to lose sleep over their killing each other now."

"When you get sarcastic like that, *you* think the mystery a whiz, Inspector," declared Kay softly.

"Well, well! You read me like a book, Kay." Joyce's blue eyes glinted with approval. "Suppose I tell the bunch of ye what's what about the business, and how Dan McCall comes into it. Don't lose track of the fact that we're talking about the Osage nation, which numbers some two thousand men, women and children, owns oil wells worth nearly half a billion dollars and today lives in luxury. Because they're public wards, the individuals can't touch their capital. The Government pays them the income. And when an adult Osage dies, his, or her, income goes for life to the next of kin. They can't make wills."

"I begin to see a motive for members of the tribe bumping off their relatives," commented Tom.

"Yeah." Joyce consulted his newspaper clipping again. "A few years ago, an old Indian widow named Eliza Bigheart died, leaving four daughters. We don't need to bother about one of the latter, who died, too, of natural causes. The other three were Anna, divorced from an Indian named John Kenny, and the widow of a second Indian husband, Joe Brown; Rita, who married a white man named Bill Smith; and Mollie, also the wife of a white man, Ernest Burkhart, a nephew of Dan McCall. Each of these women rated an income from oil of $60,000 a year.

"Pretty nearly two years ago, the body of Anna Brown was found in a woods near Fairfax, Oklahoma. She had been beaten and hacked to death with an axe. Her home in Pawhuska had been ransacked, and a small amount in money and jewels taken. Her divorced husband, John Kenny, was suspected, because he had gone to visit her the morning she was kidnapped. Kenny ducked. But Charley Whitehorn, a friend of his and related to Anna, did some careless talking. He hinted that he knew more than he was willing to tell the police. Four days later, he was found in his car on the roadside, with two bullet holes in the center of his forehead."

"Why, that's the dope on the Harry Roan killing," the Sheriff murmured deprecatingly. "The one I mentioned."

"The two deaths resembled each other, all right. The same methods used. Probably the same murderer. But Charley Whitehorn was bumped two years ago this spring, while Harry Roan didn't get his until last December. In between, there were no homicides."

"And since then?" demanded Kay.

"About three weeks ago, the home of Bill and Rita Smith—Rita being one of old Eliza Bigheart's daughters, you'll remember—was blown to hell with nitroglycerin that had been planted under the porch. The Smiths and a maid named Nettie Brookshire were killed."

"That got a little space in the New York papers, Inspector," said Kay. "It gave me the slant I had upon the whole affair. The authorities couldn't pin the guilt on any one, I believe."

"There were no clues. Dan McCall, the cattleman, was the only person who claimed at any time to have a sound theory. He got into the case several months after the death of Charley Whitehorn. The local Sheriff and the State Police had laid down on the job. Said they couldn't discover why either Charley or Anna Brown had been bumped, and officially dropped the investigation. Dan was so sore, he offered to spend his own money to run down the murderers. He argued that white bandits, who've been pretty thick in the Oklahoma bad lands since the discovery of oil, had pulled off the first crime for purposes of robbery, and had then shot Charley Whitehorn to silence him."

"Did this McCall really do anything?" Sheriff Symes inquired in a characterless undertone.

"He did plenty, according to this Kansas City paper. Took to the hills with a bunch of his cowboys and hunted bandits for months on end. He seems to have failed to prove, so far, that the Indian murders had originated in that quarter. Finally, Roan was shot near Pawhuska and the Smith family blown up in Fairfax. Dan McCall rushed back to civilization and raised the devil with the law for not having prevented these crimes. Now, he's gone to Washington to enlist big-time help."

"Why do you suppose he takes it in such a personal way, Dad?" asked Tom.

"He made his fortune out of the Indian country, and he feels like a sort of guardian of the Osages. That seems to be on the level," answered Joyce. "Besides, you mustn't

forget that his nephew is married to the last of the Bigheart girls, Mollie."

"The last of them!" repeated Kay. "She has inherited
the oil money belonging to her dead sisters, hasn't she?"

"Sure. Her income is now around $180,000 a year."

"Which makes her husband, Burkhart, a rich man. I
wonder how McCall feels about that."

"He doesn't give Burkhart or the said Mollie long to
live," retorted Joyce grimly. "Dan mentioned the point
when he was talking to me on the phone. Thinks they'll be
the next to be murdered, and then the dough will pass to
a first cousin of the Bighearts, a blanket Indian who still
wears feathers in his hair."

"Still, if Mollie does survive!" the Sheriff mumbled.

"Are you comparing her wealth to Dan's? He's far richer
than she. He holds title to half a county of grazing land,
and he could make a mistake of a thousand here or there
in counting his head of cattle and never miss it. Why, the
guy paid Federal income tax on more than a quarter of a
million dollars last year, including his own oil interests."

"It's a wonder the bandits didn't kill him first," said
Tom.

"Getting at a man who lives surrounded by husky cow-
punchers is no snap. But the Burkharts are town folks.
They could be bombed at night, the way the Smiths were.
Dan has tried to get them to remove to his ranch for safety, but they refuse to go."

The Sheriff moved his head and stared at the floor with
his blank eyes. He seemed as fundamentally lethargic and
unworthy of notice as a member of the unemployed class
who stares vacantly into an excavation on some street corner.

"If Harry Roan carried a life insurance policy for
$25,000, the beneficiary is certainly a suspect," he remarked.

"Yes. Dan's whole theory, however, is confused by
this very point. Roan's policy was in favor of a white

cowboy named Jonathan Rumsey, or Ramsey—both names are given in the newspaper stories. He was one of Dan's own cowboys, and he was the dead Indian's particular pal. Rumsey had been out with the posse, hunting bandits. But he happened to be in Pawhuska on an errand, when the news reached town that Roan's body had been found. Rumsey had a perfect alibi as to the shooting of Roan."

"He might have had the crime committed," suggested Tom.

"Then we've got to ask yourselves: 'By whom?' By the same hand which had plugged holes in Charley White-horn's forehead in almost exactly similar circumstances? Dan thinks an outlaw killed Whitehorn. But the outlaws would have had small reason to go after Harry Roan, who was a tight-mouthed redskin and had never let out a grunt about the previous murders."

"Suppose the cowboy had been double-crossing his boss, McCall. Suppose this Rumsey, or Ramsey, is secretly in cahoots with the bandits, and tipped them to shoot Roan so that he could collect the insurance money," said Kay.

"Smart girl. It would take a lot of proving, though."

"In my opinion, it's nothing but a race quarrel," declared young Tom Joyce. "The Indians are jealous of each other's riches, and they've gone bloodthirsty for the sake of gain, just as they used to do when they took the war-path with tomahawks."

The Inspector looked curiously at his son. "They fought tribe against tribe in the old days. Murder within the ranks of a nation—as with these Osages—wasn't at all their style. But never mind. Whose trail would you follow?"

"The blood that disappeared seems the suspicious customer to me. Kenny was his name, wasn't it?"

"What had Kenny to gain? He was divorced from Anna Bigheart, and no longer an heir."

"Well, he did skip. I'd want to know why."

"So would I. That he was reported to have been snooping around her before she started on her last journey was enough to scare him silly." Joyce paused, and laughed. "We have almost no dope on this case. Only the little I remember, the newspaper clippings, and what Dan McCall told me over the phone. Yet we sit here discussing it, as if the Agency had been given the job of solving it."

"I'm thinking the Agency will be asked to do just that, Inspector," said Kay.

"One of your hunches, me darlin'?" Joyce's eyes twinkled.

"More than that. McCall wouldn't have spoken to you the way he did, if he hadn't hoped to line you up."

"I haven't heard from his friend yet. I don't know what his friend wants."

"You'll be hearing any minute now."

"Maybe."

But when the telephone rang and Kay Carey answered it, her face fell. "The switchboard says a Mr. Allan Eagle wants to speak to you, Inspector."

"Eagle? I don't know the name. Jewish, I guess. Find out what he wants."

Kay spoke again into the receiver, then held the latter against her chest. "Why—why, it's the Indian from Oklahoma," she stammered. "He was on the wire himself this time, and he's got a strong English accent."

Joyce smiled. "So it's that kind of an Eagle! Whadya mean *English* accent? I'll talk."

He took the instrument, and snapped: "Hello! Michael Joyce speaking."

"Good morning, Inspector Joyce. Allow me to introduce myself," came the reply, in the perfectly modulated tones peculiar to graduates of Oxford University. "I am Allan Eagle, or, to be exact, Chief Allan Black-Horse Eagle, of Pawhuska, the individual mentioned to you this morning by my friend, Mr. Daniel McCall."

"Happy to know you, Chief," answered Joyce drily. "Anything I can do?"

"I understood that you would be willing to see me, and—er—discuss steps that might be taken to clear up an unpleasant situation in which I and my family find ourselves."

"Right. I told McCall I would at least talk things over with you."

"That is very kind. But, Inspector, I am forced to ask a special favor of you. Naturally, I should call at your office. Instead, I beg you to be so good as to come to my hotel, the Hermitage, Forty-first Street and Seventh Avenue, before noon."

Joyce frowned slightly. "I'll be up, if nothing else will do. But my time is valuable, you know."

"I fully appreciate that, and I am more than grateful, believe me." The soft and courteous voice became colored with embarrassment. "I can explain the difficulty in a word. I have brought several members of my family to New York, and at the moment their nerves are shaken to such a point that it is impossible for me to leave them."

"Yes," commented Joyce.

"You see, Inspector," declared Chief Allan Black-Horse Eagle coolly, almost negligently, "an attempt to murder me was made here less than half an hour ago."

CHAPTER TWO
"They Called It Suicide"

After Inspector Joyce had listened to the astounding assertion that an attempt had been made to murder a chief of the Osage nation in the heart of New York City, he promised curtly to get to the hotel without delay. Then he flung himself back in his desk chair and gave his assistants the gist of the information, in phrases that crackled like machine-gun fire. He glanced from the piquant Irish face of red-haired Kay to those of his son Tom and Sheriff Symes inviting comment.

"Sounds like business for the Police, rather than for a private detective," the Sheriff pronounced judicially.

"This end of it does. But the bird is hot on seeing me about his Oklahoma troubles. I'm going on up."

"What's his connection with the victims who've already lost their lives, the ones you've been telling us about?" asked Tom.

"I don't know. All the Osages are blood relations, more or less. The thing that flattens me is the way this Eagle guy talks. It's the high-fallutin' Oxford accent, no less."

"I'll bet I can explain that, Inspector," cried Kay, her eyes dancing. "He's a Rhodes scholar."

"What?" exclaimed Joyce, startled.

"A Rhodes scholar. Each State in the Union is entitled to two scholarships at Oxford, under the will of Cecil

Rhodes. Why shouldn't Oklahoma have sent an Indian? In fact, it came back to me while you were on the phone that I'd read of such an election four or five years ago."

Joyce leaped from his chair, went over to a bookcase and took down an almanac dealing with intercollegiate matters. He kept his feet moving, as he rustled through the pages. It was an idiosyncrasy of his to walk back and forth, while he read. In a moment, he had found what he wanted and slammed the volume shut.

"Damned if you aren't right," he said. "I call that swell. A brain that stores up information about people, and knows how to draw upon it, is a good detective's brain."

He stepped closer to the girl and let his big hand fall lightly upon her shoulder. "Just after the World War, Allan Black-Horse Eagle was chosen by the Committee of Selection in his State to take advantage of the Rhodes bequest," he continued, speaking at large. "Which of us besides Kay remembered that?"

The Sheriff shrugged his shoulders. "I didn't. It's impossible to remember everything, Boss," he breathed reproachfully.

Tom looked sheepish, and shook his head.

"Well, I didn't remember it myself, as you all may have noticed," said Joyce, faintly jocular. "But I'm tickled to have the tip-off. Always like to be better posted on a customer than he thinks I am. We'll be running up together to see the chief, Kay, if you'll get that little freckled nose of yours powdered as quick as God will let you."

Her cheeks flushed with pleasure, the girl hurried from the office and returned in fewer than five minutes, a miracle of make-up accomplished, and wearing a hat and a light spring coat. Joyce grinned his approval of her soldiery celerity.

The two dropped down to the street level and took a taxicab. As they lurched up Broadway, Joyce settled his large

frame comfortably in a corner, and began capriciously to
discourse on his hobby—the collecting of deadly weapons.
Above the noise and the jolting of the vehicle, he described
some of the prizes he had found recently at auctions.

"But I turn up the best items through sheer luck," he
declared. "Never knew that to fail. I'm working on a case,
maybe, in which weapons don't figure, and suddenly I
stumble on something grand. Last week, I was shadow-
ing a sea captain on that smuggling investigation for the
Green Funnel Line. I follow him into a sailors' hotel on
South Street, and right there in the lobby an old hardtack
is sitting, polishing the blade of a Zulu assegai. As soon as
the captain is safe in his room, I go after the assegai and
buy it for four bucks cash. Some bargain, I'm telling you!"

"I thought you had plenty of those in your museum
already," commented Kay.

"Assegais? The English-manufactured trade goods—yes.
But you recall the lozenge-shaped blade at the end of the
light wooden shaft—that sort of blade used to be ham-
mered out of raw iron by the Zulus. It took weeks to make
one. The spear I found the other day was a real specimen
from the ancient times. Luckily for me, the sailor didn't
seem to know the difference."

Joyce enlarged upon the subject with gusto, while Kay
stared at him, impressed by his unquenchable enthusiasm.
The fact that he was on his way to a rendezvous of excep-
tional promise seemed to have slipped out of his mind.
Yet the instant the cab stopped in front of the Hermitage
Hotel, he reverted to the business in hand.

"If Dan McCall's theory is correct, the key to the whole
plot against the Osages is the leader of the band of white
outlaws in Oklahoma. Bert Lawson, his name is; I forgot
to mention it," said Joyce, his tone an indication to the
observant Kay that one compartment of his brain had not
ceased to busy itself with the mystery.

They entered the hotel and headed straight for the desk, to phone their names to Chief Allan Black-Horse Eagle. But before they were a third of the way, they were abruptly halted by the sight of a group of persons whose exotic appearance was proving vastly beguiling to many patrons of the hostelry. Huddled in the middle of the lobby were seven American Indians, dressed in their full tribal regalia. Four of them were men of various ages, and three were women of notably advanced years. The men wore buckskin coats with fringed borders, and ordinary trousers down the sides of which had been stitched bands in a checkered pattern of white and red; on their heads were the great feather bonnets characteristic of all branches of the Sioux race. The old women were so muffled in particolored blankets that nothing showed of their costumes underneath, except the tails of their long skirts.

Joyce looked narrowly at these strangely impassive aborigines, concentrating presently upon the youngest of the men. The latter stood a little apart from his companions. He had smooth bronze-colored skin, and aquiline features of a pronounced type. The eyes were set far apart, the cheek-bones salient and the mouth wide. The perfect gravity of his expression was tempered by a certain alertness with which his glance swept the crowd. He appeared to be secretly interested, whereas the other redskins were stolid.

Followed by Kay, Joyce walked up to the young Indian. Before the white man could utter a word, the other bowed almost imperceptibly and said in the cultivated voice that had sounded so attractive over the telephone:

"Inspector Joyce, I imagine? Allan Eagle, at your service."

"Well—um—Mr. Eagle," replied Joyce, nonplussed. "This strikes me as being rather a public place for a conference."

"Of course, Inspector. You will pardon my waiting for you here. After what occurred—you know!—my people were not happy in the rooms upstairs. They did not feel safe. I thought it well to humor them. But now that a celebrated detective has arrived, they will not hesitate to go with us to my suite."

He turned and pronounced some guttural phrases. The six Indians to whom he had spoken grunted, and then stalked towards the elevator. They had been credited with "nerves," and what amounted to fear, but they exhibited not the least sign of suffering from these emotions. The mechanical contrivance of the lift must have been novel and disagreeable to them, yet they maintained an outer aspect of total indifference to its workings. Allan Eagle, suavely talkative in English, was the only one who tried to make their visitors feel at home.

On the ninth floor, the party entered a suite with windows opening on Seventh Avenue. Introductions became in order, and Eagle repeated the different Osage names in both languages. The designation "Horse" formed a part of all of them. The man closest in age to himself was Joe Yellow-Horse, while the two older men were Sam and Thomas Swift-Horse. The ancient women answered to the simple names of Sue, Jane and Mary Many-Horses. None of them spoke English readily, with the exception of Joe Yellow-Horse, and he was satisfied to leave the negotiations to Allan.

Joyce, who had been quivering with impatience, said bluntly:

"You can spring your story any way you wish, but I think you'd better start by describing the attack made upon you in this hotel."

"Very well, sir. I was standing alone by that center window, and with one hand resting on the ledge I was leaning out as far as possible to see which of the great skyscrapers

were visible. I was suddenly aware of an object flashing
in the sunlight close to me, and the next moment I felt a
sharp blow in the ribs. I jumped backwards, pretty nearly
to the middle of the room. Fortunately, it turned out that
the missile had just grazed me, ripping my coat and bruis-
ing my ribs. There were no serious results."

"You have changed the coat. Please let me see the one
you were wearing at the time," snapped Joyce.

Allan took a buckskin garment which had been thrown
carelessly over the back of a chair, and handed it to the
detective. Joyce noted a rent about three inches long, un-
stained with blood, and apparently made by an instrument
with a dulled edge.

"What became of the weapon?" he asked.

"I do not know. It did not enter the room, and must
have dropped back into the street."

"Was it a knife, or what?"

"Positively, I cannot give you a clue, Inspector. I caught
a mere glimpse of the thing, and immediately jumped away
from it. I did not return to the window for several minutes, when I assured myself that it was not to be found, on
the sill or elsewhere."

"Have you notified the Police?"

"No."

"Why not? You should do it at once. This is a Police
matter. The weapon was probably thrown—or fired—from
that office building across the street. The Police may be
able to trace the room from which it came."

A curious look of arrogance took possession of the
Indian's face. Not a muscle moved, but it was as though a
film had fallen upon his features, and his eyes hardened.

"I shall not tell the Police. I shall make no complaint,"
he asserted.

"But, look here—"

"There is no law to compel me to report an attempt upon my life," interrupted Chief Allan Black-Horse Eagle sternly. "I choose to ignore what has happened in New York. I am here to consult you about treachery and murder in Oklahoma."

Joyce fixed the Chief with the shrewd, cold stare that had been the terror of evil-doers when he had been in charge of the Homicide Squad of New York's Finest. He thought swiftly, and unexpectedly he smiled.

"Any objections to *my* trying to solve the mystery of how you were wounded?"

"None—if I engage you for the principal case."

"You mean if I *take* your case."

"Let us leave it at that."

"All right. Now tell me what you've got on your mind."

"Are you familiar with the killings which have occurred around Pawhuska and Fairfax, in my State?"

"I know about the deaths of Anna Brown, Charley Whitehorn, Harry Roan and the Smith family."

"They have not been the only ones. Twelve days ago, a venerable Osage named Flying-Horse-Tail Eagle was found dead, with a knife in his heart and his fingers closed upon the handle of the knife. They called it suicide, but I believe it to have been murder. The dead man was my uncle, only brother of my father Chief Pale-Horse Eagle. I tell you, Inspector Joyce, there is a plot to wipe out every prominent man and woman in the whole Osage nation. Some way must be found to prevent that."

"Your State authorities?" growled Joyce.

"They have shown neither sympathy nor understanding. They have failed to make a single arrest."

"I know it. But what do you expect to be able to do?"

"Get at the bottom of the plot. Upon Daniel McCall's recommendation, I wish to employ you to investigate the death of my uncle. You're an outsider, and you'll not attract too much attention if you work upon a single case—especially one that the newspapers have overlooked, believing it to have been suicide. But if you discover who murdered my uncle, I feel sure we can break up the conspiracy."

To Kay's surprise, the expression about the Inspector's mouth became frankly contemptuous.

"May I ask what object you had in bringing a whole party to New York, to see me?" he demanded. "And in Indian costume, too! Were you set on advertising the business to the newspapers, not to mention any enemies you may have?"

Allan Eagle stiffened. It was clear that his pride seldom received the shock of such brusque questioning. But in addition to being an Osage chief, he had absorbed the white man's culture and this enabled him to control himself.

"It does need explaining," he said quietly. "We have our peculiar tribal laws and household laws. Employing a pale-face detective is, to us, a very serious step. No one person could presume to act for all the branches of a family. I represent my father. These others are witnesses—even though they speak few words—for various tepees of cousins."

Without waiting for an answer, he translated his remarks into Osage, for the benefit of the elders, who replied with grunts of approval.

"And the fancy-dress?" Joyce prodded.

"It is no masquerade to us," Allan declared icily. "It is the costume of our ancestors, the clothes that mark us as Osages instead of conquered creatures glad to hide their red skins under the stuff you make in factories."

"No offense meant," retorted Joyce, smiling. "But I didn't know you cared much in Oklahoma about that race pride business. It's a new high-brow notion among Indians, isn't it. Maybe you picked it up at Oxford, Chief, and the more credit to you if you did."

Allan leaned forward, faintly startled. "You'd actually heard about my being a Rhodes scholar?"

"Sure. What important folks have done interests me. I keep posted on general principles." For Kay's benefit, Joyce caused the skin at the corner of the eye nearest to her to pucker. "But let's get down to tacks. You claim the murders in your country are part of a scheme to kill all the big-wigs among the Osages?"

"Just so."

"And you want me to save the rest as I can?"

"Yes."

"Well, from my point of view, it's the bunk. Call in United States troops, if it's as bad as you say. I'd never be able to satisfy you, and I'll not take the case."

For the first time, an emotion mirrored itself plainly on Allan Eagle's face. He looked intensely chagrined.

"I suppose you believe me to have a foolish, exaggerated view of our trouble," he said.

"Exaggerated—probably. But I'd not go so far as to call it foolish."

"If I can't convince you, I can't, Inspector Joyce."

"Hm! By the way, does Dan McCall go as far as you do on this plot theory?"

"I'm afraid not. McCall puts it down to gang murder and robbery, with little plotting. I say it's sinister that one Bigheart after another, or protector of the Bighearts, should have been picked off, and the doom then pass on to my own family. The cursed oil money is motive enough, for it would make the last survivor richer than Croesus. My father predicted this, when the liquid gold was discovered years ago. He had the gift of prophecy, and I—his son—bow down before his wisdom."

Joyce gnawed scornfully at his lower lip. "What does the Sheriff of Osages County think?"

"Sheriff Hawes has never deigned to discuss the murders with an Indian."

"Hawes!—Luther Hawes!" the detective exclaimed.

"Why, yes. That is his name."

"I ran into him on a case at Fort Smith, Arkansas, a few years back. So Luther Hawes is your Sheriff. Tell you what I'll do, Chief. I'll put through a long-distance call to him right now, and find out for myself whether he thinks you Horse-Eagles are in danger."

"It will be perfectly agreeable to me, Inspector," Allan replied in his impeccable English.

Joyce sat by the telephone table, gave his order to the operator, and then lighted a fresh cigar. The glance which Kay intercepted revealed nothing of his mood. He drummed with stubby fingertips on the top of the small, square table. The moment the connection had been established, he shouted a curt greeting over the wire to the man in Oklahoma and made his request for information in short, lucid phrases. Without stating the whereabouts of Allan Black-Horse Eagle, he asked, in effect, whether the latter and the latter's story were worthy of credence. For a full five minutes thereafter he listened silently. Then he said, "Thank you!" and hung up.

He stuck both hands in his side pockets and walked over to Allan. "Sheriff Hawes says you're crazy as hell," he declared, while still gripping the cigar with his teeth.

Allan lifted his chin, and made a contemptuous gesture with his right hand.

"Says Dan McCall is looney, too," went on Joyce. "Says the Indian murders have been routine crimes, and that he can prevent any more from occurring."

"You accept his professional opinion, of course?" interrogated Allan, his voice sphinxlike in its concealment of either resentment or irony.

"I'll tell you what I think of Luther Hawes and his opinions." Joyce snatched the cigar from his mouth, and spoke fiercely. "Hawes is the biggest fathead I ever ran into, on a criminal investigation. At Fort Smith, I couldn't teach him to tell the difference between good money and the counterfeit bills we were working to trace. He took a handful of bad twenties in change himself. If that guy knocks you, you must be all right. If he claims you're talking through your feather bonnet, said story of yours begins to have weight with me."

"Which means?" urged Allan softly.

"It means that you can count on Michael Joyce and the Joyce Detective Agency. I'm ready to go West with you to Pawhuska, as soon as you say the word."

CHAPTER THREE
The Foe Strikes Again

Triumph glowed briefly in Chief Allan Eagle's eyes as he perceived that he had made his point, and that Michael Joyce, most eminent of private detectives, would work to lift the pall of tragic mystery which brooded over the Osage nation. Subtly, the Indian's features brightened to human friendliness. For the first time, both Joyce and Kay realized that in addition to being handsome in a noble mold, he was gifted with more than the average share of masculine charm.

Allan stretched out a sinewy brown hand. "I am awfully grateful to you for tackling this," he said, the formality disappearing from his voice. "Let's shake on it.

"Oh, that's all right," growled Joyce, gripping the hand bearishly. "It's in the day's work."

"Then I'll call your offer to leave for Pawhuska on short notice. We must hop by the next transcontinental plane." Allan's accent was still that of Oxford, but he used Western idioms.

"By plane!" repeated Joyce sharply. "You want to fly your whole crowd to Oklahoma?"

"No, no! Just you and I by aeroplane, Inspector. We can put the others on the train. Joe Yellow-Horse here speaks English well enough to take care of the party."

"I see. But I want my secretary, Miss Carey, to go along with us."

Allan turned to Kay, with a shadowy smile and a slight, but gracious, inclination of the head. "Splendid! Our air trip will be made all the pleasanter. Will you and the Inspector have lunch with us, Miss Carey? I can order it sent up from the dining room?"

"One minute," interrupted Joyce. "When does the plane leave?"

"At three-thirty, from Newark, New Jersey."

"And it's after twelve now. Sorry we can't accept the bid to lunch. We've got to run home for our bags."

Allan seemed disappointed. He checked a gesture of protest, and said evenly: "You know best. When may I expect you back?"

"By two-fifteen."

The Indian escorted them ceremoniously to the elevator, and thereby caused confusion and alarm in the breasts of some New England schoolteachers, members of the vast army of tourists who pass unnoticed in the metropolis. Horrified at the sight of a genuine feather bonnet, the prim ladies stumbled backward into the rooms from which they had been emerging.

In less than five minutes, Joyce and Kay were at the street door of the hotel. The detective threw a sidelong glance at his secretary and grinned.

"What we'll do first is to snatch a quick bite by ourselves. I want to talk to you."

He led the way around the corner to a grillroom, which despite the hour and the crowded neighborhood afforded some privacy at its side tables set in alcoves. Joyce snapped out an order for hot roast beef sandwiches and coffee, and then leaned towards Kay.

"Well, what do you think of the business?" he asked.

"It's pretty complicated, Inspector." She traced vague patterns on the tablecloth with the nail of one finger. "I don't have the experience to—to see all that you probably see in it."

"Listen, Kay. I'm not asking you for a snap solution of the case. I'm a long ways from having one myself. But there's the makings of a grand little detective in you, and I want to train you as we go along. Just tell me what hits you hardest about the doings this morning." His voice was rich with blarney where she was concerned, yet had an acid undertone.

"The killings in Oklahoma have certainly been murders; we can leave the how and the why until we get out there," she answered, brightening. "The attempt this morning against Allan Eagle is really the puzzle that should be cleared up first. It's weird."

"Just so."

"There may be lots of reasons why an enemy should follow him to New York and try to put him out of the way."

"Of course."

"But no rational explanation of why he prefers to keep the attack a secret from the law. His attitude throws a doubt upon his sincerity. His sincerity with you, I mean. It suggests he may be covering up some trick of his own that went wrong."

"Now you've put your finger on it. Gee whiz, Kay, I knew I could trust that smart bean of yours to work right! We're on a case where our client goes, right off, on the list of suspects."

"Not as a murderer, surely! The Chief didn't commit the series of Osage murders," protested Kay, aghast.

"I'm far from saying he did—but he may have! Anything's possible in a homicide mystery, as you ought to know. He's a good-looker, if that's what you mean, me darlin'."

Kay shook her finger familiarly at her boss. "I'm an operative on the job, and I have no eye for handsome Indians. But if he's crooked, I can't see why he should risk consulting you."

"Dan McCall is investigating this case, too, and Dan told the Chief to come here. Don't forget that."

"A redskin bluff, eh?"

"It might be. Still, I'm taking him at his face value. I'm working for and not against him."

"Is there anything to be done, before we leave, to check up his account of the attack?"

"Plenty. I'll put the office on it. I'll do a bit of investigating myself. And if you keep *your* eyes and ears open, it won't harm."

The sandwiches had been brought while they talked, and they ate hurriedly.

"That rent in Allan Eagle's coat—it was never made by the blade of a knife," commented Kay. "The edges are not sufficiently clean cut."

"Good dope. But if the knife had spun around before it struck, the handle could have done it. Or an arrow—had you thought of that?—the head of an old Injun arrow which had gone blunt and rusty."

"Attempted murder in Times Square with a bow and arrow?" the girl demanded incredulously.

"We have a pack of braves and blanketed squaws in our midst. So why not an enemy with weapons to match? A missile seems to have been discharged from across the street at a window in the Hermitage Hotel. Since no gun was used, a bow would have been about the best substitute."

Joyce snapped his fingers to summon the waiter with the check. He paid, and stood up.

"I'll be asking you to fetch my duds, as well as your own," he said. "It won't be the first time you've packed my bag for a business trip."

"You bet, Inspector. I'll stop at your house on my way back, and old Biddy will let me up to your room. Where will I find you?"

"Nearest crossing to where we are now. Forty-first and Seventh, on the northwest corner."

Nodding briskly, Kay darted away. The detective paused near the front door of the grillroom and entered a telephone booth. He put through a call to his office, which was answered by his son Tom.

"I'll be hopping out to Oklahoma this afternoon, and taking Kay with me," he declared, and proceeded to sketch the essentials of the case. The trivial wound that Allan Eagle had received in his hotel suite was mentioned briefly.

"There's one thing I want you to get busy upon," he said in conclusion. "Try to learn through the Police Department and all lost and found agencies whether a weapon of any kind was picked up in the street this morning, in front of the Hermitage. Stick an advertisement in the papers, offering a reward for the return of an arms collector's curio dropped there—yes, put it in just those words, 'an arms collector's curio.' I'll be in touch with you by wire. That's all. S'long!"

Joyce stepped out of the booth, lighting a cigar as he came. He walked without undue haste to the office building across the way from the Hermitage Hotel, and rode up to the ninth floor. The fact that there was a row of empty offices facing the street at that level had already been noted by him, before he had quit the Osage Indians. Instead of asking the superintendent of the building to let him in, he had decided to learn whether the doors of any of the rooms happened to be unlocked. The second handle that he tried yielded, and he found himself in a bare cubicle, the dusty floor of which was zig-zagged with footprints.

He scrutinized the tracks interestedly. They had been made by feet, encased in rubber galoshes of an unusually

large size. The last-named, also, had been brand new, as
indicated by the clear prints left by the ribbed pattern on
the soles. Joyce pinched his chin and stared, surprised.

"A man who wore rubbers indoors, on a fine spring
day," he muttered.

The trail led straight to the window, which was open,
and then went away. No further clues could be discovered
there, or, indeed, anywhere else in the room. The prowler
had evidently been gloved, for the window-frame and even
the handle of the door were unmarked by fingerprints.
Joyce shrugged, and contented himself with measuring the
huge outline of a foot, using for the purpose a pocket rule
he always carried. Then he returned to the window, and
spied patiently upon the occupants of Chief Allan Black-
Horse Eagle's suite.

He observed a couple of waiters remove a luncheon
table and close the door behind them. Stalking to and
fro were the Indian men, while in an adjoining room the
women could be seen perched stolidly on the edge of the
bed. None of them appeared to be concerned about getting
ready for the return journey, their facial make-up being
primitive and their baggage scanty. But as Joyce watched,
two of the braves drew apart and began to argue heatedly.
They were sparing of gestures, yet there was no mistak-
ing the significance of their heads tilted backwards until
the feather bonnets shook, and the abnormal rigidity of
their bodies. They stood at the far side of the room in
semi-obscurity, and it was impossible to tell at that distance whether Allan was one of them. Joyce peered and
scowled, and longed for a pair of binoculars. The Indians
dragged out their dispute interminably, and he could make
nothing of it.

A little after two o'clock, he gave up and went to the
street corner appointed with Kay as a rendezvous. The girl
was late. She piled out of a taxicab with the bags at two

twenty-five, panting an account of unavoidable delays at her home and traffic difficulties. Joyce grinned aside her excuses. He seized the luggage in both hands, and the pair hurried to the hotel.

Once more, the pilgrims from the Osage country were awaiting them in the lobby. But Allan Eagle's eyes were now fixed anxiously upon the clock. It became a problem of summoning porters, lining up three cabs at the curb and distributing the passengers and their belongings comfortably. As the Indians emerged on to the sidewalk, passersby turned their heads casually and a few halted to goggle. The sensation-proof New Yorkers, however, plainly regarded the group as being part of an inferior Wild West show.

Joyce and Kay found themselves seated opposite to two of the ancient squaws. The latter gazed ahead with blank eyes, and did not utter a word. They paid no attention to the sights of the vast city through which they were riding. Even the surging crowds and the tangle of vehicles which slowed their progress seemed powerless to make the least impression upon their invulnerable stoicism.

At the Pennsylvania Station, Allan, who had arrived first, was busy marshalling his tribe and engaging red-caps. The great terminus had no terrors for him. But Joe Yellow-Horse, despite his knowledge of white men's lore, was standing around with a helpless look not far removed from idiocy.

The party moved in a straggling procession toward the ticket window. They aroused even less interest than had been the case in Times Square. Persons who are about to take trains are mentally prepared for odd traveling companions. The Pennsylvania Station sees the arrival, or departure, of some delegation of exotics almost every day in the year.

Allan gravely purchased the necessary tickets, and soon the passengers were descending to the platform, where the

electrified trains glided in and out with formidable efficiency, smokeless and clean in the half light.

Aboard the pullman, the Indians sat dolefully, with the
exception of Allan, who as soon as the train left the tun-
nel on the Jersey side, pressed his face against the window,
frankly absorbed by the view of Manhattan's skyscrapers
receding in the distance. There was no opportunity for
Joyce and Kay to exchange words with him. They watched
curiously his bronze profile, as austere and pure in type as
a medallion wrought by a sculptor of genius.

But before many minutes had passed, the train was
drawing into Broad Street Station, Newark. Allan swung
around to his people and spoke in the Osage dialect, addressing Joe Yellow-Horse in particular. They answered
him with gruff and guttural sounds, their heads nodding
slightly. Then he signed to a porter to take his baggage,
which was a canvas roll fastened with rawhide straps. Joyce
obtained another servitor for himself and Kay. The Indians left behind did not so much as glance sideways out of
the window as the three walked by along the platform.

They caught a taxicab, and gave the address of the transcontinental flying field. Bumping and jerking over the un-
even streets, they merely looked at one another without
talking. Conversation would have been too great an effort,
and the Chief's thoughts appeared to be far away.

When they stood at last beside the gigantic passenger
plane, its engines throbbing and its propeller already ro-
tating tentatively, Allan smiled unexpectedly and spoke,
his stern Osage mannerisms fallen from him like a cloak.

"My people call that the thunderbird," he said, pointing at the plane.

"The name describes it okay," growled Joyce.

"Doesn't it? You know, there has always been a thunderbird in our legends. He was supposed to come with the
storm, when he would roar and throw lightning-bolts as

arrows. He brought rain, and we pray to him in the dry season. When Indians first saw a flying ship, they thought it must be the original thunderbird. We've never quite given up the idea. Picturesque, to my mind, for the plane is the American thunderbird indeed. I've never traveled in one before, by the way."

"You're taking it pretty coolly, Chief," commented Joyce drily.

"Why not? Every new experience should be a fine adventure—even death."

They climbed a step ladder, Kay Carey first, and entered the cabin of the pulsing craft. Only then, in the few minutes that remained before the clamor of the engines would drown out speech, did Allan revive the topic that obsessed the minds of all of them. He suddenly brought his head around with a bird-like quirk and looked quizzically at the detective.

"Well, did you learn anything in that building on the opposite side of the street?" he asked.

"Not a hell of a lot," answered Joyce calmly. "Footprints that might have been made by the janitor, that's all."

"But you wondered, perhaps, why Joe Yellow-Horse and myself should be wrangling?"

"You could see me watching you?" queried the detective, in some astonishment.

"Oh, yes! Indians do have the gift of long-range vision, Inspector. Even from the back of a darkish room, I made out that part of your head which showed beyond the window frame. The quarrel, however, was not important, not worth observing. Just a little family disagreement."

"Glad to be set straight," Joyce grumbled, feeling uncomfortably as though the Chief had reversed their roles and become the detective.

"While you were absent, the case nevertheless took a new turn."

"Yes?"

"I received a telegram from Oklahoma. Ah, my friend, it is going to be more interesting for you than just looking into the stale mystery of my old uncle, dead and buried nearly two weeks ago!"

"What's in the wire?" Joyce rapped out.

Allan handed him, without further comment, a blue-and-white telegraph form, which read:

JENNIE DEERFOOT GONE TO HAPPY HUNTING GROUNDS STOP HER UN-WOUNDED BODY FOUND IN WOODS BUT MURDER FEARED STOP HURRY BACK

CHIEF PALE-HORSE EAGLE

"She was the sister of the girl, Sylvia Deerfoot, to whom I am betrothed," explained Allan grimly.

Before Joyce could answer, the spinning propeller whined in a noisy crescendo, the plane lurched forward, gathered momentum, and soaring into the air it hurtled westward.

CHAPTER FOUR
Can Murder Leave No Trace?

After a stop-over at Columbus, Ohio, the plane completed the second leg of its coast-to-coast journey at Topeka, Kansas, late the following afternoon. Inspector Joyce, Kay and Allan descended at Topeka and caught a slow train, which meandered due South to the Indian reservations of Oklahoma and would land them at Pawhuska at eight in the morning. Luckily, there was a single pullman sleeper attached, and they were able to crawl into their bunks early for the rest they sorely needed. The level prairie slipped past, formless as the ocean, and almost as sombre by night.

They awakened instinctively an hour before their scheduled arrival, made their toilets and drank coffee peddled by the Negro conductor from a thermos bottle. At the Pawhuska station, they were the only passengers to get off. An automobile was waiting for them, and this proved to be an eye-opener for Kay—and to some extent for Joyce, also—in the ways of the newly-rich Osages. The car was an enormous limousine, painted lavender, and of a flashy model that would have elicited smiles on Fifth Avenue. Its cost could not have been less than $12,000.

In the back seat alone, his arms folded, sat a venerable Indian, dressed in much the same style as Allan, with feather bonnet and striped trousers, but wearing instead of a buckskin coat a white woolen shirt and sleeveless tunic.

Embroidered on the deep cuffs of the shirt were lozenges and arrowheads in red, while on the tunic over his heart was a design which roughly suggested a spray of three-leaved clover. His two companions, however, by no means flaunted the aboriginal costume. The man at the wheel was in an ill-fitting chauffeur's uniform, immoderately decorated with piping of crimson velvet and with gold braid on his cap. The other attendant, who loafed with one foot on the dashboard, was tightly buttoned in a sack suit of a loud checked pattern; a gray felt hat rested upon black hair so lank and long behind that it was like a girl's bob.

"My father, Chief Pale-Horse Eagle," said Allan quietly, as he conducted the visitors to the car and presented them to the old man inside. "He can speak only a few words of English."

The patriarch bowed with extraordinary dignity and replied, spacing his syllables in labored fashion: "Good morn-ing, miss and sir. Wel-come."

"He is the real Chief, the head of our branch of the Osage nation," continued Allan. "I am only called Chief by courtesy, because I am his heir."

Thereupon, he turned and introduced the fellow in the checked suit: "Harry Deerfoot, brother of my fiancée, Inspector Joyce. Brother, too, I scarcely need to add, of the girl who has died so mysteriously."

His grotesque clothes did not prevent Harry Deerfoot from responding with a certain native grace. He removed his hat, and stepped forward lithely to shake hands.

"We can drive you now to our home, where you will do us the honor to live as guests," said Allan. "But perhaps you would prefer to go and look at the dead girl first?"

"Where is the body?" Joyce inquired.

"Coffin got um. She lie in her own front parlor since las' night," Harry Deerfoot volunteered.

"Turned over to you by the authorities already, eh?
They evidently don't believe she met with foul play."

"Sheriff Hawes, him say it is not murder," declared
Harry, with extreme sadness.

"Of course, I want to see her right off."

They took their places in the luxurious car, Kay Carey
beside the old Chief, Joyce and Allan on the folding seats
in front of them, and Harry beside the chauffeur. Allan
gave an order in Osage, and the limousine swooped forward in a reckless jet of speed which its perfect construction and huge, springy tires saved from being discom-
moding to the passengers. Allan caught the detective's eye
and shrugged apologetically. But Joyce cared little about
the rate at which they were tearing through the sprawling
Indian town. He was interested in noting that every interior fixture of the car was of solid silver, and that he was
sitting upon costly velvet, the nap of which was more than
an inch thick.

After burning up the ground for about a mile, the
chauffeur swung into a tree-shaded block, where he slowed
with a suddenness that was almost comical to a funereal
crawl and drew up before a frame house of no great pretensions. All the window blinds were drawn. Crepe hung
upon the doorknob.

As the party got out, a squaw in a blanket could be
seen retreating from the strip of dusty lawn into the back
garden. Allan rang the bell. There was a brief delay, and
then the door was opened by one of the most beautiful
girls that Joyce or Kay had ever set eyes upon. She was
cast in the purest American Indian mold, a little above
average height, her figure as well-proportioned and straight
as that of an athlete. Delicately flattened cheeks and a
pointed chin redeemed her from the moon-faced type. Her
eyes were black with thick eyebrows, her full lips a fruity

crimson, and her hair hung forward down her chest in two long braids. A simple skirt and bodice, hand-dyed with Osage symbols, conveyed the feeling of a choice of costume that deliberately compromised between native taste and the white man's fashions.

She and Allan clasped hands silently for several minutes, as if they were oblivious to the presence of others. Then the young Chief introduced her by her sweet-sounding name of Sylvia Deerfoot.

She murmured a greeting in clear, grammatical English, and invited them to enter. From the hallway, the half-darkened interior of the parlor was visible to the right. Several old women were sitting there like stone images around the silhouette—unfailingly sinister—of a casket upon a trestle.

Hardened as he was to scenes of tragedy, Joyce felt a peculiar embarrassment at thrusting himself upon this alien grief. But he whipped himself into a professional attitude and gave urgent orders:

"The parlor will have to be cleared. The longer I delay my examination, the less I am likely to learn."

"We understand," replied Allan steadily. He then made some remarks in the dialect, and the mourners filed out.

Joyce started forward alone, but changed his mind and beckoned to Kay. In a moment, he had closed the door behind them, and they were standing on either side of the coffin, looking down at the dead girl.

They saw a face that strikingly resembled that of Sylvia Deerfoot, though it could never have been quite so beautiful. The pinched and waxen features were now of a faded coppery tinge, against which the hair was violently black. An inferior undertaker had not done very well with molding the lips and applying make-up to such parts of the skin as remained visible. But the eyelids, with their long, curving lashes lay peacefully and naturally closed.

The detective scrutinized the corpse for several minutes, without touching it. Through a pocket magnifying glass, he surveyed every inch of the face, neck and hands. Then he straightened up, and glanced at Kay.

"See anything out of the way?" he asked.

"No, Inspector."

"There's a bruise on the right jaw, close to the ear. The discoloration is slight, and it's been dusted over with talcum powder. But it sure is a bruise."

Kay looked closer, and nodded. "I can barely make it out. She may have received a punch."

"Maybe. Her finger nails have been thoroughly cleaned. Too bad. Stuff under the nails is often good for a straight steer. I'd like to see into her mouth, but the jaws are locked tight as brass by this time. Hm!"

Kay shuddered a little at the thought of wrenching open the clamped mouth.

"We've got to see the doctor who signed the death certificate," Joyce continued. "Something can be dug out of him, perhaps. I hope he's bright."

He stepped to the door, and addressed Allan curtly: "Please call the doctor in this case. Get him to come over here right away."

He returned to the coffin and prowled around it silently, a brooding expression on his face, as he viewed the body from all possible angles.

In about fifteen minutes, the bell rang, and there followed the sound of rough-edged voices and a commotion of trampling feet, which seemed decidedly indecorous in that house of sorrow. Then Allan appeared in the parlor doorway with two white men, and promptly withdrew, shutting the door.

Joyce and Kay saw a pair of Westerners, each of whom approximated a type that has been popularized by the writers of cowboy stories. The first was a husky citizen of fifty, sun-tanned and muscular. He wore a red kerchief spotted with white around his neck, and carried a five-gallon hat. It was too bad that his rugged, clean-shaven countenance did not beam with intelligence, and that he somehow conveyed the impression of needing a bath. The second man was small and aged, his nose red and his bristly white beard hacked round and short, as if he trimmed it himself with a scissors. Except for his rusty black suit and bow tie, he could have posed for a picture of an old prospector, or desert rat.

The taller specimen was no stranger to Joyce.

"Hello, Sheriff!" he said. "I knew you as Luther Hawes, internal revenue agent, when we were chasing the Fort Smith counterfeiters in 1920."

"Why, if it ain't the great New York sleuth!" grinned Hawes. "Mornin', Mr. Joyce."

"You might introduce your friend."

"He's Doc Purdy, of this town. James J. Purdy, M.D., I had ought to have said."

"Oh, the doctor I sent for!" Joyce switched his attention to the shabby runt. "How did you happen to come here together?"

"As soon as I got the call, I notified the Sheriff, who of course is interested. He lives just around the corner from me, and he rode me down in his car," stated Purdy, with unexpected precision.

"I thought the Sheriff had laid off this death, because he couldn't see any crime in it."

"I do say it warn't murder," Hawes averred combatively.

"What did the town police say? And the coroner?"

"This body was found outside the town limits, and the police didn't have no say. It was county business. As Sheriff of Osages County, I sit as coroner, too."

"Well, you sat," remarked Joyce pithily.

"An' I brought in a true verdict. But if the family sends East for a great sleuth, I'm a-goin' to see—"

"You can see and hear all you want," Joyce interrupted. "Let me talk to the doctor now." He turned back to Purdy. "Were you satisfied that this girl died of natural causes?"

"Yes."

"Did you make a detailed examination of the body?"

"Naturally."

"Did you find any contusions, or marks, on it?"

"There was a bruise on the left leg below the knee, such as might have been caused—and undoubtedly was caused—by her tripping over the root of a tree."

"What about the bruise on her right jaw?"

"Oh, that! It was trivial, probably the result of her face coming into contact with a stone in the grass, as she fell forward. It appears she was found in some such posture."

"I kin explain," Hawes contributed. "She was lyin' with her face in a shaller puddle, where there was a rock."

"Who discovered her?"

"An Injun boy named Benny Gopher. He come straight to me."

"And then what?"

"I amble over with a couple of my deputies, and we bring the remains to my office. There's no signs of dirty work, so I tell the family to come and get her. That was late in the afternoon, day before yesterday."

Joyce controlled with an effort his impulse to voice contempt for this slipshod procedure, and swung back to the doctor. "You were summoned by the family?"

"Yes. I at once performed an autopsy. I examined the viscera for possible poison, and gave special attention to the condition of the cardiac region."

"What did you figure killed her?"

"She died of a cerebral hemorrhage. The state in which I found the valves of the heart and the arteries clearly indicated that. She had suffered what is commonly called a stroke, and must have died almost instantly. Although her head had been partly submerged in a puddle, there was no water in her lungs."

"Ever treat her for heart disease, Doc?"

"No. She was probably unaware that she had a touch of it, and Indians hate to consult a white physician, anyway."

From the moment that Purdy had answered the first question put to him, Joyce had been astonished by his succinct phraseology and his ready, if superficial, medical verdicts. The man's culture contrasted oddly with his appearance.

"May I ask where you graduated?" the detective demanded suddenly.

"Harvard, class of '86," replied Purdy in a bored tone.

"And in medicine and surgery?"

"It's none of your business, but I pursued my studies the old Indian Territory. When the State of Oklahoma was created in 1907 and this section was included within its bounds, I met all the requirements of the law and obtained my certificate."

Joyce knew what that meant. Numerous pioneer adventurers in the West had taught themselves professions from the books, and trusted to rough-and-ready experience to complete the dubious job. The Governments of new States had generally accepted such persons as *de facto* surveyors, accountants, lawyers and dentists, as well as doctors. Purdy was that kind of medico. The Inspector preferred, however, to contest the facts of his diagnosis rather than his credentials.

"I'm here to find out whether or not this girl was *murdered,*" he said slowly.

He reached for the hem of Jennie Deerfoot's dress and turned it back to the knee. On the bare shin could be seen a bluish mark about two inches across. "Yes, that could have come from a fall," he observed. "Nothing dangerous. But I tell you flat, I believe she was socked on the jaw by a human fist."

"She might have been," agreed Purdy calmly, while Sheriff Hawes snorted.

"I suppose you claim that that in itself could have brought on a brain hemorrhage?"

"Certainly, if the tendency already existed."

"Then you didn't go far enough with your autopsy. You only opened the torso. You should have made a section of the skull."

"The condition of the heart told me all I need to know."

"If there was the least reason to fear anything had happened to the brain, you should have looked at the brain," Joyce persisted. "Some other kind of injury to the head might have done the trick."

"There was no such injury," asserted Purdy.

Joyce moved to the upper end of the coffin, and deliberately thrust his left hand between the pillow and the rigid cranium of Jennie Deerfoot. He forced the head up, though this required considerable effort on his part and caused the whole body to shift its position in the casket. Then, with the stubby but sensitive fingers of his right hand, he commenced to massage the scalp, covering the domed surface inch by inch and bearing down heavily to ascertain whether the bone had been fractured at any point. The skin was clammy and like putty to the touch; the hollows which he punched into it remained there temporarily. A dreadful moisture clung to his fingertips.

His features were impassive as he performed his task. Kay Carey stared at him in professional admiration, yet horror-stricken at his cold efficiency. It seemed to her that she would rather sacrifice a year of her life than fumble and prod for everlasting minutes, in that way, at the head of a corpse.

Slowly, Joyce worked around to the back of the neck, where the flesh was thicker and consequently the more repugnant. He felt of it accurately, but with a lighter touch. A digit came into contact of a sudden with a tiny hard surface, and the detective started to grip the latter between two of his nails. He checked himself and drew his hands away, allowing the head to fall back upon the pillow. His face mirrored no emotion, and the light in his eyes did not quicken. Yet so well did Kay understand her chief, so telepathic were the reactions between them, that she knew instantly that he had made a vital discovery.

The Inspector looked right past her at Sheriff Hawes and Dr. Purdy.

"Gentlemen, I guess I'll have to accept your view of this fatality, after all," he said. "I'm satisfied that Jennie Deerfoot's skull was not broken."

"You could have taken my word for it and saved yourself trouble," sneered Purdy. "I did examine her, you know, with possible fractures in mind."

"Yeah. I apologize, Doc."

"What about me? I ain't sich a fool as you took me for," crowed Hawes. "I told you right off the gal's death was just an accident."

"Even accidents should be investigated carefully. Some of the deaths around here have been murders," said Joyce.

"Onnery murders, that grew out of Osage cussedness and jealousy. They've been killing each other since their great-great-granddaddies invented scalping. And that's something else I told you. When you telephoned me from New York, I told you there warn't no plot against the Bighearts, or the Many-Horses, or any special family. And you can put that in your pipe and smoke it."

"Quit your shouting, Sheriff, and leave me to deal with my clients," cried Joyce impatiently.

"Okay! I hope you make 'em feel they've had a good run for their money."

Hawes flourished his hand in a salute that was intended to convey sarcasm and took his departure, followed by Purdy. As soon as the door had been shut once more, Joyce glanced at Kay.

"Come over here," he directed in a low voice.

At close range, she watched him lift the dead girl's head again and part the thick black hair at the base of the skull.

"Help me hold it," he muttered.

In her excitement, she somehow did not mind clutching a handful of the hair and drawing it taut. She saw Joyce approach his finger and thumb to a dot of metal that barely protruded. He caught the end of it with difficulty, tugged and pulled out a two-and-a-half-inch length of harness needle, minus the end which contained the eye.

"This was driven in as far as it would go, and then broken off," he explained. "Deliberate murder, all right."

"The needle pierced the medulla oblongata," she gasped.

"That's it. The only part of the brain that isn't protected by bone."

Kay met his eyes squarely. "Do you have the right to keep this from Sheriff Hawes?"

"No legal right. But—"

She nodded. Vengeance would be infinitely more swift and sure, she knew, if Inspector Michael Joyce worked in his own way, unhampered.

CHAPTER FIVE
The Land of Vanishing Gold

Handling it gingerly, Joyce put the needle which he had
drawn from Jennie Deerfoot's head into an empty envelope and slipped the latter into his side pocket. He looked
around for water with which to wash his hands, but finding none in the parlor he kept his arms hanging awkwardly
away from his body. For fear of infection, he was careful
not to touch any part of his own or Kay's skin with the
contaminated fingers.

"The broken end of that needle will be a mighty important clue. We've got to find it," he said.

"How on earth can we hope to discover so small an
object? Where can we search?" she asked disconsolately.

"The murderer probably snapped it off, right there in
the woods, and threw it aside."

"Combing muddy soil and leaves for an inch of thin
steel is going to be no joke."

"Did you ever see a detective problem that was really
easy? Now open that door like a good girl, me darlin', and
let us both out."

Joyce ran upstairs without ceremony to the bathroom,
where he thoroughly scrubbed his hands. He then returned
to the group of silent Indians. With the exception of the
old Chief Pale-Horse Eagle, who still sat with folded arms
in his limousine, they had been awaiting him patiently in

the hallway. Allan met him with an interrogative glance, but Joyce shrugged his shoulders noncommittally.

"I'll talk this over with you later," he growled.

"All right, Inspector. Then allow me to take you to our home. You and Miss Carey must be starving."

"Huh! I'd forgotten about food. But we none of us had breakfast, and that's a fact."

They shook hands gravely with Sylvia, bowed to the ancient Osage women and resumed their seats in the car. Harry Deerfoot did not go with them. He stood on the sidewalk, a mournful and absurd figure in his check suit, and waved them out of sight with lackadaisical motions of his hand.

The instant the chauffeur had rounded the corner, he again threw his gears into high and strove desperately to clip a few seconds from the Pawhuska speed record. Neither Joyce nor Kay liked it; they had no desire to become casualties, and they looked about hopefully for a nonexistent traffic cop. But in the end they found compensation in studying the furrowed, imperturbable face of Pale-Horse Eagle and wondering whether he thought fast driving a tribute to his dignity, or simply accepted it because all Indian chauffeurs indulged in the evil habit.

They arrived presently at a large, rambling house on the western outskirts of the town. It was far from new, and the grounds looked like a camp, with the first tepees that Kay had ever seen standing haphazard among the trees. Several generations of blanket Indians were evidently living there contentedly in the open. The children played on the grass, the women were busy at their domestic tasks, and the men sat about, smoking. The effect was patriarchal, for the interior of the Chief's residence proved to be as luxurious as those of his retainers were primitive. A radio of the most expensive make caught the attention of the visitors. There were rich Persian rugs on the floors, heavy ornate furniture in every room and many costly *objets-d'art*.

"When my father was young, this was a frontier ranch-house," Allan explained negligently. "It is older than Pawhuska, and antedates the setting apart of the territory as the Osage reservation. My father once stormed it with a troop of young braves and took scalps here. It appealed to his vanity to buy it when the oil wells made us rich. The furniture is his idea of what would be expected of him. But he sleeps on the open back porch in a hammock."

If the veteran warrior understood this startling account of himself, he gave no sign. He did not seem able to follow English that was spoken rapidly.

They proceeded to the spacious dining room, where Negro servants brought them fruit, an excellent Spanish omelette, freshly-baked corn cakes and coffee. Joyce and Kay made the observation, which they later confirmed, that no full-blooded Osage ever works as a servant. The domestics in the Indian country are blacks, half-breeds and in some cases low-grade whites.

As soon as the dishes had been cleared away, the detective lighted a cigar and leaned back.

"I'm not figuring on keeping anything I do a mystery from you, or holding out on anything I learn," he said. "Jennie Deerfoot was knocked out with a blow to the jaw, and a harness needle was then jabbed into her brain at the top of the spinal column. I've got part of the needle."

Allan heard him stoically. "This is no surprise to me, Inspector. I assumed it was murder, though I couldn't guess at the means that had been used. What steps shall you take?"

"I want to see the boy who found the body, of course. Benny Gopher, the Sheriff said his name was."

"He's just a kid, and a sort of little vagabond. He'll be hard to find."

"It's important he should guide us to the right spot in the woods; the investigation begins there. Now, as to motive. Can you dope it out why that girl, instead of another, should have been picked as a victim?"

"No. This is the first blow against the Deerfoots, but it follows the murderous attacks upon the Bighearts and my own family. I believe, as you know, that all these crimes are of a piece. They're moves in a ghastly chess game which we don't understand, because we haven't yet put our finger upon the master player."

"Hm! How many heirs did Jennie leave?"

"Only her brother Harry and Sylvia. But they may not be allowed to benefit by her money for long," said Allan quietly.

"I get you. The Deerfoots are related to you and the Bighearts, too, I suppose?"

"We are all cousins."

"The exact links can be worked out on paper when we have time for it. Let's dig up that Gopher kid now."

"I can send a man out to hunt for him."

"We'll go ourselves," Joyce ruled. "I want to look this town over, and pass the time of day with any of your friends we happen to meet."

Allan arose promptly. He did not resume the ceremonial feather bonnet which he had worn as a badge of pride in New York City, but put on a brimless cap with a high, round crown, bizarre and clerical-seeming. This was in the true native style. The average Osage, even when he clung to the buckskin tunic and trousers with figured bands down the sides, preferred a felt hat or peaked cloth cap, the effect of which was thoroughly inharmonious.

"Shall I order the car?" Allan inquired.

"Thanks, but we'll walk," answered Joyce blandly.

The young Chief threw him an amused look. Words were unnecessary to emphasize the point that he understood perfectly the other's aversion to Indian chauffeurs.

With Kay between them, they sauntered past the tepees of Pale-Horse Eagle's hangers-on and started to descend a long, dusty street, sparsely shaded by the young pinnate leaves of locust trees. The houses varied oddly between the flashiness of fresh paint of many colors and utter dilapidation. Some of them had been improved with garages of obviously recent construction, but a surprising number of cars stood under canvas awnings or quite unsheltered in back yards. Here and there, a brand-new wooden mansion plentifully adorned with scroll-work and unneeded turrets, flaunted itself like a boastful parvenu.

Anticipating the questions that were about to be put to him, Allan swung his arm in a broad gesture.

"This is typical of Pawhuska and the villages nearby. Every Osage has money. Every one of them could have a nice house, and the things that should go with it. Many do. But some of my people are still savages at heart. They move into a house, because they think that is the proper caper. Yet after they have filled it with a lot of junk, they lose interest, neglect to paint the outside and don't even make ordinary repairs. They are apt to sleep on the floor, and use the front parlor as a pantry."

"Why the cars parked in the open?" asked Kay.

"The owners are too lazy to build garages. Besides, these new millionaires of ours make a virtue of extravagance. They don't care what the weather does to a car, since they're sure to be trading it in for another model the following month, and damn the expense!"

"They're especially bugs about automobiles, eh?" commented Joyce.

"Automobiles and radios." Allan laughed. "I could talk all day, telling you funny stories along those lines. There's a young fellow living on this street—in the red house you can see to the left—who was sued last month for $30,000 on cars he had bought from a local firm. He had taken nine machines and smashed them up, one after the other. But he refused to pay, on the grounds that the dealer should go on supplying cars at his own risk until he produced one that couldn't be smashed. The claim had to be taken to Washington, since the U. S. Government is our guardian and the last court of appeal in such matters.

"Another Osage blood bought thirteen machines in three years, paying $4,000 for the cheapest. The joke on this particular lad is the fact that he never could get accustomed to riding in an automobile. He tried all of his thirteen, and then told his friends that he preferred horses. He bought him a mustang, which promptly threw him, and he's since been trudging everywhere on foot."

"I'll bet a box of cigars that he's an exception. Easy money and high-powered cars go together. And learning to drive like hell was never a problem for a half-wit, white, black or red," prodded Joyce, coming out with his grouch.

"You're right, Inspector. Our braves are beginning to go in for aeroplanes, too. The general craze for radios has more to commend it. A man I know went to a shop in this town to buy a radio set. The storekeeper had two very expensive models, equally good at getting results from the air, but varying a lot in appearance. It proved impossible to persuade the customer that he would be as well off with one as with the other. He argued that if the first was a radio set, the second must be something else. The shopman, fearing to lose a sale, tried desperately to convince him and fix his fancy upon one of them. When he had finished talking, my Osage brother giggled and bought both of them."

"You are making up these tales to amuse us," insisted Kay.

"I wish that I were," replied Allan, with a touch of sadness. "A plague of salesmen descended upon us as soon as the oil wells began to spout. It was child's play to sell an

Indian anything that tinkled or shone brightly. Remind me to show you a grandfather's clock that stands among the tepees on our place. An old second-cousin of mine saw it in a shop. Its chimes pleased him, and when he was told falsely that it was an antique worth $2,000, he answered that he was now a rich man and that the price was no obstacle. For several weeks, it remained planted in the middle of his tepee, getting in the way of his family and scaring them when it struck the hour at night. He finally got mad at it and dragged it out of doors, where it is now quite covered with rust."

"At that rate, even a big income could be thrown away faster than it comes in," said Kay.

"How true! Some writer has called our oil flowing gold, and that is what it is: fluid like quicksilver, and just as elusive. The land is a land of vanishing gold."

"This is an important angle on the bunch I've got to deal with," observed the practical Joyce.

"You will find that there are other slants on our character. But while we're on the subject, I want you to have a good laugh. I haven't mentioned the funniest thing of all that happened here, and instead of just telling you about it I'll show you an exhibit."

Allan led the way down a side street until they came to a large house with an unkempt lawn. Standing in the middle of the lawn was a hospital ambulance.

"Well, what about it?" asked Joyce, as the Chief pointed.

"The owner is a fat widow. She thought it would be a good idea to get a car in which she could ride lying down. A large number of salesmen called upon her by invitation, but were unable to land her order until one of them had this bright idea. He sold her an ambulance."

"No fooling!" said Joyce. "Did she ever travel in it?"

"Frequently. It was not considered in the least comical by her neighbors. They looked upon her as a practical

person, and envied the showing made by such a large, long
vehicle. Indeed, a certain matron was all burned up with
jealousy, and decided to outdo her. The second woman
made a trip to Kansas City and looked over everything
that the dealers in motor specialties had to offer. She returned with an enormous carriage, which had glass sides
and the sculptured figures of angels at the four corners. It
was a hearse."

Joyce and Kay shouted with merriment. "Now I know
you're spoofing," the detective gasped.

"I swear that I am not. She still rides about in it,
stretched full length on a soft cushion, her head supported
on one elbow. The effect is much admired."

"I'll believe it when I see it," bantered Joyce, though
the sincerity in Allan's tone had already convinced him.

They had arrived within a few blocks of the center of
town, and now struck across to the main street. This was a
characteristic urban thoroughfare of the Southwest, lined
with two-story frame buildings and at intervals a taller
stone structure containing the offices of lawyers and other
professional men. The ground floors of these miniature skyscrapers were for the most part occupied by banks, insurance agencies, or automobile firms. Of the last-named,
Pawhuska clearly had more than the usual quota.

On this street, white Americans were more in evidence
than the Osages. They vastly predominated as managers
and clerks in the places of business and formed a goodly
minority of the customers. Kay thought this odd, but
Allan informed her that Pawhuska had between six and
seven thousand inhabitants, of whom perhaps half were
white. The Osages, who formed the millionaire class,
scarcely exceeded fifteen hundred, with others of their
clan in nearby villages swelling the total for that nation to
beyond two thousand. There were also a number of Chero-

kees, Creeks, Choctaws, Pawnees, Seminoles, Ottawas and Kaws in and around Pawhuska.

"Interesting dope," growled Joyce. "But let's put our finger on the boy, Benny Gopher. He's the hot lead right now."

"Benny works sometimes for a shoemaker down the street. He hangs out, also, in a poolroom close by. We'll try the shoemaker first."

They went to the dingy shop in question, where a small, stooped Cherokee proprietor named Owl-Face, upon whom the god of oil had not smiled, shook his head and complained that the boy had not deigned to do any jobs for the past two days.

"Him run with lazy Injuns an' tellum how he fin' dead girl," the decrepit craftsman grunted.

"Then the poolroom is the place to look," remarked Allan. "The ne'er-do-wells of this town are the greatest devotees of the little ivory balls. Most half-civilized Indians are."

But in the sordid parlor to which they came presently, they failed to discover the errant Benny. The players halted their games, to listen to Allan's questions and then shrug their shoulders. The mob of spectators, mostly youths smoking cigarettes and wearing rusty black hats, gathered around silently, as much as to say that any one could observe that Benny was not among them.

"Have you seen him at all today?" the Chief persisted. "If not in here, perhaps some other place?"

The vacant-eyed dumbness which serves the ignorant as a mask became more emphasized. Finally, a half-blood of some intelligence stepped forward and spoke in fair English.

"I saw Benny Gopher," he said. "He was in a Ford car with three men."

"Who were the men?" asked Allan.

"One of them was Harry Deerfoot."

"Harry Deerfoot. That's strange. Were the others Indians?"

"I could not tell. Their hats were pulled down low. The driver, he crouched over the wheel as if he did not want to be recognized."

"But when *was* this? I left Deerfoot at his house less than two hours ago."

"I see 'em maybe three-quarters of an hour ago. The Ford was on the South edge of town, headed for the prairie and going like hell."

Allan glanced at Joyce, and his lips silently formed the word, "Kidnapped!"

"Did you notice the number on the license plate?" the detective cut in, addressing the half-blood.

"No, sir. How could I know you gentlemen would be interested?"

Allan sprang to a wall-phone and called the Deerfoot residence. He asked for an account of Harry's movements, and after listening for a minute or so he hung up. As the three investigators left the poolroom, he stated bluntly:

"This is bad business. Harry went for a walk, and has not been home since. He would not have gone willingly to the country without telling his sister. He was no friend of Benny Gopher. The two were probably prevented from crying for help in that car, because guns were stuck in their ribs."

"Taken for a ride, eh?" said Joyce. "You Osages don't have much to learn from New York or Chicago."

CHAPTER SIX
The Bloody Woodland Trail

From Sheriff Hawes that afternoon, Joyce obtained a reasonably accurate description of the spot in the woods where Jennie Deerfoot's body had been found. Allan declared himself competent to use this information as a lead, and locate exactly where the corpse had lain. The project moved Hawes to laughter. He thought it a farce that the sleuth from the East should still treat this death as a mystery, and he expressed himself upon the subject uproariously.

"As I told you, I figure she may have been punched on the jaw. Let's suppose that that was the cause of the brain hemorrhage. The family would naturally be interested to know who punched her," exclaimed Joyce, with affected mildness.

"It warn't no blow from a fist. Doc Purdy only allowed it might have been. But it warn't. She hit her face on a rock."

"I feel I might as well try to follow the clue through."

"Oh, you got to earn your money! No doubt o' that."

Upon the subject of the disappearance of Harry Deerfoot and Benny Gopher, the Sheriff of Osages County was equally contemptuous.

"Injuns are always runnin' around like looney coyotes," he exploded. "I don't have no time to chase after them."

However, he grudgingly consented to send an alarm to the townships thereabouts, and to instruct his deputies to keep an eye open for the missing persons.

Joyce could have laughed in his face. On their way back to the Chief's house, he asked Allan:

"Where can I get a man to put on the trail of those two? Not a local cop. I want a guy who knows the wild country, and will work for our interests and none other."

Allan thought for a moment, then turned his car down a side street and stopped in front of a shabby frame cottage. "Al Jenkins, a quarter-breed scout, lives here. He's always ready to take on odd jobs, and he's the very man for us if we can get him," the Osage said.

In answer to their call, a gaunt personage about fifty years old came slouching from the back yard of the cottage. Jenkins had skin the color of the rind of an ancient ham, grizzled hair that fell in points over his brown eyes, and a drooping mustache. He listened silently to the meager facts available on Harry Deerfoot and Benny Gopher. Thereafter he ruminated, and ended by stating:

"Sounds like they've been took to the Osage Hills. Ef so, I kin find 'em."

"I want them located, no matter where they are," objected Joyce. "They may have been rushed clear out of the State."

"I kin find 'em," reiterated Jenkins.

"All right. I'll pay you fifty dollars a week, and a bonus of a hundred if you show results."

"Suits me, Boss."

The Inspector and Allan drove off. "The next thing is for you and Miss Carey and I to duck out to the woods pronto, and see how good we are as detectives," remarked Joyce. "We've just plain got to find the head of that needle."

"Why? The fact of murder and the way it was done have already been established."

"Yeah. But it's important to know whether it was out there in the woods that the needle stunt was pulled off. If that's where we find the other piece, we'll know it was."

"Could it have been otherwise?"

"There's no limit to the possibilities in a murder case, Chief. Jennie might have been in a coma until the needle was used—at the Sheriff's office, let's say, or the doctor's. Even the undertaker, in that event, would not be above suspicion."

Allan looked thoughtful. "I'm going to suggest that we add a fourth person to our search party."

"Who?"

"My father."

"That's an idea. But how come?"

"He had great fame as a scout in his young days. You have read about Indian woodcraft, I am sure. My father was a master at it. Such wisdom might bring results in discovering a tiny object."

"Right. And in figuring exactly what happened around there. We'll sure take the Big Chief along."

At the house, while Allan went to ask old Pale-Horse Eagle to help, Joyce and Kay sat on the front porch. The Inspector closed his eye and tilted his head backwards. His whole body relaxed visibly. In a few moments, he straightened and smiled at the girl with a gentleness that was curious in so rugged a man.

"This job among the trees will teach you a lot," he said. "But after that's over, me darlin', I'm thinking I'll be sending you back to New York."

"New York!" she repeated, shocked. "I want to see the case to the finish. Why would you send me away?"

"It promises to be pretty tough. Wholesale killings, which I hadn't quite believed in at first, and now these abductions with murder as the likely motive. If the gang acts this fast in making off with a witness, it'll think nothing of bumping detectives."

"Of course, the work is dangerous. I'm prepared for that."

"I'm the boss, Kay, and there's one girl whose life I don't want to risk in a damned Indian feud."

"What about *your* life?"

"You should know better than to ask. It's understood that I gamble my own neck every time that I go out on a hot case."

"And you're satisfied to turn me into a quitter! Inspector, you've told me time and again that I'll make a real operative if I stick close to you. That means the hard as well as the easy. A detective can't pick his assignments soft. Now, what's the answer?"

Joyce got up and brushed the tips of his thick fingers along the reddish curls above her ear. With his right hand, he reached playfully at her neck, as if he intended to choke her.

"You'd make a lawyer, too—a regular mouthpiece. There's no shaking you loose from a sound argument."

"Then I stay here with you?"

"Yes," he answered soberly. "But if harm comes to you, they'll know that Michael Joyce is on the warpath in this section, by God!"

The Eagles, father and son, put in their appearance on the porch, and Allan spoke:

"We'll go in the car; it's much too far to walk. But the chauffeur is busy on an odd job. I'll take the wheel."

"Suits me," grinned Joyce out of the side of his mouth.

They went over to the garage and climbed into the limousine, which Allan brought around with a smooth technique and drove at a modest forty miles an hour. So powerful were the engines of the great car that it seemed to glide like a gull in the air.

"We're bound for Three Mile Creek, near Fairfax," said Allan over his shoulder. "That's about twenty miles in a southwesterly direction. The first of the Osage murders, that of Anna Brown two years ago, was committed within a mile of where we're going."

"Seems funny they could have lured Jennie as far from home as that," remarked Joyce.

"She had been visiting friends in Fairfax in the morning. The killer got her on the way back. Her roadster was found parked under a tree by the creek. The Sheriff claims she must have gone into the woods to pick spring flowers."

"What has been done with the roadster?"

"Unfortunately, Sylvia sent it to a garage in Pawhuska to be washed and painted. No clues there."

They spun along without further conversation, and in half an hour had reached Jennie's halting place beside the watercourse. Locking the limousine, they left it under the shade of the same tree. Joyce looked about him for telltale footprints, but if these had ever existed they had since been erased by the soft pattering of April rains.

"The scene of the murder is described as being a hundred yards from here, where the creek makes a sudden curve," said Allan. "We are to turn to the left until we strike a clearing in the midst of black-jack shrubs."

They entered the woods, Chief Pale-Horse Eagle in the lead. The old warrior kept his head bowed, the chin touching his chest, while his downward peering eyes roved sharply in all directions. Joyce and Kay followed him, feeling a little out of their element, while Allan brought up the rear.

The trail offered no physical obstacles. It was almost a pathway, which had doubtless been used by rustic lovers. An investigator, no matter how amateurish, could not have failed to follow the shortest route to the clearing among the gnarled and stunted black-jacks. But at this point the

definite indications ceased. The ground was covered with
a litter of rotting leaves from the year before and trampled
grass. There was no puddle that could be identified as the
one in which Jennie's face had rested. Instead, a series of
tiny pools had formed at brief intervals, and every object
in sight was dripping with moisture.

It would have been impossible to conceive of a location
where one would be less likely to discover the lost head of
a needle.

After making a complete circuit of the clearing, which
was some fifteen yards long by ten wide, the old Chief
sat upon a stump at the end looking toward the creek and
studied the terrain with his sphinx-like eyes. Allan addressed a few words to him in Osage, to which he replied
laconically.

"He says that we should go ahead and learn what we
can," the young man explained. "But we are on no account
to disturb him."

"He'll not hear a cheep out of me," said Joyce. "I want
to see how a redskin works."

The detective and Allan commenced to sleuth in their
respective fashions. Methodically, the former traversed
the open space in a crisscross pattern that enabled him to
survey every inch of the soil. He adopted a cat-walk that
would displace the dead twigs, leaves and grass as little as
possible. But Joyce soon realized that his method was limited to hunting for extraneous objects and those special
signs which remain in the wake of a murder. He hoped to
find a discarded weapon, scraps of clothing, some personal
belonging dropped by accident; above all, the needle. His
keen glance sought for footprints and bloodstains, though
the chances were greatly in favor of the rain having elimi-
nated these. Of woodcraft as an art, he knew next to nothing, and it was patently by the exercise of woodcraft that
Allan hoped to get results.

Allan was scrutinizing the trees and shrubs, with attention to broken branches even at a considerable distance from the point where the deed had probably occurred. He advanced as far as the creek and then explored the environs of the clearing in a contracting circle. Exposed roots and stones interested him almost as much as branches.

"There were three men here, in addition to the girl," he whispered at last to Joyce.

"Yeah? I can understand that the bushes tell you a story of human beings having been through them. But without footprints, how do you know it was three?"

"One man slunk along parallel to Jennie, as she came from the road. Over there to the left, the disturbance is too great to have been caused by a single person, but hardly great enough for more than two. It's likely that that pair merely looked on, standing by in case their help was needed. Then the lot of them went to the creek, where they appear to have followed its course, walking in the water so as to hide their tracks."

"Can you show us some of the evidence on which you build this theory?"

"Certainly."

Allan led Joyce and Kay to several spots where the underbrush had been trampled and an occasional twig hung by a shred of bark. It was an easy assumption that some kind of living creature had crashed through, but to Joyce's eye the recent presence of man remained unproved. He could not find so much as a thread of cotton or wool, torn from a prowler's sleeve.

"What took place in the clearing is really the important issue," he commented, shrugging.

They returned to that tragic arena. Except for broad indications that the site had been somewhat churned up and then muddied over by the rain, their problem seemed, if anything, more difficult there. Even Allan was at a loss.

He stood with his chin cupped in his palm, his brows con-
tracted.

Suddenly, Chief Pale-Horse Eagle waved an arm in an
authoritative gesture that told them all to step aside. They
obeyed promptly, retreating to the fringe of black-jack
shrubs. The old man dropped forward from the stump on
which he had been sitting, and landed upon his hands
and knees. His face within a few inches of the ground, he
crawled a zig-zag trail, at times accelerating his motions
with brusque lunges. He seemed almost to be smelling out
a secret, like a bloodhound in pursuit of its prey. But his
fierce, cold eyes were predominantly active. One could
see them roll in their sockets, dart glances in every direction, and then stay fixed briefly upon some irregularity in
the contour of the tract. The noiselessness with which he
progressed was uncanny. Joyce could not help thinking of
G. Borden Symes, known as the Sheriff, his star operative in New York, who also had a talent for moving about
silently. For this reason, if for no other, he mused, Symes
was a man who would be sure to earn respect in the Indian
country.

In his own peculiar manner, the Chief surveyed the
clearing with deadly efficiency. At the end of fifteen minutes, he had covered every square foot of it. Then he resumed his seat on the stump and gave a final sweeping
look around. He pronounced a judgment in curt Osage
sentences.

"My father says he can show you exactly where Jennie's
body lay," declared Allan quietly.

"Ask him to do it," retorted Joyce with a certain skepticism.

Pale-Horse Eagle walked, without being asked, to a
point a little to the north and west of the center of the
clearing. He gathered twigs and laid them end to end on

the ground rapidly, until he had by this means created
the outline of a human form. Joyce stooped to examine
the silhouette, and his heart leaped. Magically yet convincingly, the picture had come to life. Where the head
had been indicated, there was a depression no longer containing water, but which might easily have been a puddle two days before. These pools amid the debris of the
woodland, drained and refilled capriciously. At its edge
was a half-embedded stone, in precisely the position where
Jennie's jaw would have rested against it. Further down, a
hollow corresponded to the hip-bone which perhaps had
bored a place for itself among the rotted leaves.

Joyce's face lighted in admiration. "Damned if I don't
think you're right!" he said.

"Me right," the Chief asserted in English. "No can mistake."

"I'm sold on the result, but I'd like to understand how
it was worked out."

Pale-Horse Eagle struggled for explanatory phrases,
and ended by reverting to the dialect.

"He says that if you do not see for yourself, he cannot show you," explained Allan. "His methods are the
ancient ones of Indian scouting. He found leaves and twigs
crushed in a special way. And there are small wood ants
which had gathered to eat the dead flesh, and still linger
at the spot."

Joyce nodded. He was standing over the weirdly sug-
gestive silhouette, and gradually he adjust his body to the
posture that the supposed murderer would have found
most convenient.

"Now I figure that after the guy had knocked Jennie
down, he planted his knee in the small of her back and
got busy with the needle," he expatiated. "He pushed it
into her brain, and then broke it off close to the skin of

the neck. It's possible that he was foxy enough to carry the piece away with him. But more likely he just threw it aside. It would have fallen within a yard or so."

Turning to the right, he searched the ground narrowly. A thrill of excitement communicated itself to Kay and Allan, and they, also, joined in the quest.

A cry of triumph sounded at last from the one who was farthest from the center of action. Kay pointed to a cleft in a stone, which protruded from the vegetable detritus. What looked like an inch of discolored wire rested there, comparatively sheltered from the weather. But instead of being to the right of where the corpse had lain, it was some five feet straight ahead.

"Funny," commented Joyce. "It couldn't have been discarded with a flick of the hand. It was deliberately thrown."

He picked up the precious clue. "The head of a harness needle, sure enough," he went on. "The eye is broken on one side, with a scrap of the metal missing. Looks as if it were bloodstained, which it shouldn't be. No blood would have run from a jab to the brain that stayed plugged."

"I have a suggestion to make, Inspector," said Allan. "When the killer snapped off the needle, its head may have punctured his own thumb. The blood may come from that."

Joyce looked at him admiringly. "You were one jump ahead of me there. I was just going to say the same thing. If this stain shows up under the microscope as blood, we'll be hunting for a man with a sore thumb."

Chief Pale-Horse Eagle exhibited small interest in the mechanical detail of the fractured needle and the detective theories that were being built around it. He was following his own train of thought, and he voiced it at last with difficult and chopped precision.

"I tell-ing you white men was here to harm lit-tle Deerfoot girl."

"Your son claims there must have been three men. Do you mean that all of them were white?"

"May-be no. May-be one In-jun. But I say two white men was here."

"What makes you so sure, Chief?"

"Plen-ty bush torn. Holes dig in ground—stamp, stamp! In-jun like snake. In-jun no tear bush, no walk hard."

Again, Joyce was reduced to shrugging his shoulders. It was beyond him to confirm the degree to which the soggy clearing had been trampled. But any opinion formed by the old red warrior was worth bearing in mind for future reference.

"Well, I guess there's nothing more we can do here," he said. "Let's get back to Pawhuska."

They retraced their steps along the trail which had proved so sinister a one for Jennie, and which doubtless had been trodden, too, by Anna Brown, the earlier victim.

The idea that any new surprise would develop from their trip to the woods was far from the minds of all of them. But as they reached the open road, they halted by common consent and stared. Lettered crudely in white chalk on the side of the locked limousine, they read the word:

BEWARE

CHAPTER SEVEN
When the Hand Talks

That evening, after dinner, Joyce called a council of war at the Chief's house. Other than the old man and Allan, the important members of that family were in the party headed by Joe Yellow-Horse, which was coming from New York by train and would not arrive until the following day. But the Inspector was convinced that an immediate analysis of the situation must be made, without waiting to consult Joe. He insisted, however, upon the presence of Sylvia Deerfoot. Her father being dead and her mother an illiterate invalid, Sylvia was the only available representative of the Deerfoot household. The fact that she was grief-stricken because this was the eve of Jennie's funeral did not exempt her from attending the conference.

The three Osages and the two white detectives sat in Pale-Horse Eagle's front parlor with the doors closed. Most of the questions inevitably were answered by Allan, but his father and his betrothed were there to be appealed to when necessary.

"First, let's see if I have the straight dope on the Bighearts," said Joyce. "Three of them have been murdered, including the white husband of one of the girls. The Charley Whitehorn and Harry Roan killings seem connected, due to the closeness of those men to the Bighearts and the belief that they knew enough about the plot to have spilled the beans. Right?"

"Absolutely," replied Allan.

"How many Bighearts are there left?"

"Just one of the main branch—the fourth and last sister, Mollie, now the wife of Ernest Burkhart. There's a distant relative named George Bigheart living in this town, and that's all."

"Mollie is Dan McCall's niece-at-law, since Ernest is his nephew. Dan ought to be strong enough to protect them, and if he isn't we can't make it our business. I propose to leave the Bigheart end of this mystery alone, and concentrate on your family and the Deerfoots. You told me that the first tragedy on your end was the death of your uncle, two weeks ago. What was his name again?"

"Flying-Horse-Tail Eagle, my father's brother."

"He was found dead, with a knife between the ribs. The official verdict was suicide. Wasn't that it?"

"Yes, Inspector."

"Where was he found?"

"In a small vegetable garden he worked by himself as a hobby, adjoining the backyard of this house. He patronized bootleggers, though one swallow of corn liquor drove him crazy. His bad drinking habits gave some color to the suicide theory."

"But you don't believe that if he'd wanted to kill himself, he'd have done it with a knife?"

"No. And I deny that the coup was physically possible. The wound was inflicted too high up. His fingers were clutched awkwardly on the hilt of the weapon, as if they'd been placed there after death."

"What has become of the knife?"

"Sheriff Hawes kept it. As a legal exhibit, he claimed, since suicide is a crime."

"Hm! I'll probably demand before long that Flying-Horse-Tail's body be exhumed and a proper autopsy held. How wealthy was he?"

"The oil 'head-rights' concentrated in his name were worth about $100,000 a year. Next to my father, he was one of the richest Osages."

"Who inherits from him?"

"Joe Yellow-Horse, his son, who came to New York with me, is the sole heir."

"And if Joe were to die?"

"The income would then be divided among a number of cousins whose blood relationship is equally close. The Many-Horses women and the two Swift-Horse brothers, Sam and Thomas, who also accompanied me East, would be his principal inheritors."

"That's interesting. We'll return to it later. Now, what's your father worth?"

"His revenue of about half a million a year is supposed to represent a capital—in oil wells—of between fifteen and twenty million dollars."

"You are his heir, of course. Who comes next to you?"

"Joe Yellow-Horse, with the succession again extending to the Swift-Horses and Many-Horses. The basis of our tribal name, by the way, is 'Horse,' with only the Big Chief, his brothers and his eldest son entitled to add 'Eagle.'"

"We'll now pass to the Deerfoots," said Joyce. "Are they millionaires, too?"

"Barely so. Sylvia's mother draws $40,000 a year."

"Yet, following the Bighearts and your family, these rather modest Deerfoots were murderously attacked. Can you explain that?"

"You see, Inspector, my engagement to Sylvia makes a difference. When I marry Sylvia, she will be my heir."

"Yes, I do see. The motive for killing Jennie may have been to scare Sylvia out of marrying you. But I must say it would have been simpler to destroy your fiancée herself."

"The opportunity was perhaps lacking," Allan pointed out. "It's useless deviltry, anyhow. We shall allow nothing to prevent us from marrying."

"Nothing!" the Indian girl broke in, her soft voice melodious with a singing quality. "It is impossible to frighten love."

Joyce looked at her grimly. He thought: "Poetical sentiments are swell, this side of the grave. But if death takes a hand, neither fear nor love will have much meaning."

Aloud, he said: "I'm going to suggest, all the same, that you publicly break off your engagement for the time being."

Allan stiffened. "We Osages may trick an enemy, but not with lies."

"This wouldn't be exactly a lie," Joyce argued tolerantly. "You really end the betrothal, and later on you really renew it. See! If I decide to order that done and you refuse, I may have to quit the case. But let it pass. I suppose you're wise to the upshot of the present talk. The Big Chief, yourself, Joe Yellow-Horse and Miss Sylvia here are the ones most likely marked for death. Where does that point? Who would benefit? It points to the assassin being among the nearer members of your own family, doesn't it?"

Allan brooded stonily, his eyes clouding. When he answered, his Oxford accent was strangely emphasized and his manner had all the suave formality of an upper-class Englishman's.

"I had naturally contemplated that possibility, my dear sir. But I admit to finding it distasteful, and hope we shall not be forced to accept the theory."

Joyce knew that he must prevent this sort of reserve from crystallizing. "The time's come to lay the cards on the table—face up," he said bluntly. "Who do you figure tried to kill you in New York? I can't be kept in the dark any longer about that."

"I held back no details of what happened, Inspector."

"That wasn't my question. I asked who tried to kill you?"

"I don't know."

"But you're plenty suspicious. When you refused to let the Police be notified, I doped it out that you preferred not to have some person or persons questioned. Or am I wrong about that?"

Allan remained impassively silent for several minutes. It did not take a mind reader to perceive that he was struggling between some point of pride and the obligation of candor which he owed to the detective he had employed.

"The incident occurred before your arrival at the hotel, as you will remember. You found my people gathered in the lobby of the Hermitage. But the Swift-Horse brothers had been absent for twenty minutes when the missile was discharged. They had gone for a walk, to see Times Square."

"Oh, Oh! Then it would have been possible for them to have crossed the street and made a try at you from that office building I visited."

"Possible, yes. But dressed as they were, I don't believe they could have gotten away with it unnoticed."

"I don't either. Indians in feather bonnets are looked at twice. Besides, the office I was in showed the footprints of only one man, and he had been wearing new rubber galoshes."

An expression of relief flickered across Allan's austere countenance. "I hated to doubt my own kin."

Joyce was satisfied with learning who the young Chief *had* doubted. He refrained from indicating that he himself had merely admitted that the movements of redskins in costume would probably have been observed. After the elevator had left them at the ninth floor of the office building, they might have worked quickly, one standing guard in the corridor and the other slipping to the window of the empty cubicle. Unlikely, perhaps, but quite conceivable. As for the galoshes, a cunning criminal of no matter what race might have thought of that means of disguising his tracks.

"Well, somebody was guilty," he said. "The nature of the weapon puzzles me. What do you suppose was used?"

"The nature of the tear in my coat suggests an arrow with a stone point."

Joyce exchanged a swift, smiling glance with Kay. Here was partial confirmation of the bow and arrow solution he had hazarded, when they had talked about the case at luncheon.

"I had thought of that possibility," he told Allan, "but imagined an iron arrowhead which had gone dull. The stone tip seems to come closer to the truth. A primitive Indian arrow, eh?"

"It may have been. But don't forget that I caught a glimpse of the thing just before it struck me. Even in a fraction of a second, I think I'd have identified a familiar object like an arrow. I was aware of nothing but a momentary flash."

"I get you!" He allowed himself a minute to ruminate. The evidence against the Swift-Horse brothers certainly was diminishing. They might have had arrows concealed in their baggage-rolls, but where would they have got a bow? And it was incontestable that Allan should have been able to see a feathered arrow stopped by the impact against his own body.

"We'll let this phase of it slide," he went on. "Now, tell me why were you and Joe Yellow-Horse quarreling shortly after I quit the hotel?"

"Oh, our little family argument, upon which you most legitimately spied!" exclaimed Allan, with a touch of irony. "Joe Yellow-Horse had stronger suspicions against the Swift-Horse brothers that I had. Against Sam Swift-Horse in particular. Joe wanted to do what I refused to allow. He wanted to accuse them. He said it was his right, because there was just as strong a motive for killing him as for killing me. The next blow might be aimed at him, he thought, and he wished to forestall it."

Joyce sighed. No sooner had he mentally dropped the Swift-Horses than their names were dragged back into the mystery, with new complications. It was typical of detective work.

"What had Yellow-Horse got on them?" he inquired.

"Nothing definite. He was following an Indian hunch. He believed that Sam Swift-Horse had put the evil eye on him."

"So that's it. The crowd of them won't be here till to-morrow. But it's plain that Yellow-Horse *is* in as much danger as you are—from some quarter. You and he, your father and Miss Sylvia, the four of you have got to be privately guarded."

"How will you arrange that, Inspector?"

"Miss Carey and I will stick close to you and the Big Chief. I'll send to New York for two of my best operatives, to take care of the others."

Joyce promptly walked over to the telephone table, picked up the receiver, asked for the Western Union and dictated a wire to his office. It ordered his son Tom and G. Borden Symes to hop for Pawhuska by aeroplane the next day, and report to him at Pale-Horse Eagle's mansion.

"That's that," he remarked. "There's nothing more to be done about protection until they get here. But we *can* start looking for a man with a puncture at the tip of his right thumb."

Sylvia directed a sloe-eyed look of interrogation at the detective. She had not heard the details of the sleuthing on the woodland trail, and Joyce sketched the important facts for her.

"I've examined the head of the needle, and I'm satisfied there's blood on it," he said. "The notion that the murderer wounded his own right thumb is a pretty sure bet. Keep mum about it, though."

The girl nodded, dazed, and as if troubled by this piling up of sinister implications.

"It will be hard to identify our man," observed Allan. "He's not likely to be such a fool as to wear a bandage, and a pricked finger doesn't necessarily swell."

"N-no," agreed Kay doubtfully. "He'll be carrying around a mighty sore thumb, all the same. The head of that needle went deep."

Joyce enjoined silence with a wave of his hand. He reflected briefly, and the drift of his thoughts appeared to move him to sardonic amusement.

"We had dinner early, and the evening is young. I'm game for a party before we go to bed, if the Big Chief here will help to make a success of it," he declared.

The company gazed indignantly at him, as if they suspected him of indulging a warped sense of humor.

"A party!" repeated Allan coldly.

"Sure. Invite all the second cousins and their pals from the tepees outside. Girls as well as boys. Get as many of them as you can into the house."

"But we don't understand, Inspector. This is a very singular suggestion."

"It is, eh? We doped out that we'd be hunting for a man with a bum thumb. Why not set to work on the bunch that is nearest to hand? But they mustn't be scared. I suggest that you ask 'em in, to lap tea or whatever else it is they like."

Allan wrestled with his dignity, yet could not resist smiling. "We could send downtown for ice cream. Indians can never get enough of that."

"Hop to it. Then, when the crowd has gathered, I want the Big Chief to inspire them with confidence in a little racket of mine."

"My father? What is he to tell them?"

"That I am a famous palmist—a wiz at forecasting the future from the lines in the hand," answered Joyce tranquilly.

Kay laughed outright. "A good excuse for sizing up the condition of fingertips, I'll say!"

The Indians, however, debated the subterfuge solemnly. Allan made a long explanation to Pale-Horse Eagle in Osage, for the latter found it difficult to grasp what palm reading meant. His sing-song answer was the most elaborate speech that Joyce and Kay had heard from the veteran of forgotten scalping forays.

"He says that what you propose is good medicine," Allan stated at last. "You should begin by looking at the white girl's hand, he says, and then at Sylvia's. Meanwhile, he will give the guests an idea of what you are doing, and they will all become eager to be given a turn. The way to lull the suspicions of Indians is to make them inquisitive and jealous."

"Not much difference in that respect between Indians and other folks," the detective opined.

He got up and walked restlessly about the room, leaving it to the others to make the arrangements. Kay found it prodigious to discover a palmist in her boss. It was a new angle on his versatility, because she knew that it was unlike him to essay an out-and-out bluff of this character. He would not risk encountering a customer who had some actual knowledge of the pretended science.

Within half an hour, the parlor had filled slowly with the numerous relatives, young and old, who lived in and about the house of the Big Chief. Most of them wore modified Western garments, but a few, especially among the patriarchs, were blanketed against the traditional ills of the night atmosphere and had the quills of birds stuck in their plaited hair. The chauffeur had made a speed-shattering dash to Pawhuska's main street, and had returned with cartons of ice cream variously flavored. The gastronomic treat was being enjoyed by all with gusto and gravity.

Joyce knew that the reason for his presence in Oklahoma could be no secret from this clan. But it was practicable to make them think that he was taking an evening off from his duties, to meet them socially. He confirmed this impression by asking questions about the tribal customs of the old days, and parading his rather limited knowledge of native art and music. But the white man's songs were sweet, too, he added, and illustrated by singing *Kathleen Mavourneen* in a husky Irish baritone.

The lack of emotional response did not ruffle him. Behaving like a guest who has done his part in trying to break the ice, he turned to his own special group, performed a few juggler's tricks with a coin for their amusement, then took Kay's right hand in his and owlishly studied it.

"You'll have a long, long life, me darlin'," he said. "No sicknesses or accidents worth speakin' about. I see but one marriage for you, and that's enough, God knows. The man you wed will have loved you a divil of a time before you ever dreamed of it. And—what's this?—I see a whole raft of children coming, to make the two of you happy."

He looked up grinning, but more than half serious, and surprisingly Kay Carey lowered her eyes. Behind them, they could hear the deep voice of Pale-Horse Eagle discoursing to his people about what was going on. Joyce caught at the hand of Sylvia Deerfoot and improvised a

fortune for her, pointing accurately with a stubby forefinger, nevertheless, at the Life Line, the Line of Destiny,
the Head Line and the Heart Line. Slowly, the aboriginal
Americans, child-like and curious, gathered in a dense circle about him. When he had finished with Sylvia, an old
fellow bashfully stuck out his hand.

"Sure, I'll tell each one of you a little something," announced Joyce briskly. "The right hand contains the fate
you were meant to have at birth; the left shows what you
have made of it since. I don't have the time for so many
full readings tonight. Suppose I take only the right hands."
He glanced at Allan. "Explain that to the folks who don't
understand English."

In quick succession, the detective seized one wrinkled or calloused paw after the other and endowed it with
prophecies of a general character which the owner would
find it hard to deny. His shrewd glance, however, was concerned primarily with the pad of flesh on the end knuckle
of each thumb. He avoided doing anything so obvious as
to squeeze or prod at the suspected spot. A wound, no
matter how small, would not escape his eye; he felt confi-
dent of that.

But at the end of the session, after the thirty-five or
forty Osages had passed inspection, the result was nil. He
hid his disappointment by continuing to talk hokum on
the subject of palmistry. The guests departed singly and in
groups until the original five were left alone.

"We may try this again with a new crowd," remarked
Joyce to Allan. "But, you know, while I was taking a slant
at right thumbs it struck me that I'd made a bull in not
looking at both hands while I was about it. The murderer
of Jennie may have been left-handed. A slim chance, of
course; but there's always a place for 'maybes' in murder.
A sore left thumb would have a meaning, too."

The words were scarcely past his lips when the totally unexpected happened. Sylvia Deerfoot swung away from the window beside which she was standing and placed herself directly in front of him. Her lips were taut, and her eyes though tearless were glittering with anguish.

"My brother Harry is left-handed," she said, "and the thumb of that hand is sore. He had a bandage on it yesterday, which he had removed this morning before you met him."

Joyce peered hard at her. "You're telling me that your brother—" he began.

"Yes," she interrupted. "From the moment I heard about the needle, it tortured me. But you insisted it would be the right thumb. I—I tried to fool myself. I couldn't believe that Harry might have killed Jennie."

"It's not proved that he did it," replied Joyce soothingly. "Still, the fact remains that instead of having been kidnapped, he may be a fugitive from justice. The boy, Benny Gopher, who found the body was in the car with him, and that listens bad."

"Harry Deerfoot is not guilty," asserted Allan evenly. "But for his sake and our own, we have got to find him and clear this up."

The detective stared at the expressionless Indian masks of the young Chief and his father. Behind them, he read that both men understood as clearly as he did that, in the orgy of homicide for gain which had gripped the millionaires of Pawhuska, Harry might well have slain his sister.

CHAPTER EIGHT
Dan McCall Breezes In

The third morning of Inspector Joyce's stay in Pawhus-ka found the community significantly enlarged, from the viewpoint of the baffling case on which he was working. Joe Yellow-Horse and his party of Osage elders had been the first to arrive from New York. They had scattered to their respective homes on the Big Chief's domain, the Swift-Horses and Many-Horses to tepees. Joe had gone to the house he owned in the rear, beside the vegetable garden where his father had perished miserably with a knife in his heart.

Then Tom Joyce and Sheriff Symes had slipped quietly into town, had reported to the Inspector and received their orders. Symes was to take up his residence with the Deer-foots and act as Sylvia's bodyguard. Tom had been told off to protect Joe Yellow-Horse, but a hitch had developed there. The Indian, mysteriously sulky after his journey, had locked himself in and would talk to no one. Tom had been reduced to patrolling the approaches to the premises. It was a situation which Joyce intended to clarify as soon as he got the time.

For the moment, he was more concerned with the news that Dan McCall, the wealthy ranchman and altruistic champion of the stricken Osage nation, also was back on the old stamping ground. Driving a high-powered car

which had met him in Kansas City, he had breezed in from
Washington, accompanied by two of his cowboys. They
were staying in rooms on the main street above a bank,
which was owned by the white magnate and picturesquely called the Bank of the Bad Lands. A phone call from
Joyce had drawn Dan's hearty invitation to come down and
talk things over. The appointment having been set for an
hour later, the detective devoted the intervening minutes
to checking routine details with Kay.

He had telegraphed his New York office to follow fresh
leads, and now he gave the girl the gist of the long night
letter just received:

"Dinny Sullivan got busy in that building opposite the
Hermitage. He learned from the starter that two redskins in
full paraphernalia were seen in the lobby, all right. But the
elevator men deny that they took them to any upper floor."

"They may have climbed the stairs. It would have been
the foxy thing to avoid elevators, not to mention that they
probably had no love for that way of traveling," said Kay.

"Sure. But the starter thinks—he won't swear to it—
that they walked out again in a very few minutes. And
Dinny questioned the tenants on every floor. Nobody had
seen Indians in the corridors, or on the stairs."

"Still, they might have gotten away with it."

"They might. As for the missing weapon, there's nothing new. I told the office to advertise again, mention a
stone-headed arrow and double the reward. Not a nibble,
so far!"

"And the hunt for Harry Deerfoot?" asked Kay.

"The local authorities aren't being much help. Hawes
and his boob deputies—hell, what can we expect from
them? I've wired the Police Chiefs of Dallas, Fort Smith,
Kansas City and Topeka to be on the lookout, because if
Deerfoot is running away he'll likely leave the State. If
he's really been kidnapped by other Indians, he may be

hidden a few miles from here. We can only wait for some
light to break."

"Guilty, or a victim—which?" Kay mused aloud.

Joyce waved a hand. "His sore thumb will take a lot of
explaining. I feel mighty sorry for that pretty sister of his.
She came through like a heroine with what she knew."

He got up, chewing on his cigar, and reached for his
hat: "I'll be drifting along now to see this McCall bird.
Sorry to leave you behind, darlin', but I don't want to take
either of the Chiefs, and one of us has to make good on my
say-so that they're not to be left unwatched."

"I understand," replied Kay coolly. "I can guard 'em.
My gun is loaded, and I know how to shoot."

Fifteen minutes later, Joyce was mounting by the side
stairway to the flat above Dan McCall's bank. The hilar-
ious sounds that were audible through the closed door
implied that the ranchman had lost no time in gathering
his cronies around him. It seemed scarcely necessary to
knock. The detective turned the handle and walked in.

He saw a big man sprawled across two chairs, and with
one booted foot supported by the window-sill. Behind him
stood a couple of cowboys, in their shirt sleeves and wearing capacious hats. A-straddle on small cane-seated chairs,
the backs of which they used as rests for their crossed
arms, were Sheriff Hawes, Doc Purdy and a slim, pompadoured stranger. There was a gallon of corn whiskey on
the floor. Every one held a glass in his hand, and sought
with loud guffaws to capture the center of attention. The
air reeked with smoke from cigars and the Bull Durham
cigarettes of the cowboys.

But as soon as Joyce entered, the big man jumped to
his feet. He had a pear-shaped face, the narrowness of the
chin being emphasized by the small, downward curving
mouth. His thick black hair grew high upon his forehead
and looked like a cap. Horn-rimmed glasses perched on

the bridge of a short beaked nose. He wore a sack suit with a stiff white collar, the conservatism of which was offset by a loud checkered tie. A general air of health and wholesomeness radiated from his person.

"Inspector Michael Joyce, or I'll eat a cow's tail!" he cried, sticking out his hand.

"At your service," replied Joyce. "I guess I'm talking to Dan McCall."

"The same. Glad to meet ya. We just missed running into each other when you were on that Fort Smith counterfeiting case. But we've talked over the long-distance phone, and that's something."

The detective sized up his man rapidly. He knew Mc-Call by reputation as a gun-fighting Westerner, who as a youngster had herded cattle all over Texas and the former Indian Territory, and had made big money before he was twenty-five by buying Mexican steers at bargain prices and running them to the Omaha beef market. When statehood had been granted to Oklahoma, McCall had picked the Osage country for development. He had leased huge cattle ranges from the Indians and nursed the venture to success. Then oil had been struck, and his tenant's rights in more than one section had rolled up a fortune for him. He was called "the uncrowned King of the Osage Hills."

So much for his public standing. Joyce now decided that he also was a magnetic and likable fellow.

"I sure appreciate your putting that young Allan Eagle in touch with me," he remarked, for want of something better to say.

"Don't mention it. I calculated an investigation of this kind would be your meat."

"It's interesting. I never worked among Indians before."

"Just a bunch of big children, ain't they?" Then, as Hawes snickered, he added: "I hear you had a little argument with the Sheriff and the Doc here."

"Not so as you could notice it," answered Joyce calmly. "We met on opposite sides of a coffin, and that's no place for a quarrel. I asked them for explanations of their findings in connection with the death of Jennie Deerfoot. They explained the best they knew how."

Hawes scowled and fidgeted. He seemed unable to decide whether fun was being poked at him.

"I'll tell you what I think—" began McCall, but interrupted himself and dropped a hand upon the shoulder of the pompadoured man, who had been standing by modestly. "I haven't introduced you to the rest of the crowd. Inspector Joyce—Judge Billy Vaughn."

"My pleasure," said Joyce, shaking hands. "Are you the circuit judge, sir?"

"He *is* not," McCall replied boisterously for him. "He used to be a J.P.—a sort of a magistrate for horse thieves and drunks. Now he's a plain lawyer, but we kid him along by calling him 'Judge.'"

Vaughn made a wry face, and said: "Don't you believe him. I was on the bench in territorial days."

His back already turned, McCall gestured toward the cowboys.

"Those two long-horns are named Jack Ramsey and Steve Drake. I took them to Washington with me, and first crack out of the box they pointed to the Capitol and asked me whether it was Abe Lincoln's tomb," he averred.

Everybody laughed, including the cowboys. Joyce appraised the latter as being typical plainsmen, though of the two Jack Ramsey had the stronger and more intelligent countenance, with hard, pale eyes like pebbles. And as he made this observation, the detective recalled that the news in his office had mentioned Johnathan Rumsey—or John Ramsey, as a few of them had it—as the beneficiary of the insurance policy held by the murdered Osage, Harry Roan. They had described him as being a cowboy. Here, perhaps,

was the man. He would have liked to question him, but
Dan McCall was talking again.

"I started to tell you something I thought, when I
plumb choked myself off to do the honors. So I'll tell it
to you now. I think Luther Hawes plays a wicked hand at
poker and holds his liquor like a he-man, but for getting
the lowdown on killers he's about as much use as a school-
ma'am."

Hawes bounced out of his chair, astounded. "The hell
you say!" he cried.

"Sit down. Sit down," grinned Dan. "I love you like a
brother, and don't forget it was I made you Sheriff of this
county. But I've always told you you were on the wrong
track about these Indian murders. I'm answering the
Inspector, who said kind of sarcastic that you'd explained
one of your verdicts the best you knew how."

Joyce glanced from the ranchman's mocking face to the
red and flustered one of Hawes. This was getting good.

"Tain't fair to make sport o' me before an Eastern
galoot—a book deteckative!" the Sheriff raged.

"He's a damned sight more than that. He was one of the
biggest shots in the New York Police Department before he
went into private practice," Dan retorted, suddenly grave.
"Besides, we're trying to avenge murder—murder, do you
understand? That's serious business. If you're blundering,
fear of hurting your feelings is not going to gag me, or
him either."

"I done my dooty as I seen it," Hawes muttered. "I've
took from the evidence that when there *was* murder, it was
just Injun cussedness among themselves."

"Well, why haven't you arrested some of the bad Indians?" Dan yawned. "I say that the crimes are up to pesky
white outlaws from the bad lands."

Purdy, the physician who looked like a desert rat, raked
with soiled fingers at his scraggy white beard.

"Am I to gather, McCall, that you are dubious of my diagnosis of the cause of death in the Jennie Deerfoot autopsy?" he asked, his English smoothly incongruous.

"You're not to gather anything but fees, Doc. What do I know about autopsies? If you satisfied the family and Joyce here, you satisfy me."

Purdy arose, brushing a little surface dirt from his deplorable waistcoat, and moved towards the door. Hawes followed him. The pompadoured Billy Vaughn hesitated, and then joined the procession.

"S'long, Dan, s'long!" they chorused, with varying degrees of warmth.

"I'll be seeing you in church," the ranchman jested, cocking his right eye at their departing figures.

As soon as the door had closed behind them, he looked at Joyce. "I aimed to worry them out of here, so that we could talk turkey. Guess we'd better chase Jack and Steve, too." He talked over his shoulder at the cowboys, without turning:

"One of you long-horns ring the bell in the wall by the window. It connects with the hash-house on the ground floor. I want grub. After you've turned that small trick, you can mosey to the poolroom, or your favorite cat-house for all I care."

Steve Drake, whose back was propped against the frame of the window, extended his left arm carelessly and touched the button with his thumb. But the next instant he withdrew his arm sharply. The cowboy seemed suddenly to feel the necessity of mending his manners. He straightened to a more conventional pose, swung around muttering, "Right, Boss!" and pressed the bell in the ordinary way.

"He's a self-conscious egg," Joyce commented to himself.

Both the cigarette-smoking roughnecks had sheepish expressions as they waited until they heard steps upon the stairs, and then went away, saluting awkwardly.

Dan ordered steaks, apple pie and coffee from the restaurant man. He overruled Joyce's protests. A hearty luncheon together would do them good and make talk easy. Finally, the waiter had been paid and tipped, and they found themselves alone.

"I guess you want to know what I did in Washington," said Dan. "Not so much, and yet it may lead to action. I persuaded the Commissioner for Indian Affairs, if that's his correct handle, that conditions were bad in this country. The Indians aren't being properly protected. I've been doing my best as a private citizen to stamp out lawlessness, but a few Federal agents would help."

"No doubt," replied Joyce. "But why, exactly, did you tip off Allan Eagle to hire me?"

"Because the trouble in that family struck me as being a bit different. It wasn't like the wholesale murdering of the Bighearts, with dynamite plots and ambushes on the roadside. Whenever a Bigheart was killed, there was robbery. The motive was plain."

"And I take it you feel quite sure those crimes were committed by the outlaws you mentioned just now?"

"Yep. The Bert Lawson band, as it's called. But to get back to the Eagle business. That old fellow, Flying-Horse-Tail, was no suicide. He was stabbed to death, but he wasn't robbed. It was a personal vengeance case, a mystery that your detective methods might solve. Have you been able to do anything to clear it up?"

"Not yet. I've been forced to concentrate upon the murder of Jennie Deerfoot, which occurred while you were away."

"Oh, that! I've been hearing about that," commented McCall a trifle scornfully. "I don't believe it was a murder."

"What was it?"

"Rape, probably. The girl was lured into the woods and criminally attacked. She died from heart failure, induced by fright."

"Dr. Purdy called it heart failure, which is just another name for death, by the way. But he said nothing to me about rape. Did he find evidences of it? Was it mentioned in his report?"

"I guess not. He's a pretty punk doc. If a heart is all gone to the devil, he can likely see that. But he doesn't know how to look for fine points. The rape idea is my own. A good-looking gal caught in the woods by some skunk. Why not?"

"Even if it happened as you say, men have been known to silence women by murdering them after an attack of the kind," declared Joyce, troubled.

"That's true, too. But there's no real proof of murder here."

Joyce hesitated. He had kept the facts about the needle from Sheriff Hawes, but now he concluded that there was small justification for keeping Dan McCall in the dark. The ranchman was a disinterested party battling on the side of justice, and not an ignorant official devoured by conceit. Lucidly and swiftly, he recounted all that he had discovered in the Deerfoot parlor as well as on the bloody woodland trail.

McCall listened to him, open-mouthed. The moment he had finished speaking, the big man started to pace the floor excitedly. There could be no doubt that he was profoundly stirred.

"By God, by God!" he repeated several times. "What lousy business! Let me think."

The detective sat perfectly still, to give the other a chance to calm down.

McCall looked as if his reflections were getting him somewhere. He halted in his tracks jerkily.

"I knew there was a memory stewing in the back of my brain," he cried. "I can tell you who murdered Jennie Deerfoot."

CHAPTER NINE
Pride of the Osages

It was one thing for Dan McCall to proclaim, "I can tell you who murdered Jennie Deerfoot!" and quite another for him to prove it, Joyce thought, putting a check upon his exultation. The ranchman had been far from Pawhuska when the outrage was perpetrated. Yet it was interesting that he should make the claim, and from his knowledge of these people, he might well be able to furnish a hot tip. Joyce leaned forward eagerly.

"Who did it?"

"The employer of that boy who found the body. The Cherokee shoemaker, Owl-Face."

"How come?"

"I should think you'd see the connection. He works on leather, and he uses harness needles. Damn few people would have one of those handy as a weapon, or be wise to its value."

"Some sense to that," remarked Joyce, impressed. "But it's no more than a suspicious circumstance."

"I've not finished, Inspector. His boy reports to Hawes that he stumbled upon the body, and three days later this same Benny Gopher is spirited away. Why should the finder of a corpse be kidnapped unless somebody is scared by the knowledge that he'd told less than the whole truth? I say the boy was an accomplice, or at least a witness. The Cherokee sent him to Hawes in the first place."

"Why?"

"He feared that a search party would discover Jennie dead. Then somebody might remember having seen Benny around that neck of the woods. It was safer to answer all questions in advance by having him go to the Sheriff with a story. Or so he thought. Then, when the boy began to shoot off his mouth around town, it worried Owl-Face."

"I see," replied Joyce, uncomfortably aware that he himself had not checked up the matter of Benny's presence at the scene of the murder, twenty miles from Pawhuska. It needed explaining. "But Chief Pale-Horse Eagle claims that there were three assailants in that clearing, not two," he went on.

"I've a lot of respect for Indian scouting, but with the tracks washed out by rain the Chief may have been mistaken."

"There's the brother, Harry Deerfoot, to consider," protested Joyce. "He had an injured thumb, and he was last seen in the same car with Benny."

"The boy may have talked recklessly to him, and so they were both kidnapped. If Deerfoot was the murderer, as you think, and was lighting out of his own free will, he'd have been crazy to take Benny along."

"Seems that way. We're talking through our hats, though, unless we can get something positive on Owl-Face. Circumstantial evidence has to be good to convince a jury."

"Here's what you don't know and couldn't know unless you'd lived the life of this town," challenged McCall, a note of triumph in his booming voice. "The Cherokee for years has been going to Fairfax every Tuesday, to pick up business. There's no shoemaker there. Jennie Deerfoot was killed five days ago—and that was a Tuesday, wasn't it?"

"Right. Then Benny's movements that day are account-
ed for by the fact that he hit the road with his boss." Joyce
showed his excitement by no more than the narrowing of
his eyelids and the vibrancy of his tone. "Didn't it occur
to Hawes to question Owl-Face, too?"

"Nothing sensible occurs to Hawes in a murder case. I
wish I hadn't backed him for Sheriff. He was probably told
that the boy was on his own, playing hooky from work,
and he swallowed it whole."

"I can have the Cherokee held by the local Police—not
the Sheriff's office—can't I? Material witness stuff, until
I'm ready to grill him?"

"Sure. A word from me to any cop's enough."

"Then, let's go."

McCall jumped up and put on a gray Stetson hat. He
and the detective descended to the street and walked the
few blocks to Owl-Face's shop. But they found the latter
closed and padlocked. A sense of disappointment gripped
Joyce.

"Maybe this bird has been tipped, and has flown the
coop, too," he muttered.

"It's certainly not like him to be away from business in
broad daylight," said McCall.

They continued along the street until they met a white
policeman, to whom the cattle king spoke:

"'Morning, Siegel. This gentleman is Inspector Joyce
from New York City. He's working on the Indian murders,
and he has my confidence. I guess he's got something special on his mind. Play along with him, and to hell with
what the Sheriff thinks!"

Siegel saluted obsequiously. It was plain that the ranchman was a real power in Pawhuska.

"I want you to pinch the shoemaker, Owl-Face. Book
him on some charge that doesn't mean a thing. I'll be in
to talk to your chief about it later," Joyce told the officer.

"Ah'll pick him up right smart for yew, Inspector. Ah sho' will," replied Siegel, who despite his German name was an exaggerated type of Southern cracker.

Joyce went a step or two farther with McCall, and then declined an invitation to make a round of visits to the local white celebrities whom he had not yet met.

"I've some musts to attend to with the Horse-Eagles," he said, "but I'll be keeping in touch with you."

"Maybe I'll send you a message in the afternoon. I'm going to get my ranch on the phone, and it wouldn't surprise me if news had broken up there," McCall answered.

They shook hands.

Secretly, Joyce felt worried at having left Kay alone for so long a time in the threatened Indian household. And he was anxious to straighten out the matter of protection for the recalcitrant Joe Yellow-Horse.

He hailed a cruising Ford taxi, and rode out to the Chief's feudal mansion with its dependent cottages and tepees clustered under the trees. In the parlor, he found Kay chatting with Allan as quietly as if their only problem were that of entertaining each other socially. He described briefly the developments which had grown out of his conference with Dan McCall.

"This bringing of Owl-Face into the picture is unexpected," he stated in conclusion. "But it's more than a pipe-dream. The evidence links up pretty closely."

"All the same, I think Dan is mistaken," countered Allan. "I swear by my father's woodcraft. He said that three men had been at that murder scene, and that some of them at least were white."

"We'll know the truth before we're through," snapped Joyce. "How's Sylvia Deerfoot? Have you heard from her today?"

"She just telephoned. She's perfectly well."

"Does her family get along with Symes?"

"Oh, yes! Sylvia says she has never known any one who had less to say and gave less trouble."

Joyce could not help smiling. He saw a mental picture of the Sheriff—his own Sheriff, in contradistinction to Hawes—sitting around drably, or slipping like a neutral shadow from room to room of an Osage home.

"And where's my son Tom?" he pursued.

"In back somewhere, waiting for Joe Yellow-Horse to return," answered Allan.

"What do you mean 'return'?"

"Joe insisted on going riding in his car by himself. He wouldn't allow your son to accompany him—pushed him off the running board, in fact."

"The damn' fool! Is he trying to commit suicide? Doesn't he realize I want him guarded, to save his life if possible?" Joyce raged.

"He is in a very bad, dark temper," droned Allan, curiously Indian of a sudden.

"What's biting him? You ought to know. He's your cousin."

"Joe is angry with me for crossing him in New York about the Swift-Horse brothers. It seems he quarreled with them on the train coming West. He told me as he got into his car that he would take his own vengeance on them."

"Good Lord! We've got to stop that. The Swift-Horses may be guilty, but if vendettas go off at half-cock inside the family, clues will become so tangled we'll never land anywhere."

"You are right. Perhaps my race cannot be saved. Perhaps we are doomed to be destroyed by follies of this kind," answered Allan fatalistically.

"Rot!" cried Joyce. "I'll talk to Joe Yellow-Horse as soon as he comes in."

He went out to the porch alone, lighted a strong cigar and strode up and down impatiently. The wait proved not to be long. A roadster presently came tearing up the street at the usual break-neck speed in which Indians delighted, and headed for the garage to the left of the house. Joyce followed it, and stopped Joe Yellow-Horse just as the latter was starting afoot down the pathway that led to his own residence in the rear.

It was the first time that the detective had had direct conversation with this Osage, whose face lacked the cultivated intelligence of Allan's, but who was none the less a handsome red-bronze image of a man.

"I hear you refuse to have my son around you, Yellow-Horse," said Joyce crisply. "What's the idea?"

The other drew himself up stiffly. "I need no help in dealing with my enemies, sir," he replied in good English.

"You're 'way off the track—'way off. I took this murder case because you and Allan Black-Horse Eagle and a bunch of others came to New York and hired me. Savvy? Now I've got to be let run it the best I know how. I don't want you killed, and I can't have you making plans on the side."

Joe looked at him gloomily. "I am a warrior's son," he muttered.

"Sure. And a brave man yourself." Joyce shifted his position adroitly and gave him flattery. "But the danger to your people today is like war. Many heads, many strong arms and one leader are better in war than the confusion of everybody fighting for himself."

"Yet, if a blood brother be treacherous!" The Indian spoke obliquely, as if posing a question.

"Who has been treacherous?"

"The Swift-Horses. In the great city, they fired an arrow, not caring whether it pierced my body or the body of Allan. For afterwards they would have shot again and killed the other."

"How do you know?"

"I read it in the eyes of Sam Swift-Horse."

"No more than that? You did not see him do anything evil?"

"I did not need to. His right eye was the eye of a man who casts a spell, and his left eye was full of death. Then he went walking with Thomas Swift-Horse, though the streets of the great city were strange to them and full of perils. Murder was in both their hearts."

"Oh!" Joyce was a little baffled by the Osage's mystical talk. But he seized on the fact that no real evidence was being presented against the Swift-Horses. "I don't want you to kill either of them until we know the whole story. It would not be just. They may be innocent."

"I shall not kill unless I am attacked," Joe Yellow-Horse promised tonelessly.

"That isn't quite enough." Joyce pressed his advantage. "Your life must be protected. Suppose you were attacked suddenly in the dark, without being given a chance to defend yourself. I urge you to let my son stay beside you night and day, walk and eat with you and sleep in the same room. I think it will only be for a short while."

The Osage stared wordlessly for a minute or two, then, broke into a high-pitched, fierce declamation, the phrases chopped off and interspersed with weird native cries:

"Those of my blood know how to fight and to suffer— Ha-ya! My father and his brother, the Big Chief, fought the whites in the old days and took many scalps. None were cowards—Hi-yu! When I was a boy, I knew my grand-father. Chief Tail-Horse Eagle. A bold warrior. A man who rode the far North plains and shed his blood at the Little Big Horn. He saw Custer die—Ay-ay-ay! In his last days, he say to me:

"'Yellow-Horse, danger is nothing, pain is nothing. Only the coward dies the dog's death.'" The Indian paused, to beat with both fists upon his broad chest, absurdly covered with a wrinkled blue serge waistcoat. "Haya! My

grandfather built a fire as I watched, and put his hand into
the flames. He let them burn away his hand, which was too
old for fighting. He say: 'Yellow-Horse, it does not hurt
when the heart is strong.' I always remember that lesson,
Pale-Face. If I am to be murdered in the dark, I do not fear
it. My heart, too, is strong."

Joyce sought desperately for an argument against this
splendid fanaticism.

"Listen, Joe," he said in a quiet, friendly voice. "Those
were grand days. But it's different now. You didn't have
any money to worry about in those days. The oil has made
you rich, understand! It has put bad, new ideas into the
heads of your own folks. Women are being murdered, as
well as warriors. That's why you had to come to white
men, to ask their advice. That's why you hired me. Don't
you agree it would be sort of the fair thing to let me do
my job in my own way? I'm asking for the right to risk the
life of my son when I put him to stand guard over you."

Once more, the Indian remained silent for a protracted
spell. Then he said stoically: "I cannot argue against such
talk. You may do as you will." He had evidently relieved
his feelings by getting his tribal philosophy off his chest.
A case having been made out for his pride, the practicality
which had been drilled into him in an American grammar
school took the upper hand.

Joyce felt, also, that his final argument about the risk
Tom would be running had had its effect.

They went together to Joe Yellow-Horse's house, where
they found the younger Joyce sitting on the steps, like a
sentry who knows his post has lost its significance, but
whose officer has forgotten to relieve him. The blond lad
jumped up. He suggested a football player rather than an
operative, Joyce thought critically.

"Hello, Dad! If you're going to have a conference with
our friend here, can I run over and talk to Kay?"

"Nothing doing. The conference is over, and Mr. Yellow-Horse has agreed to co-operate. Your real job has just begun. See that you don't let him out of your sight for a moment."

The Indian stretched out his hand to Tom. "I shall not be too much trouble to you. Please consider yourself my guest as well as my jailor," he said, with a touch of whimsy unusual in a red man.

Joyce left them and went his way moodily. The complications of this case were irking him. He wished he could get a report from the scout, Al Jenkins, whom he had sent up country on the trail of Harry Deerfoot and Benny Gopher. The business of exhuming the body of Flying-Horse-Tail, Joe's father, was an unpleasant task ahead, though since the cause of death had been established and this would simply be a precautionary measure in the hope of finding clues, it was not urgent. The shoemaker Owl-Face and his whereabouts took precedence. If the local Police flopped on locating Owl-Face that same day, Joyce would have to try to make the arrest personally.

Before returning to the Big Chief's house, he made a detour through the settlement of tepees, and by judiciously indifferent questioning he came unheralded to the one occupied by the Swift-Horse brothers. The two oldish men were sitting outdoors with their wives, smoking. They accorded Joyce a grave salute, and as they spoke almost no English it was useless for him to attempt a conversation. He had simply wanted to check up on their activities, which had all the appearance of bucolic innocence. Impossible, of course, to tell what schemes were stewing in a blanket Indian's mind, but he found it difficult to take seriously Joe's accusations against this pair.

He struck back across the garden and had reached the corner of the porch before he saw that a man was lounging there in a cane-seated chair, awaiting him. Al Jenkins. The

quarter-breed was precisely one of the persons he expected
to hear from, yet his physical presence was astonishing.
He had supposed he would phone in from an outlying
township, if he had news. Bounding up the steps two at a
time, Joyce said as much to his scout.

Al scratched his head above the left ear and looked
foolish. "Snakes, Boss," he said, "I plumb hate to use them
instruments! I can't hear a word of what the other feller
is saying to me, I get so rattled. Man to man talk is more
my style."

Inspector Joyce, alert crime hound, groaned. "Well,
have you brought me anything?" he asked resignedly.

"Sure have. Your two Injuns are prisoners in a camp at
Beaver Dam in the Osage Hills, fifty miles from here."

"What sort of camp? Whites or redskins?"

"Whites. A mob of outlaws, but they have some no-
good Injuns along with them."

Joyce said to himself: "By God, Dan McCall is right!
The whole plot ties up with the bandits." Aloud, he inquired: "Did you see Deerfoot and the kid?"

"No. Couldn't get that close. But I met a pal who gave
me the fac's positive. You can trust that info'." Al Jenkins
grinned in a manner that suggested he had his own secret
alliances in the bad lands.

"You've done a good job. Hang around. I may have
something else for you."

"Thankee kindly. But I got more to tell right now."

"Yes? What?"

"This morning I met Owl-Face, the Cherokee, on a
pinto pony and riding licketty-split in the direction of
that there same Beaver Dam."

Joyce started to say something, but the quarter-breed
drawled straight on, as if he had read his employer's mind:

"How the hell could I know you wanted the coyote?
You should of told me. But the minute I hit town I hear

you're after him, and the best I can do is to give you the
low-down. Owl-Face will be in the Osage Hills by tomorrow morning."

CHAPTER TEN
Joe Yellow-Horse Pays

Joyce went directly to the telephone after leaving the scout, and called Dan McCall. He was too good a strategist to reveal the crux of his story without feeling the other man out, and he began by asking what Dan knew about the Beaver Dam section, as well as the outlaws who lurked there.

"Why, hell, it's on the edge of one of my ranches," the cattle king replied breezily. "Can't say I get much good out of the nearby runs, because if I put steers to graze anywhere handy to the Dam, I wouldn't have a one of them left in a week. It's a nest of real tough hombres."

"Is that the Bert Lawson gang I've been hearing about?"

"Yes, and no. Lawson hangs out deeper in the back country, but I guess he has a hold on this crowd, too."

"I wanted to know, because a hot report has just been made to me," said Joyce quietly. "Harry Deerfoot and Benny Gopher were taken to Beaver Dam by the men who kidnapped them, and Owl-Face has been seen galloping on horseback in the same direction."

"The hell you say! Is this straight goods?" Dan's hearty voice quivered with excitement.

"I think so. It comes from a special agent I put on the job."

"Who's he?"

"I prefer not to give his name over the phone."

"Oh, all right! It doesn't matter to me. I can tell you that if kidnappers were in cahoots with those outlaws, Beaver Dam would be the first place they'd head for. But I figure now that only Deerfoot is a prisoner. They may have collared him because he began to get wise to how his sister died. In that case, they probably won't let him live long. But Benny was sent away to stop his gabbing, and now the Cherokee has gone to join him. Scared out of town by your work, I should say."

"You have quite some bunch of ideas," commented Joyce. "I've got to work this out for myself, of course; but you can take it from me, I won't let the murderer of Jennie Deerfoot escape by flight. Thanks for the dope on Beaver Dam."

"Hold on there. Don't ring off yet. Let me think," cried Dan. He could be heard over the wire clicking his tongue, and presently he said:

"You're going to find that all trails lead back to those bad men in the hills. Except probably the Flying-Horse-Tail stabbing, which I still think was a personal affair. Why not come out to the ranch house as my guest? You'll get a great line on things that way, and maybe you'll be able to help me in my fight against the outlaws."

"Thank you," answered Joyce, startled, "but I'm taking the Big Chief's money, and his family troubles right here in town come first with me."

"Well, bear what I said in mind and visit the ranch whenever you're able."

"I will. Thanks. Did you phone your foreman, by the way, as you said you were going to?"

"Sure did. But he had nothing much to report."

"When are you leaving for the ranch?"

"Tomorrow afternoon."

"Well, I'll be in touch with you again. Good-bye." Joyce hung up.

He transferred the center of action to Allan Eagle and Kay, who had listened to him, astonished, while he conducted his conversation with Dan over the telephone in the parlor. "We must let Sylvia Deerfoot know about her brother," he said.

"It begins to look less likely that he killed Jennie, doesn't it?" inquired Allan.

"If he's actually held captive, yes. But that may be a stall. He may have taken refuge with the bandits, so that the word could be passed around that he had been kidnapped. The point that worries me is why Owl-Face should beat it up there to join them."

"You don't put a great deal of stock in the theory of Owl-Face being the murderer?"

"No more than I did this morning. It's possible, but the motive is kinda far-fetched. Rape. That old Cherokee. Hm! I'm going to question Doc Purdy about it, and Hawes, too. But let's go see Sylvia first."

They called the old Chief, got out the car and started for the Deerfoot home, with Allan driving. On the way, Joyce mentioned another angle.

"I'll be wanting to visit that trick Sheriff at his office, any how," he said. "He hung on to the knife with which Flying-Horse-Tail Eagle was killed, and it's important I should lamp that. Gee, it's no cinch trying to solve two separate murder mysteries at the same time!"

Sylvia herself opened the door to them and stepped back, her copper-brunette skin paling as if she feared that the whole crowd would not have come except to break bad news. But Allan reassured her in a few words.

"Harry's life is safe, so far," he asserted in conclusion. "And nobody would dream of accusing *him* of a crime until it's known whether or not he's been victimized himself."

She led them into the parlor, empty now of that mournful coffin which had been lowered into its grave the previous day. But they stood around restlessly, troubled, unwilling to sit and talk there. The spell was broken when there materialized, apparently from nowhere, the colorless figure of G. Borden Symes. He came slipping around a bookcase, his narrow, unimportant face preoccupied with business which no one would feel interested to question, and his dark gray suit of clothes merging into the background.

"Howdy, Inspector," he said lackadaisically.

"Hello, Sheriff! Anything to report on the assignment here?"

"Not a thing. All quiet, night and day."

"That's good."

Symes moved off noiselessly, but stopped. "I've been talking to some of the folks that come visiting at the back door. This may amuse you, Inspector—" the lack-lustre eyes brightened a trifle—"but it seems the local Sheriff is sore at me."

"Hawes sore—at you. What for?"

"A man who's friendly with the cook asked me who I was. Knew me for your operative, of course, but wanted to be told what I'd done in the detective business. I said I'd been Sheriff of Algonquin County, New York, and that that had qualified me for Agency work."

"I don't see anything about that piece of information to get Hawes's dander up."

The ideal shadow grinned. "Well, I happened to mention that everybody still called me 'Sheriff.' The guy took the word back to Hawes, and he got sore as a pup. Others have posted me that he's saying he won't stand for a second person with the title of Sheriff in this County."

Despite the tragic atmosphere of the parlor, Joyce doubled up in sudden, explosive mirth. This story, as told by the dry and unemphatic Symes, served to release the tension under which he had been laboring. When he had caught his breath, he said:

"We're going down to see Hawes now. Suppose you come along with us."

"You don't think it unwise to irritate him?" Symes murmured.

"That big bluff!" exclaimed Joyce. "He needs to be razzed. I'll get more out of him that way." He turned to Sylvia. "If your bodyguard goes, you'll have to come, too. A spin in the fresh air will do you good."

The girl agreed readily. The talk between Joyce and his assistant had moved her to cryptic Indian amusement, and now she seemed brighter than she had been for days. She put on a smart little hat with feathers that was only partly white-American in character, and Symes fetched the gray cloth cap he wore by preference. A cap somehow made him thoroughly inconspicuous, like a second-rate salesman, or an honest mechanic out of a job. They all piled into the limousine and drove to the center of town, where the Sheriff's office was located above a hardware store.

Hawes's voice could be heard through the open windows, orating. A deputy who was sitting in the frame of one of the windows with his knees crooked shouted that visitors had arrived, and Hawes poked his head out. A look of disgust spread over his sun-tanned countenance when he saw who they were.

"There you are," growled Joyce to his companions. "He's pulling a party. I knew he wouldn't be attending to business, so we might as well land here in a bunch."

He led the way up the creaking stairs and invaded a room murky with tobacco smoke. In addition to three deputies, McCall's cowboys, Jack Ramsey and Steve Drake, Doctor Purdy and the so-called Judge Vaughn were keeping the Sheriffs company. Joyce was pleased, at all events, to see Purdy.

Hawes waved a shirt-sleeved arm. "Callers welcome here on business or pleasure, boys or girls, white skins or red," he cried sarcastically. "The emporium of justice for the Osage country, that's what this is."

Joyce came right to the point: "I'd like to see you and Doctor Purdy alone, if you can spare a few minutes."

The curt, cold voice had a sobering effect.

"Okay." Hawes straightened his rangy form and entered a private room, followed by Purdy and the detective. The only pieces of furniture in there were a desk, three chairs and an iron safe of very ancient vintage. The men sat down.

"I won't keep you long," said Joyce. "It's been suggested to me that the motive for the killing of Jennie Deerfoot was rape. You both examined her body. Can you confirm or deny the rumor?"

"I can state definitely that no such outrage was committed," answered Purdy quickly. But Joyce knew that he might be lying, to cover up his incompetence.

"My expert testimony is teetotally similar," stated Hawes, with a leer which a devastating stare from the Inspector caused to vanish.

"Very well," conceded Joyce, who had checked the matter in this quarter by way of routine. It was a partial reassurance that both Purdy and Hawes should deny that rape had occurred, and he hoped from the bottom of his heart that he would not be forced to exhume the corpse later on to make sure. If the murderer could be convicted on different evidence, so much the better.

"There's one other thing," he continued. "I want to see the knife that was found plunged into Flying-Horse-Tail Eagle's side."

Hawes bridled. "Still snooping after that suicide, are yer?"

"I don't care what you call it. I represent the family, and I have the right to look at the weapon."

"Here, get an eyeful," said Hawes sourly. He turned to the iron safe, unlocked it and drew out a repellent, be-smeared object which he slammed upon the desk.

Joyce gave the knife close scrutiny for several minutes. It was simply an old hunting knife, with a worn handle and a blade about six inches long. The dirt and dried blood upon it had blackened, and was now coated with dust. All fingerprints had certainly been erased by time and careless handling. The only feature of some slight interest was a fresh nick in the blade, presumably caused by contact with the victim's ribs.

"Who owned the knife?" the detective asked.

"Flying-Horse-Tail himself, o' course. Half a dozen Injuns swore to that."

"In which side had he been stabbed?"

"Left side—where the heart is."

"And which of his hands was clenched on the weapon?"

"The right hand. I noticed particular. He'd reached across his chest to plunge it in."

"That will be all, thank you," said Joyce, and stood up.

The three men returned to the outer office. Hawes's friends and the party consisting of the old and young Chiefs, Sylvia Deerfoot, Kay and Symes had not frater-nized. The Osages and Kay were still in a little group by the door. But Symes had been sauntering around unobtru-sively, and was now contemplating with a sad, harmless expression a colored print of a group of Mack Sennett bathing beauties, tacked to the wall.

"Here's a man I've been wanting you to meet. You two have a lot in common," remarked Joyce maliciously to Hawes. "One of my most trusted assistants—Sheriff Symes. Shake hands with the law officer of Osages County, Symes."

The Oklahoman jumped a step backwards, and his jaws began to work furiously, as if he were chewing gum.

His neck and temples flushed brick red. Nevertheless, his courtesy challenged by a guest and colleague, he stuck out his hand. Symes took it limply, with a reproachful side glance at Joyce.

"Meaning no offense," said Hawes, "where the hell are you the Sheriff of?"

"Nowhere. They just call me that. I used to be one, though, up near the Vermont border in New York State."

"Dew tell! I'll not deny I've been a-hearin' this yarn about you." Hawes, ponderously ribald, appealed to his own satellites with a guffaw. "Can you shoot a gun?"

"I've done it plenty."

"Real quick on the trigger?"

"I don't pretend to beat the stunts in a Wild West show, if that's what you mean," said Symes, starting to get mad.

"Stunts! Show!" Hawes repeated the words wrathfully. "We're plumb in the West, brother, and don't need no shows. I'm askin' whether you figger you could round up a bunch of hell-roarin', gun-shootin' bad hombres in this man's territory and fill the hoosegow with them?"

"How do I know?" snapped Symes. "I never was in such a situation."

"Then don't call yourself a Sheriff in these parts. It listens foolish. You may be an Eastern Sheriff—"

"I've informed you that I'm not a Sheriff at all," the other interrupted, as close to a state of frenzy as Joyce had ever seen him. "I'm a detective—a dick—a gum-shoe artist—get me? And I don't have to care whether you like my name, or my face either, thank God! I'm not working for you, Mister."

"Nor couldn't be at any price," blustered Hawes. "My last kid deputy is more of a two-fisted he-man than you are. Sheriff!—huh!"

"Oh, shut up!" said Symes.

Joyce interposed, choking back his mirth with difficulty. "I'm the one who's responsible for his nickname, and I won't use it again in your hearing," he promised the disgruntled title-holder. "Let's all shake hands, and no hard feelings!"

Hawes glared, but ended by exchanging grips with a show of magnanimity. He saw them to the head of the stairs, and before they had reached the sidewalk, they could hear him boasting to his cronies of the victory gained.

Joyce and his entourage departed in good humor for the Indian homes. Even G. Borden Symes could see the comedy of the role he had been jockeyed into playing, and at intervals his narrow face cracked in a quite soundless laugh. But a let-down followed. The net result of the visit to Sheriff Hawes's office had been essentially sinister. No one except Joyce had seen the murder knife, and it was far from clear in his mind as yet whether it had conveyed a clue to him. But somewhere there most surely had been a clue. Everybody felt that. Was it, indeed, related to the knife itself? Or did they have a hunch that Hawes and the shady Doctor Purdy were in some conspiracy of silence, that the intimacy of all these white men, including McCall's cowboys, could bode no good for Osage interests? Joyce recalled again that one of the punchers, Jack Ramsey, had benefited from an assassinated Indian's insurance policy.

Sylvia Deerfoot and Symes were deposited at the Deerfoot house, and the others returned to the Big Chief's. Looking at Kay reflectively, Joyce said:

"I don't believe we'll be able to learn much more today or this evening. Tomorrow may bring developments. I'm going to work up a scheme with Al Jenkins for penetrating to the Beaver Dam hide-out."

The crushing surprise that the morning was destined to bring, however, was remote from his dreams.

Shortly after dawn, he was awakened by a heavy pound-
ing on his door. He leaped out of bed, and opened to his
son Tom. The latter stood on the threshold, his hair rum-
pled and his face distraught.

"Dad," the young fellow mouthed, struggling for breath.
"Dad, Joe Yellow-Horse was killed during the night."

Joyce's first reaction was one of icy contempt. "You *let*
him be killed?" he accused, almost before his brain had
had time to grasp the information.

"My bed was right beside his. Yet I didn't wake up.
I—I've failed you, Dad. I only just discovered he'd been
stabbed to death."

"Stabbed, eh! Joseph and Mary! You should have heard
that kind of struggle." Joyce was thinking fast now. He
rushed to Allan Eagle's room and aroused the young Chief.

"Joe Yellow-Horse has been murdered," he threw at him
baldly. "I want you to locate the Swift-Horse brothers,
pronto. I'll be dressing."

Allan slipped his feet into sandals, drew a blanket about
his shoulders and was gone in a flash, without uttering a
word. He returned as Joyce was buttoning his coat.

"The Swift-Horses went away during the night," he reported. "The women in their tepee say they do not know
where they have gone."

CHAPTER ELEVEN
Stabbed to the Heart

The circumstances of Joe Yellow-Horse's death afforded Joyce one notable advantage and simplified his task, he felt, in solving the murders of the latest victim's father and of Jennie Deerfoot. For the first time, he had a chance to examine the body and the scene of the crime before any one else had tampered with them. If, as appeared probable to him, all the killings had been perpetrated at the behest of a single plotter, or group of plotters, he should now be able to get a true line on their methods and identity. If, as was even more likely, Flying-Horse-Tail and Joe Yellow-Horse, had been slain by the same hand, he stood a fair show of discovering evidence that would pin the guilt upon that person.

Without allowing them even the leisure for breakfast, he took Allan, Kay and Tom to the dead man's house, to aid him in a preliminary investigation. The local Police would have to be notified pretty promptly, and it was vital that he should steal a march upon their ineptness. Hawes, he realized thankfully, would have only secondary authority within the bounds of the city of Pawhuska, and would be out of this.

As they entered the bedroom where the tragedy had occurred, Joyce noted instantly that there were remarkably few indications of violence. Clothed in an old-fashioned

white nightgown, the body lay on its back in bed, with one
arm flung out and the other hand crisped upon the cover-
let. The last-named and the sheets had been pulled back,
exposing the chest and most of the left side, and they
were still in a fairly orderly condition. Joe Yellow-Horse
undoubtedly had rolled over once or twice before he died,
but he had finished on his back and his legs were stretched
out straight. His rigid, upturned toes made a little mound
draped with bedclothes.

A deep and gaping wound was visible over his heart,
though the torn nightgown and clotted blood partly veiled
it. His torso was weltering in a veritable pool of blood.

Joyce began by making a quick search for the knife, or
dagger, with which the ghastly business had been accomplished. He was scarcely disappointed at not finding it.
This had not been planned to look like suicide, and the
murderer had made off with the weapon.

He then scrutinized the wound. It had been inflicted
with a curious upward stroke, beginning at the seventh
rib and apparently driving to the heart at a sharp angle.
Several of the ribs seemed to be fractured, but it would be
impossible to know that for sure until after the autopsy.
No fingerprints could be detected on the sheets, pillow or
nightgown.

The next obvious leads would be footprints and other
evidence to show how the miscreant had entered the room.
The inquiry in this direction proved to be more fruitful. A window giving on the vegetable garden had been
pried open. It was on the side near Yellow-Horse's bed and
away from Tom's. The Indian inevitably would have had
the window closed, both as a precaution and because when
Indians sleep in a house they paradoxically shut out the
night air. But it had not been locked. Joyce marked this
as a point against Tom's efficiency. Even an insecure lock

could not have been worked loose without arousing the
light-slumbering redskin.

Between the window and the bed there were tracks,
huge, clumsy footprints which the detective deduced had
been made by sandals or boots wrapped in burlap. He
picked up a strand of the coarse cloth, but felt that it
would be of little service as a clue. Burlap bags were to be
found in almost every household.

More interesting was a piece of waxed thread, some
eighteen inches long, very dirty and crumpled into a loose
ball. Joyce exhibited it to Kay.

"What do you make of that?"

She shook her head. "Not a whole lot. It may have belonged to Yellow-Horse."

"Maybe. It was on the floor where the killer had passed,
and it seems to say something special to me. I don't know
what yet." Joyce folded his silk handkerchief carefully
around the piece of thread and put it in his pocket.

He continued to rove the room, peering into every
corner and halting to observe how bits of furniture were
standing and whether there was dust upon them. His nostrils vibrated oddly. Finally, he did something which completely mystified the others. He approached the grisly bed,
stooped down and smelled at the pillow, his cheek within
a few inches of that of the corpse.

"Tom," he asked, "have you got a headache?"

"A slight one—not worth mentioning," his son answered self-consciously.

"A little tight about the temples, eh?"

"Yes, that's it."

"I thought so. The murderer used chloroform on both
you and Yellow-Horse. That was the only way he could
have pulled off the job without a struggle. You just couldn't
have slept through it normally." Joyce held his head on

one side and measured the distance between the window and the bed. "I figure that after he got the window open, he doused chloroform on a pad tied to the end of a stick and shoved it against Yellow-Horse's face. He likely did the same to you subsequent to entering the room, but too hurriedly for it to affect you seriously. Then he knifed our friend."

"I'm lucky he didn't stab me, also," muttered Tom.

"Lucky is a mild word for it! Your patron Saint must have been watching out for you. Perhaps you stirred around, and he thought you were coming to. Wanted to make his getaway without risking a fight. Hm!" Joyce reached abstractedly for a cigar and lighted it.

"The piece of thread you picked up," remarked Kay thoughtfully. "It's waxed. I should say he was a man accustomed to carrying a supply and employing it in place of string. He probably bound the chloroform pad to the stick with waxed thread."

"Sound reasoning, me darlin'. Now Owl-Face, being a shoemaker, would fit the ticket. Leather is always sewed with coarse waxed thread. But Owl-Face, according to Al Jenkins, was headed for the Osage Hills last night."

"Let me give my opinion," put in Allan Eagle. "Nothing about this crime suggests that it was committed by an Indian. The use of chloroform is beyond the imagination of the average Osage. And once he had entered this bedroom, a killer of my race would have certainly destroyed both men."

"I think you've got the right dope, Chief," declared Joyce grimly. "But there never was such a thing as a sure deduction about murder. We must find the facts."

"How?"

"Do I know? The next move is to give the Pawhuska Police their innings."

On orders from his father, Tom went to the nearest telephone and called up the local Headquarters, reporting the fact that a man had been done to death, but furnishing no details. Within half an hour, there arrived Thad Calkins, Police Chief, the patrolman Siegel and a hayseed plainclothesman named Pitta. To stall meddling with his private investigation, Joyce had deliberately avoided meeting Calkins, whom he now discovered to be an energetic, if amateurish, officer, noisily respectful of the former head of New York's Homicide Squad.

Calkins fussed around and proclaimed it to be "as plain as a pikestaff" that Yellow-Horse had been stalked by some enemy, undoubtedly a native, knifed in his sleep and slain so instantly that his guard had not been awakened. He submitted this simple diagnosis to Joyce with ejaculations of disgust for redskin bloodthirstiness. The Inspector nodded. There was slim hope of catching the murderer, said Calkins, for as every Oklahoman knew, the reasons for Indian feuds were pretty impenetrable. However, he was going to do his darndest.

"No hard feelings, I hope, over my working along my own lines?" queried Joyce.

"I'm honored to see you on this here case," cried Calkins expansively.

"Fine. Then, will you do this for me? Have an autopsy performed by the best surgeon on your list, and furnish me with an exact, detailed description of the cause of death?"

"Of the knife wound?"

"Yes—the dimensions, the injury to bones and tissues—everything."

"I'll be glad to have it done, though it don't seem necessary. Plain as a pikestaff how this Injun checked out."

"All the same!" shrugged Joyce. He waited until the surgeon arrived, so as to make sure that it wasn't Dr. Purdy.

The body of Joe Yellow-Horse was then transferred to
the room in the rear of Police Headquarters which served
as the city morgue of Pawhuska.

Family breakfast that morning was a dreary affair,
though no one would have been able to tell from Big
Chief Pale-Horse Eagle's stoical countenance that a new
and ruthless blow had been dealt to his household. Asked
for an opinion, the hardening of his keen old eyes was the
only sign that he had heard.

"With us, blood bro-ther no kill bro-ther," he declared
at last, and would say no more, even when urged to hazard
a guess where and why the Swift-Horses had departed.

Joyce, also, remained moody. He experienced a sense
of personal defeat in connection with this latest murder.
If he had not been able to protect Joe, how could he hope
to save the Chiefs at whose table he was sitting? How
guard the lovely Sylvia Deerfoot from the fate which had
overtaken her sister? Short of bringing his whole force of
operatives from New York, he lacked the man power to battle with the widespread plot that clearly existed. He could
demand the help of State troopers, but if he did that before
he had put his finger on the key to the mystery he would
have flopped as a detective. Allan Eagle might as well have
taken his troubles to Oklahoma City in the first place.

His uneasy reflections were interrupted by the sound
of an automobile drawing up at the front door, and in a
moment the bell rang. A servant answered it. The loud and
dynamic voice of Dan McCall reverberated in the hallway.

Accompanied by Kay and Allan, Joyce left the table
to greet him. He found the ranchman flanked by his two
cowboys, Ramsey and Drake. Dan strode forward a few
steps, his hand outstretched.

"I've heard what has happened here. By God, this
slaughter of Indians is a disgrace to the County! You and
I have got to put a stop to it, Inspector."

"Yeah! But how?"

"Root out the bandits, lock, stock and barrel, from the Osage Hills."

"You think a bandit killed Joe Yellow-Horse in his house in this backyard?"

"Sure do."

"I'm kind of tired of hearing that explanation," said Joyce tartly. "What bandit? How would he sneak in and out of Pawhuska without anybody noticing him? Until this morning, you thought the murder of Yellow-Horse's father was an exception to your theory. Now you say the son was stabbed by a bandit."

"The death of Joe is precisely what's made me change my mind about Flying-Horse-Tail. Everything is of a piece, I guess. I blame the outlaws, and by the right hind leg of the Lamb of God, I'm going to get them for it!"

"Maybe you're right. But around here we're worried by the disappearance of two of Joe's cousins who'd been scrapping with him—the Swift-Horses."

"That so? Tell me about it."

Joyce sketched the essential details, and Dan listened intently. Frowning, he weighed the implications.

"This fits in with what I proposed to you yesterday, and what I'm proposing again. Your latest Injun suspects have fled to the hills, it's safe to bet on that. Deerfoot and Benny Gopher are there. Owl-Face, too. Even if they're not tied up with the outlaws, they're in the same territory. Come out with me to the ranch, Inspector, and you can hunt your game while I hunt mine."

With Yellow-Horse dead, the argument now seemed forceful to Joyce. "I'd do it in a minute, if it weren't for leaving my clients unprotected here," he said frankly.

"I thought you'd spring that, and I've got the answer ready," grinned Dan. "We'll take them all along—the two Chiefs and the girl, Sylvia—your operatives—everybody."

Not a bad solution, if they'll come." Joyce swung around, and interrogated Allan with a glance.

"It is excellent," the Osage replied promptly. "I can speak for my father and Sylvia. They will do anything that both you and I think best. In fact, my father has already expressed the opinion that he and I would do well to follow the trail to Beaver Dam."

Joyce nodded to Dan. "There you are! I guess we'll be accepting your hospitality. When do we start?"

"Three o'clock this afternoon." The ranchman jumped up and down in what was almost a caper of delight at making his point. "I've been hoping for co-operation of this sort. Now we're all set to get somewheres."

"We sure are, with big Eastern deteckatives to help," remarked the cowboy, Steve Drake.

"'Way better than the Federal agents we were after in Washington. Remember, Steve?"

"I reckon I do, Boss. Those tenderfeet in Washington can't see no farther than the end of their nose."

"Do you mean to say that the Government refused to send agents?" asked Joyce curiously.

"Not exactly. The Indian Commissioner allowed he'd be giving us one or two, but I don't believe they'll be much use. Couldn't get him to say neither when they'd be showing up for work."

"I see." Joyce became interested afresh in observing the cowboys, and especially the one who had spoken. This Steve Drake was an awkward fellow, perpetually supporting the small of his back against the nearest wall and given to keeping his hands in his pockets. His eyes lacked the hard, pebble-like quality of Jack Ramsey's, but were none the less those of a rough-natured plainsman, a competent herder of cattle no doubt, but a man who was probably ready to pick a fight for a good excuse or a bad one. He chanced at this moment to bring his hands to light, and started to roll a cigarette clumsily.

"Try a made cigarette," said Joyce, producing a package.

But Steve frowned at the suggestion. "I can't smoke 'em, thankee. They smell like dried cow-dung to me."

"They're too good for you, you damn' long-horn," laughed Dan McCall. He looked at Joyce:

"We've got to be blowing along, Inspector. But we'll call back here for you at three sharp."

"Okay, Dan."

When the men from the cow country had gone, Joyce gave orders for the journey. Allan was to notify Sylvia and bring her and Sheriff Symes to the house. He sent his son Tom to look up the scout Al Jenkins, whom he had decided to add to his party. Then he touched Kay on the arm.

"I'll be taking half an hour to study a bit of the evidence," he said, "and I want you to sit in on it, me darlin'."

They went into a small room that opened off the parlor and sat by a window through which bright sunshine was pouring. Kay valued enormously these occasional interludes with her chief, when technical procedure was explained to her along practical lines, yet with the touch of intimacy that Joyce gave to none of his assistants except herself. Such moments rewarded her for many days of difficult and arid sledding.

Joyce took out the piece of waxed thread he had found beside Joe Yellow-Horse's bed, arranged it carefully on a sheet of white paper and held over it the powerful magnifying glass he always carried. For several minutes, he observed the exhibit silently, moving the glass a fraction of an inch at a time.

"Now you look," he said, and shifted his bulk to permit of her leaning close to him so that their cheeks were on the point of touching.

Kay saw the thread enlarged many-fold. The wax with which it was covered had the appearance of a coarse paste, and clinging to the latter were a multiplicity of tiny objects. Grains of dust resembled sand and dark stains of perspiration were like gum embedded in the wax. Most easily recognizable were small, pale-yellow squares of tobacco leaf and a number of stiff hairs from the pelt of an animal.

"Well, what's your verdict?" asked Joyce. "What type of man carried this in his pocket?"

"He was a smoker, of course, and he had a dog. I should say those short, brownish hairs were dog's hairs."

"Maybe. We'd need a microscope to be sure. But there's no making a mistake about the tobacco." Joyce resumed his scrutiny, and prolonged it interminably. At last he leaned back in his chair.

"Kay, if it weren't for one contradiction in the evidence, I'd swear I knew who murdered Jennie Deerfoot and Joe Yellow-Horse," he stated calmly.

"No?" she exclaimed, thrilled. "Tell me who you think it is."

"You tell me," he countered. "I want you to work it out for yourself. I'm not ready to make an arrest, because I don't have complete proof, a case for the jury. But any time you bring me a theory, we'll talk it over."

"Are we at least on the right track in going to the Osage Hills?" the girl demanded.

"Unless I don't know a clue when I see one, the Osage Hills will be the very place to get the rest of the dope on the murderer," averred Inspector Michael Joyce.

CHAPTER TWELVE
The King of the Osage Hills

Dan McCall's ranch, which was bigger than the average county in an Eastern State, was located in the rolling country to the Northwest of Pawhuska. The Osage Hills, as their name implies, are far from being mountains on the scale of the Ozarks or Cumberlands, much less the imperial Rockies. But they are rugged and inaccessible in comparison with the immediately adjacent territory, and the pioneers passed them by. It had remained for Indians driven from the rich plains to lay a shadowy claim to them, and this same McCall in our own times to exploit them on a practical basis.

The ranch-house stood in a valley which it is said that explorers have circled three and four times without finding the entrance. For the valley is pocketed in the hills as neatly as the pit of a disappearing coast-defense piece. One trail runs in from the North and one from the South, and both are veiled in the vast monotony of scrub and stunted oaks. Rocks jumbled together like the toys of Titans cause the unguided traveler to lose his sense of direction. The scarcity of grass and fruitful vegetation along the way discourages his progress. Yet the valley is fertile. A stream rises there, and the herds of grazing cattle are fat. Numerous other valleys, similar in character

though not so fantastically hidden, are scattered throughout the region, The party, consisting of Joyce, Dan and
their respective followers, had come up in a parade of old
Ford cars, which must have seemed strange indeed to possible onlookers whose memories dated back to frontier
days. The Indian Chiefs, even the cowboys, found it simpler to journey at ease in the battered caravan. But Dan
assured his guests that once on the ranch they would see
plenty of horseback riding.

He had named his place Lone-Star, he added, not because that was descriptive of the brand he used on stock,
but in honor of Texas, the State of his birth. Actually, his
cattle were marked with a circle, barred twice.

Arriving after nightfall, the company sat down promptly to supper in a mess hall a hundred feet long. A small
regiment of punchers were there ahead of them, and Jack
Ramsey and Steve Drake merged into the mob, their indi-
viduality erased for the moment. Joyce wondered curiously
what there had been to prevent these efficient-looking
huskies, each with a gun on his hip, from extirpating any
ordinary band of outlaws.

He, Kay and Tom ate with keen enjoyment of the novel
setting. Symes appeared to be less happy; he glanced about
him warily, exactly like a worthy white-collar clerk who
suspects he has blundered into company a little too fast
for him. The Osages remained as emotionless and impenetrable as usual.

But when supper was over, they all went to the spacious
living room and sat down with Dan to discuss eagerly the
plans for the next day. The ranchman, they learned, was
unmarried. He scorned the custom of the country to the
point of having no avowed half-breed mistress, though
he remarked negligently that a number of his illegitimate
children were knocking around the premises.

"Well, what's your scheme for tomorrow?" asked Joyce.

"We'll form an expedition, broken up into two or three sections and raid the Beaver Dam outfit from several directions at once. How does that strike you?"

"I'd call it a military maneuver that might rid you of the bandits," retorted Joyce drily. "But where does the detective work come in?"

"Afterwards. The way will be clear for you to dig for evidence concerned with past criminal deeds. And of course we'll try to take alive the Injuns you want."

"That's not good enough, Dan. I haven't enlisted with you for a young war. I'm here to do undercover work."

"Write your own ticket, then. What do you suggest?"

"That we creep up on the outlaws and observe them. See whether Deerfoot and Benny Gopher are really prisoners. Locate Owl-Face, if we can. Figure a way of prying them loose from the whites. Put a finger on the leader you claim is back of the whole business."

"A straight scouting proposition, eh?" Dan tilted his pear-shaped head on one side and thought, his glasses balanced queerly on his hawk-bill nose. "There's no reason why we can't do that. I guess it's the best way to begin."

"From my point of view, it's the only way," said Joyce, and glanced at his Osage friends.

The Old Chief pronounced a few guttural sentences, which Allan translated:

"My father says it is good medicine."

"We'll calc'late it's decided, then. The details can wait until the morning."

But in the morning a flood of business obligations overwhelmed Dan McCall, and it became evident why this man was popularly known as the uncrowned King of the Osage Hills. Cowboys arrived from distant runs, to report stock sick, strayed or stolen. An office executive and clerks whose existence Joyce had not suspected, descended on the boss with problems of financing which bored him insufferably, but to which he was forced to give attention. The foreman of an oil well he owned on the banks of the Arkansas River galloped up to the door, to get emergency orders and ride madly off again. There was even a delegation of tepee Indians, who brought family troubles for arbitration, in preference to appealing to a mistrusted resident agent for Indian affairs.

A huge domain, to most of which he held property title and whose inhabitants were dependent upon him for a living, gave seemingly willing allegiance to Dan McCall. Joyce felt like a spectator. His concerns were of minor interest here.

After the midday meal, however, Dan snapped into action with the Inspector.

"You might think I could never break away from these pesky plagues, but to hell with them!" he cried genially. "I'm ready for Beaver Dam. Suppose we get up three parties. You'll lead the first. The second will be under me, and I'll put my puncher, Steve Drake, in charge of the third."

"Will I have none but my own people with me?"

"Better not, though your scout Jenkins certainly knows the country. I'll give you Jack Ramsey."

"And I'll put one of my men with each of your parties—my son Tom with you, and Symes with Drake."

"Great! Are you taking the girls along?"

Joyce thought that a peculiar question. He did not want to be hampered with girls on a perilous foray, and had assumed that Dan would be the last person to be tolerant of the idea. But before he could answer, Sylvia Deerfoot spoke quietly:

"I beg for the privilege of going. My brother is a prisoner out there. I must go."

"You know what that means, Inspector. Me, too!" Kay pressed her bluff jauntily.

"Why, you're all crazy," said Joyce. "Consider the danger."

"Oh, danger!" Dan laughed. "In this country, the women aren't scary. An Indian girl knows how to look out for herself when guns are popping."

"And I'm a detective with a chance to get experience along new lines," Kay pleaded. "I hoped I'd won you over for good when we last talked about that in Pawhuska."

Joyce shrugged, and his eyes narrowed. Kay, who read him like a book, perceived that she would carry her point. But she had no way of telling that at the last moment he admitted reasons for not leaving her alone at the ranchhouse. The touching virtue and sentimentality ascribed to cowboys by writers on the Wild West did not, he feared, hold water with the roughnecks of Lone-Star.

"So now we're set!" exclaimed Dan. "No reason why we shouldn't start within an hour. We'll have to camp out one night—maybe two or three." He paused and cackled. "I only hope we're back in time to have the laugh on the Sheriff."

"Which Sheriff?" asked Joyce, thinking of Symes.

"Luther Hawes, of course. When that galoot gets wise to the fact that you're with me, he'll come stampeding out here pronto. He'll suddenly get a fever for bandit hunting, such as hasn't hit him for months."

"That might be awkward. His foolish tactics would tip them off to scatter, and they'd probably kill their prisoners."

"Sure. So let's try to do our job as quickly as possible, and double on our tracks. It's a safe bet he'll stop at the ranch-house first, and if we're home with results already, we can give him the he-haw! Not bad, eh? The he-haw on Hawes!" Dan roared at his own feeble pun.

"I agree with you that we must beat him to it at all costs."

The cattleman bobbed his head up and down vigorously, and departed to issue instructions for horses and supplies.

Joyce beckoned his people into a corner of the living room for a hurried conference. He addressed himself to Al Jenkins first:

"What do you think of the plans, Al?"

"They're all right, 'cept that you don't need McCall and his boys," the quarter-breed drawled. "I could show you all you'd want to know about the outlaws. Your gang's strong enough to push in right close."

"Perhaps. But I can't refuse McCall's help."

"Well, he's okay. A fust-rate citizen, Dan McCall is. I was just remarkin'."

Joyce stared at Tom. "You have an easy assignment, son. Stick close to McCall, that's all I ask of you. Now you, Sheriff—" he turned—"this is your chance to perform a big service. You're to be with cowboys, and I figure them as a pretty irresponsible lot. Get a line on their private opinion of the bandits. It wouldn't surprise me if they'd been in the habit of pal-ing with them at times when the boss didn't know it. Watch Steve Drake. I'll want a full report on him, because he's the leader. You've not laid eyes on Deerfoot, Gopher or Owl-Face, so you're not likely to be of much use identifying them. Work as an operative who's looking for any sort of clue that might be valuable—savvy?—and forget the scouting."

"I never thought I'd be out to rope cowboys, but I guess they're no tougher than New York racketeers," replied Symes mournfully.

"You'll do a good job. I know you. And, by the way, try to learn if any of the punchers played hooky in Pawhuska while McCall was in Washington."

Joyce swung around to Kay. "Are you sure you can stick on a horse?" he asked, a little coldly she thought.

"Oh, yes! I've done a lot of riding, every vacation I ever had. Early mornings in Central Park, too, this spring."

His eyes softened. "Fine, me darlin'. I'll not be doing any more crabbing, only don't let me lose sight of you."

They left the house, crossed the great dusty yard and approached the corral, where the last of twenty-one mounts were being saddled. Each party would consist of seven persons, those to ride with Joyce being the Big Chief and Allan, Al Jenkins, Jack Ramsey and the girls Kay and Sylvia. As an afterthought, Dan suggested an additional cowboy to balance the weakness of the women, but Joyce declined. He had a hunch that the smaller and more mobile the group the better.

At half-past three o'clock, the expedition rode away from Lone-Star ranch and followed the North trail out of the valley. It was decided that they would keep together for the rest of that afternoon until they reached an outlying section belonging to Dan, where half wild cattle roved. This would be within striking distance of Beaver Dam, but they would make a pretense of inspecting the cattle and then go into camp for the night. It was important that some stray outlaw should not take alarm at their movements and spread the word. Before dawn, the three parties would organize and be off in different directions.

The novelty of their initial impressions remained long stamped upon the memories of both Joyce and Kay. They rode side by side—or when the trail narrowed, in single file—through scenery that was not vividly picturesque, yet almost inconceivably wild, lost and forgotten upon the map of the United States. The rich watered patches were quite overshadowed by pinnacled bad lands. Streams gushed unexpectedly from caverns and tore their way down invisible gullies. Woods stretched like serpentine ribbons across the face of the panorama, marking the course of the illusive water without which they could not have flourished. The whole scheme of things was topsy-turvy, irrational, like a patchwork quilt that the gods had not completed.

In the valley of their objective, the stock fled before
them like deer. Dan grinned and said that the beasts had
undoubtedly been treated as game for a long time by the
bandits. The cowboys started a perfunctory round-up, lassoed a few head, lighted a fire and branded them. But with
the falling of twilight the bluff was abandoned, and the
fire converted to the uses of cooking supper.

A shack stood in a clump of trees. It had been built for
the sheltering of occasional range-riders, and now came in
handy as a place for the girls to sleep. The men wrapped
themselves in blankets and lay on the ground, with their
saddles for pillows. Joyce had roughed it often enough
before, but never in this Western fashion. Kept on the
alert by an intuition of brooding menace rather than the
strangeness of the setting, it was a long time before he
slept.

The summons to get ready for the next day's activities
came, however, without any nocturnal move having been
made against the campers. It was still pitch dark, except
for a faint rosy flush on the eastern horizon. The business
of breakfast and the saddling of the horses occupied an
hour, and the atmosphere had then paled to a pearly twilight. Dawn was at hand.

The members of the scouting party mounted and formed
their three predetermined groups. It had been agreed that
McCall and Drake would go to the right and left respec-
tively, make wide detours and converge on Beaver Dam.
Joyce would advance in a straight line, and was due to get
there first. This arrangement suited him, because he had
no faith in the discretion of cowboys. A fight would start
soon after they arrived; he felt sure of it.

With farewells reduced to a minimum of muttered sig-
nals, the outfits loped away from each other.

Joyce held as close to Kay as the difficulties of the
trail would permit. That he should have brought her into

this exotic peril made him willing almost to believe in
the working of blind fate. Barely a week ago, redskins
had come to New York to offer him a case—a weird thing
to happen, say what one pleased—and now he was riding
through the wilderness with Kay under conditions fully as
serious as those of warfare. The Inspector pinched himself
ironically.

He looked ahead to where Al Jenkins was blazing the
path, and then behind him at the taciturn Osages, with
Dan's cowboy Ramsey tagging along as a rear guard. Well,
there was no sign of disaster, so far!

At about ten o'clock, they reached a plateau where
cottonwood trees grew in a clump and thorny scrub masked
the edges of a pool. Al Jenkins halted abruptly, and stated
when Joyce rode up to him:

"This is the best place to work from, Boss. The mob
have their camp on the next plateau, and you kin look
across to it. The gulch between is full of thorns, but any
Injun kin crawl through them. The Horse-Eagles and I
will make it, if you give the word."

Everybody dismounted. The ponies were tethered among
the cottonwoods. Guided by Jenkins, Joyce and the others
advanced to a spot where, screened by gigantic boulders,
they could command a close-range view. At a distance of
some thousand yards, and at an elevation about equal to
their own, they observed a settlement rather than a camp,
consisting of tents, tepees, shacks and a few fairly preten-
tious log cabins. Housing existed for between fifty and
seventy-five persons. Some of the latter were Indian wom-
en, who could be seen in the open engaged on domestic
tasks. Armed men walked here and there, and the majority
of these were white.

"They don't seem to have any notion that we're around,"
commented Joyce.

"No, sir! We've snuck up on 'em."

"Who's the leader?"

"I ain't sure. But I think it's Slim Cooney, a bank buster what escaped from the State Penitentiary two years gone."

"Slim Cooney is right," commented the cowboy Ramsey.

Joyce flashed a look at him. "Why is that camp called Beaver Dam?"

"There's water on the far side, and beavers used to build there," replied Ramsey.

Through a pair of pocket binoculars, Joyce studied the location for a long time in silence. He wished he had stronger glasses, though it would have been too much to hope that he could spot Harry Deerfoot or the boy Benny. The last-named was a stranger to him, and he doubted whether he would recognize Harry at the distance.

Ramsey spoke again: "What do you reckon we should do?"

Impatiently, Joyce turned. He was about to tell the cowboy that there would be orders when he was good and ready, and he stretched out his arm to pass the binoculars to Allan Eagle. An unexpected diversion arrested both the words and the gesture.

Walking towards the group, as if he had nothing to fear, as if no one ever whispered the suspicion of crime against him, came Owl-Face, the old Cherokee shoemaker.

CHAPTER THIRTEEN
An Ambush in the Dark

Owl-Face made the Indian sign of greeting and respect as he approached boldly, and as this was the first time Joyce had seen him outside of a half-darkened shop, the detective gave his appearance a swift appraisal. He was more than sixty years old, and stoop-shouldered as a result of long years at a cobbler's bench. But he was by no means broken down physically. Under the open sky, he ceased to seem decrepit. His face was abnormally lined, but his body was sinewy and his step had a firm spring to it. It would have been well within the scope of this man's powers to accomplish the murder of Jennie Deerfoot.

Returning his salute gravely, Joyce demanded: "What are you doing here, Owl-Face?"

"Me huntum bad man—bad Injun—bad pale-face. Want to catchum boy."

The English he used was so stammering and tangled that Joyce asked Allan to question him in the dialect and make a report. This method also had its difficulties, because the shoemaker spoke only Cherokee, a variation of the tongue with which the young Osage chief was not fluently acquainted. Eventually, after a deal of roundabout talk, Allan stated:

"He says that he came to this place to rescue Benny Gopher, for whom he has great affection. When he saw us, he recognized us as friends and hastened to greet us."

"Hm! Doesn't sound like a bluff," Joyce muttered. "Ask him why he supposes Benny was made a prisoner?"

"The boy talked too much about the body of the Indian girl he had found," Allan translated. "Owl-Face thinks that certain of the outlaws must have murdered the girl. So they captured Benny to close his mouth, and since they have not killed him they probably intend to train him as a robber and bring him up as one of their band."

"How does he know that Benny is still alive?"

Allan held long converse with the Cherokee, and finally announced: "He says that he crawled through the outlaw camp twice last night. He located the shack where the boy is held, and even talked with him through a chink in the boards. But there was a guard sleeping there, and he could not venture to cut a larger hole to bring about his escape. He says he is able to return any night, and take an Indian with him. He would not risk it with a white man."

Ramsey snorted, but Joyce silenced him with a downward sweep of his hand. "Get the old fellow to explain how he located the shack."

"He says he hooted like an owl," reported Allan. "Benny put his lips to the chink and replied softly. So they drew together, little by little."

"Ask him if he can tell us anything about Harry Deerfoot."

"Harry Deerfoot is also a prisoner, but not in the same shack. Benny knows he is a prisoner, because of the way they were both treated in the car that took them away from Pawhuska. White men drove that car."

"Well, it helps to be on to that much. But why was Deerfoot kidnapped?"

"Owl-Face inquires by what means it would be possible for either himself or Benny to know? Deerfoot is no friend of theirs. It may be that since the outlaws had killed his sister, they feared the vengeance of Deerfoot and are now amusing themselves with him before they put him to death with cruel tortures."

Joyce thought rapidly. He did not want to put into Owl-Face's head the idea that Harry might have been the slayer of the girl, nor share even a hint of that theory with the listening Ramsey. "Question him about the chance of Deerfoot being really on good terms with the bandits and pretending in Pawhuska, for appearance's sake, that he was being dragged off against his will."

But the complications of this proposition were too much for the Cherokee. He frowned, shook his head and made helpless gestures with both his hands. Allan interpreted:

"He feels that Deerfoot would never have had anything to do with men who had murdered his sister."

"Put it to him in just those terms."

Allan complied, and translated: "He says that that is naturally what he meant. No Indian could be so false to his family honor."

"I'm inclined to think he's right. But that's on the assumption that the outlaws killed Jennie," Joyce commented. "This Owl-Face appears to be very much on the level. Tell him to stick by us until I work out a plan."

He moved a dozen paces to one side, beckoning to Kay, Allan, Jenkins and Ramsey. The Old Chief stayed behind to talk to the Cherokee.

"There's no sense at all in our trying to break into that camp, especially by daylight. We've learned a lot just by coming here, getting the lay of things and finding Owl-Face. I'll let him pull off the stunt he suggests—the night scouting—him and one of the Horse-Eagles, together. Meanwhile we lie low for the rest of the day. What do you think?" demanded Joyce.

Al Jenkins nodded.

"It should work out fine if Dan McCall's men don't start a commotion when they arrive," said Kay.

Ramsey jerked his head from side to side in savage impatience. "What's the idea of letting a woman butt into man's talk?"

"I'll have you remember that she's a detective, and my assistant," snapped Joyce. "We need detective brains in this. What she said was good sense. Suppose your cowboy pals do raise hell! We've got to have sentries out, to notify us if the outlaws seem to have had a scare thrown into them."

"My mistake," sneered Ramsey, bowing elaborately.

Suddenly, Joyce both disliked and mistrusted the man. But he kept the animus from his voice: "It would be a smart turn if Benny Gopher could be rescued tonight. Deerfoot, too; it's not impossible. Will you be Owl-Face's side-kick in the attempt, Allan?"

"My father will insist on going," answered the young Chief sadly. "He's three times better a scout than I am."

"It's easy to go rusty on woodcraft at Oxford, I guess. Well, Pale-Horse Eagle will be grand at the job. I propose that we rest and eat—no cooking, because of the smoke—and afterwards I'll post sentries. We'll leave the horses saddled."

By the time they had set out the cold food, it was noon of a scorching day. The undeflected rays of an almost tropical sun poured straight down upon the plateau. They ate in the meager shade of the cottonwoods, and killed an additional hour puffing at cigarettes which they lighted in their cupped palms. Lethargy took possession of them, but Joyce would not tolerate the impulse toward slackness. He ordered Al Jenkins to the thorn-choked gulch between their position and the camp of the outlaws. Ramsey he sent to the head of the rough trail by which they had forced an entrance to the plateau. The cowboy would be more trustworthy, he felt, at a point where any diversion that might occur would be visible at a long distance.

Joyce walked part of the way with Jenkins. "You see," he explained, "the bozos across the way may very well have got on to us. You said yourself that it was no trick to worry through the gulch, and if they want to spy on us this is the route they'll choose. It's important to watch it.

"You're dead right, Boss," the quarter-breed agreed. "Kin you make out that dwarf oak inside the thorns, but close to the edge? That's where I'll take my stand."

"Yes," replied Joyce. He was destined before long to congratulate himself that Jenkins had pointed out the oak.

Returning to the spot where they had eaten lunch, he found every one of the Indians sleeping. Owl-Face, who on his own showing, had been in action all night, was curled up like a wolf at the foot of a cottonwood. The Horse-Eagles and Sylvia were reposing with their heads on fallen logs, recouping the slumber they had lost as a result of the early start that morning. It seemed a good idea to Joyce. The midday atmosphere tended to somnolence, and certainly every one would have to be on the *qui vive* after sunset.

He grinned at Kay, and stretched himself out at full length. It was his intention to nap with half an eye open, but as the girl followed his example, and the sound of her rhythmical breathing came softly to his ears, he discovered that he was excessively sleepy. With two sentries on guard, it would be safe for him to relax, he mused.

The next thing he knew, he was awakened by a series of staccato explosions, and started up to find that it was dark. A glance at his wrist watch showed that it was after six o'clock. The early spring dusk had fallen while he slept. On both sides his companions were rousing. Then the explosions came again, and he knew them to be rifle shots. The sound of horses' hoofs could be heard galloping over the stones in the direction where Ramsey watched. A single yell rang out. Another volley sent bullets tearing through the cottonwood grove, and twigs whipped from the trees fell about the heads of Joyce's party. Their own horses plunged frantically, and bursting their tethers escaped to right and left, whinnying.

The four Indians and Kay had crowded close to Joyce. Revolvers were the only weapons they carried. Only Ramsey and Al Jenkins had had rifles. It was useless to attempt resistance at the spot upon which the attackers were obviously centering.

"Down into the gulch!" the Inspector ordered in a low voice, and led the way.

His fine sense of direction enabled him to follow accurately the path he had taken with Al Jenkins a few hours before. Even in the dim light, he was soon able to make out the branches of the dwarf oak protruding above the barrier of thorns. Lacking this sign post, he might easily have missed making a contact with his scout. But as it was, he led his followers straight into the arms of Jenkins, who had emerged a short distance from his hiding place. In their rear, they could hear renewed shooting and the wild confusion of mounted men careering back and forth among the cottonwoods.

Jenkins started to draw his friends back into the thorn thicket, but abruptly with an impatient muttering of Cherokee talk, Owl-Face took charge of the situation. He guided them some twenty yards to the left, parted the tangle of spiny bushes and shepherded them to an unsuspected oasis.

"Safe here. Injun him know, but not bad man. Bad man go other way," he grunted.

For many minutes, none of them uttered another word. They heard the intruders come blundering down the gulch and skirting the thorns. An odd silence prevailed among their foes, also. Occasionally, a man growled something under his breath, and that was all. Retreating footsteps finally seemed to leave the coast clear. But faint sounds that drifted down indicated that the plateau was still occupied.

Joyce conferred softly with the rest. It was agreed that Jack Ramsey had almost certainly been killed, or taken prisoner. At the best, he had been cut off from them and would be forced to make his way to safety in the opposite direction. Nothing could be done to help him. There remained the problem of their own evasion, without horses and with no assets except their guns.

A parley in the native tongue between Allan and Owl-Face brought out some practical suggestions.

"He says that he can take us under cover of the thorns into a valley where the outlaws will be unlikely to find us," the young Chief reported. "We will find water there, and we can kill a steer for food. After that, we should be able to reach a section where we'll run across cowboys riding the range for McCall."

"Sounds like a tough prospect, but we don't have much choice," answered Joyce. "Maybe Dan himself will pick us up, or the party led by Steve Drake."

"That is so. Owl-Face makes another suggestion. He points out that the bandit camp is now half deserted, because of the raid against us. He thinks it an ideal night to attempt the rescue of Harry Deerfoot and Benny Gopher. So he wants to go ahead with that project, taking my father with him."

The coolness of the proposition, in view of the difficulties they were in, startled the detective. Neither Allan nor Owl-Face seemed troubled by the idea of dividing their forces and risking the loss of two men on a desperate enterprise. "What do you think?" he countered.

"We should not hesitate. We came here to learn the truth about those prisoners, and this may be our last chance to do it."

"Damned if I can deny that! But if it's pulled off successfully, it'll be a miracle. I don't want your father to get killed."

"No Indian would give that a second thought. If the time has come for him to die, he must die," replied Allan stoically.

"If that's the way you feel about it, it's okay with me. Are we supposed to wait here until they return?"

"Oh, no! Owl-Face will take us to the head of the valley, where it is safer. He expects to be back before dawn."

"Then let's go."

They bored a pathway laboriously through the thorn bushes, the Cherokee in the van. It was hard sledding for a while, and they did not escape without receiving a few scratches on their faces, hands and ankles. The importance of making as little noise as possible delayed their progress. But in a surprisingly short time they came out upon a rocky slope, down which they slided rather than walked. They rounded a huge boulder, advanced along a narrow ridge for a quarter of a mile and at last dipped into the promised valley. There they found trees and thick grass on which to lie. The rippling of a stream came pleasantly to their ears.

Joyce and Kay had no sooner thrown themselves upon the ground than Owl-Face and Chief Pale-Horse Eagle turned right about and began to retrace their steps, uttering no word of superfluous comment. Their task having been agreed upon, they tackled it in true Indian fashion, silently and swiftly. On that moonless night, they were almost immediately lost to view.

Staring upwards at a ridge that was silhouetted sharply against the sky like a rough sketch drawn in sepia against a background sprinkled with stars, Inspector Michael Joyce did not feel pleased with himself. This was not his sort of adventure. He had come to Oklahoma to solve a detective problem, and the thing had developed into a campaign of guerilla fighting. He saw no logic in the course to which Dan McCall had persuaded him. If Deerfoot and Benny were rescued, that would be so much gain. But how had Dan expected to pin former crimes upon a crew of outlaws by practically challenging them to battle? There was a catch in it somewhere.

For himself, he regretted, above all, having brought Kay into a situation from which she would be lucky to escape with her life. He reached out his hand and let it fall upon hers, where she lay beside him on the grass.

"You're getting a raw deal, me darlin'," he said. "But you asked for it. Not such a smart girl, this time."

"Don't try to fool me. You're blaming yourself when you put it that way. You mustn't. I—I like this. I'd never imagined anything so thrilling could happen to me." Her upturned palm clung briefly to his, and was withdrawn.

"You put up a brave front," he replied sadly. "But you nearly stopped a bullet or two, and if those blackguards had taken you alive it would have been worse still."

"They didn't take me. In life, it's always win or lose, Inspector, and I'm willing to bet that before we're through with this case we'll both be winners."

He did not answer, but shifted his gaze to the dome of sky. Velvet-black, it was like an inverted bowl that had been clamped upon the world, and the glittering stars were so large and close that it seemed he could have reached up and touched them.

It would have been impossible for him to sleep after his injudicious slumber of the afternoon, and he no longer wanted to talk. The night slipped slowly away.

At a little after four o'clock, the sound of cautious footsteps was heard, and advancing figures loomed in the darkness. Joyce jerked out his revolver, assumed a crouching position on one knee and cried: "Halt!"

The voice of Pale-Horse Eagle responded simply: "Friends."

Without a sign of emotion, as quietly as though they were returning from a stroll, the Old Chief, Owl-Face, Harry Deerfoot and Benny Gopher walked into the circle.

"By God, you did it! Some stunt!" growled Joyce.

"We find strange thing," said Pale-Horse Eagle in his hesitant English, and ignoring the personal triumph of having snatched two prisoners from a camp full of enemies. Unable to continue fluently, he broke into a long speech in the Osage language.

Allan, whose voice seldom shook, repeated the gist of it with a touch of excitement:

"My father declares that the outlaws were not the ones who attacked us. He found them in a dilemma over the fighting which had taken place on our plateau. Many of them were scouting between the two positions to learn what it was about. It was largely because of their confusion that the rescuing of Harry and Benny could be accomplished."

"If it wasn't Slim Cooney's outlaws who attacked us," said Joyce, thunderstruck, *"who was it?"*

CHAPTER FOURTEEN
Sheriff Symes Gets His Man

The amazing information that unknown and unsuspected foes had descended upon them with intent to kill left the whole party gasping. It was easy to say that a second outlaw band, perhaps the one led by Bert Lawson himself, had stumbled across their trail. But Lawson had close relations with the Slim Cooney outfit, and would certainly have communicated with the latter either before or after the attempted coup. The theory of the sudden emergence of a new lot of independent bandits scarcely held water. It was a remote possibility, no more than that.

Who, then, had tried to murder them, and for what motive? The hope of gain could not have cut much ice, argued Al Jenkins, because there had been nothing worth stealing from such a group except the horses, and that would have been foolish in the Osage Hills, where mustangs could be had for the trouble of roping them.

"It may have been the doing of Sheriff Hawes," suggested Kay. "You know, Dan predicted that he would follow us to this section. Suppose he and his deputies mistook us for the Cooney outlaws, and attacked blindly."

"I'd not put it beyond him," said Joyce.

They debated the wisdom of sending one of their number back by daylight to find out, but Jenkins advised against this. The maneuver would take hours and risk a man's life unnecessarily. It probably was not Hawes. They were hungry, and their immediate problem was to find food and get back to civilization.

In the end, every one accepted this view of the matter. The Osages were particularly opposed to returning to the plateau. They seemed to have some mystic hunch, which they explained only by averring that whatever persons might be there, they were enemies with superior arms.

Joyce then switched to the question of Deerfoot and Benny Gopher. In the past twenty-four hours, they had fortunately been transferred as prisoners to the same shack, a new one on the edge of the camp which Owl-Face had easily located. By a persistent repetition of his owl-cry, the Cherokee had induced the guard to come to the door, when the Old Chief had jumped on him from behind and killed him silently by breaking his neck with his crooked arm. The escape thereafter had offered few difficulties.

"Why were you kidnapped in the first place?" Joyce flung at Harry Deerfoot.

"No can say," the young fellow answered dazedly. "I think they want to scare my family and make um pay ransom."

"How did it happen—your capture, I mean?"

"Two white men stop car at sidewalk, and tell me they have news. I come up close, and one point gun at me, tell me to get into car. Afterwards, they pick up Benny."

"Have they treated you badly?"

"First day, they beat me. Then no more sticks, or hard words. Plenty food, plenty drink."

"Corn liquor?"

"Yes."

"Trying to get you soused, eh? Did they question you about Jennie's murder?"

"They ask who kill her. I answer, no can say. I explain great detective has come from New York, and will find out some time. They laugh at me."

"Here, give me your left hand," ordered Joyce abruptly, and as the bewildered Harry held it out, the Inspector took the hand in the darkness, struck a match and held the light close to the thumb.

He saw the scar of a recent wound on Harry's thumb.

But it was no puncture inflicted by the head of a needle. Obviously, the Indian had cut himself with the blade of a small knife, the hurt being on the side of the finger at right angles to the nail. Joyce let the hand drop with a meaningless growl.

Turning to Benny Gopher, he posed a few queries. The boy had nothing to add to the evidence. Haltingly, he told his old story about finding Jennie Deerfoot's body and gave an account of his kidnapping which corresponded with Harry's.

"One thing is clear," Joyce told the company at large. "The outlaws had some kind of interest in the death of the girl and some knowledge of the circumstances. We need no better proof of that than the way these kidnappings were handled."

"Surely it looks as if the killer were a member of the band!" urged Allan.

"Dan McCall thinks so—and I don't know," replied Joyce. "The mystery has not been solved yet, not by a damned sight!"

It was getting light enough now for them to walk without missing their footing, and to distinguish the main features of the landscape. In agreement with Jenkins and Owl-Face, the two who were most familiar with the Osage Hills, Joyce gave the command for forward march. The plan was to aim for one of the grazing sections which constituted the productive part of McCall's vast ranch. These were scattered over the whole region, though often widely separated. Jenkins thought that he remembered a short cut which would bring them to cow country within twenty-four hours.

They were all sorely in need of breakfast, and on empty stomachs they found the going hard. But after they had progressed about five miles they had a stroke of luck. They ran across one of their own fugitive horses, still saddled and bridled. Bags containing food were attached to the saddle, and there was even an unbroken flask of whiskey. The animal, a tame pinto, responded to their call by trotting towards them, pricking its ears and shaking its tail with joy at the prospect of human companionship.

The chance to eat was not the only gain from this encounter. They now had a mount for the two girls, and were able to make better time. By following the course of a stream, they avoided the rougher trails and soon left the region of plateaus far behind them.

In the afternoon, Al Jenkins shot a mountain goat. A fire was built, and they dined on broiled cutlets without salt. A little dry bread remained from the store they had found in the saddle-bags. They drank water with a nip of whiskey in it, to stimulate them for the hike that was immediately resumed.

Camp for the night was struck at the foot of a ridge which Owl-Face insisted was the last barrier separating them from a large, fertile valley. An additional hour of toiling forward would have proved whether this were so, but they were too exhausted to make it. They lay down like wild beasts and slept until the chill of the early morning hours penetrated their bones and brought them, one after the other, to their feet, shivering.

This was Nature's signal, and really advantageous to them. For it was best to start traveling at dawn before the rays of the sun became oppressive. They ate some more goat's meat, cold from the preceding day, and trudged on. The ridge was conquered slowly. But the view from the top fulfilled the Cherokee's promise. They looked down into the widest valley they had seen in the hills, and the descent to it took on the character of a joyous lark.

They had arrived at civilized territory. An immense herd of cattle wandered there, and although no cowboys were in evidence at the moment they could be expected to show up sooner or later. Several days often passed without the herders being able to visit any given section. A shack intended to be used as a rest-house would probably be found, its larder stocked with emergency provisions. There might also be a corral, where riding horses were kept.

In a little while, the voyagers came to a well-beaten road running the length of the valley. This was all that Jenkins needed to orient himself fully. They were on one of the main trails to Lone-Star ranch, which was not more than thirty miles distant, he announced. Persons connected with Dan McCall traversed it almost every day.

Notably cheered, Joyce and his tattered crowd pushed ahead. By noon they had located the anticipated rest-shack. A thin wisp of smoke was rising from the hole in the roof that served as a chimney. They hastened their steps, their stimulated imaginations scenting a hot meal. When they were within a hundred yards, Jenkins shouted. The door of the shack opened, and a man showed part of his head around the jamb. But the head was quickly withdrawn. They wondered whether this spelled new trouble for themselves, yet continued to advance. At a distance of ten feet they stopped, for the man suddenly emerged and stood blinking at them in the sunlight. It was the Sheriff, G. Borden Symes.

"Howdy, Inspector," he said colorlessly, as if he accepted as a matter of course the arrival of Joyce on foot and weather-beaten.

"Why, Sheriff, you damned slippery shadow! How come? Where's the crowd you were with?" cried Joyce, who thought he had never been so delighted to see any one in his life.

"I lost that crowd, all right. Lost them on purpose," Symes murmured. "I was on my way to the ranch, but it's broken right, your coming up like this. I've got two birds in there for you."

"Who are they?"

"A couple of Indians—the Swift-Horse brothers."

"The hell you say! What's it all about?"

"It's a long story."

"No longer than mine."

"Better come inside, Inspector, and we'll talk. You look as if you needed food. I've got some cooking."

Joyce led the procession into the shack, where sure enough the brothers Sam and Thomas Swift-Horse sat tranquilly smoking their long native pipes. They greeted the Old Chief and Allan in guttural, monosyllabic phrases, and the Osages launched into mutual explanations. Ignoring them for the present, Joyce sat at the table with Symes and told him about the surprise attack on the plateau and what had happened afterwards.

The Sheriff chewed his lower lip and stared at the floor.

"Holy smoke, Inspector, there's been mighty funny business going on!" he said, on a note of agitation that was exceptional with him. "The way things broke for me sort of fits in. Maybe not, but it's an earful."

"Well, spill it. Make a speech. I know you hate to talk more than one sentence at a time, and three's your limit. But this is where you hang up a record."

Symes grinned faintly. "After we separated from you, I rode off with that Steve Drake's gang and didn't like their actions from the start," he asserted. "They did an awful lot of kidding, poking fun at me for a tenderfoot and what not. I felt they weren't trying to arrive anywhere in particular, and about noon they blundered across McCall's own party, which was supposed to be headed in the opposite direction. I must say McCall seemed taken by surprise, and he bawled out Drake.

"Then McCall decided on a new line-up. He pulled me and a certain cowboy away from Drake, and gave him two of the men who had been with himself. The gangs cut loose from each other again, and the last I heard of that Drake he was whooping like a madman."

"Why the devil should McCall have shifted you? My idea was that you and Tom should report to me on what results were had by each party," said Joyce.

"I know. I kicked to him, but he overruled me. Said his cowboys were tough customers who didn't think much of Eastern detectives, and that he couldn't vouch for my safety unless I was along with him. It's a fact that Drake acted as if he'd enjoy bumping me. Fired his gun right beside my ear once."

"Senseless noise, eh? And he was supposed to be scouting! Go on with the story."

"McCall was all for getting to the bandits quickly. But he met up with some of his range-riders, and they delayed us with a report about sick cattle. This took up the rest of the afternoon, and we camped for the night. In the morning, McCall said it was too late to go on with the expedition, because you and Drake between you would have thrown a scare into the outlaws. I kicked again, but he dusted for home along this trail."

"It's as lousy a deal as I've heard of," said Joyce furiously. "Why should he take it for granted we'd scare them? Our plan was to creep close and observe. It was possible, however, that we'd get into trouble—as we did—and he should have figured on being on tap to help us."

Symes shrugged. "I can only give you my part in it. Now, about the Indians. We met them at the head of this valley some three hours ago. McCall stopped them and asked questions. They didn't tell much, but admitted to being from Pawhuska. Said they were going to visit friends in the hills. Their English was awful. McCall didn't seem to know who they were, or put any stock in them, and he said they could beat it.

"But the minute I heard them mention Pawhuska, I had my suspicions. You'd told me about the disappearance of the Swift-Horse brothers, of course, though I'd never seen them. I put it to McCall straight that I had business with those Indians, and I left his party to pursue them."

"Did he object?" asked Joyce.

"Yes. Claimed I'd get lost. But I let him know that God Almighty Himself couldn't prevent me from going, unless He struck me dead. We had quite an argument, until Mc-Call ended by telling me to go to my death if I wanted."

"What about Tom? Did he stick by you?"

"At first—y-yes," answered the Sheriff, embarrassed. "But Tom and McCall had got very thick. That ranchman certainly catered to Tom, as if he'd taken a great fancy to him. Told the boy stories about the West, and painted himself as one grand hero. When Tom wanted to go with me, McCall argued that he mustn't be such a fool, that there wasn't anything to my idea about the Indians, and that you had ordered him, any way, not to go off on side issues. He bullied and laughed Tom out of it, and I went alone."

Joyce's face remained impassive, but his heart burned. There was a technical excuse for his son's action. Just technical, seeing he had been commanded to stay with McCall. That was the trouble with Tom; plenty of energy, but no sense of judgment. Would he ever make a detective?

"Well, I rode after the Indians and didn't have a hard time catching them. They weren't trying to escape, I guess. I asked them whether they were the Swift-Horses, and they said yes. So I told them to come along with me. That was when they began to resist. I pulled my gun on them, and forced them as far as this shack. Idea was to get them to the ranch-house, Inspector, so that you could grill them on your return."

"I came damn' near not returning," remarked Joyce grimly. "But you've done a swell job, Sheriff. Who said you'd fall down on sleuthing in this land where men are men!"

Symes cackled sheepishly. He relapsed into the inconspicuousness that was his natural role, and began to set dishes and food noiselessly upon the table.

Turning to Allan, Joyce asked: "How do the Swift-Horses explain their action in fleeing up here?"

"They became tired of the killings and the investigations, the suspicions and the rumors of new trouble in Pawhuska," replied the Young Chief. "It was not the kind of warfare in which they had been reared. They decided to run out on it all. A white man would call it going primitive. They insist that they did not even know that Joe Yellow-Horse had been murdered when they left."

"Do you believe them?"

"I do. Nothing they have said or done implies guilt, except their unwillingness to turn back with Symes, and that is excusable."

"Inform them that they'll have to go to Pawhuska with us now. Their evidence has a bearing in connection with Joe's death. I'll arrest them unless you can guarantee that they'll come quietly."

"It is guaranteed," promised Allan.

Symes's meal had been served by this time, and the company ate ravenously. No one spoke until the last cup of rank coffee had been drunk. Then Joyce asked at large: "Who would you now say attacked us on the plateau?"

"Steve Drake and his mad lot of hoodlums," retorted Allan promptly. "They may have taken us for bandits, and charged without bothering to check up."

"You're generous with them," commented Joyce. "Suppose they hated us, anyhow!"

"If they killed Ramsey, they'll have a tall lot of explaining to do to their boss," remarked Al Jenkins.

"No doubt about that—if they killed him!" said the Inspector cryptically.

"We'll know when we reach the ranch-house, maybe," put in Kay.

"Yes, and we'd better head for there as soon as possible. There's a bare chance to beat Drake's arrival, and I'd like to do it," Joyce announced.

Destiny intended otherwise. The words were barely out of the Inspector's mouth when the high-pitched droning and drumming of engines was heard above their heads through the roof of the shack.

Allan Eagle, who was nearest to the door, made a foray and returned swiftly.

"It's an aeroplane," he said. "It just came over the ridge we crossed this morning, and apparently it's going to land in the valley."

CHAPTER FIFTEEN
The Thunderbird Once More

Everybody stepped outside and watched with astonishment the beautiful, slim aeroplane like a monster dragonfly, which was soaring above that lost pocket in the Osage Hills. The reason for its presence was unimaginable, and still less its object in landing at this spot, as it evidently proposed to do. The plane was not experiencing engine trouble. Perfectly under control, it dipped and then soared again, as the pilot looked for a favorable stretch of level ground. The motor hummed more softly, and the cut-out exploded in little jets of sound.

With the exception of Allan who stood haughtily apart, the Indians of Joyce's party huddled together as if for protection in a tightly-packed group, and gazed at the thing in the sky with expressionless faces.

"Thunderbird!" they muttered. "Heap-big thunderbird!"

"It is good medicine. No enemies of ours would come that way," Allan told them. But they did not answer.

The plane, which was now flying very low, glided definitely in the direction of an expanse of grass a couple of hundred yards to the south of the shack. It dropped easily, and with a long swoop made an excellent landing, its wheels bumping over the turf for a short distance and its tail sinking gracefully as it came to a full stop.

Joyce hurried towards it, followed by the whites and Allan Eagle. The other Indians remained frozen in their conservatism. Even the Old Chief showed plainly that he could not bring himself to accept a thunderbird as a harmless and normal creature.

A jaunty young aviator had already stepped out of the cockpit when Joyce arrived. He smiled and waved a hand. His passengers, a middle-aged man and a much younger one, needed his assistance to disembark, but in a few minutes all three were standing side by side.

"My name is Hubert Gallatin," said the middle-aged man. "Meet my assistant George Dunham and Flying Lieutenant Curtis Grant. Are we correct in thinking that this is Daniel McCall's Lone-Star ranch."

"It's part of it," replied Joyce. "But you are thirty miles from the ranch-house."

"Do you work for Mr. McCall?"

"No. I'm in the hills on business of my own. Michael Joyce at your service."

"Not Inspector Michael Joyce, the famous private detective, and formerly of the New York Police Department?"

"The same. How did you guess it?"

"There's no guesswork about it, Inspector. I'd heard you were in Oklahoma, and I hoped to meet you. I am attached to the Indian Bureau of the Department of the Interior."

"Oh, that's who you are, Mr. Gallatin!" exclaimed Joyce, his interest flaming up. "Sent from Washington to report on the killings and disorders here, eh?"

"Exactly. We started from the capital by plane yesterday morning, intending to land at the McCall place. But Lieutenant Grant lost his bearings among the hills."

"Now you're this far, you don't have to be in a terrible hurry to see Dan McCall, do you?"

"Why, no. I fail to understand exactly what you mean, however."

"I thought you and I might have a little talk. We're on the same general case, from different angles. My dope could be useful to you, and yours to me." Joyce hoped that his blunt phrases would break down the reserve of this gray-mustached Federal agent, whose manner somehow suggested the red-tape and sealing-wax of Government offices. Apparently, the approach was the right one.

"A first-rate idea, Inspector," said Gallatin, thawing. "But we'll exchange views, if you don't mind, without witnesses."

They walked to the shack, entered it and closed the door, leaving Dunham and the Flying Lieutenant to the pleasing occupation of attempting flirtations with Kay and Sylvia Deerfoot.

Joyce sketched the bare facts of the murders on which he had been working, as well as all the murders of Osage millionaires which had occurred during the past two years. He expressed no theories and aimed no suspicions of guilt at individuals. He ended by inquiring simply:

"Does this jibe with the information that you have?"

"Very much so, though I had not heard about the more recent deaths."

"Well, what line of action do you intend to follow?"

"I shall look into the bandit situation. It appears that the State of Oklahoma and our resident Indian agents have been shamefully lax. Outlaws have been stalking and butchering the wretched Osages, almost unchecked."

"You folks in Washington absorbed that notion straight from Dan McCall, didn't you?"

"His personal protest to my chief forced us to think about it urgently. But rumors of the same order *had* been reaching us."

"Well, take it from me," said Joyce solemnly, "you're all wrong. If you confine yourself to digging up evidence against the bandits, you'll get nowhere. In the first place, they're outlaws rather than bandits. You haven't heard of their turning any tricks of highway robbery, or raiding towns, have you? They seem just to live off the country, which boils down to their stealing cattle from McCall. I'm returning from a contact with those bozos, and I tell you flat: they haven't been guilty of the Osage murders!"

"You think McCall lied to us?" Gallatin gasped.

"Let's say that he's playing a phony hunch."

"Or a shrewd game," the agent shot back, with a flash of insight. "He would stop losing cattle if the Government could be spurred into doing what is really a State job and wiping out his rustlers for him."

"Maybe. But that's not the big point. Some dozen murdered Indians is what should worry us. How do you feel about the Indians, Mr. Gallatin?"

"They have never received full justice from the United States," replied the Federal man frankly. "We tell them they are wards of the nation, and then we put their affairs in the hands of second-rate politicians who are sent out here as residents. Even the rich Osages have had cause for complaint in the way we have winked at tricksters and exploiters in their midst. They have little confidence in Uncle Sam, and I'd be the last to blame them."

"You notice that when one family was enterprising enough to look for outside help, it came to me, a private detective, and not to the Indian Bureau," Joyce prodded.

"I know it," said Gallatin sadly. "But I'm here to try to remedy that, to win confidence."

"Then steer away from the bum slant of pinning the murders on to outlaws. Listen to McCall's line; don't antagonize him. But look closer to home for the criminals."

"Won't you help me? Who do you think is guilty?"

"I'm not prepared to accuse any one yet." Joyce hesitated. "In less than a week, I expect to have solved the mystery, so far as the Horse-Eagle and Deerfoot families are concerned. If you'll hunt me up in Pawhuska, I'll tip you off privately."

They shook hands, and emerged from the shack. The afternoon was young, and the sun shining brightly. Lieutenant Grant, who had been straightening out his landmarks with Al Jenkins, announced that it would be a cinch hop to the ranch-house in less than half an hour. On horseback, it would take hard riding to make it by midnight.

"Unluckily, the plane is too small to accommodate extra passengers," remarked Gallatin apologetically.

"That's all right. Don't disturb yourself about us," replied Joyce. "There are a few horses in a corral here. We'll do it by easy stages, some mounted and some walking, and be satisfied to get in tomorrow morning."

"But I insist on being disturbed on this young lady's account." Gallatin bowed to Kay, and the tardy introduction was made. "About this lovely Indian girl, too." He smiled at Sylvia. "I have an idea. Both of them could squeeze into Mr. Dunham's seat. They shall ride with me, and Mr. Dunham with you."

"Fine, fine!" Joyce gripped Gallatin's hand, and then gave the dispossessed assistant agent a playful shove. He felt keenly elated at the manner in which this and other problems were being solved. Splendid to get the exhausted girls back to civilization quickly.

As for his murder case, his logical mind leaped ahead to the conclusion and supplied Xs for the missing links in the evidence. But until those tough links had been forged, nothing would have induced him to state to his closest confidant what man, or men, he expected to hang.

The aeroplane took off with a great whirring of the propeller and roaring of the engine. Soon it was a darting

silhouette against the azure sky. Terrified cattle galloped
here and there in the wake of its departure, and the Indians stared after it gloomily.

But now that the party was composed only of men,
Joyce whipped more energy into it. No saddles were available, but mustangs were lassoed and the journey made a
little easier by bareback riding. A halfway pause for the
night helped. The men were up before sunrise, and at eight
o'clock they had completed the last lap.

They found the Lone-Star ranch-house and its environs
in a state of commotion. The plane, grounded in the nearest pasture, was an object of wonderment even to the white
cowboys, who crowded about it to feel it all over. There
were also an unusually large number of horses in the corral, and accoutrement was piled beside the stable door. A
row of Ford cars had been parked to the left of the house.
Dan McCall was entertaining visitors on a large scale.

Travel-stained and wearing a four-days' growth of
beard, Joyce strode to the front door. It was flung open before he reached it, and a dozen men tumbled out, McCall
at their head. The cattle king's welcome was exuberant,
and his hand-clasp hearty.

"By God, I'm glad to see you safe, Inspector!" he cried.
"I was worried sick until Mr. Gallatin landed here, bringing the women and good news of you."

Joyce mumbled a reply. But McCall interested him less
right then than the rangy figure tagging behind him. There
was Sheriff Luther Hawes, exaggeratedly Western for the
occasion, the crown of his five-gallon hat picturesquely
dented and his torso garbed in a flannel shirt startling-
ly checkered in red and white. Hawes even wore chaps,
though according to the best usage these belonged strictly
to the costume of working cowboys.

"It's the New York detective, or I'm a fried sinner!"
shouted Hawes, indulging his usual flair for the obvious.

"Yeah! Business makes me pop up where you'd least expect me," replied Joyce sarcastically. "How about yourself?
Doing well in these parts?"

"I've been on a tour of inspection," the Sheriff said,
frowning uncertainly. He was never quite sure when fun
was being poked at him. "These bad lands would become a
hot bed of lawlessness, if I didn't jump in once in a while."

"You don't mean it!"

"Sure do. I had a running fight with some skulkers a
couple of nights ago."

Joyce started. *"You* had a fight?"

"That's what I said."

"How many deputies did you have with you?"

"Eight. What are you getting at, anyway?"

"I'll tell you in a minute." Joyce turned to McCall. "Is
Steve Drake back yet, and was he in a scrap?"

"Yes, he's here, scrap and all under his belt. We've been
puzzling our heads trying to figure how it happened. We
thought at first that Steve and the Sheriff might have got
into a tangle unbeknownst. Then Miss Carey arrives in the
place and tells you've been in trouble, too. Be damned if I
can make it out," the ranchman declared.

"It ought to be easy to solve," Joyce snapped. "I know
what kind of fight I was in. I was attacked in the dark between six and seven o'clock. My horses stampeded, and I
had to get out without firing a shot. Does Hawes's story
correspond to that?"

"Hawes says that the shebang started with a shot being
discharged at him. Then there was plenty of gun-play on
both sides."

"At what hour of the night?" asked Joyce, addressing
himself to the Sheriff.

"Oh, a little after dusk," answered Hawes uncomfortably.

"Did you lose any men?"

"No. And nary a one wounded."

"Kill anybody, or take prisoners?"

"No."

"Where did the fight take place?"

"I can't say exactly. We'd lost our way. But hell, I'm not going to stand for your hinting I tried to wipe you out. A shot was fired at us first, I tell you. If one of your men did it, you've got to take the blame."

Joyce recalled his sentry, Jack Ramsey, and was staggered at the manner in which the Sheriff's story fitted the facts. Ramsey might well have opened the affray without stopping to challenge.

The Inspector glanced about him for Steve Drake, but failed to locate the cowboy. "Where's Drake?" he asked.

"Steve's taking it easy. He was wounded," replied McCall.

"Sorry to hear that. Badly?"

"Oh, no! One arm grazed by a bullet."

"What account does he give?"

"He was in a general mix-up, something like the Sheriff's. But he swears none of his boys let loose the first shot."

"Can he locate the scene of the scrap?"

"Sure. It was on rough land at the head of a valley we call Chickasaw Gulch."

"Anywhere near Slim Cooney's camp of outlaws?"

"Quite a ways from there. He didn't push on to Cooney's after the fight."

"Prisoners?"

"No."

"Kill any one?"

"Not that he knows of."

The thing became more and more of a jumble in Joyce's mind. Earlier, after listening to the report by Symes, he had been convinced that the attack on the plateau had

been launched by Steve Drake, with malice or otherwise.
Now it looked like Hawes. But in that event, with whom
had Drake fought? The cowboy had a wound to prove that
he had been in action.

"There's another angle to this—the fate of Jack Ramsey," Joyce told McCall. "He was standing watch for us at
the point where the shindy started. We lost him."

"So I've heard." The ranchman's countenance fell.
"That touches me in a soft spot. Jack was more than a
hand around here; I regarded him as a pal."

"Aren't you going to send out a searching party?"

"I've done it already. Six punchers have left, to try
and find him, dead or alive. They'll comb that plateau of
yours."

"Who gave you the location?" asked Joyce quickly, and
with crafty intent.

"Kay Carey and Sylvia Deerfoot," answered McCall
promptly.

Abruptly, it seemed to Joyce that what he needed more
than anything in the world were a shave and a cup of strong
coffee. He was weary of talking and wanted to think. But
after he had finished with the razor and was seated at
table, a whole pot of coffee in front of him, he became
aware that Gallatin, the Federal agent, was hovering at his
elbow, eager to discuss the case. He felt it to be the wise
thing to keep in with Gallatin, and, for half an hour they
raked over the various accounts of events that the Federal
man had overheard at the ranch-house door. They were
not getting anywhere in particular, when Joyce happened
to remark:

"I am sorriest about Ramsey, because it might be said
I was responsible for his safety. He was one of the two
cowboys McCall took to Washington with him, you know."

"Two cowboys," repeated Gallatin. "There was only one
cowboy with McCall in Washington."

Joyce turned and stared. "Are you sure of that?" he asked quietly.

"Yes. The pair were widely commented upon in the Department. There were not three of them."

"Can you give me the cowboy's name? Would you recognize him if you met him here?"

"No, to both those questions. I saw McCall in Washington several times, but the cowboy only once, and then he had a hat over his eyes. Most cowboys look alike to me."

"At what hotel did they stop?"

"I cannot say. But Commissioner Jessup's secretary would know. He frequently got in touch with them."

"Okay. Now, one thing more. Do you happen to remember whether McCall came West directly from Washington?"

"I am pretty sure he did not. He told Jessup that he was going to New York a week ago last Sunday."

"Oh, McCall went to New York first, and was probably there Monday morning, he and his cowboy!"

"That is my impression."

"Thanks," said Joyce. He felt that he had put his finger upon two very valuable pieces of evidence.

CHAPTER SIXTEEN
Mysteries of Lone-Star Ranch

In the afternoon, Joyce went to visit Steve Drake in the bunk-house, and took Gallatin with him. He found the puncher lying on his back on a special cot that had been rigged up for him, his sullen eyes fixed on the ceiling, and his right hand engaged in manipulating the cigarettes that he smoked one after the other. Drake's left arm was swathed from the elbow down in a thick, amateurish bandage which covered the hand. It looked like a huge, clumsy fin, the way he held it lying across his chest.

"How are you feeling, Drake?" the detective asked, with impersonal solicitude.

"Hello, Mr. Joyce! I heard you was back safe. I'm pretty good, thankee." The other turned his head on the pillow, but his face wore an expression that was not so amiable as his polite words. He seemed feverish and angry.

"Where did the bullet nick you?"

"Just above the wrist. I'm lying low so I can get back the use of my hand quick."

"Did a doctor put on that dressing?"

"Hell, no! We ain't got no doctors around here."

"You'd better be careful of blood poisoning. I'm familiar with this sort of thing. I'd be glad to bind it over for you."

"Thankee, but I know all about dressing wounds," said Drake, a disagreeable note in his voice.

That subject was closed. Joyce hesitated, then demanded bluntly: "Do you think there's any chance it was your men who got into a scrap with us near Cooney's outlaw camp?"

"I'm damn' sure it wasn't," replied Drake wrathfully. "We was miles away, and anyways Jack Ramsey would of reckernized my outfit. Pore Jack—my pal—dead maybe, because of you tenderfeet!" The cowboy groaned. "Sheriff Hawes shot you up, from what I've heard tell."

"Then who wounded you?"

"How the hell can I say? Injuns—horse thieves—any kind of bad men."

The prospects of getting helpful information from the disgruntled and suffering Steve Drake were nil, and Joyce left the bunk-house. He then put a single question to Gallatin:

"Is there a possibility that that is the cowboy you saw with McCall in Washington?"

"A possibility, yes. But to be honest I don't think so. On the witness stand under oath, I should certainly refuse to identify him as being the man," replied the Federal agent uncomfortably. "May I ask why you are so interested in this?"

"Just a hunch," Joyce evaded, and they both let it go at that.

The Inspector felt that it was now of paramount importance for him to get back to Pawhuska as quickly as possible. In the persons of Harry Deerfoot, Benny Gopher, Owl-Face and the Swift-Horse brothers, he had rounded up all the Indian witnesses whose absence in the hills had been either enforced or voluntary. They should be removed to town, where they could be kept under close surveillance. The murders in the Old Chief's family and that of Jennie Deerfoot were, after all, the crimes which Joyce had been hired to solve. The autopsy report on Joe Yellow-Horse awaited him. He was anxious besides to do some long-distance telephoning under conditions of assured privacy.

The one thing that he regretted was, that he would probably be forced to leave before he had learned whether Jack Ramsey had survived the ambush.

He informed McCall that he would need cars for an early start in the morning, and was told genially that three would be at his disposal. Meanwhile he concluded that a limited amount of sleuthing could still be accomplished at the ranch. He went at the task systematically, questioning and giving instructions to one of his assistants after the other.

The first man he summoned was Al Jenkins. "You're a smart old fox," he said. "I want you to mosey around among the hands, draw them out and take notice on just one point. Learn if you can whether they have friends in the Slim Cooney gang, whether there's any visiting between the ranch and that camp. Not the bigger Bert Lawson outfit, you understand; we think there's a real war on between McCall and Lawson. Just the bunch of cutthroats we were scouting after, and from whom we rescued the two Indians."

"I get you, Boss," replied Jenkins. He winked, and went strolling in the direction of the corral.

Joyce then cornered his son Tom. He did not reproach the lad for his failure to cooperate with Symes in the matter of the Swift-Horse brothers. He talked to him about Dan McCall.

"You got along with him pretty well, didn't you?" he said. "I suppose you were keeping your eyes and ears open. Did he drop anything that might have a bearing on this case?"

"I'm afraid not, Dad. He seemed to have made up his mind to avoid the subject of the murders—with me. Once when I asked him straight for an opinion, he said he cared to discuss it only with you."

"But he spieled along some line. He must have."

"Oh, sure! He told me reams about his adventures as a cattleman and oil prospector, and about this country."

"Nothing else?"

Tom considered, frowning. "He laid off Oklahoma and Texas stories once, and even so it was to tell me a similar sort of yarn. It appears he spent two years in Australia as a young man."

"Australia! That's funny. What was he doing out there?"

"He'd heard it was a newer and bigger Wild West, and a paradise for stock raisers. So he worked his way on a sailing ship, and got him a job herding cattle in the interior of Queensland. He didn't like the conditions. But the Australian bushmen amused him, and he studied their customs. He gassed a lot to me about them."

"Australia, and bushmen!" Joyce repeated the words slowly, reflectively. "A queer chapter in Dan McCall's life, all right. But I don't just see how it could furnish us with a clue to the present case."

"Nor I," answered Tom. "I mention it because you want to know everything that passed between us."

"Well, son, keep on being friendly with him. He may yet drop a hint that he's forgotten to give me, or that he'd prefer to keep to himself for that matter."

To Kay and Symes the Inspector did not assign any definite duties. He had decided to tackle Sheriff Hawes himself, and he took along with him the courageous young girl operative and the ideal shadow.

They found Hawes roosting on a fence with his deputies, some of whom were professional gun-toters attached

to his office in a vague capacity, and some Pawhuska busi-
nessmen who got a thrill out of riding into the wilderness
with him now and then.

"Well, Sheriff, I'll be returning to town tomorrow,"
Joyce announced. "I'm wondering whether you have plans
for going after the bandits for revenge."

"Revenge!" countered Hawes suspiciously. "They ain't
done nothing special to me."

"You don't admit that you shot it out with my party,
so maybe you ran into bandits. And if you didn't, Steve
Drake must have. Seems to me, bad actors are mighty live-
ly in this county of yours, and you'd want to get even with
them."

"I'm up here lookin' for evidence, if that's what you
mean. Guess I will hit the trail again." Hawes began to
work his jaws vigorously, and glanced belligerently over
his shoulder at a vague point on the horizon where Lawson
and Cooney might be supposed to be busy at their dirty
work. "Let me once clap eyes on them, and I'll slaughter
the buzzards."

"We're rooting for you, Sheriff."

"Might be able to do you a little service, too. I'll keep
my eye peeled for them two Injuns you claimed had been
dragged to these parts."

"Deerfoot and the Gopher boy," said Joyce innocently.
"Why, Sheriff, I sent a couple of my men—redskins, but
grand scouts—right into the Cooney camp, to fetch them
for me. They're all set to ride back to Pawhuska in the
morning, in one of McCall's Ford cars."

"The hell you say! Don't believe they were prisoners,
anyhow. Injuns work with each other, and are in cahoots
with the lawless elements of our population." Hawes
mouthed the last phrase with difficulty.

"That might be called a theory, Sheriff. But what have
you got to say to this? I wanted still another pair of Osages,

who were up here traveling. Nothing pinned on them. I needed them as witnesses, but they didn't know that, and they were independent, scrappy old boys. Mr. Symes here met them on the road, and brought them in single-handed."

Hawes, who had not deigned before to notice the presence of Symes, hopped off the fence and started to prance about like an infuriated ram. "Bunk!" he cried. "Bunk, bunk! Bushwah! That white-collared, hollow-chested sissy never pulled off no trick like that in this man's country."

"I'm telling you, the arrest of the two desperate Indians was entirely due to Mr. Symes," declared Joyce, emphasizing the "Mr." maliciously. "He turned them over to me when I caught up with him in the valley where the plane from Washington landed."

Symes looked very unhappy. He had dug his favorite cloth cap out of his bag, and the humble headgear made him resemble a suppliant clerk as he hovered unobtrusively between the Sheriff and Joyce. He murmured:

"I persuaded them to come along without much of an argument."

"I thought so," roared Hawes. "Lucky thing for you. I'll bet you'd have been slow on the trigger if the coyotes had turned ugly. By the right hind leg of the Lamb of God, it takes a Westerner to deal with 'em! 'The only good Injun is a dead Injun,' as old Gin'ral Scott used to say."

"We'll all cut this out, if you don't mind," said Joyce, suddenly freezing. "I'm here to help the Indians, and your old-time frontier race prejudice doesn't go with me."

The Sheriff was too startled to resent the cutting words. He half turned his back, and chewed with energy. The conversation was resumed on a more serious note, but it soon became apparent that there was little hope of extracting any evidence pertinent to the Osage murder plot from Hawes. Joyce earnestly suspected that he knew nothing.

The Sheriff was on a junket in the name of law enforcement, and that let him out.

The afternoon drifted uneventfully toward supper time. McCall's huge mess hall became jammed with the motley company of punchers and guests, and shortly after the meal had been eaten the tired investigators were glad enough to tumble into bed.

They arose at six o'clock. Breakfast was on the table by seven, and the three cars stood in a row at the front door. Dan McCall, in his role of an expansive host, buzzed around Joyce and Kay to see that they were properly served. Finally he had to depart to give orders to his foreman, and Al Jenkins who had slipped quietly into a seat beside the Inspector spoke under his breath.

"I worked on the boys since you gave me my orders, Boss. Cain't say as how they confessed anything to me, though they dropped a few right friendly words about the outlaws. Said Slim Cooney and his gang wasn't such bad fellows, and that everybody had to find a way to live."

"That sort of talk is to be expected," replied Joyce indifferently. "Folks in a wild country always half sympathize with outlaws."

"But though I couldn't dig up nothing for you myself, I got help from the right galoot," pursued Jenkins, who enjoyed creating suspense.

"Yes?"

"I sung our song to Owl-Face—Oh, I speak a little Cherokee!—and that old bird brings me something hot before the evening is over."

"Spill it."

"He allows that there's a man from the Cooney outfit right here at the ranch, passing himself off for a cowboy."

"I couldn't ask for anything hotter," whispered Joyce, delighted. "But how can Owl-Face be sure of it?"

"He did a lot of skulking around Cooney's, ahead of us. Daytime as well as night. He swears he saw the son-of-a-gun out there three days ago, and now he's here."

"And McCall's hands are friendly with him?"

"Sure. He's their pal."

Joyce analyzed this information rapidly. There was little to be gained by making a hullabaloo and trying to arrest the bandit. The latter probably would be protected long enough by his cronies to effect an escape. The significant point was, that the existence of such a person could be sworn to in due time by both Owl-Face and Jenkins. It would prove at least that McCall's employees had been in close and comradely contact with bad men. A jury would be impressed to learn that.

"We'll let it ride, Al," said Joyce. "But you've done a swell job, and I shan't forget it."

The party left the breakfast table, stood around smoking for a while and then took their places in the cars. Joyce would drive the first one himself, Jenkins the second and Allan Eagle the third. Their baggage was stowed about their feet, and only the fact that Hubert Gallatin, the Federal agent, had just emerged from the house to say farewell delayed the order to start. This was the moment chosen by Fate for the final development at Lone-Star ranch. There suddenly appeared from around a corner in the trail running northward a mounted man, bearing down on the ranch buildings at a smart canter. Somebody shouted, and the man threw up his left arm in a salute. His answering "Halloo!" came on the wind, faintly.

"By God, it's Jack Ramsey!" cried McCall. "I'd know him at twice the distance." The cattle king capered with glee, like a schoolboy.

Then a dozen cowboys began to clamor their joy. In fifteen minutes, Ramsey had arrived in their midst and had thrown himself off his sweating horse.

Joyce got out of the car, and approached the group. He heard McCall ask:

"Were you hurt, Jack?"

"No, just lost. And it took me some time to catch one of the runaway horses. I'm fine and dandy."

"What's your version of what happened when we were attacked the other night, Ramsey?" the Inspector inquired.

"The bunch was upon me before I knew a thing. I fired to warn you. They cut me off, and I ducked to cover. Later, I couldn't find out where the hell you'd gone, and I had to fend for myself."

"Did you get a line on who they were?"

"Nary a line. Tough hombres, that's all I know." Ramsey was sulky and impatient of questioning. He turned his back with a brusque movement, and spoke to one of his comrades.

Joyce wavered, and then drew Gallatin out of earshot of the cowboys.

"Was this Ramsey the man in Washington with Mc-Call?" he asked.

"His face seems a little bit more familiar than that of the other fellow. It might have been he. But I assure you, Inspector, I couldn't swear to it," replied Gallatin in a distressed tone.

"If you can't, you can't. But I'm going to put one hell of an important proposition to you. Will you co-operate?" Joyce's voice was very cold and incisive.

"I'll do anything that seems honorable and reasonable," the Federal agent agreed.

"Okay. I want you to show up in Pawhuska within three days. I want you to induce Dan McCall and those two cowboys, Jack Ramsey and Steve Drake, to come, too. Don't give them a reason connected with me. Don't let them suspect that there is such a reason. Just persuade

them to come, and I shan't care how you do it or what you
tell them."

Gallatin thought for a moment. "I might request that
they go with me to visit the resident Indian agent."

"If that argument will work, use it. If not, it will be up
to you to find a better one."

The agent bridled a little. "I am on a confidential
mission for the Government, and you ask me to accept a
course of action without even explaining its purpose."

"My dear sir, if you'll do what I say I'll have evidence
ready that will make your job look a darned sight simpler.
I promise you that."

Gallatin studied the face that had never failed to inspire confidence in Police circles and among all champions
of right and justice.

"You may depend on me. I'll phone you when we reach
town," he said.

They shook hands.

Joyce returned to his seat in the car, and the three
machines headed towards Pawhuska.

CHAPTER SEVENTEEN
Joyce Tightens the Net

Back, at the house of Chief Pale-Horse Eagle, where they arrived late in the afternoon. Joyce promptly organized his forces for the last phase of his inquiry into the three brutal murders of members of his clients' family circle. He sent Symes with Sylvia Deerfoot, to resume his guardianship of her person and home. The Swift-Horse brothers had given their promise not to leave again, but Tom was told off to keep in touch with them, and to watch that no attempt was made to do them harm. Joyce himself and Al Jenkins would act as bodyguards for the Old and Young Chiefs.

The Inspector's next move was to telephone Thad Calkins, the local head of the Police, and ask for the autopsy report on Joe Yellow-Horse's body.

"I've got it ready for you," answered Calkins. "In a short while I've got to be going out your way. Suppose I bring it to you."

"That's fine," said Joyce.

He spent the intervening time in reading mail that had accumulated. There were several letters and reports from Dinny Sullivan on the New York end of the Osage investigation, but they cast no light on the still unsolved mystery.

At seven o'clock Thad Calkins came stalking in. He greeted Joyce heartily, and handed him a document which

the Inspector noted with satisfaction was not signed by
Dr. James J. Purdy.

The medical examiner's report was simple in character.
It testified that the Indian Joe Yellow-Horse, aged forty-
one, had come to his death by a knife-wound in the left
side. Traces of the effects of chloroform had been discovered in the lungs. The wound was described as an opening
six inches deep which had squarely attained the heart. It
had evidently been inflicted by a knife with a blade from
six to eight inches long and an inch and a half wide, such
as a common hunting-knife. The weapon had been driven
in at an upward angle of about forty-five degrees, and
with extreme force so that three ribs had been fractured in
the course of its passage. A scrap of metal splintered from
the blade had been found in the wound, and was submitted therewith. Otherwise, the condition of the body had
offered no unusual features.

Joyce read the report aloud, and then glanced at Kay.
She nodded understandingly. The fact that the knife had
been nicked created a marked resemblance between the
Yellow-Horse murder and that of Flying-Horse Tail. The
weapon in the possession of Sheriff Hawes also showed a
recently damaged blade.

"This is just what I wanted," Joyce told Calkins. "And
now I'll be asking a service of you. I need to have some red
tape cut—pronto."

"Anything to oblige," the provincial chief constable
replied with alacrity.

"You remember the case of the other Indian belonging
to this same family—Flying-Horse Tail, his name was? He
was adjudged a suicide, and buried."

"I sure do remember it."

"Why did the Sheriff handle that case, instead of yourself? The man died within the town limits."

"It was reported to Hawes first, and he sort of took it away from me. O' course, I was in on the inquest and approved what was done. But Hawes, he always did claim that bein' Sheriff of the whole county he was free to jump in on criminal cases along with me."

"Very interesting. I'm not questioning the past at all. I care only about your power to act now. That corpse has got to be exhumed tomorrow. I want you to jam through a permit and be present to help me with your autopsy surgeon."

"Exhumed?" repeated Calkins, dazed.

"Yes, dug up for a post mortem."

"The Sheriff is away in the hills, and *he* can't kick; but I'm tellin' you, you're askin' to take on the nastiest job you ever tried. That Injun has been in his grave nigh on three weeks, and he won't be a pretty sight."

"I know it," said Joyce impassively. "But it's got to be done. Will you work with me?"

Calkins threw out his chest. "Yes, sir. The Injuns may not like it, though. These folks here are eddicated; I'm sayin' nothin' about them. But the common blanket Injuns, they don't like to see graves disturbed."

"Have a Police guard at the cemetery, then."

"That's the ticket. I'll turn out half a dozen of my best men. What time o' day do you reckon you'd like to start?"

"Let's say ten o'clock in the morning."

"Suits me. I'll stop by for you, Inspector." Calkins strode away, looking important.

Kay and Tom did not so much as comment upon the gruesome chore which Joyce had shouldered. They were accustomed, around a detective agency, to hearing demands for the exhumation of bodies when the cause of death was beclouded.

The investigators had dinner with their Osage hosts, and Joyce then proceeded to the second move which recent

developments had made logical. He got the personal representative of his firm in Washington on the long-distance
telephone.

"Craddock, this is Michael Joyce speaking from Pawhuska, Oklahoma," he said crisply. "I require information as
fast as you can get it for me. About ten days ago, a ranchman named Daniel McCall, from this place, was in Washington accompanied by a cowboy. They had business with
Indian Commissioner Jessup, of the Department of the
Interior. Find out the cowboy's name for me, that's all."

"The Government offices won't be open until ten
o'clock tomorrow morning, Inspector. I'll surely be able
to get the info' then," replied Craddock.

"There are other ways. You can maybe do something
about it tonight. McCall and his man stayed at one of the
hotels, probably a big one, since McCall is a rich guy. Take
a look at the registers in the likeliest places. Oh, yes! and
here's another lead: If you can get Commissioner Jessup's
private secretary on the phone at his home, he'll be able to
tell you what hotel it was."

"You want the cowboy's name, eh? Have you any idea
what name it might have been?"

"John Ramsey or Stephen Drake. But if you can't find
either of those, don't let that stop you. The bozo may have
used an assumed name. Learn how the man accompanying
McCall was registered, and if possible get a personal description of him. I can tell you that he always dressed in
full cowboy regalia."

"All right, Inspector. I'll attend to it."

Joyce hung up, and then sent a telegraph night letter to
his office, as follows:

TRACE PHONE CALL RECEIVED AT TEN
FORTY-FIVE A.M. MONDAY THE FIFTH

INST. STOP WAS MESSAGE TO ME DIRECT
FROM DANIEL MCCALL WHO STATED
WAS SPEAKING FROM WASHINGTON, D.
C. STOP REPORT AT EARLIEST POSSIBLE
MOMENT

JOYCE

"And that's all I can do for this evening," he said, throwing himself back into the softest armchair. He grinned at Kay, a little wearily, and added:

"I haven't been taking you much into my confidence, have I, on the way suspects are shaping up?"

"It's clear that you think McCall's men may have had a hand in the murders. But I don't get to what extent you tie them up in your own mind with the Cooney outlaws," answered Kay judicially.

"Well, ask yourself! You heard Jenkins tell that one of the gang was actually at Lone-Star ranch passing himself off as a cowboy. The two outfits are in cahoots somehow— or maybe I should say individuals in the outfits. The bandits kidnap Deerfoot and the Gopher boy, not for a purpose of their own, you may bet. They would have killed or ransomed such small fry in quick order. They are playing the game of their Lone-Star friends."

"Which is?"

"It's still too deep for me, but I'm getting there. Let's say that in addition to closing the mouths of Deerfoot and Gopher, the real criminals wanted to puzzle us. If they did nothing but kill, kill, kill, we'd have one straight notion about our problems. But if they mixed in a few kidnappings—by outlaws—we'd be forced to entertain another."

"I see. Now as to the 'real criminals,' as you put it, Inspector. You evidently suspect Jack Ramsey and Steve Drake, one of them, or possibly both. But what motive

could they have had for murders that brought them no
plunder? What good does it do them to cause the millionaire fortunes of these Indians to pass from one set of hands
to another?"

"There might be a motive," replied Joyce, "but I'm not
ready yet to state it."

"And I thought they had alibis. Weren't they in Washington with McCall?"

"Mr. Hubert Gallatin assures me that only one of them
was in Washington," said Joyce, passing on this knowledge
to Kay for the first time.

"Oh!" The girl was dumbfounded. "Then the other was
keeping under cover in Pawhuska at the time Jennie Deerfoot was killed!"

"He may have been. We're safe in working on the
assumption that he was."

"In that case, his alibi was deliberately prepared. And
McCall helped him to maintain it. Why should McCall do
that?"

"It is possible that Dan McCall was given a phony reason by his man—debt-dodging, or a love affair, or something like that. Possible, I say, just possible. McCall is a
democratic sort of cuss, who'd think nothing of obliging a
cowboy in that way."

"Jack Ramsey, or Steve Drake," enunciated Kay slowly.
"Which one of them do you think went to Washington—
and which stayed here?"

"I've put a man on the job to find out. But there's no
harm in guessing, me darlin'. You guess first."

"Ramsey remained in Pawhuska," asserted Kay without
hesitating. "The man is a harder type than Drake, and
when we were on that expedition in the hills he showed
that he wasn't any too friendly to us. He was our sentry
at the point of attack. I believe he either betrayed us, or

ducked without trying to help. Didn't he return without a scratch?"

Joyce smiled. "Those are reasons, but they're a woman's reasons, Kay. I've been looking for evidence connecting the man with the three murders that interest us, and I'm more suspicious of Drake."

"You have something on him?"

"Yes, and no. It will have to be checked; but I'm prepared to do that when he hits Pawhuska."

They both remained silent for several minutes, commenced to yawn and decided to go to bed.

In the morning, Joyce went coldly about his preparations for the trip to the Indian cemetery. Allan Eagle would identify the body. But Joyce felt that witnesses of his own would be desirable, and selected Al Jenkins as one of them. His son Tom was on the spot, but he decided in favor of an older and more experienced man.

"I'll take Symes, and send Tom to the Deerfoot house in his place," he told Kay.

The orders were issued, and within half an hour the Sheriff had reached the mansion. He loafed on the porch without saying anything, his narrow face wearing its customary look of mild indifference to hardships.

Finding a minute to spare for him, Joyce remarked:

"The Old Chief's brother was no suicide, of course. He was bumped, but I'm compelled to root him out of his grave to prove it."

"Exhumation often clinches a tough case, not to mention bringing the unexpected to light sometimes," said Symes gravely. "I remember when I was Sheriff of Algonquin County, I had reason to exhume the body of a minister who had died abroad, and whose body had been shipped to his home town for burial. When we opened that coffin, we found a dead Chinaman inside."

"That was a hot one," commented Joyce, too preoccupied to ask for the details.

He had noted the approach of Thad Calkins and his policemen, six in number, as well as a surgeon and four gravediggers. They were in cars, and they had a truck along. Joyce, who had borrowed the roadster once the property of the late Joe Yellow-Horse, signed to his two assistants and made haste to join the procession. Saved the necessity of getting out to ring the doorbell, Calkins turned his car about and they all speeded along the outskirts of town in a southeasterly direction.

They came presently to a fenced enclosure on slightly rolling ground where there were trees growing.

"This here's the cemetery," said Thad. "It's right old. Time was when the Injuns used to lay their dead on platforms made of crossed sticks, and leave 'em to the wind and rain. But we put an end to such unchristian business many years ago."

The cars discharged their passengers, and the Police chief set two men to stand guard at the gate where they descended. The rest advanced on foot along a shady path bordered by tombstones. Thad left a sentry at a point midway in the burial ground, and despatched two others to take posts a hundred yards to the right and left of their objective. It was simply a measure of precaution, because not a single onlooker was visible in any direction.

Under a stunted sycamore tree, they found a recently turned mound of earth, the resting place of Flying-Horse-Tail Eagle. The body of his son Joe Yellow-Horse would presently be brought to lie beside it. Surrounding the spot were many older graves of the numerous and important Horse-Eagle tribe.

"Guess we'd better pitch in and be done with it," grimaced Calkins, taking a chew of tobacco.

"Yes," said Joyce. He lighted an especially strong cigar, which he had put in his pocket for the purpose. He expected to smoke not less than three of them that morning.

The Police chief waved to the gravediggers. The latter, who were half-bloods, seized their spades and attacked the mound of earth. Because of the soft spring weather, the soil was loose and moist, making their task comparatively easy. The spadefuls flew to right and left. In half an hour, a hole six feet long and nearly three deep had appeared in the ground.

"Should be striking the casket pretty soon," mumbled Thad Calkins through his tobacco juice.

Joyce stepped back to avoid a shower of earth, and Symes who had been standing wordlessly at his elbow retreated still farther. A few minutes later, a dull thud as of iron colliding with wood was heard within the hole.

"Trust Injuns to have their graves shaller. The deeper they plant a corpse, the worse they think it is for his soul," said Thad, and laughed nervously.

Joyce said nothing. He listened to the muck being scraped from the top of the casket, and watched the preparations for prying the latter from its trench with stakes as levers. In time, the stained box began to make its appearance above the edge of the excavation.

"We'll be taking the whole shooting match to our morgue in the truck. Can't hold an autopsy here," explained Calkins. "But I suppose you want to take a look at the face first."

"It's very necessary," rasped Joyce. "That's why I came. That's why Mr. Eagle is here. An exhumed body has to be identified at the graveside."

"Unscrew that lid," Calkins ordered the sole policeman who was not doing sentry duty.

Behind him, Joyce became aware of the sound of retreating footsteps. He turned to see Symes scurrying in the direction of one of the officers who had been put on guard.

"Hey there, Sheriff!" he called after him. "Hey!"

Symes did not answer, and Joyce went in pursuit of him, shouting. "What the hell's the idea?" he asked, when he had caught up.

"I'm going to talk to that cop," the other muttered.

"Are you crazy? We've got a job to do. You're on duty."

Symes turned a suddenly pallid and emotion-racked face. "Honest to God, Inspector, I can't look at the stiff. Don't ask it of me. It's the one thing I never could stomach in this business."

"But—but you were telling me this morning about digging a Chinaman from a minister's grave in upstate New York." Joyce felt bowled over by the weird pusillanimity of this man, who was fresh from arresting two Indians in the Osage Hills and who thought nothing of tackling the most sinister racketeers in their dens of crime.

"Inspector, you misunderstood me," said Symes earnestly. "As Sheriff of Algonquin County, I was *Sheriff,* see, with a whole flock of deputies to do what I told them. I never saw that Chinaman. I went by the certified reports that were turned in."

"So you're scared of corpses. I'll be damned!"

"I don't mind 'em until they're buried. But after they've been underground a week or longer—ugh! You wouldn't want me to puke, or faint, would you?"

Joyce shook his head helplessly, and departed. Experience had taught him that good detectives, like other artists, were subject to temperamental quirks.

The group around the grave, mystified, had halted operations during the interlude. They now went to work again on the lid of the coffin and lifted it.

The face of an old Indian, dreadfully stricken by mortification, was laid bare. Eyes deeply sunken in their sockets and swollen, gaping lips would have been bad enough. But the necrosis had attained in purplish patches all visible parts of the flesh, cheeks, neck and hands.

Joyce puffed heavily on his cigar, drawing the acrid smoke into his lungs and expelling it through his nostrils in rapid jets. The deodorant qualities of nicotine helped to make the ordeal bearable. He gave Allan Eagle an interrogative glance.

The Osage's countenance was like a hard copper mask. "That is the body of my uncle," he declared.

"All right. Cover it up."

"Sweet job for me, this is going to be," the surgeon complained.

"Not so difficult, anyway," said Joyce. "Poison isn't in question, and you don't have to touch the viscera. I want only a description of the wound, with a statement as to whether it could have been self-inflicted."

"Okay."

Leaving it to the town officials to conclude the details, Joyce and his party moved away. They were joined shamefacedly by Sheriff Symes, and all walked to the gate of the cemetery, where they climbed into the roadster.

At the door of the Old Chief's house, Kay met the Inspector with a telegram. He opened it eagerly, and read:

DANIEL MCCALL AND COWBOY NAMED STEPHEN STAYED AT HOTEL HARRINGTON HERE STOP CHECKED OUT SUNDAY APRIL FOURTH

CRADDOCK

Joyce handed the wire to Kay. "You win," he said. "Looks as if Drake went to Washington, and Jack Ramsey skulked in Pawhuska."

CHAPTER EIGHTEEN
Millions Are at Stake

While he waited for the autopsy report on Flying-Horse-Tail Eagle, Joyce made a brief but exact inquiry. He went to the office of the resident Indian agent, where he obtained a list of the individual fortunes of the Osage millionaires. He noted particularly the sums which had been inherited from persons who admittedly had been murdered, or who had died in suspicious circumstances. He learned the names of the beneficiaries, and going further he jotted down the degrees of relationship and the names of those who stood to benefit, in the event of the sudden taking off of leading members of the nation still in the flesh.

Much of this information was already known to him, but for the first time he collated the whole record and posted himself on the ramifications of the tribal hierarchy. Since the Osages numbered about two thousand, and their wealth was estimated at about half a billion dollars, evenly divided in theory but concentrated here and there because of previous deaths, the killing of a mere handful of them could change the ownership of vast sums. Literally, millions of dollars were at stake.

Armed with these statistics, he returned to the Old Chief's house in the afternoon. He had just sat down to study them when a Police messenger arrived with the expected report, and thereafter things moved fast.

The autopsy surgeon had found that the death wound of Flying-Horse-Tail resembled amazingly the one by which Joe Yellow-Horse had subsequently perished. There was evidence of the same powerfully delivered stab, which had resulted in the fracturing of ribs. The peculiar upward direction of the blow had been a salient feature in both cases.

"It would have been totally impossible for the deceased to have stabbed himself in this manner," wrote the surgeon, "especially as the wound occurred on the left side of the body. It was noted at the original inquest that the dead man's right hand had been found gripping the handle of the knife. Manifestly, Flying-Horse-Tail could not have thus reached across his body and driven the lethal weapon upwards into his left side. It is to be doubted whether even an individual of immense physical strength could break his own ribs with the thrust of a knife, and this Indian was an old and feeble man. He came to his end by means of a blow which had behind it the momentum of a long and crushing drive. I recommend that the coroner's verdict be reversed and this death be adjudged a willful and premeditated homicide, instead of a case of self-destruction."

"So that's that," said Joyce, after he had read the report to Kay. "It's only what we looked for, only what we agreed was as good as certain when you and I last talked about it. But this is going to help when the time comes to draw up an indictment."

"We know that the same person killed the two Horse-Eagles," asserted Kay. "But was he also the murderer of Jennie Deerfoot?"

"I think so—" began Joyce. He was interrupted by the ringing of the telephone. Kay, who sprang to answer it for him, announced:

"The New York office speaking. Dinny Sullivan on the wire."

Joyce took up the receiver and heard his assistant say:

"Howdy, Chief. I've got a report to make to you on that telephone call you wanted us to trace."

"Yes. Spill it."

"The call was put in through the Lackawanna exchange, New York City."

"Are you sure? Did you get to the 'Phone Company's District Superintendent himself for a tracing order?"

"You bet, Chief. And I used Police Department pull with him. We were given quick service."

"Was there any call from Washington, D. C., to my office that morning?"

"No. I made a point of asking that."

"Did you question the girl at our own telephone switchboard? When she buzzed me, she said I was to stand by for a long-distance message."

"I took it up with her, all right. She remembered the call perfectly, because when she took it a man's voice told her it was long distance. She thought that queer. The regular thing is for the woman central to announce it. But since there was no comeback, Miss Kennedy—our girl—didn't give the matter any more attention."

"Some monkey business! McCall himself, in New York, said he was talking from Washington and got away with it. Not the least doubt about that, is there?"

"The Telephone Superintendent says the customer must have pulled a fast one. No operator would have dared to do such a thing. I'm of the same opinion myself," replied Sullivan with meticulous accuracy.

"I'm pleased at your getting the dope on this right off the bat," said Joyce. "Anything else to report?"

"Well, about those Indians in the office building across the way from the Hermitage Hotel. Another check-up seems to prove they were there for only a few minutes. I don't believe they went above the ground floor. And I found an orange juice stand in Times Square, near Forty-seventh, where they stopped for a couple of glasses within the half hour."

"You can quit bothering about them, Dinny. I guess they were on the level. Any luck in finding the weapon that fell in Seventh Avenue?"

Sullivan seemed to hesitate. "You counted on some-body having found an arrow, didn't you, Chief?"

"Not necessarily. Any missile that could be discharged from one ninth story to another, the width of the Avenue."

"I get you. We advertised in the newspapers, as you told us to, and inquired at different Lost and Found bureaus and through the Police. Now there hasn't been any arrow, or sling-shot, or bullet showed up—nothing of that kind. But a man brought in a sort of club he'd picked up that morning in the middle of the street, between Forty-first and Forty-second."

"Yes," said Joyce curiously. "A club? It doesn't sound very hopeful."

"No, sir. I scarcely thought I'd mention it to you. The thing isn't even a club, in a right manner of speaking."

"What is it like? Describe it."

"It's some three feet long, and very much curved. I'd not figure it for a club, except that it's polished and has criss-crossing on one end to give a grip for the hand."

"Go on. Go on," snapped Joyce. "Tell me more about the thing."

"Well, it's thicker in the middle, and the two ends taper off. It's shaped a bit like a bow, but made of a hard, black wood that doesn't bend. You couldn't shoot arrows from it. Besides, the center part is at least three inches thick. If it's not a club, it's a freak walking stick, though a broken-backed shillelagh like that would look real foolish in a man's hand."

"I know what you mean," replied Joyce, his voice tense with interest. "You say a man brought it in? To our office?"

"Yes, Inspector."

"Did you pay him the reward, and hang on to it?"

"It didn't seem to be what you wanted, but I told him if he cared to leave it, you'd pass upon its value—to you—when you got back."

"For God's sake! My instructions were that any weapon found in Seventh Avenue near Forty-first Street was to be accepted. Did the guy leave his crooked stick?"

"He did. It's on your desk right now."

"Do you have his name and address?"

"Yes, Inspector."

"Well get in touch with him at once, and give him ten dollars as reward. If he asks for more, pay him anything within reason—say up to fifty bucks. Make him write out a receipt for settlement in full, so there won't be a chance for a comeback later. Hang on to that club. Fight for it, if necessary. I want it for my collection."

"Okay, Chief. Trust me!" answered Sullivan briskly, but with a shade of astonishment.

"Good-bye, then. I'll probably be back in New York this week, and I'll wire you when to look for me."

"Good-bye, Inspector."

Joyce slammed down the telephone receiver, and turned to Kay. Succinctly, he gave her Dinny Sullivan's report, that half of the conversation which she had not been able to hear. His ordinarily cold blue eyes had the light of victory in them.

"Now, what do you get out of that kettle of fish, darlin'?" he asked eagerly.

"McCall fooled you on a supposed long-distance call, when he was actually in New York. He asked you to take Allan Eagle's murder case, but wanted you to think that he

himself had not left Washington, D. C. A chunk of curved
wood is discovered in front of the hotel," she recapitulated.
"If those facts help to solve the mystery, I don't see it yet."

"Chunk of curved wood!" Joyce seized upon the phrase.
"Surely you know what that is, darlin'."

"No, I don't," she replied, a little shamefacedly.

"And you've visited my museum of deadly weapons a
score of times. Kay, I'm ashamed of you."

"I—I'm afraid I can't identify it. A weapon, you say? Is
that stick a weapon that could have been used against the
Indians in the Hermitage Hotel?"

"Just so. It's a boomerang."

"The thing the Australian bushmen use in hunting?"

"Yes. Any dictionary will tell you that a boomerang is
a missile that can be hurled so that its flight will bring
it back to the place from where it was thrown. Does the
idea click now? If Allan Eagle had been hit squarely by
the thing, it would have fallen at his feet, stopped by the
impact; but he would have been killed. It only grazed him,
and sailed back part of the way, to drop in the middle
of Seventh Avenue. That's the devilish ingenuity of the
boomerang. A miss, and it returns to the hand of the person using it! A half-miss, and it still has enough momentum to remove itself to quite a distance!"

"Great stuff!" said Kay. "But where's the connection
with Dan McCall and a lot of Osage Indians? Have we got
to look for an Australian suspect now?"

Joyce leaned forward. "I didn't tell you the clue that
Tom picked up in the hills. I'll confess it passed over my
head until Dinny Sullivan started to describe the boomerang just now. McCall spilled to Tom that he'd spent two
years in Australia, and studied the customs of the bushmen."

"Which means that he's one of the few men in the United States likely to know about boomerangs!" gasped Kay.

"Or to own one. Sure!"

"But you don't claim that McCall tried to murder Allan Eagle a few minutes after he'd telephoned you to recommend him and his case! That's fantastic!"

"I claim nothing. He'll have to disprove it, though."

"I can't imagine what object he could have had to attempt such a crime."

"That will come out at the show-down. It won't be long now."

"Drake!" cried Kay, her mind leaping to a conclusion. "Steve Drake, the cowboy who went East with him. If Jack Ramsey could commit three murders in Pawhuska, Drake might have been in the plot with him to kill off members of the same family in New York. They're buddies."

"Why do you credit Drake with knowing how to employ a boomerang?"

"He's thick with McCall, isn't he? He and Ramsey are the two ranch employees who seem closest to their boss. Suppose McCall taught him the trick."

"A little far-fetched, Kay darlin'. It's one thing to learn a queer stunt like that from a whole slew of natives who practice it, and another to teach it to an Oklahoma cowboy. Neither professor nor pupil would be likely to apply themselves very hard in a country where lassoing and gun-shooting are much more fashionable. However, it's possible that Drake was a boomerang expert, and that he stole the weapon from McCall."

Joyce made his last statement without conviction. He fidgeted in his chair.

"Anyway, Inspector, we've boiled down the suspects to men who are close to that cattle king person."

"And of what do we suspect them?"

"Of guilt in the cases we came here to investigate—the deaths of Flying-Horse-Tail Eagle, Jennie Deerfoot and

Joe Yellow-Horse—of the attempt in New York and the kidnapping of essential witnesses here—of, of—"

"Of what else?"

"Of trying to murder you, also, in the Osage Hills," Kay burst out. "I don't know whether Sheriff Hawes lent himself to it, or some other gang of cutthroats was put on the job. But that night on the plateau, you were deliberately attacked with the idea of wiping out your whole party, and I don't think it was done by bandits."

Joyce slapped his thigh. "If you hadn't understood that, you'd have been dumb—which you aren't."

He leaped up, and strode about the room, puffing furiously at a cigar. "But the affair is bigger than even you are able to see as yet. In the past twenty-four hours it has entirely changed its character, in my mind. The three murders in this family—hell, they're solved! That's the least of it. I know right now who to arrest."

"Jack Ramsey!" the girl said under her breath.

He ignored that. "The larger phase of it is what bothers me. I haven't made up my mind exactly where my duty lies. I'll have to sleep over it."

Kay knew better than to prod him with questions when he was in a mood of this sort. He would tell her everything in his own good time.

"Millions are at stake," he said, repeating a thought which had come to him earlier in the day, after he had examined the records of the wealth of the Osages. "And that's only part of it. Dozens of lives and the self-respect of two races are involved."

He continued to propel his robust frame from one end of the room to the other. Then his reflections went off on a new tack, and he cried brusquely:

"I must know whether that Federal agent will make it to Pawhuska tomorrow, or the day after. Get the Lone-Star ranch on the phone, will you?"

Kay moved over promptly to the instrument, and asked for the connection. A minute or so later, she said:

"Here they are, Inspector."

Joyce took the receiver from her. His voice gone suddenly matter of fact, he stated that he wished to speak to Hubert Gallatin.

Kay could hear the resonant buzzing of a shouted answer, without being able to distinguish the words.

Joyce listened to the end, said "Thanks," and hung up.

"We're all set," he declared. "Gallatin started fifteen minutes ago. He has McCall, Ramsey and Drake with him. They'll be here some time during the night."

CHAPTER NINETEEN
A Plot Against a Nation

Early in the morning, Gallatin phoned from the South-western Hotel, where he was staying, and announced that he was at Joyce's disposal. The Inspector asked him to come over without delay. He countered with the suggestion that his traveling companions be included, and was told to come alone. Joyce was quite satisfied to know that the ranchman and his two cowboys were safely installed in the rooms where he had first met them, above McCall's colorfully-named Bank of the Bad Lands. That they should be in Pawhuska, without his having been forced to go after them with warrant or subpoena, was in itself a triumph.

Waiting for the Federal agent to appear, he was un-communicative to the point of glumness. He had scarcely spoken to his Osage hosts the night before, and now he looked through and beyond them, as if unaware of their presence. They had become symbols to him, impersonal figures in the drama of justice he had conceived, thought Kay, who knew him like a book. She did not mind that for the moment he was also ignoring her.

Her faith that he would not shut her out of the final elucidation of things proved justified as soon as Gallatin entered the house. The gray-mustached representative of the Government looked solemn and somewhat at a loss. He began by volunteering that he had failed to learn anything of interest during the preceding two days at the ranch.

"That's all right. I didn't expect you to bring me any news," replied Joyce. "You and I are now going into a huddle, and I'm prepared to give you dope you never dreamed of. It will be a private conference, with the Indians left out of it. But I want Miss Carey to be present. I call her a secretary, but she's really the smartest woman assistant that a guy in my business ever had."

Gallatin bowed. "I have no objection to her hearing our discussion."

"She'll be taking down a record in shorthand, for my future reference, anyway," Joyce explained.

They went into old Pale-Horse Eagle's parlor, and closed the door behind them. Joyce plunged into his subject without further preliminaries.

"The first thing I heard about the trouble in the Osage country was, that it was a widespread conspiracy. The newspapers said that more than a year ago, repeating the gossip of this town. Then Dan McCall came out strong with the theory that it was to be laid at the door of the outlaws in the hills. Allan Eagle, the Indian who engaged me, also was sold on the idea of a plot; but I think he suspected people of his own race. Members of his own family, he'd have said, if he'd been willing to be frank. Wanted me to pin the guilt on the right parties, if I could, without his having made an accusation. I'm repeating these points so that we'll have them clear in our minds."

"They are perfectly clear," answered Gallatin. "It cannot be doubted that a plot exists. I hesitate to assert that it is of white bandit origin, but I still lean toward that interpretation of the whole succession of tragic events."

"McCall got to you again, I see, after you and I talked on the ranch."

"He did give me a complete account, from his point of view." The agent looked uncomfortable.

"Well, you can safely ignore it. McCall is a liar."

"A deliberate liar? You can't mean that."

"He knows the truth, and he is concealing it. He has known it from the very beginning."

"Do you have proof?"

"Not watertight proof—not yet—but circumstantial evidence strong enough to make any District Attorney sit up and take notice."

"Really? Evidence of McCall's bad faith?"

"Yes."

"Are you prepared to give it to me?"

"Nothing else but! Now listen. I'll start off with that ranchman's public actions and his dealings with me. A year and a half ago, he jumped into the Osage murder cases with a bitter complaint that they were being mishandled by the State, county and town authorities. He sprang the bandit theory, and proclaimed that he was scouring the hills with posses formed of his own cowboys. Yet he never brought in a single prisoner."

"It would be difficult to lay hands on the right person in such wild country."

"McCall claimed to be the sworn enemy of all outlaws," Joyce scoffed. "He's mentioned the big Bert Lawson gang in particular, and for years he's lived cheek by jowl in those hills with Lawson and the smaller Cooney crowd, too. Not once has he grabbed a bandit and turned him over for questioning. Not once has he killed a son-of-a-gun of them in a fight, so far as I've been able to learn."

"That indicates that he has been pretty lax."

"Lax, eh? What will you say when I tell you that a member of Cooney's band was at the Lone-Star ranch-house, dressed as a cowboy and on friendly terms with everybody, at the same time that you and I were there?"

Gallatin leaned forward, startled. "You can prove it?"

"By two witnesses, yes. But let's take up some other angles. McCall objected to the administration of justice in this county, and yet he backed for Sheriff the incompetent Luther Hawes, his man Friday, who's better at running errands for his master than catching criminals. I don't know what you made of that attack on me when I was scouting. I lay it either to Hawes or to McCall's cowboys, and I say they intended to kill me. It was no blunder in the dark. It was planned."

"But why, Inspector, why? I understand it was McCall himself who had you hired for the investigation, when you need never have known anything about it officially."

"That brings us to his Washington trip. He went with a grand hurrah to plead the cause of the Indians, yet he was full of lies and deception. You saw him there with one cowboy. He told me that there were two—"

Joyce proceeded to give a summary of his information that Drake had gone East, while Ramsey lurked in Pawhuska; of the falsified telephone call to arrange an interview with Allan Eagle; the attempt on the latter's life, with the piquant detail that an Australian boomerang had been retrieved in the middle of Seventh Avenue.

"The object of all this, the object?" the astounded Gallatin queried, in his somewhat helpless, repetitious way.

"It's simple. McCall felt he needed to bolster his reputation, so he nervily took his story to the Indian Bureau in Washington. He also wanted one quick conviction here, for the look of things. He tipped Allan Eagle to engage me, figuring I could be fooled into hanging a murder charge on to some poor egg like Harry Deerfoot or Owl-Face the Cherokee. Meanwhile, a cowboy had been left behind, and that man pulled off some new killings; he had to be protected. McCall saw that I was getting too near to the truth in the Jennie Deerfoot affair, and he invited me to the ranch in order that I might be bumped without a comeback. The same sort of fate would have been arranged for you, if you had shown signs of striking a hot scent."

The Federal agent gasped. "And the blow at Allan Eagle in New York?"

"A last-minute inspiration, because it seemed as if it could be done safely. Allan, next to his own father, is the wealthiest of all the Osage millionaires."

"But where is your argument getting to? Can you possibly think that Daniel McCall is the master murderer?"

"You have ears and a good logical brain, Mr. Gallatin. You've followed my drift, and you don't honestly doubt what my answer to that last question is going to be. I've given you circumstantial evidence, as I promised. There's more to come, and it's the most damning yet."

"Yes—yes—yes!" the other stammered.

Joyce pulled out the sheaf of notes he had made at the resident Indian agent's office. "Everybody knows that McCall's nephew, Ernest Burkhart, married one Mollie Bigheart, a daughter of the first Osage family to be attacked in this murder campaign. After her sisters had been removed—violently—she fell heir to a fortune of about $180,000 a year. Burkhart benefited, and a juicy sum like that must have looked good to his Uncle Dan. But McCall was clever enough to shout to Heaven that he feared Mollie and her husband were next in line to be eliminated. Actually, they're safe and sound today, and enjoying their jack.

"The McCall propaganda that he was out to save the Indians, and especially Mollie, fooled me at the beginning. There didn't seem to be any reason why that ranchman should covet money. He was tremendously rich already, what with his cattle and his oil holdings. Then I checked up on the inheritance results of other deaths in this section, and I found this:

"I found that in every case, the Bighearts were in the direct line of succession. The first heir might be a son or brother, aunt or sister, but if that one and perhaps still another were to be removed later, the beneficiary would be the former Mollie Bigheart. Take the Horse-Eagles, for whom I am working. Flying-Horse-Tail and Joe Yellow-Horse are dead. Their money goes to the Swift-Horse brothers and some old women. But with the last-named out of the way, the next of kin would be Mollie Bigheart. The same is true of the Deerfoots, only in that case the tie-up is even closer. Sylvia and Harry Deerfoot are first cousins of McCall's daughter-in-law, their immediate heir. The Old and Young Chiefs themselves are fairly close blood relations of the Bighearts."

"Isn't that true of the entire Osage nation?" muttered Gallatin.

"More or less. There are degrees, however. The group attacked is tightly knit, and is the wealthiest group. A little more judicious killing, and through the Burkharts McCall will control half the resources of the race. . . ."

"Well, why does he want that? What can additional millions mean to him?"

"Power. I've been studying him, and I tell you he's drunk with self-conceit. They call him the 'uncrowned king of the Osage Hills.' He glories in the title. He'd certainly enjoy bossing this county more than piling up the fortune of Rockefeller, but money is the short-cut to it. He's half-cracked, too. Only a criminal maniac is capable of wholesale murder to gain his ends."

Joyce, who had been pacing the room, halted, to beat on the table with the lower part of the fist that held his eternal cigar.

"Call what I've been saying unproved deduction, if you like. But the facts will bear me out. Of course, the case has to be worked up. It might take months. The judge

would want to know when and how McCall gave his orders
for a murder, and to whom. There'll have to be material
evidence. The business of the outlaws will have to be fully
studied. He's been using some of them as allies. Which
ones? Is his nephew Burkhart in on the plot? Are some
of the Indians traitors to their kind, and scheming with
him?"

"We have a terrific task in front of us," said the Federal
agent, finally convinced.

Joyce stared at him moodily. "I could go out and beat
you on this exposé. I have a running start. But I don't
intend to. You're to make free use of all that I've told you,
or may be able to tell in the future. I've decided to let you
make the arrests—with one exception—and take the entire
credit."

Kay, who had been listening open-mouthed without
saying a word, found it impossible to restrain herself any
longer.

"Do you realize what you're doing, Inspector?" she
cried. "This is the greatest opportunity you've ever had
in the business. If you, a private detective, were to convict McCall of this slaughter of the Osages, you'd be three
times as famous as William J. Burns was after the San
Francisco graft investigation."

"Yes, I realize it. But I don't feel I have the right to be
selfish. Not in this thing. It's altogether too important to
the whole United States."

"How so?" asked Kay, wondering.

"Uncle Sam didn't give the Indians a square deal in
the old days. They don't believe in our good intentions
now, and who's to condemn them for that! McCall, a white
man posing as their friend, has betrayed them as badly as
they've ever been betrayed before. If a detective, paid by
Indians, brings him to book, it will only confirm them in
their idea that they can't get justice from the Government.

The Federal agents have got to clean this up, for the sake of establishing confidence. I shouldn't be satisfied that I'd done my duty, if I failed to help along those lines."

Gallatin jumped from his seat and stretched out his hand. "You are a patriot, Inspector Joyce. I've never heard a finer sentiment expressed since I joined the Department of the Interior twenty years ago."

"Aw, cut out the bouquets!" mumbled Joyce, his honest Irish face flushing brick-red with embarrassment. "I made up my mind to this during the night, and I've said my say. Now, let's get down to the next piece of business."

"I only hope I can be of service to *you* in it, whatever it is," exclaimed Gallatin.

"You have already, by bringing McCall and his two pet cowboys in from the ranch."

"I don't quite understand."

"Well, I'm going to arrest one of them this morning."

"Which one?"

"That would be telling. I'm none too sure myself. But you'll remember I stated just now that I made a single reservation, in turning the Osage cases over to you. I've got to fulfil my contract with Allan Eagle, and hang the man who murdered his uncle, his cousin and Jennie Deerfoot."

"Can't I help?"

"Yes, by keeping away from me, from now on. McCall mustn't suspect that we've been in cahoots. You just go back to your hotel, Mr. Gallatin, and I'll handle my little affair in such a way that McCall thinks it an individual bit of sleuthing, and that I intend to lay off himself."

"I can do this at least. I can drop in at the flat above the bank, make sure that the three of them are there and telephone you from outside."

"So you can," agreed Joyce, with a certain admiration for the Federal Agent's persistence. "It would be useful to know whether they're alone, or if a crowd of visitors have blown in."

"I'll make a report to you on that within the next half hour."

"And I'll start down as soon as I hear from you."

They shook hands, and Gallatin departed.

Joyce moved over to the telephone and summoned Symes from the Deerfoot home. Then he glanced at Kay quizzically.

"All that concerns us now is to pinch the guy who committed the triple murder. But it would be a mistake to do that until we have a case for the jury."

"Don't you have it yet?" she asked, astonished.

"No, me darlin'."

"What are you going to do, then?"

"Complete the case on the spot, a few minutes before we pinch him. You'll see."

CHAPTER TWENTY
The Case for the Jury

Joyce received in due time the promised telephone message from Gallatin. McCall, Ramsey and Drake were having an early luncheon in the cattle king's rooms, and they were alone. The Inspector thereupon assembled his aides, consisting of Kay, Tom, Symes and Jenkins and left in a car borrowed from Allan Eagle. On the way, he met the local policeman Siegel, whom he invited to come along. Hypnotized by the respect which his superiors had shown the New York celebrity, Siegel accepted without asking questions. When they reached the side entrance of the bank building, Joyce ordered him to post himself on the stairway.

"I may have trouble upstairs," he said. "If you hear a rumpus begin, bust into McCall's flat and help me. If anybody tries to shoot his way out of this building, stop him."

"Ah reckon yew can depend on me. Yew sho' can," replied the officer with the German cognomen and the cracker accent.

Joyce then spoke to Kay in a whisper. "I'll let you go in with us, because I want you to see the finish. But if there's gun play, you must promise me to duck fast—out of the door, or under a table, depending on circumstances."

"All right," the girl promised a trifle unhappily. She was carrying a perfectly good revolver in the side pocket of her coat.

They mounted the stairs and knocked at McCall's door. A genial shout advised them that they could enter, which they did bunched, with Joyce slightly in the lead.

"Why, hello, hello! Glad to see you," the ranchman boomed; but his eyes narrowed behind their horn-rimmed glasses, as though he perceived in a flash of intuition that this mass invasion was of a menacing character.

"'Morning, Mr. McCall," said Joyce. "I've come here hoping to get co-operation from you. A bit of funny business I want to investigate, and you can be of assistance."

"I'll be glad to help the law in any way that's reasonable," answered McCall slowly.

His big frame, which had been sprawled in an armchair, straightened to a sitting position and his right hand moved unobtrusively across his lap until it was close to the .45 Colt in his belt. The line of the small, downward curving mouth tightened.

The two cowboys were loafing in their favorite places at the window behind him. Jack Ramsey, with his hard, pale eyes set in a cruel face. Steve Drake, the weaker type apparently, his countenance brutish and devoid of sentiment, like that of a moron schoolboy. Their right thumbs were hooked in their trouser-pockets, and thus already near to their six-shooters. But Drake's left forearm and hand were swathed in a bandage, less cumbersome than the one he had worn at Lone-Star ranch. Self-rolled cigarettes dangled from their lips.

The table at which they had breakfasted stood covered with dishes between the three cattle men and the detective's party.

"First, I wish you'd tell me why Ramsey and Drake have been spreading the word that they were both in Washington with you a couple of weeks ago?" demanded Joyce.

Craftily, he put the blame for the story upon the punchers, and not upon their employer from whom he had heard it. And as he spoke, his own right hand was held tensely, ready to spring to his arm-pit, where he had slung his automatic. Joyce always maintained that a gun carried that way could be drawn a full second more quickly than a plainsman could jerk his from a holster. It was a trick learned from the gangsters of New York and Chicago.

"Because they *were* both there, I guess," drawled the king of the Osage Hills.

"I know you must have a reason for covering the man who stayed behind. But suppose he wasn't on the level with you, Dan McCall. Suppose he pulled some rough stuff, when he likely had told you it was private business that held him here. Would you still want to protect him in a false alibi?"

McCall brushed aside the implication that he was personally blameless. "I've told in Pawhuska that the two boys were East with me. Are you calling me a liar?"

"No. I'm not accusing you of anything, so it doesn't matter to me what you may have said. But I want to know which of the boys lied, and why."

As he pronounced this statement, Joyce narrowly watched Ramsey and Drake. He was well aware that cowboys, no less than their bosses, made a fetish of resenting the stigma of "Liar!" The pair, however, had evidently been trained to await orders. Their faces were masks of savage wrath, yet beyond gazing beseechingly at McCall they held themselves in check.

"If they did lie," the latter said, biting off his words, "they're the ones to do the telling. Ask 'em."

Kay Carey wondered in a frenzy of excitement why Joyce did not arrest Jack Ramsey first and question him afterwards. To her increased amazement, the Inspector turned to the rougher of the two punchers and inquired mildly:

"Were you in Washington?"

"You bet your life I was."

"And you, Drake?"

"The same goes for me."

"From now on, you'd best not insist—unless you have proof," McCall warned grimly.

"I'd not be here talking this way unless I had something. Only one name was registered with yours at the Hotel Harrington, Washington. It was Steve Drake's."

"Whether that's true or not, you had a hell of a nerve putting a dick on my movements in Washington," said McCall with complete aplomb.

"It wasn't on your movement, but on those of the cowboy. I was forced to identify the one who had gone there. How else would I find out which of the pair had remained in Pawhuska? The latter may have been guilty of the rough stuff I've hinted at."

"What sort of rough stuff?"

"Unlawful entry of an Indian house, the home of a client of mine. Motive and details will come out in the wash. I need to take a slant at the guy's fingerprints, so that I can compare them with evidence previously obtained."

Kay was thunderstruck. At no stage of the game had fingerprints been a factor in their inquiry, and she was baffled by the drift of Joyce's tactics. He might be employing a new ruse, though this no longer seemed necessary to her, to get a look at the fingers without causing suspicion to flame.

"Oh!" The exclamation passed McCall's lips with a subtle inflection of relief. The mental strain under which he and his men had been laboring relaxed almost visibly. "So you want a daub from Jack's dirty hand! I'm sure he'll give it to you. Both hands, if you like. Will a print on the back of an envelope be good enough?"

"Maybe, if it's clear."

"Step forward, Jack," McCall instructed.

Ramsey swaggered over.

"Do you still say you were in Washington?" asked Joyce, as he went through the motions of taking a faint and practically worthless set of impressions.

"Sure!" But the cowboy winked. "If one of us galoots did hang back in Oklahoma, you'll find it was to make love to his divorced wife—and not in Pawhuska, nohow!"

"Haw-haw!" laughed McCall.

Joyce had achieved one of his main objectives in getting Ramsey separated from his pal. With a slight movement of his head, understood by Tom and Symes, he signaled that the man was to be collared at the least sign of an outbreak. Then he walked straight toward Steve Drake.

"I'd be obliged if you'd let me have prints of your fingers, too. Please take the bandage off that left hand."

Drake jumped and flushed. "No siree! I've got a bad wound."

"You were shot above the wrist, you told me. There's no reason why you shouldn't uncover your hand."

"But what the hell!" wrangled McCall. "Why bother this bird? You've got the dope on the man you suspect."

"I demand to see his fingers," cried Joyce sharply. He was within a few feet of Drake, and was entirely prepared for what followed.

The cowboy grabbed at the handle of the gun in his belt. He did it with his right hand, and the movement was strangely clumsy and ineffective. He abandoned it with a curse. Joyce's automatic was already out. Yet Drake hurled himself toward the detective.

Joyce leaped to one side and struck him with his clenched fist behind the ear. The plainsman stumbled. It would have been absurdly easy to fill his body with bullets, but this was far from being what the Inspector desired. Instead, he kicked him on the shins and then tripped him. Drake fell to the floor, the bandaged arm under him. He howled with pain, and as he rolled over he found himself staring into the barrel of the automatic held within a few inches of his face.

"One more false move from you, and I'll shoot!" Joyce grated.

Steve Drake lay still. Every muscle in his face sagged, and his mouth fell open. There was fear in his eyes.

Over by the door, there had been a short, stiff tussle with Ramsey. He, too, had reached for his six-shooter, but Symes and Tom had covered him with revolvers before he could draw it. He was standing now with his hands held above his head.

Throughout the mêlée, Dan McCall had not left his chair or made a single aggressive gesture. He was sitting now with his arms crossed, his pear-shaped head tilted to one side, his eyes like pin-points and an expression of almost clinical curiosity upon his face.

"Come here, Jenkins, and cut the wrappings from this cowboy's fin," Joyce ordered. "Not only the hand. Rip the whole bandage off."

The scout advanced swiftly, drawing a long hunter's knife from its sheath. He inserted the blade under the first layer of cotton and sliced it all the way down. Then he hacked off the crude knots which held the wrappings at the wrist. With a jerk that elicited a groan from the prostrate man, he tore the cloths loose and threw them on the ground.

Steve Drake's exposed arm was innocent of the least trace of a bullet wound. But the tip of his left thumb was enflamed and seriously swollen. Jenkins caught him by the wrist and lifted the hand for Joyce to examine.

"That's all I need to know," the latter stated after a moment of electric silence. "I arrest this man for the willful and premeditated murder of Jennie Deerfoot. Put the handcuffs on him, Tom. Jack Ramsey may go."

The detective's son advanced and clamped irons upon the wrists of Drake.

Dan McCall still had not budged from his seat. He lifted one forefinger and rubbed it along the side of his chin.

"You are not arresting him merely on suspicion, are
you? Where is your evidence?" he asked smoothly.

"This." Joyce took an envelope from his pocket and exhibited the section of harness needle which he had found
in the woods at Three-Mile Creek, the scene of Jennie's
death. "I've told you how a needle was driven into the base
of the Deerfoot girl's brain and the end snapped off. I figured that the killer had injured his own thumb, and I've
been looking ever since for a thumb that filled the bill.

"Right here in this room a little more than a week ago,
I first suspicioned Drake. You'd asked him to ring the bell
in the wall by the window, and he touched it with his left
thumb. Then he pulled the hand away kind of sharply,
swung his body all the way around and used his right
hand. Do you get what that meant to me? None but a
left-handed man would have employed his left thumb in
the first place. But if it hurt him because it had recently
been pricked, he'd switch to the right.

"I watched Drake after that. He went to a lot of trouble
to act as if he was right-handed, but once in a while he'd
give himself away in little things. The finger was healing
okay. Then, when we were on the scouting trip, he must
have got it infected. To fool me, he wrapped up his arm
from the elbow down and pretended he'd been shot."

"Fooled me, too—about the gun wound," drawled Mc-
Call. "But it's a bit hard to understand the charge you're
making. You said you wanted a man for 'unlawful entry.'"

"That was just a stall, to prevent him from catching on
to my intention at the go-off."

"Furthermore, I thought you claimed to have proved
Drake went to Washington with me and Ramsey stayed
here!"

"There's two answers to that, Mr. McCall," said Joyce, masking with difficulty his loathing of the hypocritical arch-plotter. "First, *I* knew it had to be Drake who'd remained in Pawhuska to do murder, because his thumb was sore and Ramsey's wasn't. Second, you knew—seeing you were there—that Ramsey signed Drake's name to the hotel register, so as to provide said Drake with a watertight alibi. I'm not hinting, of course, that either you or Ramsey had the least notion that he'd use it to cover up a foul, dastardly crime."

McCall slapped his thigh. "By God, you're smart!" he boomed. "I wondered whether you'd see through the juggling of the names, but if you hadn't I'd have told you. I should never have stood for that trickery in Washington. Drake swore he intended to pass the time with his divorced wife, and Ramsey and I believed him. He begged us to do everything we could to make it seem he'd gone East, so the boys on the ranch wouldn't kid him."

"You're telling the shallowest, cheapest lie, McCall, that a man ever told to squirm out of a tight fix," Joyce said to himself. But his face was expressionless.

Drake, who was now on his feet, handcuffed, between Jenkins and Tom, burst out suddenly:

"I'm getting a lousy deal. I won't stand for it. I—"

"Just remember, Steve, that the law has got you now, and whatever you say may be used against you," interrupted McCall, talking like a stage cop. "If you're guilty, shut up and take your medicine."

The other's lips parted for a reply, then clamped together in the taciturnity regarding his confederates to which he adhered until the State executioner claimed him.

"It's not hard to figure, me darlin', that this Drake was also the murderer of Flying-Horse-Tail Eagle and Joe Yellow-Horse," said Joyce to Kay later. "But whether we'll

ever be able to pin those killings on him is something else
again."

"Why do you think it was he did those other jobs?" she
asked.

"The piece of waxed thread we found in Joe Yellow-
Horse's bedroom, for one thing. Cowboys use that kind of
thread to mend saddles, boots and other equipment. Besides, the thickness was just right for the broken eye of the
needle that's our chief clue in the Jennie Deerfoot case.
When you and I looked at that thread under the magnifying glass, I knew that it had been carried in a cowboy's
pocket. Horse hairs and Bull Durham tobacco were sticking to it."

"That says a lot, Inspector. But how do you link him
with old Flying-Horse-Tail's death?"

"You've been with me through this whole business. You
saw how closely the autopsy reports on the two Indians
resembled each other. Similar knife wounds, and the blade
of the weapon nicked by the violence of the stab, in each
instance. Pretty strong circumstantial evidence that the
same man bumped both victims."

"I know. But I wanted to hear you state it positively,
Inspector."

"And that's as far as we'll get, I fancy. Legal satisfaction
for the Horse-Eagles seems to be out, because we'll have
to try him on the strongest charge—the murder of Jennie
Deerfoot."

Following his conviction, however, Drake broke under
the merciless pressure which Joyce brought to bear upon
him and confessed to the other killings. Then, growing
boastful, he cleared up a moot point that had long piqued
his prosecutor's curiosity, if nothing else. On the scouting
expedition in the Osage Hills, it had been Drake who had
fired upon both Sheriff Hawes and the Joyce party. The
blundering Hawes, he stated, had forced the matter by

treating the first mounted men he had met in the dark as bandits, and bellowing threats of destruction. Afterwards, Drake had ridden forward with the deliberate intention of wiping out Joyce.

"Why did you want to get me?" the latter asked.

"Because you were too hot on my trail," the doomed cowboy replied, and would say no more. He never acknowledged his motive for the apparently senseless slaying of the three Osage millionaires.

Nearly a year later, the Government completed its case and arrested Daniel McCall, his nephew Ernest Burkhart and a score of co-plotters, including the outlaw leaders Bert Lawson and Slim Cooney. The trial caused a nation-wide sensation, the public finding it incredible until absolute proofs were read into the record, that the megalomaniac "king of the Osage Hills" had schemed to murder every prominent Indian in his section and concentrate their wealth in his own hands. Through a technicality, the principals received life imprisonment instead of the death sentence. But redskin confidence in Uncle Sam was created in Oklahoma. And the Departments of Justice and the Interior knew that without the constant, secret collaboration of Inspector Michael Joyce they never would have been able to plumb to the bottom of this tenebrous affair.

ABOUT THE AUTHOR

Little is known about the author, Louis Cornell, assuming that that was his actual name. Publicity blurbs in 1930s newspapers mentioned that he had actually been a private detective in a top New York agency. As he dedicates the second novel to well-known detective George S. Dougherty, it's likely he worked in Dougherty's agency (and just as likely that he patterned Michael Joyce after Dougherty). Dougherty was a character himself, and even wrote up newspaper stories of his own true exploits in criminal investigation.

The bookstore-publisher, Brentano's, noted that *Kidnapping Case Number 7* and *Espionage Case Number 1* were in preparation. Unfortunately, they never appeared.

No Face to
Murder

EDITH HOWIE

COACHWHIP PUBLICATIONS
ALSO AVAILABLE

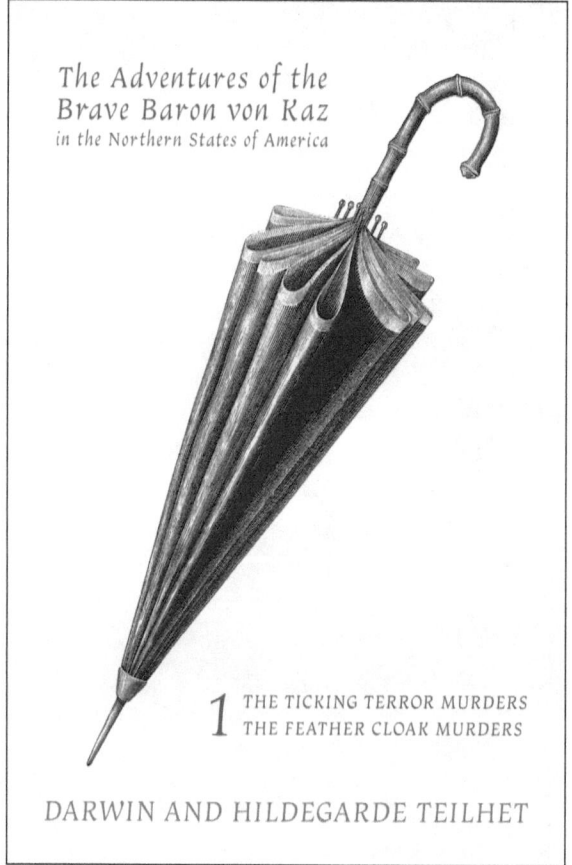

The Adventures of the
Brave Baron von Kaz
in the Northern States of America

1 THE TICKING TERROR MURDERS
THE FEATHER CLOAK MURDERS

DARWIN AND HILDEGARDE TEILHET

COACHWHIP PUBLICATIONS
ALSO AVAILABLE

A SULTAN'S HAREM MYSTERY

Drink the Green Water
The Milkmaid's Millions

HUGH AUSTIN

COACHWHIPBOOKS.COM (PRINT)
COACHWHIP.COM (EPUB)

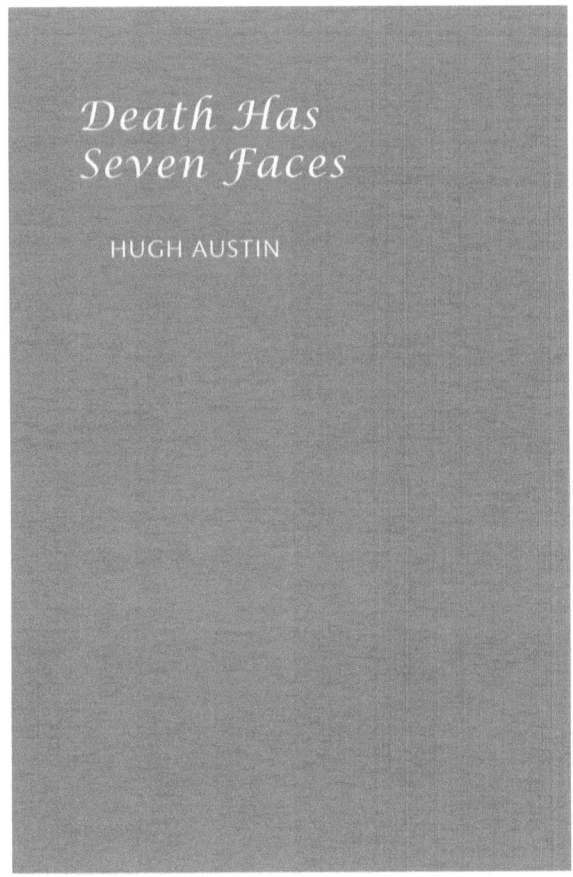

Death Has
Seven Faces

HUGH AUSTIN

COACHWHIPBOOKS.COM (PRINT)
COACHWHIP.COM (EPUB)

DEATH
ON THE CAMPUS
ADDISON
SIMMONS

MURDER IN THE FAMILY

NICE PEOPLE MURDER

Mary Hastings Bradley

Death at
Windward Hill

Murder in the
French Room

HELEN JOAN HULTMAN